# TALES FOR THE
# CAMP FIRE

# TALES FOR THE

# CAMP FIRE

## EDITED BY LOREN RHOADS

*A Charity Anthology Benefitting Wildfire Relief*

Tomes & Coffee
PRESS

TOMES & COFFEE PRESS, SAN FRANCISCO

Tales for the Camp Fire

Copyright of this edition © 2019 by Tomes & Coffee Press.
All individual contributions copyright by their respective authors.

Regarding "The Ninth Skeleton" by Clark Ashton Smith, the text that appears here is from *The Collected Fantasies of Clark Ashton Smith* (2007), Volume 1, edited by Scott Connors and Ron Hilger, Night Shade Books. It is published with permission of CASiana Enterprises, the Literary Estate of Clark Ashton Smith.

Cover art: Helge Balzer
This image is owned by Petersen Games LLC and is used by permission.
Cover design: Deirdre Spencer
Interior design: E.M. Markoff
Ebook design: Nada Qamber and L.S. Johnson

10 9 8 7 6 5 4 3 2 1

Available on Amazon in paperback and ebook.
ISBN 9780997195194 (pbk.)
ISBN 9780997195187 (ebook)

Library of Congress Control Number: 2019901804

Printed in the United States of America

Check out author readings and other events at ellderet.com/campfire.

# TABLE OF CONTENTS

# IN THE FACE OF THE FIRE

**MY FATHER WAS** five when his home burned to the ground. My grandparents had been sitting up one evening when a chicken incubator caught fire on the porch. As flames licked up the outside of the house, they rounded up their three kids—my dad was the oldest—and fled into the cold Michigan night. Somehow, in the process of doing what they could to fight the fire, my grandparents lost track of my dad. He wandered back into the burning house and went back to bed. He was too young, too sleepy, to understand the danger. My grandfather braved the flames to rescue him. Grandpa was burned coming back down the stairs, but thankfully, they both survived.

Not only did the family lose everything beyond the clothes on their backs, but Grandpa hadn't trusted the bank. He'd had a thousand dollars in cash hidden in the house. In an instant, everything they'd owned and all of their savings were gone.

I'm not the only contributor to this collection whose life was shaped by fire. Gene O'Neill's family lost a house on Mount George, on the eastern side of Napa Valley, in one of California's wildfires. Gary Clark wrote in his submission letter, "A woman who lost her home in the Camp Fire has just moved into the mobile home park where I live."

All of us in this book remember the terrible smoke from last year's Camp Fire. Not only could the blaze be seen from space, but smoke blanketed the San Francisco Bay Area from Napa in the north to San Jose in the south. Because of the unusually still weather last November, smoke poured through the passes surrounding San Francisco Bay and got trapped by the coastal mountains. Although San Francisco itself is almost 200 miles from Butte County, we had the worst air quality in the world for almost a week.

Even while it wasn't safe to breathe the outside air and people roamed the city streets in masks like something out of a Mad Max movie, our hearts went out to the people of Butte County—those who were evacuated from the fire zone and waited in shelters to hear if their homes survived, those who lost everything including loved ones and pets, and those who could not outrun a fire that traveled ten miles in ten minutes, devouring everything in its path before people could even begin to grasp the danger they were in.

In the weeks after the fire, the San Francisco Bay Area Chapter of the Horror Writers Association decided to assemble this volume as a way to raise money to support the survivors of the Camp Fire. The initial idea was put forth by Ben Monroe. I volunteered to edit. E.M. Markoff stepped forward to act as publisher. Ken Hueler helped get the word out to the members. Submissions flooded in.

Horror is the perfect genre to grapple with questions raised by disasters of this magnitude. What, in the end, is truly important in life? How can we face death? How does one continue when confronted with unimaginable loss? Is it possible to find light in the darkness? Can humor save us? One hopes that catharsis will cause us to value our common humanity all the more.

I am immensely honored to present this collection of short horror stories to you. Many of these tales have been published previously, but others appear here for the first time. You'll find everything from straight-up horror to science fiction to fairy tales: stories to frighten, awe, and cheer you.

I'd like to call out the team who made this project come together so quickly. Thank you to the Contracts Committee (E.M. Markoff, Gabriel Markoff, L.S. Johnson) who worked out the finer details of how we were going to make this happen. Thank you to Arthur Petersen at Petersen Games for his generous contribution of Helge Balzer's amazing cover artwork and to William A. Dorman, executor of the Clark Ashton Smith Literary Estate, for contributing the master's story—and thanks especially to Ben Monroe, who served as liaison in both cases. Thank you to L.S. Johnson, who handled the Library of Congress details, served as proofreader, and along with Nada Qamber designed the ebook. Thank you to Ken Hueler, who provided bonus proofreading. Thanks to James Chambers for advice on promoting the book. Thanks to the Social Media Coordinators (Ben Monroe, L.S. Johnson, E.M. Markoff) and the Promotions Committee (Ben Monroe, Ken Hueler, Chad Schimke, and Anthony

DeRouen) who got the word out about the book and all the ways we are going to present it to the world. Very special thanks to E.M. Markoff, who researched charities and made the connection with the North Valley Community Foundation, who will receive the profits from the sale of these books.

Finally, deepest thanks to the contributors of the stories that follow. In every case, they donated their work to raise funds for our fellow Californians. I have been deeply touched by their generosity.

Loren Rhoads
San Francisco
March 2019

# CALIFORNIA'S WORST NATURAL DISASTER

## CHAD SCHIMKE

**FROM THE GREAT** Fire of 1849 to the 1906 Earthquake, from the live World Series broadcast of 1989's Loma Prieta Earthquake to the Tubbs Fire of 2017, San Francisco (and the surrounding Bay Area) is no stranger to natural and unnatural disasters.

Power in Northern California is provided by Pacific Gas & Electric (PG&E). The utility has a long and storied history in San Francisco, going back to the days of gaslight in the Gold Rush era. The PG&E Building, the company's headquarters, is located in the Financial District in downtown San Francisco. PG&E's infrastructure is far-reaching, providing electricity to all of Northern California from the Oregon border to Bakersfield.

After the 2017 Tubbs Fire in Sonoma County was caused by downed powerlines during a windstorm, the power company was nervous about its thousands of miles of back-county powerlines during extremely windy weather. Prior to the Camp Fire, the National Weather Service issued warnings about high canyon winds and unusually low humidity.

The day before anything happened in Butte County, Betsy Ann Cowley, a retreat owner near the town of Pulga, notified PG&E about sparks coming from a nearby utility tower. As a public utility, PG&E bore the responsibility of operating the electrical equipment in Pulga.

In the early morning of November 8, 2018, a PG&E worker observed a fire under powerlines at Camp Creek Road above Poe Dam, near Pulga. This is the alleged origin of the Camp Fire and the significance of its name.

Ten minutes after the fire was discovered, Fire Captain Matt MacKenzie, first to arrive on the scene, issued an urgent warning to evacuate the area. His quick action is credited with saving countless lives. Fire began to consume the canyon between Pulga and Paradise. Gridlock impeded traffic on the way out and vehicles were eventually forced to a standstill. Video footage posted to social media depicts flying ash, trees burning overhead, and flames licking embankments as fleeing evacuees panic. Wind gusts up to 70 miles per hour sped fires along.

Needing to flee at a moment's notice, families and ranchers rushed to save pets, working animals, and livestock. Many animals were not lucky enough to escape and were burned alive. In addition to homes and farms, hospitals, nursing homes, disabled care facilities, and schools needed to be evacuated. While volunteer firefighters fought flames, many of them lost their own homes.

Under an orange sky filled with roiling smoke, evacuation must have been a harrowing experience. Efforts to put out the fire were understandably chaotic at first. Abandoned cars blocked roads, forcing evacuees to get out on foot. They dodged raining embers. Initial responses to the disaster were reflective of the chaotic circumstances, with early reports of 250 missing persons presumed dead.

Twelve days later, the fire was only 70% contained. Animal shelters filled up across the state, as they took in rescued and injured pets. The impact on wild plants and animals will never be truly known.

President Trump initially withheld Federal Aid, erroneously blaming environmental laws, poor forest management, and misuse of funds for the disaster. The decision was quickly reversed and FEMA, the Federal Emergency Management Agency, provided assistance upon declaration of an emergency.

In the week prior to Thanksgiving break, students as far away as San Francisco were kept indoors as air quality elevated to Purple Alert, the most hazardous of all warnings. Many school districts in the wider Bay Area closed for one or more days. Air quality was deemed to be hazardous to everyone, prompting closure of many businesses and services throughout Northern California.

More than a thousand firefighters had been brought in to contain the blaze, with three becoming injured themselves. The Camp Fire displaced more than 250,000 people and decimated the Butte County towns of Paradise, Concow, Pulga, and Chico. An estimated 14,000 residences, 500 commercial buildings, and 4,000 other structures were destroyed.

Slowly, eventually, the disaster was brought under control.

Cal Fire, the California Department of Forestry and Fire Protection, announced on November 25, 2018 that the fire was 100% contained. The Camp Fire surpassed the state's previous record for its most deadly blaze, which occurred in Los Angeles' Griffith Park Fire in 1933.

It would be impossible to assign a precise cost to the property damaged by the Camp Fire. Estimates range upward of $16 billion, with a final toll of 85 people confirmed dead and around 10 still missing. At the time of this writing, class action lawsuits and fire investigations haven't confirmed whether or not PG&E is ultimately responsible for starting the wildfire

As a result of the displacement of Paradise, the city of Chico has been overwhelmed by an influx of new residents, pushing it into the top real estate market in the nation. In the aftermath of the Camp Fire, Paradise looks like ground zero of World War III. In some locations, nothing but concrete foundations and broken brick fireplaces remain. Cars were burned so badly that their tires were completely obliterated, leaving behind rivulets of molten metal flowing from under engine blocks. Injured dogs and cats wandered the burned-out neighborhoods, desperate to reunite with their misplaced humans. They found nothing but charred boards, broken rubble, and remains of lives once lived.

What have we learned, if anything, from the Camp Fire?

The devastating incident takes its place amongst the worst natural disasters in US history: the Peshtigo, Wisconsin Fire of 1871; the Johnstown, Pennsylvania Flood of 1889; and the San Francisco Earthquake of 1906. Peshtigo remains the top spot, resulting in the death of 1,500 people.

What do survivors have in common?

They heed the earliest warning signs, don't remain ignorant to changing conditions around them, and react immediately at the first sign of danger. Climate science has certainly advanced in the century between Peshtigo and the Camp Fire. However, as the nation's most populous state, California needs to do so much more to equip citizens with lessons and tools to survive disaster. In times of dire need, outside help *might not be coming.*

This is earthquake country, after all—and with fresh memories of occurrences in Sonoma and Butte counties, fire country as well. First, don't wait or delay . . . your life may depend on it. Care for yourself, then turn your attention to those surrounding you, responding *immediately* to the crisis. Learn first aid, put together an emergency supply kit, monitor escape routes, and remain vigilant to surrounding conditions.

Ourselves, our children, our significant others, and our animals—all our precious loved ones—deserve nothing less.

# TALES FOR THE
# CAMP
# FIRE

**NANCY ETCHEMENDY'S** novels, short fiction, and poetry have appeared regularly for the past 40 years, both in the US and abroad. Her work has earned a number of awards, including three Bram Stoker Awards and an International Horror Guild Award. *Cat in Glass and Other Tales of the Unnatural,* her collection of short dark fantasy, was named an ALA Best Book for Young Adults. She lives and works in Northern California, where she leads a somewhat schizophrenic life, alternating between unkempt, introverted writer/photographer/gardener and gracious (she prays) wife of an eminent Stanford professor.

# COOKING WITH RODENTS

## NANCY ETCHEMENDY

**THERE ARE RATS** in the soufflé again! What cook has not blushed with pride at this happy exclamation from pleasantly astonished dinner guests? Once regarded as unsuitable for human consumption (as was the much-maligned tomato when first introduced in Europe), rodents—and particularly the succulent Norway rat—have recently come into their own as a tasty staple in the finest kitchens of the Western world.

### 1. *Know Your Ingredients*

A trip to any black market yields a bewildering array of rodents intended for cooking. How does one make a sensible choice? Perhaps the most well known of edible rodents is the once-humble rabbit, which, due to the collapse of the domestic livestock industry, is now one of the primary sources of protein in the northern hemisphere. Unfortunately, this upsurge in popularity has led to high prices and undependable quality, even in government-sanctioned outlets. Many of these so-called "farm-raised grade A" animals are actually trapped on the toxic prairies of the agricultural heartland, where, owing to poor diet and heavy exercise, they develop a stringy, fatless texture and gamey flavor. To buy a rabbit for eating under such circumstances is to take one's culinary reputation in one's hands. Mice, hamsters, guinea pigs, and gerbils—though widely available— are so small and generally unpalatable as to render them virtually useless for serious cooking. Many traditional game rodents, such as the porcupine, beaver, and squirrel, are now virtually extinct.

### 2. *About Rats*

Where does this leave us? A moment of observation solves the problem neatly. Generally speaking, a high-quality rodent is plump and the flesh slightly marbled with fat. The best indicator of premium quality, however, is the condition of the fur, which should be well arrayed, glossy, and free of insect damage. It is thus always advisable to buy rodents unskinned. Make sure there is no unpleasant odor and that the ears and paws are soft. Stiff ears and paws are a sign of advanced age.

A glance among the stalls at any local market quickly reveals one fact. The best eating rodents for sale anywhere—and those that fit the above description most closely—are invariably Norway rats. These wonderfully adaptable creatures thrive in landfills and the lower levels of urban sprawls. They will eat anything at all, which means they tend to be very well fed, and they can attain truly marvelous size. A friend of mine recently purchased a lovely five-pounder, the flavor of which was simply indescribable.

### 3. *Procuring the Best Meat*

Fresh meat available at sanctioned outlets has become steadily scarcer, lower in quality, and higher in cost as a result of corporate raiding, government deficits, and climate trauma. It is therefore recommended that these outlets be avoided if possible. While high-quality edible rodents can be obtained at established black markets, the process is generally time-consuming and expensive. One remedy is to purchase them directly from the trappers.

In my own neighborhood, enterprising waifs wander from door to door offering fresh rodents of many varieties, and prime rats in particular. It is true that the quality of these rodents varies. Care must be exercised in selecting them. The knowledgeable cook can count on these suppliers quite confidently and the prices are often unbeatable. I myself dealt with one young trapper for many months last year who obviously knew a great deal about the habits of rats and could thus provide a steady supply of extraordinarily high-quality meat. He arrived at my door promptly three mornings a week until, through some unfortunate oversight, he succumbed to typhus. It is clear, however, that a good deal of time and expense can be saved by dealing directly with trappers. They are frequently the only reliable source of better rats.

### 4. *One Way to Skin a Rat*

Many cooks find themselves at a complete loss when it comes to skinning a rat. Some may be lucky enough to have a butcher who will sell them rats fresh from the trap, then skin them while they wait.

However, the demands of the modern marketplace make skinning and dressing invaluable skills, even for the culinary hobbyist.

There are many ways to skin a rat, but the following method is certainly one of the most efficient and least messy. It requires a very sharp knife and a large working area, preferably out of doors. Covering the floor with used newspapers, if they are still available in your area, is highly recommended.

Begin by treating the fur with a common pet spray (such as Annihilate or Ecosnuff) to kill any fleas, nits, or other insects. Then cut off the forefeet at the first joint. Slice through the tailbone from the underside, but be careful not to damage the skin on top, which must remain intact. Turn the rat over and make a transverse cut the width of its behind. Place the rat on its back and step firmly on the tail while grasping the hind legs. By pulling slowly and steadily upward, the skin can then be worked over the head and front legs. The hind legs must be skinned individually by cutting around the first joints, slitting the undersides, and turning the skin back until it is removed.

Cut off the head and remaining feet, then remove and discard the internal organs. (Use of the liver, heart, and kidneys in cooking is not recommended, as they tend to concentrate toxic compounds which rats consume on a regular basis.) Although it is true that rats carry many diseases communicable to humans, this is a minor problem as long as reasonable care is exercised in the clean-up procedure. The floor and all surfaces which have come into contact with the rat, including one's hands, should be swabbed immediately with a broad-spectrum disinfectant. The skin and offal should be sealed in a water-tight bag and incinerated as soon as convenient. The carcass itself should be washed inside and out with water to which a tablespoon of vinegar (or, if vinegar is unavailable, a .5% battery acid solution) has been added for each cup.

5. *The Use of Rat in the Menu*

Served as a hearty main dish, rat may be braised and the gravy seasoned with Walnut Vinaigrette, page 281. Or it may be stuffed and roasted *à la orange*, page 426.

The real strength of rat lies in the mildly fetid nut-like flavor it imparts when combined with more delicate ingredients, such as those of a soufflé. The soufflé is an ideal method for serving rat, not only because the taste of eggs harmonizes so well with the meat, but also because many of the ingredients for this once-common gastronomic *tour de force* are now rarities which, once obtained, lend an air of particular festivity to the dish.

The average soufflé calls for between three and nine eggs and a considerable amount of cow's cream and/or butter. With hen's eggs selling at upwards of $20 per ounce, available only on the black market and of unreliable age, it is tempting to substitute Eggomax. This is definitely not recommended. While Eggomax is a very useful substitute for eggs in baking, it has its shortcomings. Among these is the fact that the finely milled insects from which it is made cannot be beaten to the frothy consistency necessary for a successful soufflé. At any rate, the "yolks" cannot be separated from the "whites." It is better to spend the extra money and use the genuine article.

Cow's cream and butter present similar problems in availability. Sheep, goats, horses, and cattle have become so nearly nonexistent that sweet cream and butter, essentials for the serious cook, are practically impossible to find at any price. An innovative way to overcome this problem is to find one or two reliable young mothers and feed them regularly in return for their milk. Though human milk contains less fat than that of a cow, the cream from a carefully nourished mother compares quite favorably with cream from a dairy goat.

### 6. *Soufflé Rattus Norvegicus*

To make a soufflé of Norwegian rat, begin by reading "About Soufflés," page 113.

Clean, dress, and cut up one 2-3 pound Norwegian rat. Boil till tender, reserving the broth. When cool, strip the flesh from the bones and set aside. (Since the bones will have been sterilized by the boiling water, there is no need for special disposal methods. It is quite safe to get rid of them in whatever way you prefer. I usually leave them out for our local scavengers.)

If cooking in an electric oven, preheat to 350° F. If cooking with landfill pressings, stoke the firebox moderately.

Prepare 2-3 cups of Heavy Béchamel Sauce, page 48. For half the milk, substitute rat broth. If using mother's milk, feed the mother garlic and onions for three days before milking to impart a delicate, piquant flavor. Rat lard may be substituted for the butter if necessary, though it has a slight detrimental effect on both the flavor and texture of the finished dish.

When the sauce is hot, stir in 2-1/4 cups of the minced, cooked rat meat along with 1 cup canned pureed certified chestnuts. I suggest certified because of a recent trend among black marketeers to substitute processed botanical tumors, heavily salted and inferior in every way. (It is possible to use acorns instead of chestnuts, as long as the tannic acid is soaked out prior to use.) Add 1 cup each chopped raw celery, carrots, and onions. Do not substitute other vegetables (particularly the readily available phosphor mutant tomatoes, cucumbers, or potatoes), as they contribute too much liquid to the mixture.

When these are hot, remove from heat and whisk in 7 egg yolks, one at a time. Remember never to use Eggomax in this procedure. Season with salt, as well as pepper and nutmeg if available. If pepper and nutmeg cannot be obtained, try a mixture of ground dried roaches and silverfish. They have a surprisingly tangy flavor.

Let cool slightly. Beat 9 egg whites until stiff but not dry. Stir a few spoonfuls into the rat mixture, then carefully fold in the rest. Pour into a greased (again, rat lard can be used) 6-cup soufflé dish, as explained on page 114. Bake until firm. Serve immediately.

Rat soufflé goes beautifully with Mildew Sauce, page 361, or for a true *coup de maître*, try Hanged Man Glaze (*Glaze Homme à Pendre*), the ingredients for which are discussed at length from page 509 onward.

**CLARK ASHTON SMITH** (January 13, 1893–August 14, 1961) was an extraordinary literary figure whose homeland, so to speak, was Northern California. He has been described, along with Robert E. Howard and H.P. Lovecraft, as one of the "big three" writers for *Weird Tales*. He was born near Auburn, California and lived much of his life there, although he spent the last years of his life on the Monterey Peninsula in Pacific Grove. Although he was largely known for his fantasy, science fiction, and horror writing, Smith considered himself to be a poet and has been grouped with the early West Coast Romantics.

# THE NINTH SKELETON

## CLARK ASHTON SMITH

**IT WAS BENEATH** the immaculate blue of a morning in April that I set out to keep my appointment with Guenevere. We had agreed to meet on Boulder Ridge, at a spot well known to both of us: a small and circular field surrounded with pines and full of large stones, midway between her parents' home at Newcastle and my cabin on the northeastern extremity of the Ridge, near Auburn.

Guenevere is my fiancée. It must be explained that at the time of which I write, there was a certain amount of opposition on the part of her parents to the engagement—an opposition since happily withdrawn. In fact, they had gone so far as to forbid me to call. Guenevere and I could see each other only by stealth, and infrequently.

The Ridge is a long and rambling moraine, heavily strewn in places with boulders, as its name implies, and with many outcroppings of black volcanic stone. Fruit ranches cling to some of its slopes, but scarcely any of the top is under cultivation, and much of the soil, indeed, is too thin and stony to be arable. With its twisted pines, often as fantastic in form as the cypresses of the California coast, and its gnarled and stunted oaks, the landscape has a wild and quaint beauty, with more than a hint of the Japanesque in places.

It is perhaps two miles from my cabin to the place where I was to meet Guenevere. Since I was born in the very shadow of Boulder Ridge and have lived upon or near it for most of my thirty-odd years, I am familiar with every rod of its lovely and rugged extent, and, previous to that April morning, would scarcely have refrained from laughing if anyone had told me I could possibly lose my way. Since then—well, I assure you, I should not feel inclined to laugh.

Truly, it was a morning made for the trysts of lovers. Wild bees were humming busily in the patches of clover and in the ceanothus bushes with their great masses of white flowers, whose strange and heavy perfume intoxicated the air. Most of the spring blossoms were abroad: cyclamen, yellow violet, poppy, wild hyacinth, and woodland star; and the green of the fields was opalescent with their colors. Between the emerald of the buckeyes, the gray-green of the pines, the golden and dark and bluish greens of the oaks, I caught glimpses of the snow-white Sierras to the east and the faint blue of the Coast Range to the west, beyond the pale and lilac levels of the Sacramento valley. Following a vague trail, I went onward across open fields where I had to thread my way among clustering boulders.

My thoughts were all of Guenevere and I looked only with a casual and desultory eye at the picturesqueness and vernal beauty that environed my path. I was halfway between my cabin and the meeting place, when I became suddenly aware that the sunlight had darkened. I glanced up, thinking, of course, that an April cloud, appearing unobserved from beyond the horizon, had passed across the sun. Imagine, then, my surprise when I saw that the azure of the entire sky had turned to a dun and sinister brown, in the midst of which the sun was clearly visible, burning like an enormous round red ember.

Then something strange and unfamiliar in the nature of my surroundings, which I was momentarily at a loss to define, forced itself upon my attention, and my surprise became a growing consternation. I stopped and looked about me, and realized, incredible as it seemed, that I had lost my way; for the pines on either hand were not those that I had expected to see. They were more gigantic, more gnarled, than the ones I remembered; and their roots writhed in wilder and more serpentine contortions from a soil that was strangely flowerless, where even the grass grew only in scanty tufts.

There were boulders large as druidic monoliths, and the forms of some of them were such as one might see in a nightmare. Thinking, of course, that it must all be a dream, but with a sense of utter bewilderment which seldom if ever attends the absurdities and monstrosities of nightmare, I sought in vain to orient myself and to find some familiar landmark in the bizarre scene that lay before me.

A path, broader than the one I had been following, but running in what I judged to be the same direction, wound on among the trees. It was covered with a gray dust, which, as I went forward, became deeper and displayed footprints of a singular form—footprints that were surely too attenuate, too fantastically slender, to be human, despite their five toe-marks. Something about them, I know not what, something in the nature of their very thinness and elongation, made me shiver. Afterwards, I wondered why I had not recognized them for what they were; but at the time, no suspicion entered my mind—only a vague sense of disquietude, an indefinable trepidation.

As I proceeded, the pines amid which I passed became momentarily more fantastic and more sinister in the contortions of their boughs and boles and roots. Some were like leering hags; others were obscenely crouching gargoyles; some appeared to writhe in an eternity of hellish torture; others were convulsed as with a satanic merriment. All the while, the sky continued to darken slowly, the dun and dismal brown that I had first perceived turning through almost imperceptible changes of tone to a dead funereal purple, wherein the sun smoldered like a moon that had risen from a bath of blood.

The trees and the whole landscape were saturated with this macabre purple, immersed and steeped in its unnatural gloom. Only the rocks, as I went on, grew strangely paler; their forms were somehow suggestive of headstones, of tombs and monuments. Beside the trail, there was no longer the green of vernal grass—only an earth mottled by drying algae and tiny lichens the color of verdigris. Also, there were patches of evil-looking fungi with stems of a leprous pallor and blackish heads that drooped and nodded loathsomely.

The sky had now grown so dark that the whole scene took on a semi-nocturnal aspect and made me think of a doomed world in the twilight of a dying sun. All was airless and silent; there were no birds, no insects, no sighing of the pines, no lisping of leaves: a baleful and preternatural silence, like the silence of the infinite void.

The trees became denser, then dwindled, and I came to a circular field. Here, there was no mistaking the nature of the monolithic boulders—they were headstones and funeral monuments, but so enormously ancient that the lettering or figures upon them were well-nigh effaced; the few characters that I could distinguish were not of any known language. About them there was the hoariness and mystery and terror of incomputable Eld. It was hard to believe that life and death could be as old as they. The trees around them were inconceivably gnarled and bowed as with an almost equal burden of years. The sense of awful antiquity that these stones and pines all served to convey increased the oppression of my bewilderment, confirmed my disquietude. Nor was I reassured when I noticed on the soft earth about the headstones a number of those attenuate footprints of which I have already spoken. They were disposed in a fashion that was truly singular, seeming to depart from and return to the vicinity of each stone.

Now, for the first time, I heard a sound other than the sound of my own footfalls in the silence of this macabre scene. Behind me, among the trees, there was a faint and evil rattling. I turned and listened; there was something in these sounds that served to complete the demoralization of my unstrung nerves. Monstrous fears, abominable fancies, trooped like the horde of a witches' sabbat through my brain.

The reality that I was now to confront was no less monstrous! There was a whitish glimmering in the shadow of the trees and a human skeleton, bearing in its arms the skeleton of an infant, emerged and came toward me! Intent as on some ulterior purpose, some charnel errand not to be surmised by the living, it went by with a tranquil pace, an effortless and gliding tread, in which, despite my terror and stupefaction, I perceived a certain horrible and feminine grace.

I followed the apparition with my eyes as it passed among the monuments without pausing and vanished in the darkness of the pines on the opposite side of the field. No sooner had it gone then a second, also bearing in its arms an infant skeleton, appeared and passed before me in the same direction and with the same abominable and loathsome grace of movement.

A horror that was more than horror, a fear that was beyond fear, petrified all of my faculties, and I felt as if I were weighted down by some ineluctable and insupportable burden of nightmare. Before me, skeleton after skeleton, each precisely like the last, with the same macabre lightness and ease of motion, each carrying its pitiful infant, emerged from the shadow of the ancient pines and followed where the first had disappeared, intent as on the same cryptic errand. One by one they came, till I had counted eight! Now I knew the origin of the bizarre footprints whose attenuation had disturbed and troubled me.

When the eighth skeleton had passed from sight, my eyes were drawn as by some irresistible impulse to one of the nearer headstones, beside which I was amazed to perceive what I had not noticed before: a freshly opened grave, gaping darkly in the soft soil. Then, at my elbow, I heard a low rattling, and the fingers of a fleshless hand plucked lightly at my sleeve. A skeleton was beside me, differing only from the others through the fact that it bore no infant in its arms. With a lipless and ingratiating leer, it plucked again at my sleeve, as if to draw me toward the open grave. Its teeth clicked as if it were trying to speak. My senses and my brain, aswirl with vertiginous terror, could endure no more: I seemed to fall and fall through deeps of infinite eddying blackness with the clutching terror of those fingers upon my arm, till consciousness was left behind in my descent.

When I came to, Guenevere was holding me by the arm, concern and puzzlement upon her sweet oval face, and I was standing among the boulders of the field appointed for our rendezvous.

"What on earth is the matter with you, Herbert?" she queried anxiously. "Are you ill? You were standing here in a daze when I came and didn't seem to hear or see me when I spoke to you. And I really thought you were going to faint when I touched your arm."

**JOHN MCCALLUM SWAIN** has lived in Canada, Germany, Scotland, and the United States, where he now shares his home with a small herd of cats. His tales, ranging from graphic horror to alternate history, have appeared in *Weird Menace: Volume 2, Spawn of the Ripper, Peeling Back the Skin, Blood Sweat & Fears, The Stars at My Door, Death's Garden*, and many other anthologies. His own titles include the horror and speculative fiction collections *My Vile Bounty* and *Califhorrornia* and the novellas *Smile* and *The Unicorn Man*. You can find them on Amazon.

# THE WOLF WHO NEVER WAS

## John McCallum Swain

**NOT LONG BEFORE** *the seasoned actor Oliver Reed died, I traveled to Ireland to work on a book with him, sharing notes and discussing the structure and substance of the book over pints of Beamish's Irish Stout in his favorite pub.*

*This would not be another biography, but it* would *be biographical: a collection of short tales that Reed had withheld sharing until that point in his life—when I suspect he suspected the end was near—for fear of offending or hurting those close to him or subjecting himself to legal action.*

The View from the Edge of Reason *would have been a wonderful collection of tales. Unfortunately, most of them now exist only as tantalizing hints of what could have been, as Oliver, at my suggestion, scribbled potential titles for his many anecdotes on a legal pad—titles as intriguing as* The Night I Beat the Blessed Jesus Out of George Lazenby *and* How to Bake an Elephant Shit Pie.

*The single tale that survives, the tale that would have been the crown jewel of the collection and the tale I will tell here, may explain why a promising young actor would soon become known for raucous behavior and regrettable outbursts of violence.*

*It may reveal why a man from a respected family already established in theater would lead British actor Michael Crawford to recall in his own autobiography that there was 'a tension about Oliver Reed, a certain aura of danger.'*

*And it may finally offer a reason why that singular man's life ended in such a sordid fashion, a death grimly detailed by Russell Crowe, the star of* Gladiator, *the film in which Oliver played his last part: "He drank himself to death. He sat on a bar stool until he fell off it and carried on drinking . . . lying in his own piss and vomit, he continued to drink till he passed out."*

*This tale is set during a time when Britain was bristling with promise and excitement. After two decades of war and recovery, the children of the men and women who fought the Axis powers were coming into their own, leading a wave of entertainment that would give the world everything from the Beatles and the Rolling Stones to Monty Python and Dr. Who.*

*From that time of great change comes a chronicle of great change, a memoir that begins with a thoroughly saturated Oliver leaning over a table in the corner of O'Brien's Bar in Churchtown and saying, "When we were filming* Curse of the Werewolf *at Bray Studios, Terence Fisher brought an actual wolf onto the set, and the mangy fucking thing bit me."*

*This is Oliver's Tale.*

## 1

"Are you a Mod?"

Oliver Reed tried not to gape at his costar like an imbecile. "What?"

"Are you a Rocker, or a Mod?"

"Sorry?"

The young woman laughed and put a delicate hand on his arm. "I'm asking if you prefer jazz, or rock and . . . Oliver, are you staring at my bosom?"

"Guilty as charged, your honor," he replied, trying and failing to wrest his attention from her incredible figure. He shifted gears, effortlessly moving into charming mode. He extended a leg and executed a low bow before her. "I'm a weak man, my love. It is impossible for me to resist the beguilements with which Mother Nature has graced you."

"Aren't you the roué." And she blushed, a dusky red glow.

Oliver Reed was twenty-two years old. After years of extras work and bit parts, this was his first film role of substance. Yvonne Romain was his age and, despite the dusky looks that would see her cast again and again as Mediterranean maidens, she was every inch a proper young Englishwoman.

She was nearly done with a costume-fitting. Oliver knew he should be focusing on his own lines for a pending read-through of the script instead of Yvonne's low-cut outfit, but . . . Mary, mother of Jesus, that *body*.

All Oliver could think about was trying to get Yvonne into bed, which was *insane*. He had been married only a year to a lovely model named Kate Byrne, he had only just met Yvonne, and this Hammer Films production of *Curse of the Werewolf* was his first big job. He simply could not botch it; he was certain this picture could be a career-starter.

Hammer was putting out films like a mouse passes turds. Last year's *The Brides of Dracula* had been huge in horror circles, despite catering to an audience that seemed to consist for the most part of spotty-faced imbeciles and bed-wetters.

If he worked hard and things worked out, he could become established when the film was released next year. 1961 could become *his* year, but that would not happen if he could not resist getting his leg over, no matter how fetching Yvonne was.

She's playing your mother, he thought. Think of your mother.

Thirty-eight, twenty-two, thirty-six, he'd heard the gaffer whisper earlier in the day.

Dancing, prancing *Jesus.*

Oliver was still bent low with a panty-soaking come-hither smile on his face as his lighter and darker natures savaged each other, when a wolf snarled behind him and sank its teeth into his jutting posterior.

Later, he would recall director Terence Fisher mentioned something about a wolf, in passing, but this was *film,* so Oliver had assumed Fisher was talking about a stuffed animal prop or a large dog with a menacing appearance, not an *actual wolf.* But no, the wolf was real.

Later, Oliver would hear people around him say, *no worries, the thing is certified rabies-free,* and *the beast's teeth were only in your arse for a tick, let's not make a fuss or our insurers will crucify us,* and *I thought there'd be a lot more blood than that.*

Later, Oliver would wonder if rabies wouldn't have been more merciful.

## 2

It was autumn in Berkshire, the lovely country west of London. The studio was set on the bank of the Thames, between the villages of Bray and Windsor. The weather was grand, all warm days and crisp nights, and the locals were of the right sort, with Windsor Castle only a few miles away.

The world would have been Oliver's oyster, if he wasn't bleeding from a pair of puncture wounds in his left buttock.

"Christ Jesus," Oliver hissed, as his wounds were cleansed with an ointment that had to have come from a bottle labeled Liquid Fire.

"Honestly," the studio nurse said. She was a stern old matron with gray hair and a bosom like a bulwark. "It's just a nip."

"Then let me raise your skirt and nip *your* nether regions, ma'am, that I might find inspiration in your endurance."

"Cheeky thing," the nurse said, slapping Oliver's bottom. "Pull your trousers up, we're done here."

The burn of the ointment began to ease, as did the pain of the bite.

Walking with a bit of a limp, Oliver stepped out of the infirmary and onto the grounds of Bray Studios. He saw Terence Fisher speaking with a man in a gray overcoat.

"Do keep me informed," the man said. He gave Oliver a nod and walked away.

"Ollie," Terence said. "I've been waiting for you."

"Who was that man? He looked rather grim."

"Yes," the older man said. "That was Detective Chief Inspector Schaap, the local constable, if you will. He said someone was murdered a few miles from here."

"Murdered?"

"Indeed. He implied it was rather brutal and bloody and asked if we would all be on the lookout for suspicious characters. I tried to tell him that this is the *film* business and I'm surrounded by suspicious characters. He didn't so much as break a smile."

Oliver did smile. "Shouldn't you be on set directing a film? That *is* why we are here, isn't it?"

Under normal circumstances Oliver would never dream of talking to a director like that. Terence had shot three dozen films; he was one of the men most responsible for making Hammer Films a production company of note. Yet there was something fatherly and familiar about Fisher that put Oliver at ease with the older man, and besides, Oliver was grumpy.

"You are correct," Fisher said. "The second unit is busy on set with a bit of business, and that gives me time to be certain you are not ailing."

"My arse hurts."

"Sorry, Ollie. Take the rest of the day off. We'll shoot around you."

Oliver nodded. "So, this bloody wolf. What was that all about?"

Fisher shrugged. "I thought it would enhance the film if we could show a wolf howling at the moon. We have stock shots of the moon, of course, but the wolf footage in our film library is abominable. I got in touch with a local man who said he had a trained wolf available for productions. A *tamed* wolf. You can imagine my horror when the creature attacked you as I was walking wolf and owner to the production office."

"Well," Oliver said, and then paused, wondering what he could possibly say to Fisher, who was clearly upset by the incident. *Don't let it happen again?* No. "Where is this fellow with the wolf?"

"I put him outside the gate," Fisher said. "I'll not have him on the grounds."

Oliver thought about this. "I think I'll have a stern word with him. What is his name?"

"Sebastian Fleuter," Fisher said. "You can't miss him, he's a scruffy red-headed man with a well-groomed wolf, but Ollie, please be careful. You don't want to get bitten. *Again.*"

Oliver forced out a laugh, hoping to sound unconcerned as he strode down the path to the studio's main gate, all the while wishing he had a shotgun.

❦

Oliver stepped through the gates onto the street and spotted the man instantly. Fleuter was hard to miss. He had a wolf on a leash, and the wolf was huge.

"You're the one Edward bit on the buttock," the scruffy red-headed man said. He pronounced it *BAH-tuck*. "I can tell by the way you're limping."

"Now see here, you simpleton," Oliver said, brandishing a threatening finger at Fleuter. "That beast could have killed me."

The wolf growled at Oliver, a deep rumbling sound that trickled into the most primitive part of his brain and left his scrotum as compact as a walnut.

"Easy," Fleuter said to the wolf. To Oliver he said, "Naw, he wouldn't have done that. Edward was doing what must be done. Edward was spreading the gift. Edward was careless, doing it in broad daylight—naughty Edward!—but he was following his blood."

Confused, Oliver asked, "What the hell are you on about?"

"Buy us a pint and I'll tell you all about it," Fleuter said, pausing to put on sunglasses before crossing the street and entering a pub.

3

By the time Oliver stepped into the dimness of the pub, Fleuter was arguing with the barman.

"Hey, you can't have that fucking dog in here," the barman said, brandishing a Theakston bar towel like a weapon.

Fleuter tapped his sunglasses with one finger and said, "I happen to be fucking blind, you bastard."

Part of Oliver suggested he walk away, but part of him wanted answers. He slid a five-pound note across the bar and said, "I'll keep an eye on both of them, my good man."

That seemed to mollify the barman.

"Now about this wolf business," Oliver said as Fleuter sat on a stool.

"Have a drink," Fleuter said.

Oliver looked at his watch. "It's only two o'clock in the afternoon. I may have the occasional tipple at the end of the day, but drinking this early would be boorish."

"Gi'us a pint," Fleuter said to the barman, pointing at the closest font.

"I'll have a sparkling water, please," Oliver said primly.

"And a Jameson," Fleuter said.

When the drinks had been set on the bar, Oliver paid for them with another five pounds, told the man to keep the change, and then waved the barman away as if he were a pesky insect.

"Now stop pissing about, you halfwit," Oliver said in the most severe tone he could muster. "What is this *'following his blood'* business? Are you letting that bloody wolf follow its every whim instead of restraining the beast?"

Fleuter swallowed the shot of whiskey, looked up and down the bar, and then leaned close to Oliver. He had to fight the urge to recoil; the man smelled like a meat pie that had gone off.

"That *wolf* is my father," he said.

Fleuter did not say wolf. He said *wulf,* as if talking about something alien and dark and older than memory.

Oliver glanced at the empty whiskey glass. "How many of those have you had today?"

Fleuter waved off the suggestion that he was drunk. "My father is a werewolf. I am a werewolf. Everything I've learned, I learned from him. Now that you've been bitten, you are a werewolf, too."

Oliver leaned back on his stool. He was wondering how dangerous a genuine madman could be. He'd never encountered one before.

"Werewolves?" Oliver asked with a disdainful sniff. "Don't be absurd! This is 1960, not 1660. You're a bloody lunatic."

"Exactly," Fleuter said. "That is grammatically correct. Like my father, I am a humane creature. Most wolves are. Despite man being the easiest prey to run down, I only feed on wild game when I've gone all fours—"

Oliver tried, but could not conceal his dubious expression as he asked, "All fours?"

"From man to wolf, from two legs to four. When you are first bitten, the moon is your master and it drives your transformation. You never overcome some of those changes. The most visceral of those is feeding. Wolves need raw meat, living meat. We need blood. But we are still able to choose the source of our meat: animal or man."

"Preposterous," Oliver said, spitting the word in Fleuter's face.

"Really?" The man smiled. The wolf at his feet seemed to be smiling as well, a tongue like a slab of ham dangling from powerful jaws. Fleuter reached into a pocket and took out a bronze cigarette case. He opened the case, holding it so the contents faced away from him.

Oliver saw what looked like a Roman coin nestled in the felt lining of the case. Then his stomach rolled and his head felt as if it had just been split open with an axe. Pain and nausea unmanned him. He would have toppled from the stool if Fleuter hadn't reached out and grabbed his arm.

"Steady," Fleuter said, holding Oliver upright with one hand while flipping the bronze case closed with the other.

When Oliver found his equilibrium, he gasped, "What the fucking hell was that?"

"A bit of ancient lore put into practice," Fleuter said. He noticed the barman hovering nearby and signaled the man for two more shots of whiskey. When the barman set down the drinks, Fleuter said, "Cheers. Now piss off."

"Charming," Oliver said, swallowing his drink and relishing the way it soothed his agitation.

Fleuter made his own dram disappear and then held up the bronze case.

"This case is made from bronze forged in antiquity. Inside is a silver coin struck with the image of the Emperor Hadrian. The coin is over eighteen hundred years old. The case is three times as old. The coin is pure silver. *Old silver.* Silver is the element of the moon. Bronze is an element of Man, so this old bronze case protects us from the silver inside."

Oliver shook his head. "What are you talking about?"

"My history. Your history now. *Our* history."

"This is a load of bollocks," Oliver said. "I haven't time for—"

Fleuter lifted the lid of the case for just a moment, exposing the buttery gleam of ancient silver before covering it again.

Oliver turned and vomited onto the floor. The wolf darted out of the way with an angry growl.

"Ahh shit," Fleuter said with a bray of laughter. "Let's be off, eh?"

He took Oliver's arm again as they left the pub. The barman was grousing in their wake as they stepped outside and into early evening, slanting shadows merging into pools of darkness on the street.

## 4

Fleuter steered Oliver to a park bench. They sat for a while without speaking, watching people pass by. Oliver waited for his stomach to settle. Fleuter lit a cigarette. The wolf sniffed the wake of every person who walked by.

"The moon is rising," Fleuter said, "and the moon does not have to be full to affect you, my newfound friend. It will not be full for a week—and by then you will be full wolf—but for many nights as the moon waxes and wanes gibbous, you will feel the change coming and receding . . . the hunger for fresh meat, the desire to run, and the simple joy of *smelling* the world."

He reached down and scratched the wolf behind the ears. "Depending on the wolf, other things can initiate a change as well: lust, rage, powerful emotions."

"Assuming for a moment that any of this madness is true," Oliver said, "why would you let that beast bite me? Why would you infect *me* with this disease?"

Fleuter appeared hurt by this. "My father always loved the movies and I'm between jobs and need money. And despite what those silly horror films say, this condition is not a curse. It is a *gift,* a part of this island's history."

"What?"

Speaking slowly, as if trying to share great wisdom with a halfwit, Fleuter said, "We were *always* here. On this island. Why do you think the Romans so often described their labors in conquering Britain as battles against savages and animals? *Because that is what they were fighting half the time; wolves!* In fact, Hadrian built his wall not to keep out the barbarians, but to keep *us* out. It's said he was inspired by God, which sounds like a tall order of shite, if you ask me."

"Wait a moment," Oliver sputtered. "The Roman conquests are recorded in rather explicit detail. Nowhere is there mention of battles with mythological monsters!"

"I know," Fleuter agreed. "One of the popes did that, the bastard. Wolf legend says he *sanitized the record.* The meddling ninny."

A young woman walked by. Oliver's nose took on a life of its own as he basked in her scent.

"My God," he said, "she smells . . . "

"Warm?" Fleuter suggested. "Ripe? Fertile?"

Oliver was salivating to excess and he had a furious erection. He crossed his legs and swallowed a mouthful of spit as a voice in his mind whispered *fuck and eat and fuck and eat and fuck and eat!*

Fleuter nudged him with one elbow. When Oliver looked at him, he pointed to the horizon, where a moon two-thirds full hung low in the twilight sky.

"Why was your father a wolf *before* the moon appeared in the sky?"

Fleuter looked both amused and sad when he said, "My father chose to be full wolf always. That is how he will spend the rest of his life."

Oliver worked his jaws. His teeth were aching. "You said your father was *following his blood.* What does that mean?"

"It means that the more time one spends in wolf form, the more one *must* share the gift, or one will live a life of misery. If one remains a wolf and does not share the gift, one withers and dies."

"Did your father bite you?" Oliver asked this wetly, spittle running down his chin.

"No," Fleuter said. "My gift is inherited."

Oliver was looking at the moon, unaware that his legs were twitching. An old man passing by saw Oliver's drooling and spasms.

"Are ye' all right, son?"

Oliver bared his teeth and said, "Fuck off," appalled by his own actions when the old man scurried away.

"The older the werewolf, the greater the control it has over the transformation," Fleuter said. "Recently converted werewolves will only change when the moon waxes full, and they cannot withstand that change. In a few years, you will learn how to resist becoming a wolf when lunar influence is at its height. If you live long enough, you will master the art of changing at will, night or day. My father willed himself to be wolf forevermore, and so he remains."

"I'm hungry," Oliver said. That was an understatement; he was ravenous.

"Where are you staying?" Fleuter asked. He took a handkerchief from one pocket and wiped clots of foam from Oliver's face.

"A hotel not far from here," Oliver said. "Most of the cast and crew have rooms there."

"Well then," Fleuter said with a grin, "Let me show you to a wonderful little pub with meat pies that will satisfy your just-awakened craving for flesh . . . for now."

"I don't know if I should drink any more," Oliver said.

With unmistakable earnestness, Fleuter said, "My friend, these are the most important words you will ever hear me say: *drinking keeps the wolf at bay.*"

## 5

The next morning, Oliver was late for the car that would take him the short distance from hotel to studio. His head was raging and his stomach was sour. He had drunk five more shots of whiskey, *five*, and had virtually inhaled a large meat pie. That sort of dipsomania and gluttony was unbefitting a Reed.

He had the most tenuous wisp of memory: Kate calling from home to ask about his day and him ending the call with, "Night-night, lovey-dovey, I need to go and vomit."

During the day's shoot at Bray, Oliver remembered snippets of conversation at the pub with Fleuter. When he asked what would become of a woman who inherited the werewolf curse when she was exposed to a full moon during her time of the month, Fleuter seemed truly afraid as he whispered, "They become *ravagers*." And as Fleuter left Oliver at his hotel, the man had smiled and said, "Looks like someone is following me. If it's some poor yobbo looking to snatch my wallet, he's in for a surprise."

Oliver had said goodnight then and somehow stumbled to his bed. As another day came to a close, he had conflicted feelings; he was sure the whole werewolf thing was a colossal joke. After all, he was here shooting a werewolf film, yet he was also coming to like Sebastian Fleuter. The man might be crude, but he was amusing and showed genuine affection for the wolf he insisted was his own father.

As the day's shooting was winding down and Oliver shambled to a dressing room to get out of his costume, he saw Detective Chief Inspector Schaap again. The tall policeman was in a huddle with producers Michael Carreras and Anthony Hinds, a man wearing a black wool trilby, and Terence Fisher. When the group broke up, Oliver asked Fisher what was happening.

"There's been another murder," Terence said. "Apparently a wild dog tore apart a young boy. Terrible. The government has dispatched someone to take care of the beast, but Schaap still wants us to stay alert for any strangers in the area, which is quite odd. The castle, I suppose."

Oliver nodded. Windsor Castle was only two miles from Bray Studios. Since the Royal Residence housed the private apartments of Queen Elizabeth, the extreme caution of the constabulary was understandable.

When Oliver left the studio, all he could think of was a quick dinner and bed, until he saw Fleuter waiting for him. It was dark and Sebastian was alone under a streetlight. The man looked miserable. His eyes had been blackened and his nose was swollen and crooked.

"It's my da'," Fleuter said. "Someone shot him. They shot him dead."

Fleuter fell into Oliver's arms. After a moment's hesitation, Oliver held the man and tried to comfort him the best he could.

Soon enough they were seated at a table in the pub Oliver thought of as the pie place.

"Tell me what happened," Oliver said.

Fleuter took a sip from a pint of beer and said, "We have a small house in Fifield, just my da' and me. My mum left him when I was young. He likes to sleep inside the door. To protect me, I suppose. After all those drinks last night, I was fast asleep. It was after midnight when I heard the sound of a gunshot, and my da's cry of pain. When I reached the foyer, someone hit me in the face. The last thing I heard was a horrific cry from my da'."

Fleuter started to cry. Oliver looked about, feeling awkward. "There-there," he said.

"I guess it was just a robbery gone wrong."

That didn't sit well with Oliver, not in such a peaceful setting; a robbery with a *gun?*

"Can you help me bury him?"

Oliver was taken aback. "What? If your father was murdered, why aren't the police involved?"

"When wolves are dying in all fours, they revert to their human form. My da' only got halfway through that transition when he died."

As outrage overwhelmed him, Oliver felt his lips peeling back as if he had too many teeth in his head: larger, longer teeth. He clapped a hand over his mouth until his indignation and that odd physical sensation subsided in his jaws.

"My poor da' must have crawled into the woods to try and hide, but whoever shot him finished him off there."

Oliver was wondering how he had ever become entangled in such a grim business when Fleuter asked for his help again.

"Help me bury my father," Fleuter said.

It was after midnight when Oliver and Fleuter reached a small wood down the road from Sebastian's home. Oliver was carrying a pick. Fleuter was carrying a shovel. They both had torches with fresh batteries in them. A fine mist crept along the ground. Oliver felt like he was in another Hammer production, this one with spectacular set dressing.

Fleuter picked his way between the trees, then stopped in a clearing near a stream. "Here we are." Sebastian brushed a blanket of fallen autumn leaves away from Edward's body.

Oliver asked, "How did you find him?"

Sebastian seemed surprised, as if the answer was obvious. "His scent."

When Oliver saw the remains of the elder Fleuter, he recoiled in horror. The man was nude, his neck ended in a raw stump, and he was half man and half wolf.

Oliver put a hand over his mouth, certain he was going to vomit on the corpse. He belched a ball of rancid air and took a deep breath.

Fleuter offered him a flask full of scotch. Oliver accepted it and took a pull, thinking that he didn't want this recent, near-constant drinking to get out of hand.

"Oliver," Sebastian said, "I'm sorry you had to become one of us in such a fashion. I honestly had no idea my father was going to bite you. He always said he would only share his gift with those he felt were worthy, and I try to do the same. He must have sensed . . . *virtue* in you."

Oliver wanted to say something glib, like *no harm done,* but damn it, harm *had* been done, so he said nothing.

"My father always said werewolves were created by God to protect mankind." Fleuter was smiling, though his eyes were full of tears. "We were the shepherds of men when the world was young, protecting human beings who were like sheep, not in ignorance, but in their innocence. We protected good people from those who would do evil, and from other ultra-human creatures—"

"Other creatures?" Oliver interrupted, "There are *other* creatures?"

"Oh, yes," Fleuter said. "But somehow, men who would harm their own kind are worse. It was men who would do evil who maligned the wolves and spread the fearful stories that led to us being perceived as horrors, not saviors. We *react* to evil. We cannot help it. That is why my father and I lived in such a peaceful hamlet as Fifield, so we could live our lives without being at the beck and call of our purpose."

"Have there ever been any bad wolves?"

Fleuter sounded almost resentful as he replied, "Sometimes, on very, *very* rare occasions. Sometimes . . . wolves go bad."

Oliver didn't like that at all.

It was as they were digging a hole that Oliver noticed something gleaming in Edward's flesh.

"What are all those glittery bits?"

Sebastian shone the light on his father. "Buckshot? Is that what it's called? He was shot with a shotgun."

"Buckshot doesn't look like *that,*" Oliver said, his intrigue overcoming his revulsion.

He took a fifty pence piece from his pocket and used the coin to pry loose a glittering bead embedded in the dead man's skin. The tiny metal sphere dropped into Oliver's palm and he bit back a scream as it began to burn him. He threw the shining bead into the stream and gasped, "Silver."

Fleuter stared at him, confused.

"That was no robbery gone wrong," Oliver said. "It was no random murder. Whoever killed your father knew he was a werewolf. He was armed with silver shot."

## 6

During the next day's shooting, Oliver tried to hide his fatigue. He had only gotten a few hours' sleep after that unpleasant business in the woods and seeing Fleuter to his home. The poor man was distraught and Oliver was both worried about his new friend and irritated that he considered the man a friend under the circumstances.

He was awakened the following morning by another call from Kate. She hadn't been able to reach him the night before and was concerned: was something wrong with him?

"Fit as a fiddle, my love," he'd said.

During the night, he had absolutely shredded his bedding. He left the chambermaid two notes: one was a short line of apology and the other was twenty quid. He'd passed the woman in the hall once or twice and given her a quick smile each time, the smile that made women melt. He hoped she wouldn't raise a fuss.

Makeup artist Frieda Steiger had never been moved by Oliver's charms. She made a brusque remark about the dirt under his fingernails. Fortunately, the grime was appropriate, as he was shooting scenes where he was locked in a grotty prison cell.

At noon, on his way to the restroom, he passed Yvonne Romain on the set. Just as Oliver's role required more and more of him, she was almost done with shooting. Once he was alone in a toilet stall and set about doing his business, he found himself getting aroused at the thought of his costar, regretting that she had no actual scenes with him. As he shook off, he looked down to see that the hand holding his engorged organ was covered in hair.

Mere minutes after that disturbing episode, he was back on set beside Catherine Feller, who played Christina, the love of his life, a woman who has just spent the night with the titularly cursed Leon Corledo, locked in his cell. In a scene in which he asked her if he had *changed,* if his face and hands had *changed,* his emoting was no act; what audiences would one day see onscreen was his very real concern that something was happening to him. And when his character says that she prevented him from changing, that she saved him, he wondered what could save Oliver Reed out in the real world . . . and then he remembered Fleuter saying *drinking keeps the wolf at bay.*

After sneaking out of the studio during a lunch break, Oliver bought a half-pint bottle of scotch and spent the rest of the day ever so slightly sloshed. He hid his inebriation well, as well as he hid his darker secret.

When Oliver was done for the day, he was exhausted from the previous late night and a day spent drunk. He felt as if he was sleepwalking as he walked down the dark street to his hotel.

He didn't notice the man in the black wool trilby until they literally walked into each other. The man grabbed the lapels of Oliver's coat and breathed deeply before letting go and moving on. The fact that the man had apparently inhaled his scent only occurred to Oliver after he was in bed and drifting off. At the time, he had been too startled by the man's appearance. Under the shadow of the trilby's brim, the left side of the man's face seemed a horror of old wounds—as if the flesh had been harrowed, or *clawed.*

## 7

The next day's shooting was curious. The mixed emotions surging through Oliver fueled his performance, thrilling and terrifying him.

He felt he did some of his best work, but he was terribly on edge. When Terence Fisher proudly displayed some of the art work that would be the basis for *Curse of the Werewolf* movie posters—a lurid scene showing a wolfman holding a woman in his arms while surrounded by torch-bearing villagers—Oliver snapped, "I don't look like that!"

Terence laughed it off, saying, "Ollie, aren't you a bit young for that kind of vanity?"

The night before, Oliver had dreamed of the moon. He had dreamed of Yvonne. He had dreamed that she was running, crying out in fear. And he had dreamed of looking into her lovely, horrified face and smiling as his hands, no, his *claws* sank into flesh and parted it like bread dough, the smell of fresh blood filling his nostrils as he pried apart the bones of a sturdy ribcage and leaned forward, sinking his elongated canines into a frantically beating heart.

He had torn apart his sheets and blankets again. When he had departed for the studio in the morning, he left behind forty pounds for the chambermaid, thinking if this kept up, he'd have to sleep in the bloody bathtub.

When his day was done, he shambled back to his hotel. As he was walking upstairs to his room, the clerk said he had a phone call. Oliver took the call in his room with great reluctance, until he heard an agitated Sebastian on the line.

"Oliver, you have to come quickly. I've discovered something absolutely *macabre!*"

One of his first jobs in his tender youth was that of a bouncer in an underground strip-tease club in Soho. Things were so much more uncomplicated then. If someone got out of line, you popped him on the snout and tossed him into the street. Now, though . . .

"I'm on my way," Oliver said. He tried to shake off his weariness as he stepped out of the hotel into twilight. The light of the moon made his bones ache and his skin crawl.

On the street Oliver bumped into the man in the trilby again. He couldn't help growling at the man, "Who *are* you?"

"Who am I?" the man asked. In contrast with his facial disfigurement, the stranger's accent was polished and refined—people who spoke so regarded men like Oliver as *not of our class.* "I am William Lucanus Walmstead, Royal Dogcatcher by appointment to her majesty Queen Elizabeth II. Now who in blazes are *you?*"

"I'm Oliver fucking Reed," Oliver said, no longer trying to hide his chagrin. "I am an actor; I'm shooting a film at Bray—"

"A *thespian,*" Walmstead said, his upper lip curling with distaste. "I should have known."

Oliver pushed by the man and went on his way. If he had looked back, he would have seen the man enter the hotel.

He reached Sebastian Fleuter's home after a brisk walk that left him invigorated instead of tired. Sebastian had called a cab and was waiting for him. "Get in," Fleuter said. His face was as pale and twisted as a handful of fresh cheese curds.

The ride was brief. They got out at the end of a lane leading to a farmhouse. Sebastian asked the cab driver to wait for them.

They walked down the lane. When they were a dozen paces from the home, Oliver stopped and sniffed the air.

"What is that *smell?*"

"The blood of our siblings," Fleuter said.

Sebastian opened the door and Oliver reeled under the rank tang of spilled blood and something else, something that smelled like the sickly light of polished silver: *fear.*

"What is this place?" Oliver asked.

"When wolves live alone or in small groups, their abode is called a den," Fleuter said as he stepped inside. "A place where wolves meet in greater numbers is called a rendezvous site. This is where wolves from Greater London and the Southeast would gather from time to time: for meals, holidays, good times. The owners of this home were dear friends."

Oliver followed, snuffling. He could smell and *taste* the odors inside, scents he instinctively knew as the bitter stench of dying badly: a miasma of blood, shit, piss, tears, and adrenaline.

There was little decoration in the home, save for a poorly done oil painting hanging over a long dining room table: an image of many wolves among many sheep, all of them side by side on a hill overlooking a green vale.

"Peaceful coexistence," Fleuter said softly. "That was the goal of this pack. It's the goal of all packs, really."

Sebastian stopped then, trying to hold back tears. He gestured to a door and stairs leading downward into sour yellow light.

Oliver did not want to go, but part of him had to, the same part of him that was alive now that the moon was riding high.

He found a congregation of English wolves, all of them dead. There were men, women, and children, six little ones bound together in a far corner, and somehow Oliver *knew* that whoever had done this had taken the children first and used them to lure the adults to their doom.

All of them, even the little ones, had been cruelly disfigured by blasts of silver shot.

One of the dying wolves—who looked as gentle and human as anyone Oliver had ever known—had drawn an image on the painted cement floor in his own blood. It was a crude human face, obscured by crimson lines.

A face scarred, as if by a harrow.

"Someone is hunting us," Fleuter said.

## 8

Sebastian called the police before sending Oliver away in the cab. "I'll tell them I discovered my friends when I arrived for a dinner party."

"Will you be all right?"

Fleuter only shrugged.

When Oliver got back to his hotel room, he was depleted. He desperately needed rest and collapsed onto his bed. He felt he was asleep only a moment before there was a knock on the door. He opened the door in a foul mood and saw the night clerk. "This had better be worth my time," he said.

The clerk took a fearful step back, reaching out and offering a stiff sheet of paper in one hand. "I was told to wait until midnight to give you this."

Oliver snarled and snatched the message from the clerk's fingers, watching the man scurry away without a tip.

He closed the door and read a hand-written note inscribed in impossibly fine script.

*I have the pretty one.*
*Come to the soundstage tonight.*
*Come alone, or she dies.*

The note was written on photo paper. When Oliver turned it over, he was looking at a glossy studio portrait of Yvonne Romain.

He felt his jaws elongating. A bone in his face snapped like a dry twig. "Damn it all," he tried to say. "Not now!" The sounds that came out of him were less than human.

Christ, he thought.

He subdued the wolf inside with a knock from the bottle of scotch in his coat pocket. When the phone rang, he growled.

It was Kate. Again. "Oliver, I'm worried about you."

"Can't talk, Sweets," he said. "Call you later."

As she cried, "Are you having an affair?" he hung up the phone and put on his coat.

When he stepped out of the hotel, a police car pulled up. An officer in uniform got out of the car, along with Detective Chief Inspector Schaap. "I wonder if I could have a word," Schaap said. It did not sound like a request.

"I'm just on my way to the studio," Oliver said. "I've . . . forgotten my copy of the script."

"Fine," Schaap said. "We'll give you a lift. We can talk on the way."

"That's hardly necessary," Oliver said. "It's such a short walk."

"I insist," the Detective said.

Oliver got into the car, settling into the back seat with both policemen up front. Was he sweating? He felt as if he was sweating. What if they saw him sweating? Jesus, he thought. I'm falling apart.

Schaap spoke over his shoulder. "Are you all right, sir?"

"Long day," Oliver said, forcing a smile.

"You film people work the most curious hours."

"Said the pot."

Schapp looked back at him. "Come again?"

"Pot, kettle, black," Oliver said, feeling silly. "Never mind."

The Detective nodded and then asked, "Do you know a Sebastian Fleuter?"

"I recently met him, yes," Oliver said, knowing the police had been coming and going and that he had probably been seen talking to Fleuter.

"Were you with him tonight?"

Oliver shook his head. "No. I had a very long day on set and had only just got back to my hotel when I realized I had forgotten my script."

Schaap thought this over.

Oliver had to struggle to remain calm. "Is something wrong?"

"Mr. Fleuter was killed tonight," Schaap said. "He called us to report the discovery of a crime scene, a multiple murder. When we got to his location, *he* was dead as well. His head was all but blown off by a shotgun blast. Nasty bit of luck, that."

At a complete loss for words and feeling he should respond *somehow,* Oliver asked, "How do you know it was a shotgun?" He instantly regretted asking that question when he saw the interest it kindled in Schaap.

"Because the poor man was riddled with these," the Detective said, holding up a gleaming metal bead.

Oliver could not hide the horror on his face, horror of the pain that miniscule portion of silver could cause, and the horror of his friend's demise.

As Schaap mulled this over, Oliver realized his own horrified reaction was the last thing the Detective expected. Until that moment, Schaap had likely thought Oliver was guilty of the crime.

"That's just awful," Oliver said. "Who could have done such a thing?"

"That is what I intend to discover," Schaap said, as the car came to a stop. "And here we are."

Oliver got out of the car and wished the policemen luck. "I hope whoever did that terrible deed gets what is coming to him."

As the car pulled away, no doubt Schaap thought *that* over as well.

With nothing but a half-empty bottle of whiskey in his coat pocket, Oliver nodded to the night shift security guard and stepped through the gates of Bray Studios.

## 9

It was a scene right out of a film: a shoddy second-rate thriller penned by an amateur. The man who had Yvonne Romain in his clutches was the man in the trilby, the man with the scarred face: William Lucanus Walmstead. The *Royal Dogcatcher*. Now Oliver knew what kind of dogs this man had been commissioned to deal with.

Walmstead stood in the street that was part of the *Curse of the Werewolf* film set. He had an arm around Yvonne's neck, a brutal chokehold. In his other hand was his shotgun. He had switched on some of the Klieg lights in the rigging overhead so that his face was hidden in the shadow of his hat.

"Step a little closer, beast, so I can see you."

Oliver stepped closer. They were now within spitting distance.

"Show yourself, you blighted thing, you diseased beast," Walmstead said.

Oliver tried to hold the wolf in as claws pierced the tips of his fingers and his snout and jaws began to elongate. There were more changes happening *inside* him than out; it was as if his body had posted a casting call for torment; the sharp pain of muscle and bone changing shape, the brute agony of internal organs shifting into new positions. He was now half man and half wolf. When Yvonne saw what had happened to his face, she screamed in terror and tried to escape Walmstead's grasp, knocking off the man's trilby.

No longer obscured by shadows, the utter ruination of the man's face was revealed. The flesh had been brutally gouged long ago and had healed in deep furrows.

"I suppose a wolf did that do you," Oliver said. "One dog bites and all dogs must die? We are no longer like that. We never were. I wouldn't be surprised if *you* had provoked an otherwise peaceful wolf until it lashed out and—"

He struck a nerve and Walmstead shrieked a command. "Silence!"

"Let the girl go," Oliver said quietly.

"I will. As soon as you *kill* her." The man gave Oliver a wide grin, clearly unhinged. "Or at least that is how it will appear: you savaged the girl and I stepped in and put you down, but alas, too late!"

"Why are you doing this?" Oliver asked. "Wolves are a peaceful people. What could you possibly gain from this?"

That struck another nerve.

"People may suggest that I am doing this simply to secure my outdated, archaic position and to shore up my own self-worth. To that I say *bollocks*. You wolves are evil through and through. You may heel like well-trained hounds now, but there will come a day when you will turn on us. I am not the sort of man who will wait for that day."

"And so you've been killing werewolves," Oliver said. "You've been killing my kind."

"Yes."

"Well, then," Oliver said, taking the bottle of scotch from his pocket. The motion made Walmstead raise the shotgun, the barrel pointed at Oliver's broad chest but just beyond his reach.

"I'll have a final drink, and then we'll get down to business."

"To your health," Walmstead said with a sarcastic sneer, as Oliver drank deep.

Before swallowing that burning mouthful of scotch Oliver waited, and waited, and *there*—Walmstead's eyes flicked in Yvonne's direction for just a moment. That was all Oliver needed.

He lunged forward and spit that deep mouthful of alcohol right into Walmstead's face.

Like the villain in a play performed by children, Walmstead screamed, "My eyes!"

Oliver grabbed the barrel of the shotgun, pushing it up and away as Walmstead squeezed the trigger. It discharged and a Klieg light shattered overhead. Bits of glass rained down on them.

Yvonne pulled free and ran away as Oliver and Walmstead engaged each other.

The shotgun fell to the street. Oliver head-butted the man, dazing him.

Walmstead's eyes were still rolling as Oliver tore open the man's coat and shirt, raking skin and muscle with his claws. Walmstead wailed.

Flesh seemed to part effortlessly under his touch. Oliver pried open the man's ribcage amid a horrid chorus of wet snaps and cracks. There it was—the miscreant's wildly beating heart—completely exposed.

Walmstead was still conscious, still aware, as Oliver said, "It appears the catcher has been caught," before leaning close and biting deep. There was a burst of hot blood. It splashed the street like water spilled from a bucket. Then Oliver was chewing living muscle as sweet as it was tough.

**10**

After that, things were *vague,* as if Oliver had been drunk on blood.

He remembered Yvonne coming to him and wiping blood from a face that felt like his old face again, not some distorted monstrosity.

He remembered Schaap appearing from nowhere and saying, "You'd best be on your way. Leave this mess to me. I'll clean it up."

He remembered asking what would happen to him now and Schaap replying, "Nothing, if you are a good boy from this point on. Her Majesty only punishes the wicked."

Yvonne got him back to his hotel, put him in bed, and left him to sleep.

The following day, it was as if nothing had happened. Oliver went to the studio, to the street where he had stood the night before. There was no blood, no broken glass, no sign anything out of the ordinary had occurred.

He supposed handlers for the Royal Family covered everything up; Schaap was probably one of them. They were reputed to be quite good at this sort of thing. It was as if William Lucanus Walmstead had never existed.

Oliver shot his scenes and left the studio at day's end to walk under the moon. When he returned to his hotel room that night, with a bottle of gin in hand, Yvonne was waiting for him.

He was already drunk and she noticed. "I never thought you were a drinker, Oliver."

"I never was, until now. Now I have to be, to keep that beast at bay. I never want another person to see what you saw."

"What . . . what *did* I see, Oliver?" she asked. "What was that beast that saved me? Was that really *you*?"

"It was a side of me that must never again be free. It can either be indulged, or restrained and caged. I choose to cage it. And the only way to restrain it is with drink."

Yvonne touched his shoulder. "But what sort of life would that be, drunk all the time, it—"

"It must be done." He stepped away from her. "It *must* be."

"Oliver, I can't let you make that sacrifice."

"But I must," he said, "for the safety of everyone I know."

As though she thought of the road that lay ahead of him, she wept. "Is there anything I can do for you?"

"Yes," he said, taking her hand and kissing it gently, thinking *like meat like meat she smells she tastes she feels like meat.* "Never speak of this to anyone. There could be other men like Walmstead out there. Keep this secret, Yvonne. The wolf in me must never be awakened and allowed to run free."

He turned away from her then and raised the bottle of gin to his lips. He drank deep, not hearing her sobbing as she left the room.

Oliver looked out the window at the night sky. The moon had yet to rise and the fragile radiance of the stars quivered in the dark.

"To the moon," he said, slurring his words as he raised the bottle in a toast to a companion he would never escape for long. "You will seek me, always. And I will turn away from you, always."

*Was the wolf real, or was it simply a fearsome delusion? We will never know now, but I suspect poor Oliver believed the wolf was real, that he was haunted by his belief that the wolf in him would strive to be released whenever the moon was full, or whenever he encountered the corrupt and the malicious. That the beast in him followed the ancient imperative to protect the likes of you and me against those who would do us harm.*

*I once asked him if he had ever let the wolf out to follow its nature. He gave me a grim smile and said, "Never. I was too afraid it might hurt someone innocent, someone I cared about."*

*He had never forgotten Sebastian Fleuter saying* sometimes . . . wolves go bad.

*The wolf had to be restrained, lest it harm someone Oliver loved, and so my friend drank, and drank. He drank through the nights and he drank through the years and, aside from the rare snarl or nip, the wolf inside him slept. And when Oliver Reed died, he cared not a whit for what others thought of him, for he had kept his promise. He had kept the wolf at bay.*

**BEN MONROE** grew up in Northern California and has spent most of his life there. He lives in the East Bay Area with his wife and two children. His most recent published works are *In the Belly of the Beast and Other Tales of Cthulhu Wars* and the graphic novel *Planet Apocalypse*. He can be reached via his website at benmonroe.com and on Twitter @_BenMonroe_.

# THE QUARRY

## BEN MONROE

*SUMMER, 1984*

It was the height of summer and stifling boredom had descended like webs of cotton candy melting on hot sand. In that no man's land between the excited rush of vacation's start and the strange excitement of seeing friends again as school began, Stacey and Mike's mom had a deadline to hit, so she'd told the kids to go play outside. Ellen was a graphic artist. Stacey didn't really know what that was, sort of assuming it had something to do with drawing graphs like in her math book. Stacey's dad had been out of the picture since before she was born. Mike's dad came around occasionally, but, according to Ellen, only when he needed money. So it was pretty much just Ellen, Mike, and Stacey, and that was okay by them.

It was too hot to play outside, but Mike and Stacey had been messing around out front when J.D. swung by on his gleaming Mongoose dirt bike. As usual, they heard him before they saw him. J.D. had a Sony tape deck strapped to his handlebars and the Scorpions' "Rock You Like a Hurricane" was blasting from it. As he pulled to a stop in front of their house and clicked off the music, Stacey noticed he had a towel wrapped up and strapped to the top tube of his bike with a bungee cord. "Hey Mike!" he yelled, then saw her. "Sup, Squirt?" he said. Stacey blushed sort of with embarrassment, but also sort of with excitement that he'd noticed her at all.

"Hey, J.D.," Mike said. "What's up?"

"Going swimming. Too hot to stay inside today," J.D. replied. "You want to go?"

Mike nodded as he approached J.D. "To the pool? My mom told us to get out of the house; I bet I could get her to spring for a couple of ice creams just to get us out of her hair."

J.D. smiled. "Yeah, that'd be cool. Go grab your stuff and we'll jet over."

Mike turned and ran back to the house, slamming the front door behind him as he barreled through. Stacey rolled her eyes in a way she thought made her look more like one of the Big Kids. "He's always slamming that door," she said. "Mom hates when he does that."

A moment later, the door erupted open. Mike charged out of the house, down the brick steps and back to the street. Slightly winded, he huffed, "Yeah, Mom's cool with me going to the pool. But she says we have to take Stace with us." He looked at J.D., as if waiting for a wisecrack or for J.D. to take back the offer.

"Yeah, that's cool," J.D. said. "As long as she can keep up."

"Ugh, Mike, I don't want to go to the pool!" Stacey said.

Mike turned to her, a frustrated look in his eyes. "Mom says I can't go unless I take you with me, so come on, will ya?"

"Sure, Stace," J.D. said. "We'll have fun. Trust me?" He winked at her. She suddenly got shy again.

"Yeah, okay," she said. "We'll have fun."

Half an hour later, they were on their bikes and on the road. They'd swung by to pick up Jenny and Paul, neighborhood kids who hung out with Mike and J.D. and lived on the way to the pool. Stacey liked Jenny a lot. Jenny was pretty and nice. Stacey was pretty sure Mike had a crush on her. Stacey thought that was gross, but they were teenagers. Stacey thought Paul was a little weird, but he wasn't mean or creepy. He just wouldn't ever shut up about wizards and dragons and his dumb games. He'd tried to explain *Dungeons & Dragons* to Stacey once, and she said it sounded like playing Barbies with math, and he didn't bother talking to her about it again after that. Stacey couldn't believe he was wearing jeans on such a hot day, but that was Paul for you.

J.D. led the group, as usual. They rode their bikes down Sycamore Lane, turned left at Oakes, and were pumping their legs hard, laughing and enjoying that warm golden summer day. Mike veered to the right as they approached Hayes Street, which would take them the back way to the pool. J.D. kept going straight, shot past the intersection, and blasted past the sign to Hayes.

"Hey!" Mike called out. "Hey, dumbass! You missed the turn!"

J.D. looked back over his shoulder and smiled. That mischievous smile that Stacey loved, although she knew it meant he was up to something. "Change of plans!" J.D. called out. "Just follow me!"

Jenny pumped her pedals harder, trying to catch up to where J.D. was gliding along the warm asphalt. "What are you talking about?" she called ahead to him. "Where are we going?"

J.D. laughed. "This is better than the pool. Trust me," he shouted back at her.

Paul sat up and pointed ahead, like a wobbly knight on his trusty steed. "Tally ho, fellow adventurers," he shouted, and pounded his pedals, zooming after J.D.

Jenny slowed a bit and as Mike closed on her, they exchanged a quick look. Jenny looked back at Stacey and smiled. "You up for an adventure, Squirt?"

Stacey, who was already getting tired, nodded. "We have to be back by dark, though, Mike. Mom said!"

"We'll be back by then, don't worry. Right, J.D.?" Mike called out.

J.D. looked back and rolled his eyes. "Oh, sure. We'll be back by dark, no problem."

The group continued down Sycamore for almost a mile before turning onto a dirt road with no sign. Two ramshackle houses faced each other on either side of the dirt road. One had a rusty, broken-down pickup truck on the lawn in front. When Stacey looked toward the house across the road, she saw a flash of movement as a curtain closed behind a window. She had a brief glimpse of a hand retreating behind the curtain.

Past the houses, there was nothing but scrub and long grass, summer dry and golden, and the occasional oak tree behind the barbed wire fence which paralleled the dirt road. Stacey looked around nervously, not sure where they were. She had a tingling in her gut that told her maybe she shouldn't be here. That maybe following Mike and his dumb friends wasn't a great idea.

She didn't have a chance to worry, though, as Mike, J.D., Jenny, and Paul rocketed ahead of her. Pedaling her bike hard, she struggled to catch up to them. "Dammit, guys, wait up!" she called ahead. The older kids were talking and laughing, but Stacey couldn't quite make out what they were saying from where she was.

Stacey pedaled harder, her face getting red. Sweat poured down her back. The others were slowing down too because suddenly she was gaining on them. A moment later, they'd stopped entirely. She came skidding to a halt in a cloud of trail dust next to Jenny.

"Holy cow," Jenny said. "You're really a good rider for a little kid."

"I'm only three years younger than you, Jenny," Stacey said, puffing between deep breaths.

Paul flicked the kickstand of his bike down, leaned it, and got off the bike. "So what's the big idea, J.D.?" he said. "You asked us to go to the pool, and then suddenly you've got some big surprise going?"

Mike straddled the top bar of his bike, holding it steady between his knees. "So, what's the big surprise?"

J.D. took an old two-liter Coke bottle filled with water out of his saddlebags and took a long drag. Stacey had noted in the past that many of J.D.'s actions seemed kind of dramatic, like he was trying to draw out the suspense of his Big Idea with the water bottle. He lowered the bottle. A glistening drop of water spilled down his chin and caught the sunlight in a brief sparkle before he wiped it away with the back of his hand. "You guys know about Founder's Quarry?" he asked.

Stacey's stomach flopped. Of course, she'd heard of it. And nothing good, either. Her best friend Casey had a cousin whose friend's brother had drowned in the quarry.

"Are you kidding?" Paul said. "Yeah, we've heard of it. Everyone has."

"And nobody's allowed to go near it," Jenny said. "It's too dangerous, that's what they say."

"Come on, J.D., let's go to the pool," Mike said.

Stacey's eyes went from each of the big kids to the others in turn, finally settling on J.D. She didn't think she wanted to be here any more and would just as rather ride home.

J.D. rolled his eyes at them. "Aw, come on. I found the trail out to it and rode it there myself. Don't you guys want to see it? It's totally safe."

"When'd you find the trail?" Mike asked. "How far is it?"

"Couple weeks ago. I was messing around and found the trailhead. It's only a couple miles further, guys."

Paul looked back in the direction they'd come. Back toward home. "I don't know, dude. Every time it comes up, my folks get all mad, and make me promise never to go near the place."

"Right," Jenny said. "It's supposed to be unstable from all the hydraulic mining hella long ago."

J.D. smiled, but Stacey could see he was getting exasperated. "Guys, seriously. It's just a big damn hole in the ground. Full of water now, and you have to come check it out. It's seriously awesome."

Mike was dubious. "Just a couple of miles up the road, right?"

"Right!" J.D. said. "We'll be there before you know it."

"Ah, what the heck." Paul flipped the kickstand back up and mounted his bike again. "Let's go check it out."

"Sure, I'm game," said Jenny. She glanced at Stacey. "What about you, Squirt?"

Stacey turned to her brother, her eyes were wide open. "Mike," she said, barely above a whisper. "Mom'll be mad if she finds out."

Mike looked back at her and smiled. "Oh, it'll be fine. We'll have fun, right? And be back home before dinner." He lifted one foot into the rubber stirrup of his bike pedal. "Come on, let's do it."

The four teens barreled off along the trail, kicking up clouds of dust in their wake. Stacey muttered, "Mom's gonna be so mad . . . " before stomping the pedals of her bike and powering off after them.

The sun was high and bright in the sky by the time they reached Founder's Quarry. They pulled their bikes up to the edge of the trail, just before it disappeared under a chain-link fence and into the water-filled quarry. Across from them was a tall cliff of bare brown rock. Atop the cliff, a verdant swath of gnarled oaks loomed like a row of silent green giants glaring down. Water flowed from a stream to the side of the cliff wall, poured into the quarry and then sluiced away to their right. The air was still, aside from a cool fresh breeze which drifted across the surface of the water.

The chain-link fence skirted around the half of the lake which wasn't bordered by the low cliff. A large metal sign hung from it and proclaimed that they should KEEP OUT! and the area was UNSAFE FOR SWIMMING. The sign was peppered with bullet holes, but Stacey could still see a graphic silhouette of someone in the water with a big red crossed-through circle around it. Stacey still felt like this was a bad idea. "Are you sure, Mikey?" she said.

Mike smiled back at her, but she could tell that even he was nervous. Something in his eyes said he wasn't sure either. "I don't know," he said. "But J.D.'s been here before, so I guess it's okay."

Stacey stared at the sign, the stick figure guy with his hands over his head like he was drowning. "I guess," she said, unconvinced.

A gate in the fence bowed outward, like someone had tried to bend it open before. The three boys climbed off of their bikes and let them crash to the dry, packed dirt amongst knee-high weeds.

"It's weird, right?" Jenny dismounted her bike, swinging one of her long legs over the frame, and then lowering the kickstand to the ground, letting her bike lean in a graceful freestand. "Like something from a whole different world."

They managed sneak under the lock and chain with just a little effort. Mike had to hold the opening a little wider for everyone but Stacey, who snuck right through. Jenny walked toward the lake, stepping gingerly around the slick rocks on the shore.

What Stacey couldn't get over was how silent it was here. "It's so quiet," she said, just above a whisper. The low rumble of water trickling into and out of the quarry muttered a susurrant hiss in the background. Over that drifted the faintest whisper of wind, the occasional croak of a frog in the distance. But aside from those intermittent natural noises, the quarry was void of sound.

Mike hustled over to stand next to Jenny where she stood at the water's edge gazing toward the center of the quarry, down into the cobalt blue deeps. She toed off her checkerboard Vans, flipping them to the side and then dipped her feet into the water. "Ooh!" she squealed. "It's cold!" She stepped back a few feet from the water. "Way too cold. I'm not going in there!"

Mike laughed. "Well, yeah it is. Who knows how deep this hole is, right?"

Paul walked closer, his eyes narrowing as he peered into the water. "Gotta be damn deep, I suppose." He picked up a fist-sized rock from the shore and tossed it underhand in an awkward arc toward the center of the lake. It landed with a *plop*! Ripples shimmered out from the point of impact.

Stacey heard crunching footsteps approaching behind her. She whirled around and J.D. was running right at them. He was laughing as he yanked his Van Halen t-shirt off over his head. The neck hole got stuck and he danced around for a moment with his face covered by the shirt.

Jenny turned to see him, and a smile played across her face. "Oh my God, you are nuts!"

Then J.D. had the shirt off, tossed it aside, and ran straight for the water's edge. He tackled Mike as he reached the shore and they both tumbled into the clear blue water. A splash of frigid cold geysered up in their passing. They vanished under the lake's surface.

Paul, Stacey, and Jenny scrambled to the water's edge. Jenny and Paul were laughing, but Stacey wasn't so sure this was funny yet. She could see Mike and J.D. below the surface, swimming toward the center of the pool, away from the water's edge. Stacey noticed that the light didn't reach the bottom; it was just darkness under them. After a moment, J.D. and Mike broke the surface of the water. Mike spat out a mouthful, coughed, and hacked up more water. Then he reached out for the shore, swimming toward it with strong, even strokes. "Holy shit!" he said. "The water's freezing!"

J.D. had swum a dozen feet beyond him and broke the surface, treading water. He shivered, rippling the surrounding water. His teeth chattered. "No!" he shouted toward the shore. "It's . . . it's great! Come on in, guys!"

Jenny laughed and kicked water towards him. "You're crazy!"

As Mike came to the edge of the pool and climbed out, Stacey watched him lower his feet onto a rocky shelf, just a yard from shore. "Careful, guys," he said. "There's a hell of a drop-off, straight down." Mike walked back toward shore through knee-deep water, but within a few strides, he was back on dry land.

J.D. was treading water and visibly shivering. Lake water lapped at his shoulders, splashing as his arms stirred to keep him afloat. "J.D., come out of there, man!" Mike called out to him. "It's too cold. You're going to get hypothermia or something."

J.D. smiled. "Yeah, I know . . . It really is hella cold." He swam toward shore, kicking up sparkles of crystal water drops.

Stacey watched him swim closer, his arms pulling and legs kicking against the water. But then she caught other movement on the edge of her vision. Ripples of something pale, sinuous, slithered in the water beyond him. She grabbed Jenny's arm and pointed to the other side of the lake. "Jenny! What is it?" she cried out.

Jenny turned, startled. "What? Ow, you're hurting my arm!"

"Look!" Stacey cried. "Look there!"

Jenny looked. J.D. stopped abruptly, his forward motion halted as if he'd hit an invisible brick wall.

Stacey waited for him to look up, to take a breath, do something.

But he floated, motionless. Dead man's float, she thought, and remembered taking swimming lessons a few summers ago where they'd learned that float for if they got tired. But J.D. didn't look tired. He looked dead.

"Paul! Mike! Help!" Jenny shouted, then jumped into the water, swimming toward J.D.

"Jenny! No!" Stacey cried out. Behind J.D. but getting closer, she saw a pallid mass below the surface of the water. It drifted toward him through the rippling water like a large mass of ghostly pale eels or worms.

Jenny continued swimming toward J.D. Then she saw them, too. The water churned around J.D., as ridged eel-like shapes wrapped and entangled him. They swarmed him, engulfed his body, and squeezed. Jenny thrashed in the water, pushing away from the nightmare squirming mass, swimming toward shore with strength born of panic.

Stacey, Mike, and Paul were calling to her from the shore, yelling for her to hurry. Their eyes fixed on her as she pulled away from the deathly pale, frothing knot that had swallowed up J.D.'s prone form.

The ropy tentacles continued constricting his body, squirming around him, engulfing his torso and limbs. One as thick as his arm slid around J.D.'s neck like a noose, then strangled him tighter and tighter. His unseeing eyes opened as his tongue lolled from his mouth. His face grew red, then purple. With a juicy wet pop, his head fell free of his body. Crimson blossomed around J.D.'s body as it sank. Stacey shrieked.

J.D.'s head bobbed once, twice. Lifeless eyes stared up at the sky until the head sank into the gloomy depths. Paul watched it sink and then fainted, falling face-first onto a chunk of rock, gashing his cheek.

At the sound of Stacey's cry, Jenny slowed her strokes. The water churned around her. Before she had a chance to shout in surprise or terror, she was dragged below.

Stacey watched wide-eyed as the pale, squirming mass sank deep below the water's surface. A thin hiss escaped her open mouth: the last soundless vestige of a scream. She took a half-hearted, shuffling step back from the water's edge. When her heel hit a rock, Stacey stumbled, but caught her balance before toppling over. Ass over tea-kettle, she thought, and squealed thin, nervous laughter.

"Paul! Paul, get up!" Mike yelled from behind her.

Stacey turned to see another of the long white tentacles inching toward Paul, who lay face down in the grit and gravel at the water's edge. The pale mass reached forward, inch by inch. It pulsed toward Paul somehow, grew toward him. A sequence of visible masses slid along the growth, forcing themselves forward, like a snake regurgitating a squirming pack of fat rats one by one. Then, as it approached the terminal point of the tentacle, the mass dissipated and it grew a few more inches forward.

Mike ran toward the viscous horror. The tentacle pulsed forward again, reaching toward Paul's ankle, prodding around the cuff of his pant leg. Mike leapt and came down with both feet on the loathsome thing. His Chuck Taylor high tops smashed the searching length against the rocky shore. He stomped again and the skin of the thing burst open. The tentacle pulled back, slithering along the shore, leaving a trail of glistening yellow slime in its wake. A froth of bubbles churned the water, releasing a foul stench: an angry, sour smell. Then the eel-like tentacle vanished, pulled back into the deep of the quarry. Mike grabbed Paul under his armpits and dragged him back from the water as fast as he could.

Stacey ran to them, grabbing Paul's legs and trying to help Mike. She'd only taken a few short, awkward steps when she tripped over a rock and fell. She landed on her knees, skinning them. As the blood began to flow, she began to cry. "Mike, I want Mom!"

"I know, Squirt!" Mike replied through teeth gritted closed by exertion. He put his hands under Paul's armpits again and yanked.

"What the hell, man?" Paul mumbled, rising from his stupor.

"Get up, dude! Move," Mike shouted. He let go of Paul and stood up. "Come on! To the fence!"

Paul got up. He moved. "Where are Jenny and J.D.?" he asked, as he booked toward the fence.

Stacey got to the gate just before Paul and Mike. Blood trickled down her shins, mixing with sweat into watery pink runnels. She dove through the opening, scraping her legs further. Fear had numbed her. She turned to hold the gate open as Paul squirmed through. As she did, she saw a knot of muscle and pale gray flesh heave itself onto the quarry's shore. And eyes. Lidless black eyes, shiny and glistening with hungry malevolence. Stacey saw the shimmering formless thing reaching out with pulsing tentacles toward them. "Miiiiiike!" she shrieked. "I'm scaaaaared!"

Mike turned to see the roiling mass bearing down on him. He picked up a handful of rocks and threw them dead center at the nightmare form. A rock the size of his fist hit one of the thing's black eyes, which popped, releasing a trickle of thin, yellow, custardy slime. "Run!" he shouted. "Run, Stacey! Get help!"

Paul shoved his way through the gate, but the chain-link fencing caught on his jeans, catching him fast. "Help me!" he shouted, as his fingers scrabbled in the dirt and gravel on the far side of the fence.

Stacey pulled hard, pulled with all the strength she had left, but he wouldn't budge. After a terrible scream, a fear-shriek, Stacey saw a multitude of thin white tentacles surround and engulf her big brother. They wrapped around him until he vanished from her sight, and the great pale mass once again seethed its bulk back to the water.

Paul grabbed at her hands, his eyes frantic. "Help me, Stacey! I'm stuck, help me!"

She shook off his grasping hands. "I can't! I can't get you unstuck!" She spun around, trying to find anything she could use to help get him loose. But the gate was too tight—she couldn't force it open like Mike had when they went in. *And oh, God, Mike's in the water with that thing,* she thought, still not ready to face the reality of the situation.

Then she saw their bikes. "I'm going to get help!" she said, running toward her Huffy. "I'll be right back, promise!" she called back as she ran.

"Stacey!" Paul cried. "Dammit, you can't leave me! Don't leave me!"

She got on her bike, kicked the pedals and rode back down the path toward home, leaving Paul, the monster, and the whole awful place behind a cloud of dust.

"Stacey!" she heard Paul's terrified shout from a distance. "Stacey, pleaaaaase don't leave me!"

With every ounce of energy left in her tired little legs, she pounded the pedals as hard as she could, and rode as fast as she could, and prayed as hard as she could that the grownups would know what to do. Grownups always knew what to do.

Stacey's legs wobbled like jelly by the time she got back to the trailhead. She knew she'd never make it back home in time to get help. The handlebars juddered in her grip as the bike bounced over every rock and rill in the dirt. Up ahead, she saw the street sign and the heat-shimmer off the asphalt of Sycamore Street. The two ramshackle houses up ahead loomed closer as her bike rushed over the rough trail.

She brought her bike to a crashing halt before the small structures. As she spilled to the ground, a new wave of pain shot up her leg, into her hip where she'd landed, pinned under the bike frame. "Help!" she called through her tears. "Somebody help me!"

Stacey pushed the bike frame away with her hands and one foot. She crawled out from under it, and then sat in a defeated heap, fat tears of despair rolling down her cheeks and plopping off her chin. "Won't anyone help me?" she whispered, looking from one house to the other. She saw a hand at the curtains in the house across from her. She waved toward the window and stood up.

There was a click and the door opened just an inch or two. A woman's face peered out from the darkness beyond the crack. Stacey waved at the woman. "Please, can I use your phone?" she asked. "My friends are . . . " and then she burst into tears once more.

The woman stepped onto the small porch. She was old, Stacey saw, maybe even older than Stacey's grandmother. She cast her gaze down the trail toward the quarry, then back at Stacey. Her face softened, almost into a look of pity. She rushed down the steps from the patio to the front yard, then over to where Stacey stood, bloody and teary-eyed in the street. "Of course, Dearie. Let's get you inside and we'll call your parents."

Stacey flung her arms around the woman's aproned body and crushed her in a desperate hug. "Oh, thank you!"

The woman ushered her inside, into the front room. A threadbare sofa sat near one wall. A series of photographs leaned on the mantle. Next to the sofa was a black plastic rotary dial telephone on a side table. She sat Stacey down on the sofa. "You call your parents, let them know where you are: 8898 Sycamore. My name is Gloria Goodman, and you're safe here."

Stacey nodded, then said, "My friends, and I were at the quarry! Something . . . something dragged them into the water. Paul was stuck in the fence and I left to get help . . . "

"It's okay, little one," Gloria said. "You call your parents. I'll get some things to get you cleaned up. And then we'll call the fire department. We'll get help for your friends."

Stacey wanted to tell the old lady that was dumb, that they needed to get the police, and the ambulances, and the army out there. But grownups always know what to do, so she said, "Yes, ma'am," and called her mom.

❧

By the time Stacey's mom came banging on the door, Stacey's adrenaline had crashed hard. She sat at a small table in Gloria's meager kitchen, hands wrapped around a warm mug of tea. Her head was dozy and felt filled with cotton. Gloria ushered Ellen in to see her daughter.

"Mom?" Stacey said quietly. "Mom, something bad happened . . . "

Ellen pulled up a chair and sat next to Stacey. "What's going on, Pumpkin? I thought you were going to the pool with Mike and his friends?" She looked down to see Stacey's knees, now cleaned and wrapped in cotton bandages. She turned her head to Gloria. "What's going on, Gloria?"

Stacey's eyes went wide. "You guys know each other?"

"Yes," Gloria said. "Your mother and I go way back. But let's hear the story again."

"Oh, Mom!" Stacey cried. "There's something in Founder's Quarry! Something big, and weird, and it dragged Mike and Jenny and J.D. in, and I had to leave Paul to try to get help, and, Mom, it was just awful!"

"What have I told you about the quarry, Stacey?" Ellen said. "You know better to go near that place. I've told you and Mike to stay away from there."

"I know, Mom," Stacey said, a pleading whine in her voice. "I told Mike, but his friends wanted to go, and he wanted to go with them, and he said it would be okay. And Mom, it wasn't okay! We have to go help them!"

Ellen and Gloria shared a brief look. "You go," Gloria said. "I'll call 911 and get the police and an ambulance on the way."

"Come along, Stacey," Ellen said. "Show me where all this happened."

"Can't you go, Mom? Do I have to go with you?"

Ellen stood and held out a hand. Stacey took it and they walked across the living room and outside the small house. "Yes, Stacey," she said. "I think it's best if you come with me. Gloria will send for help."

Soon they were in Ellen's car, a sky-blue Datsun that was more sun-faded than pastel. "Do you know how to get there, Mom?" Stacey hoped the answer would be 'no' and they could just wait for the cops to take care of everything.

"Yes, Sweetie," Ellen replied. "I've been there plenty of times before."

Stacey's eyes grew wider. "But you said it was dangerous, and we shouldn't go there . . . "

"That's true," Ellen said. "And I wish you'd listened." She started the engine and popped the car into gear. "Let's go see what we can see, shall we?"

Stacey buckled in and locked the door, something she almost always forgot to do. With a lurch, the car sped off down the dirt road, kicking up a cloud of golden-brown dust as it barreled toward the quarry.

Within ten minutes they were in sight of the chain-link fence surrounding the quarry. Ellen drew the car to a slow stop right in front of the gate, opened the car's door, and got out. She walked toward the fence, looking through it at the slow lapping of the quarry pool. Bending down, she put one leg, then her body through the opening in the gate. It was a tight squeeze for a grownup, but she made it through.

Stacey sat up straight in her seat, looking over the dashboard. At the bottom of the gate, she could see splatters of darkening blood on the gravel. Strips of torn blue denim fluttered in the chain-link of the fence just above. She felt her stomach flip and scrambled to unlock and open the door. When she got out of the car, she caught the green, clean scent of the quarry water in the breeze. Something about how pure it smelled, yet knowing what slithered below the surface, filled her with abject dread.

She searched around for her mom. "Mom," she whispered. "Mom, where are you?" Then Stacey took a few halting steps toward the fence. Each step was hesitant, as she knew it took her that much closer to the water.

Up ahead, she saw her mom standing at the quarry's edge, water lapping at her feet. Stacey looked behind her, over her shoulder, hoping the cops would be here soon, straining to hear any hint of a siren, or engine. But she heard nothing. Nothing but the wet slap of water on the shore, and wind in the trees. Stacey took a few more steps forward. "Mom, I'm scared!" she called.

Ellen held her hand out toward Stacey. Her brows were furrowed, but she wore an apologetic smile across her face. "It's okay, Honey," she said. "It'll be fine, come see."

"I don't want to, Mom . . . " Stacey said, barely above a whisper.

Ellen held out her hand. "Come on, kiddo," she said. "I want to explain it all to you."

Stacey didn't want to go anywhere near the water. She wanted to turn and run away as fast as she could. But she walked forward, toward her mom. She squeezed through the gate and crept toward the water's edge. "I don't want to see it, Mom. I want to go home," she said, approaching her mother.

Ellen reached out and took Stacey's hand. "It's okay, Honey," she said. "There's nothing to be afraid of in the water. Come see."

As they stood at the lip of the quarry, the water before them churned. Pale white slithering shapes rose from the darkness of the deep water, bubbling toward the surface. Stacey screamed. "Mama! It's the monster! The monster!"

Eel-like tentacles broke the surface of the water, dripping with slime and algae. They slithered toward Ellen and Stacey. First one, then another, and another, wrapped around Ellen's leg then crept to her face, caressing it and leaving a trail of greenish-gray slime along her cheek.

"No, Honey," Ellen said, smiling. "It's not a monster." She turned toward Stacey, her eyes huge, pupils dilated so wide the irises were little more than black voids. "It's your daddy."

"Seven Seconds" arose out of **ERIKA MAILMAN'S** fascination with what happened to the multitude of bodies guillotined during the French Revolution. Similar shades of this history are found in *Betrayed*, her Young Adult novel under the pen name Lynn Carthage. She has written two other novels under that name and three under her real name, including *The Witch's Trinity*, which was a Bram Stoker finalist and a *San Francisco Chronicle* Notable Book. Her latest is *The Murderer's Maid: A Lizzie Borden Novel*. She holds an MFA in poetry, has been a Yaddo fellow, and is co-director of the Gold Rush Writers Conference. Learn more at www.erikamailman.com and www.lynncarthage.com.

# SEVEN SECONDS

## Erika Mailman

**YOU KNOW WHEN** a guy just *gets* you and it's such a relief after all the drama? That was how it was with Diderot, an international student I met in my junior year of college. Maybe it was because he was French, but he seemed so much more mature than anyone else I'd ever been with. He seemed unconcerned by the minor disagreements that arise naturally in any relationship and evinced a Gallic sort of adultness. Which made me feel like an adult, too.

His hair was black with an adorable overhang of bangs that characterized that time period. Intelligent dark eyes, a generous face, yet all around he was perhaps an inch too thin for what Americans consider a sturdily made man. I was also on the thin side, with curly brown hair and eyes I liked to call green but were really light brown.

Many things had made me feel childish throughout my life. Strange happenstances that underscored how different I was from my classmates. Dumb things. Queasy things.

In third grade, at the end of October, a teacher had once gathered us children in a circle. This demonic woman dimmed the lights as much as possible. I tried to take confidence in hearing shouts from kids on the playground on second recess drifting through the windows. She told us a ghost story.

It was about a woman who always wore a choker around her neck. I think you know this one. The woman's husband couldn't bear that she always wore the tight necklace. Although she had warned him not to, one night he undid the ribbon—and her head fell off. She was one of the walking dead, still alert and marriageable after her beheading.

My classmates squealed at this story in a carefree kind of way. Mary Stebbins asked to go to the bathroom but then refused to go by herself. We were all unsettled until our parents picked us up. Me most of all.

Because the story was disturbing—but more than that, I was upset because our teacher winked at me twice while she told the story. That day, I was wearing a necklace with a big fluorescent green daisy on a purple velvet ribbon. I always did wear something.

My necklaces were slobbered on as I grew older, with loose-lipped kisses from boys who sought my neck like dogs attacking a swan. My first boyfriend wrapped the loose chain of a pendant around his fist, enterprising enough to lightly choke me while he kissed me. One time, he also gathered up my hair and circled under my jaw with the curly brown strands, quoting lines from "Porphyria's Lover" that we had just learned in Mrs. Fenno's AP English class.

It continued like this. Guys teased me in the shower as they soaped me down, pleading with me to take off my necklace, or watching solemnly in the mirror as I put one on before taking off the old one. My index finger and thumb knew exactly how to manipulate the tiny hook and eye of any finding.

For that was what I had learned it was called, browsing the craft aisles at Michael's: a jewelry *finding*.

Diderot was the only man who never troubled me about the omnipresent scarves and necklaces. He also didn't care about various qualms I expressed . . . let's say, things I couldn't talk about. I guess it's rare for a 20-year-old to have a list of taboo topics.

We went to dorm parties and International Club get-togethers (he was the president of the club that year, increasing his power in my eyes) where we sipped or gulped sangria; you can guess which verb goes with which individual. He got all As seemingly without studying, and several times I blew off preparing for a test myself because I was obsessed with him.

I could wax at length about his voice in my ear, the French words that came out only when we made love. I won't.

We had a year, a year that seemed the start of a lifetime. But when school ended in May, he returned to France.

He was regretful; I was destroyed. I almost felt tricked. I knew he was there just for his "junior year abroad" or whatever that equated to in French schooling (O levels?), but I'd hoped our coming together would've changed his plans, entailed rearrangements to stay another year.

My senior year passed with me resentful, in a daze. I attended those parties, aced those exams I could study for. I even took up choir and we sang Poulenc's "La Grenouillère" based on

Apollinaire's sordid little poem, all in French. I bit off every word. I did not investigate Poulenc's other works at that time, which might have put me a little further ahead on my journey of discovery.

This story predates the technology you have grown up with. Computers were new; we called them "word processors" because we couldn't imagine they would process anything other than the simplicity of language. If I'd heard the term "cell phone," I would have thought it was something so tiny a nucleus and cytoplasm would band together to make a call on it, taking turns with their microscopic mouths.

So, I did not "Skype" or "Facetime" with Diderot. Did not even send those charming things we called letters. I purchased a calling card and called him every Sunday until there was a night he was not home. I took it as a sign. He never returned the call.

I graduated and he sent a gift, a silver acorn on a silver chain. What did it mean? The accompanying card did not explain. I wished it was a light gift to say, "I'm nuts for you." I wore it because it felt like a Victorian mourning emblem, as if I were a woman all in black wearing a locket containing a strand of my deceased lover's hair.

I worked two years in a law firm until I had been named office manager, by simple dint of being able to stand the attorneys and thereby possessing what seemed to them like longevity. At this office, I was first given the thing called an email address. And because my name was listed in the caption of a photo that showed all of us members of the team, Diderot was able to search for me and email me. (We were all asked to wear red and gray that day, and my jaunty red jabot—it was the late '80s and I thought it was gorgeous— must've made him either wince or smirk.)

His email read:

*"Dear Cressida,*

*It has been many years but not one day goes by without your face on my mind. I removed myself because I was supposed to. But would you come? Here to Paris? I will send you a ticket if you say yes.*

*Yours always,*

*Diderot."*

You can imagine the effect this had on me. Don't we all think that the mistakes of youth can be overcome by nostalgia? I was several years out of college and thought myself so much wiser. It hadn't been a devastation; it had just been a misunderstanding.

I went to Paris. I climbed into bed with him. Inside a hotel room, stories above a twisty street in Montmartre, he sucked my pendant into his mouth.

The silver acorn on a silver chain, inside his rows of teeth. In the dim light from the window, I watched it flashing between his teeth. He bit down on the pendant and I smiled lazily. But when his tongue pulled it further in and he began biting on the chain itself, I grabbed it like a mother snatches foreign matter from her child's mouth.

"It still plagues you," he whispered.

"What do you mean?"

"You can't let your neck be free. Always something encircling it. Why is that?"

I rolled onto my side, facing the window with a sense that seconds earlier, heads had been at the glass, watching us, even though we were on the fourth floor.

"It is so disappointing that you asked," I said.

He laughed. "Ever allow yourself to examine why?"

"Like . . . through therapy?"

"Yes."

"I never thought it deserved that kind of attention."

"It's obsessive-compulsive. Even when you swim, you wear something. You wake up in the morning with little dents in your skin from the links."

"So what?"

"Wouldn't you like to be free of it?"

This was a thought that shocked me so much I dropped the silver acorn and it bounced down onto the pillow beside me, still tethered to my neck.

"I brought you to Paris for a reason," he said. "I think I know what's behind your problem."

"I don't want to hear it," I said and burst into tears. Which of course I worried he could interpret as any number of humiliating scenarios. I thought it best to pretend to fall asleep after sobbing.

What an agony, to lie beside him all that night, thinking that his reaching out after so many years was not driven by love, or even lust, but by the desire to fix me. It was a long evening but it wasn't until midnight, when bells from Saint-Jean des Briques rang out, that I realized what he must be thinking. My neck, Paris . . . .

The Revolution, of course, with nobles lined up, telling jokes as they awaited their turn at the guillotine, to show the peasants that their revenge was not to be sweet.

He thought I was reincarnated from someone whose head rolled into a basket.

I went down the hall to the shared bathroom on the floor, stared into the mirror. I remembered an eighth grade art project where we had to weave a simple bowl basket. I had thrown up in the middle of the teacher's instructions and gone home that day.

Myself, in the mirror, looking at the vulnerability of my neck.

The next day, he didn't mention it. We ate breakfast quietly like reproved lovers. Tentative smiles over the croissants in the breakfast room with all the other couples and families.

Because he knew Paris and I didn't, he took me to the Place de la Concorde, a city square you will have seen in many movies—except that it is not square, but circular. In its center stands an Egyptian obelisk. It was one of a pair that fronted Luxor Temple, he explained, sent to France by the Egyptian government as a gift.

"The temple is now asymmetrical?" I asked.

"I suppose so."

"It's like chipping Teddy Roosevelt out of Mount Rushmore and sending him overseas."

We walked around the obelisk, looking at the golden images on the base that showed how the monument had been shipped by a French paddle ship towing an Egyptian barge. On the side facing the Arc de Triomphe, I saw a plaque stating that the obelisk stood on the square where the guillotine had once severed the heads of Marie Antoinette and Louis XVI. I bit my lip, trying to decide whether to be angry or funny.

"Oh, was that supposed to bring on an epiphany?" I asked him, pointing to it.

He ran his index finger down my throat. "You don't remember? You, me, the rest of the court?"

I laughed—but he didn't. "You're joking, of course."

"Let me just say this," he said. "For five months, my hand ached. Shooting pains from wrist to fingertip. And then my mother was bitten in the hand by a rabid dog. Would've died if she hadn't gotten the shot. After that, my hand was fine. Except for once in the Métro—I was getting off and a woman was boarding. I was in pain until her train left the station. I've never known what it was about, but it meant something."

He held his left hand up, turning it back and forth to show me. His hand displayed no evidence of the traumas he had just described.

"So you have The Gift?" I asked, trying to keep the derision out of my voice.

"Something," he said. "And I knew as soon as I set eyes on you that your neck was the site of great agony."

"Did any . . . visuals . . . come along with this insight?" I asked.

"Blood," he said instantly.

I sidestepped a little boy so intent on his *glace* that he nearly walked into me. "Tell me what you saw. No, wait, I changed my mind, *don't*, I don't want—"

"A line across your throat. Then, as if it had forgotten to bleed, all of a sudden bright blood gushed out of the gash. And since the line was so clean . . . I thought it was from a single blade. Like a guillotine might make."

I watched the tourists, trying to collect my thoughts and suppress the scream that kept bubbling up in my throat. I could only be grateful we were having this discussion here in broad daylight, with witnesses, rather than in the claustrophobic hotel room with its dismal and livid wallpaper.

"When?" I finally managed to ask him.

"Twice. The first time I saw you . . . and the first time we made love."

I shuddered. "*While* we were making love?"

He bit his lip and slowly nodded. "It was just a flash and before I could react it was gone. You were coming."

I started walking because I couldn't run. He kept pace with me as I struggled to keep bile down. "I'm sorry," he kept saying. I don't know how many blocks we walked, but it was many. I wove in and out between other people, like a clumsily choreographed street scene. I hated him for being there, but also knew I'd be completely lost by now if he wasn't with me. I didn't speak enough French to get directions anywhere. I caught a few women's gazes as I passed and saw there the timeless, nationless glance of solidarity: sympathy for the woman bristling down the street, visibly nauseated, pursued by a regretful man. It is a trope.

Finally I plunked down at a bistro table when I thought I might otherwise faint.

We sat in silence until after the waiter greeted us and took Diderot's order for Kir.

"You are disturbed," he said, after the waiter went inside. "But as I have come this far, I will continue with my theory."

I said nothing.

"The guillotine was used throughout history. Famously, by the Nazis. Enough time has passed that you could be taking on a body abandoned in the 1930s. You're not necessarily a French noble. Although . . . ."

He waited for me to opine.

"All right," he said. When it came, he drank his aperitif in silence, and then pulled my glass over and drank it as well.

On the long walk back, I still refused to talk. My feelings were complicated. I did not appreciate being confronted with these strange musings, as if I were a specimen in a lab he was studying. His interest in my suffering seemed self-involved, as if he would congratulate himself if he was right sooner than embrace me in sympathy.

I wanted to lick my wounds in private and possibly try to forget everything he had suggested.

"I'm taking you home," Diderot said. "Even though Pierre's there. I can make you a real meal." Pierre, his housemate, was the reason we'd holed up in the hotel.

"No," I said. "The hotel is fine for me. Just drop me off. I'm not hungry." I had an exhilarating sense that I *could* be left alone. I could call a taxi to the airport and leave early. He'd never know.

"Let me make you something," he said again. "It is not really living when you are dining at restaurants for each meal." His accent had always made him sound so formal. I used to love it, but now I was uncharmed.

"I want the hotel," I said.

"Eat first."

"No."

But I was helpless because I didn't know Paris. He led me to his apartment, which was on the third story of an old Haussmannized building. I thought of refusing to go up the stairs, but went anyway. Have you ever felt the agony of not being able to stick up for yourself?

When he keyed into the apartment, Pierre was there leaning against the wall of their tiny kitchen, indolently waiting for something to cook or boil or otherwise draw his attention. Wickedly handsome, he glanced over at me and smiled briefly. "Bonjour," he said.

I stood frozen at my first glimpse of him. "Oh, shit," I said, and bolted.

"Whoa!" said Diderot, grabbing at my arm. He caught me and I lashed around in terror. "Where are you going?" he demanded.

"Let go," I gasped. "Please!"

Pierre approached, all grins and a big sloppy handshake that instantaneously became a hug, as I writhed in his arms. My skin crawled. He didn't seem to notice that I was unwilling.

"I have heard your name, but please remind me? It is . . . Celine?"

"No, it's Cressida," said Diderot. "Are you okay?"

"*No*," I said. "Is your hand aching?" I glared at him until he understood.

"Ohhhhh," he said. "*Pierre?*"

I nodded.

"What am I missing?" asked Pierre.

I looked at him and tried to figure out why he was making me want to hide behind Diderot. He looked harmless enough—a loose flannel shirt over black jeans, and sandals that made him look very French. He had straggly five-o'clock shadow and brown hair that was a little too long, and soft brown eyes that hid no malice. He also conveyed an air, through his stance and facial expression, of being overtly gay.

"Tell me what you saw," Diderot urged, ignoring Pierre.

"I didn't *see* anything, but I just knew he was . . . He had something to do with it," I said.

"Clarification, please," said Pierre.

"He did it," I said, and hated myself for accusing him.

"Well . . . you mean, some other incarnation of him. Some past ancestor or something."

"Yes," I said.

"Please," said Pierre. "This is not French and I do not understand it." He smiled helplessly.

There was something in his bafflement that made me bite my lip and then laugh at myself. Diderot put his hand on my shoulder. It wasn't *him* . . . Like Diderot said, it was some other version.

"Sorry," I said. "It's kind of *Twilight Zone* time here. Diderot's been 'counseling' me through some—"

Before I could finish my sentence, Pierre was pulling at my scarf. "This is beautiful silk," he said. "What an insane design, I have been working with textiles and—"

I beat his hands away. "Never touch me!" I screamed. "Get your goddamn hands off me!"

I clawed frantically at my scarf. Diderot lunged between us and placed one hand on my chest and the other on Pierre's shoulder, separating us. Pierre still held one end of my unraveling scarf, as if I were a dog and he held the leash.

I snatched at it and he finally let go. "*Never* touch me," I said again.

He said something in a string of French so quickly that I could not even catch a single word.

"She doesn't like people to touch her neck," said Diderot.

"Or for him to touch anything!" I snapped.

"Okay, okay," said Pierre. His eyes narrowed and they no longer looked so soft.

"I want to go back to the hotel."

"Oh my *God*, you have found yourself a drama queen."

"Hey," said Diderot warningly. "You have no idea what her story is."

"Well, if someone can't touch your scarf without a holocaust coming with it, it's irresponsible to be out in the world. Please medicate yourself, Darling," Pierre said to me.

I spun around and again raced toward the door. Soon Diderot and Pierre were at my sides, flanking me like silverware. "I apologize," said Pierre. "I do. I'm sorry. Please stay."

I eyed Diderot, who was twisting his mouth in the expression of someone who knows he will have to sacrifice something. It stopped me up short.

"Don't worry about me," I said to him. "Honestly. I can get back to the hotel on my own." It was a lie, but I didn't care.

"No," said Pierre. "He won't be happy without you. Come with us. I promise to behave myself. I'm sorry about touching your scarf."

His smile was absolutely genuine. I stared at him, stared at Diderot, and felt foolish. Pierre had committed the terrifying act of trying to examine pretty silk, for Christ's sake. He could have just as easily exclaimed at my skirt, and then there'd have been no issue.

I tried to relax. Here was a man I was deeply in love with, who was giving me a second chance, and his best friend, who I'd have to win over to stay in his life. I'd messed it up once before by not being what he wanted. Or not enough of what he wanted.

A week later, we were a triumvirate. We had gone everywhere together and sat hours on end at cafes, watching the world walk by, telling tales about ourselves. Diderot introduced Pierre to the idea of my former death at the guillotine. Pierre was intrigued that I felt he had something to do with it. "I don't think we have any headsmen in our family," he'd said. "Don't you think they would tell me that?"

We told him about Diderot's aching hand and the dog's frothy jaw, about the vision he'd seen of blood at my neck. Pierre refused to get creeped out by any of this. In fact, he wanted to do an art installation about it, a three-dimensional diptych with a stuffed dog and a three-quarter size guillotine. We poked into a Latin Quarter taxidermist shop, only to find that a dog was too expensive for Pierre's artist wallet.

One night, we stayed out too late and got drunk to the extent that Pierre crashed in our bedroom, legs slung over the arms of the armchair next to our bed. In the middle of the night, I woke to find him standing over me, grinning, checking to make sure something was still covering my neck. But I was easy with him now and simply gave him a sleepy punch. The warning signal hadn't sounded since the initial time I set eyes on him.

One morning, I loaned him the scarf he had liked so much. He wore it fearlessly around his neck. "You're definitely gay," I said that afternoon at a café near the Pantheon. "This clinches it. A man who can wear a woman's scarf and not care?"

"You're stereotyping," he said. He leaned over so that the scarf tickled the neck of its original owner. He put his hand fully around my neck, his palm clamped down over my trachea, and gave me the softest kiss I had ever had. Lips barely there, the feather of his breath.

Diderot was in the restroom and saw nothing.

I pulled away and he instantly released me. "What was that?" I asked, half-angry, half-excited.

"Proving that I'm not gay," he said.

"But . . . yesterday you were talking about your boyfriend Jean, who cheated on you," I stumbled. My lips were still tingling.

"You're so eager to categorize," he said. "Is it impossible to believe that I find you attractive?"

He nodded subtly, his eyes darting over my shoulder, to let me know that Diderot was returning. He leaned back in his chair, the wind lightly toying with the ends of the scarf.

I touched my acorn necklace. Its chain seemed warmed by his palm.

❧

Inside the Pantheon's lobby, as Pierre insisted we go see, was a painting of poor beheaded Saint Denis walking around carrying his own head. We decided not to enter and therefore didn't see Foucault's pendulum, which Pierre said, rubbing his hands in ghoulish delight, would put one in mind of a blade swishing away.

When Diderot and I peeled off and said goodbye, Pierre gave me a special wink.

That night as we got ready for bed, I asked the question I'd been wondering about for the entire week: "Did you and Pierre ever . . . . You know?"

"Excuse me?" asked Diderot. He was half-undressed, one leg coming out of his pants. I cringed at what an awkward moment I'd frozen him at.

"You know . . . did you guys ever?"

"Ever what?" His voice was icy.

"Ever have . . . uh . . . a relationship."

"He's gay and I'm straight," said Diderot flatly. He threw his pants over the armchair Pierre had slept in several nights ago.

"Oh."

He climbed into bed and looked at me. "Coming?"

I undressed and joined him. "How did you meet him?" I asked.

"We went to school together. You know that." He turned out the bedside lamp.

"Did he ever make a pass at you?"

He sighed heavily. "No," he said. "Are you done?"

I wanted him to return the question, ask if Pierre had ever make a pass at *me*. I ran a finger across my own neck, feeling the muscles and cartilage beneath—and the big vein that carried blood to my head.

The next afternoon, we were to meet Pierre above the Denfert-Rochereau Métro station to line up for the Catacombs tour. I wore the scarf that I had lent Pierre. All morning, his masculine smell had wafted up from the flimsy scrap of fabric.

As we emerged from the station, Diderot pulled me in for what seemed to be a spontaneous kiss, but I couldn't help thinking that it was meant for Pierre to see.

"We haven't made love since Tuesday," I said when he released me.

"I'll fix that tonight," he said, squeezing my hand. Then his eyebrows lifted and he raised his head, almost as if he was arranging his face, and we set out to find Pierre.

The line to enter the Catacombs, where millions of Parisians' bones were stacked underground, was very long, and I was disturbed to see such a display of morbid interest. Paris truly did revolve on its little bloody pedestal.

Pierre sat on the grass of the micro-park, waiting for us. He stood up with a huge smile to give us both French-style kisses on our cheeks. "The Goths have beat us here," he said, "but we'll walk faster than them once we're down there. They never, you see, wear sneakers."

In line were several teenagers with pale white faces and ragged dyed-black hair, wearing long black dresses, including the one boy. As Pierre pointed out, they wore heavy-soled boots that required them to walk in a stolid, Frankensteinian manner.

We waited in the line together, saying nothing. I was thinking that if Pierre had managed to kiss me without Diderot knowing, the reverse could easily be true.

"It looks better on you," said Pierre, leaning over Diderot to pay the compliment.

"Well, it's a girl's scarf," I said.

"And on you it's doing more than simply being pretty," he added.

I looked at Diderot, who cocked his head to the side. "It's covering the marks of the Revolution," he said quietly. I saw him watch my face to make sure I wouldn't be upset. "The gash of liberté, égalité et fraternité!"

They both stared at my neck. "You're like hyenas!" I said. "Stop looking!"

"I've been her lover, and yet I've never fully seen her neck."

"That's not very trusting," said Pierre.

"And taking her to Place de la Concorde to see the site of the guillotine had no effect, so maybe she's just faking the whole thing," said Diderot.

"Maybe she *wishes* she had been a noble," said Pierre.

"Fuck you both," I said.

We reached the ticket window and I paid the 5 Euro admission, leaving them to pay singly. Every other time, we'd paid as a group. I began descending the steps to the Catacombs, welcoming the colder air that greeted me as I went.

"Wait, Cressida!" Pierre called from above. "Diderot forgot his wallet!"

But I kept going down into the muskiness of subterranean air, faster and faster, not caring if they followed. At the bottom of the staircase, I walked through a room with explanatory materials, heading beyond it to the hallway of stone, as if the bones were calling me. The air got even chillier and the rock-hard dirt beneath me continued sloping down: I was still descending.

There were others around, but by walking quickly, I reached a point where the voices behind me receded, where even their echoes faded.

When I finally reached the ossuary, where the millions of skulls and femurs were arranged in aesthetic rows with the bulk of other bones tossed behind, I felt kinship. The shortness of these people of the past who once stood in their low doorways, shedding their skirts and breeches and blouses, their brief gusts of laughter, the lovemaking so their genes would scrape through the centuries . . . I felt their headaches, their sore teeth, their scuffed knuckles, their hunger. How could any Jeanne or Sabine forecast that her bones would be exhumed from the small churchyard where her family had laid them, to be brought here for the world to gawk at? I felt discomfort radiating from the bones, tumbled amongst those of their neighbors, their enemies, and pure and constant strangers.

While I stared at a tiny infant skull, a hand clamped down on my shoulder. With a half-shriek, I turned to see Pierre's delighted grin.

"I thought if I was quiet, I could catch you," he said.

"You bastard!"

"I had hoped to get a *real* scream out of you," he said. "You're too collected."

"All I need is for the ossuary police to come arrest me for sacrilege," I replied tartly.

"A scream is nothing. *This* is sacrilege." Pierre pushed me backwards until I felt the dome of a forehead press into my spine. My bare arms raked against other skulls. He pushed his tongue into my mouth and instantly began pulling my skirt up one leg, his hand spanning my hip and then pulling my panties to the side.

I pushed back, hard, and he careened into the facing wall of bones.

He righted himself, smiling faintly, and walked back to me. "Sorry about that."

"What exactly *was* that?" I was shaking, aware that though we were surrounded by hundreds of human remains, no one was around to help me. Sabine and Jeanne had not the means to even wring their hands. Tourists were far away, lingering with their cameras in other parts of the ossuary.

"That was me, trying to evade all this death," he said.

"You're fucking ludicrous," I said. "You need to *leave me alone.* Where's Diderot?"

Pierre visibly shook off my anger. "He forgot his wallet," he said calmly. "We were trying to explain, but you dashed off. I only had enough money for one entrance. I was sent ahead to rustle you along and make sure you didn't get lost down here."

"Goddammit, why didn't you just stay up there with him?"

"The catacombs terminate far from where they start; you'll emerge back onto another street and have no idea where you are. I'll bring you back to the beginning. I know Paris a little better than you," he said.

I stared at him, warily.

"Didn't you read the information at the beginning, about the guy who went down here with a torch, and when it blew out he stumbled around these passageways in the dark for *weeks* until he died?" said Pierre. "We simply couldn't trust the catacombs with our dear Cressida." He reached out his index finger and very lightly touched my throat. "I don't know if I can trust Pierre with my dear Cressida," he murmured.

He lowered his head again. This time, with a wrench in my gut, I welcomed the fleeting softness of his lips. The kiss deepened and the dank underground smell faded, replaced by Pierre's earthy, ruddy scent.

I felt oddly comfortable finally, after all the anger, and the fear: kissing Pierre was like hearing my own voice talking or dabbling my hand in water the exact same temperature as my skin. His heart beat against my chest and I entered that vital sound, adjusting my own heartbeat to its dictates, giving my breath unto his breath. I was like that man stepping through the miles of twisted darkness, his dead torch abandoned, going only by sound, by sensation.

Finally, a British family, with a young daughter talking as loudly as possible to dispel her own terror, came upon us and we broke apart. I leaned my forehead against his shoulder, my eyes closed.

"Did you know," said Pierre conversationally, "that two severed heads were once seen to kiss in the basket?"

When we emerged, we were indeed far from the starting point.

"We'll jump on the Métro here and return to Denfert-Rochereau," said Pierre.

"You mean we walked an entire Métro station underground?"

"Further. We have to go two stops and then transfer. And remember, darling, we only saw a very small portion of the catacombs. It's 200 miles."

I winced when I thought of Diderot somewhere leaning against a wall, cooling his heels waiting for us.

That night, Pierre knocked on Diderot's door while we were having sex. "Go away!" Diderot called raggedly, and we heard Pierre walk away without saying anything. I knew Pierre knew. It wasn't until a nightmare woke me up that I realized that Pierre had thrown down a 20 Euro bill to buy our Métro tokens, after he'd said he didn't have enough to bring Diderot into the Catacombs.

The next day, I washed my scarf in the bathroom sink to rid it of Pierre's scent and hung it to dry, see-through in its wet state, on the hook with the shower nozzle. I was back to wearing the acorn necklace. As I left the bathroom, I listened to the apartment; Pierre must have already left. I sat down to the baguette, cheese, and jam that Diderot had prepared.

"What was it like when you and Pierre first started being

friends?" I asked carefully, remembering how this discussion had foundered the last time I tried it.

"We were lab partners in biology," said Diderot. "We'd get together in the library to study. We just became friends."

"Was he flamboyant back then?"

"No. I mean, he was an art student, dressing like what he wore really mattered. But I didn't realize he was into guys until sophomore year."

"How'd you find out?"

"He told me."

"How?"

"God, Cressida, why do you even care? He just told me he was seeing someone, and that it was a male."

"Were you freaked out?"

"I tried not to be."

I watched his face carefully, but he met my gaze openly, smiling a little sheepishly.

"Did he ever date women?"

"What do you think?"

I put the last bit of croissant in my mouth and shrugged. "Not everybody's strictly one thing or the other," I said after I swallowed.

"And?"

"And nothing. Just pointing it out."

"Okay. Got it," he said lightly. "How about going to the Louvre today?"

I groaned. "Seriously? We haven't been bored enough?"

He smiled indulgently. "How about this . . . I'll call the artist to go with me. You know, the one who dates men? The "um" in our triumvirate? And you can sit alone at a café and smoke your heart out."

"But—" I stopped as soon as I realized I had no reason to protest.

"But?"

"No, go ahead. Good idea."

By late afternoon, I had played out the glamour of sitting at a café pretending I was a Parisian. I went back to the apartment, dim because its one window faced east, and lay down on the bed. My head was pounding: too much coffee, too many Gitanes.

Someone knocked on the bedroom door. I raised my head and looked at the closed door, wondering what to do. It could only be one person. I waited so long that he knocked again.

"Cressida?"

I sat up, put my feet on the floor. It was a contest of sorts. If I could move slowly enough, he might give up and go away. I pushed myself up to standing, looked toward the window. A bird went by. I straightened my dress, tucked my hair behind my ears. And then, step by step, listening to the silence on the other side of the door, I walked over and unlocked it.

We stood there, the door closed between us. I didn't touch the doorknob, but I knew he'd heard the lock. After a few moments, the knob turned and he pushed inside.

"Diderot's still at the Louvre. He'll be back soon."

"So why are you here?"

He looked at me and shook his head. I continued those soft, slow steps that had brought me to the door. I pressed against him, tore my fingers into him.

As one animal, we lunged for the bed. He was inside me before I even touched one of his shirt buttons. We fucked like a clock oversaw our ordeal, ticking the moments between clenched teeth.

Ordeal? It was agony, like Saint Therese pierced by a flaming arrow again and again, the angel lifting my garment to thrust with a smile. The delicacy of his torture. God's own handiwork.

And of course the clock won, with Diderot appearing in the door we'd never closed.

He joined our savagery, pulling us apart, punching and kicking until Pierre crashed into the bedside table and lay dazed on the floor.

He straddled me and put his hands around my neck, kneeling on my arms. The acorn pendant burrowed into my larynx. "I will kill you," he said. His eyes were wide, looking more amazed than enraged. I twisted my legs underneath me until I could knee him in the side. It was like using an egg as leverage to move a statue.

"You bitch," he breathed. "I'm going to *kill* you."

He continued the pressure on my neck and I began to wheeze. My legs scrabbled for purchase on the soft bed, trying to get space to kick him. The pressure on my neck abated a little bit as he withdrew one hand to fondle the acorn with his thumb. "I gave this to you," he said. "You and your fucking neck."

He gathered the pendant between his thumb and the side of his index finger, as a beekeeper might trap a bee so it couldn't sting. He was about to yank it off my neck. He was going to break the chain.

Pierre reached up from the floor and clamped onto Diderot's leg. I watched the muscles in his forearm surge as he pulled with all his weight, and suddenly Diderot was off me. He fell with a grunt against the wall.

"Go!" shouted Pierre. I crawled off the bed in speeded-up time—now the clock was mine—like a beetle flustered by its rock being lifted. I ran out the door, pulling my dress back down over my hips.

"They're going to kill each other!" I wailed as I ran down the stairs. "Someone help! Someone!" I had seen people on the stairs before, winding their way to their own apartments, but it seemed empty today. When I reached the ground floor, I ran to the phone that sat on a marble table. But I didn't know what number to dial. I couldn't even remember how to say "Help" in French.

I screamed and then started to sob, feeling where the acorn had bruised my trachea. Nobody came. Nobody. I went back to the foot of the stairs and looked up, trying to listen to what was happening two floors above.

When Pierre came down to the lobby, I crept out from the chair I had hidden behind. He looked like a ghost, hair wild. Already black shadows were forming on his pale skin. His shirt was torn. There was blood spattered on it.

"He's okay," he said. "I think his nose is broken. There's a lot of blood."

"What should I do?"

"Well, don't go up there, that's for sure." Pierre mustered a weak laugh. "It seems the relationship between you two has suffered a setback."

"But he needs a doctor, right?"

Pierre took my elbow and led me towards the front door. "His ego's probably in worse shape than his nose. Trust me, he doesn't want to see you."

"But what am I supposed to do?" I asked again. "All my stuff, my passport . . . "

"We'll figure it out. But we've got to go now."

"Are you all right?"

"As much as you can be when you've just beat up an old friend."

"And slept with his woman," I added angrily. We were out on the sidewalk now, heading for the Abbesses station.

Pierre gave me a funny look and drawled, "You made the first move."

"No!" I shouted and came to a stop, so suddenly that a couple walking behind us bumped into us. "Sorry," I said as they walked on. "I mean, je suis dés—"

"Got it, you're sorry," snapped the woman as they brushed past. Other Americans.

I resumed walking, glaring at Pierre. "The first move was coming to the bedroom."

"Which you could have played off. We could have talked about 'I love Pernod' and 'Where's Diderot?' but we didn't. Your choice."

"You were trouble since the first day I saw you," I said darkly.

"Right. *I'm* trouble," he said sarcastically. "The day Diderot's hand 'went off,' I guess a little self-awareness would have let him know that *he'd* be the one chanting, 'I'm going to kill you,' while kneeling on top of you."

I shuddered and reached up to touch my necklace, an old comforting gesture. As always, it was there.

For the first time, Pierre took me to his studio. It was everything I'd thought it would be: gossamer fabrics rippling from the ceilings, odd juxtapositions of color and texture, rugs so drenched in pigment they were works of art. It was a small chamber with a single futon mattress on the floor for when he worked late on a painting.

We sat down on it and I saw the layer of dust on the floor shining from the slant of the attic window.

"You know that we belong together," he said.

"No, I don't know that."

"But we do."

"There's nothing about us that works," I said "You're gay. I'm with—*was* with—another man. We live in different countries."

"You're so attached to labels," he said. "I identify as a gay man, yes. You were in another relationship—but look how quickly *that* fell apart. Nothing's ever set in stone."

"What are you proposing? That we take this fuck-up of a situation and actually make a real relationship out of it?"

"Yes," he said.

Since there wasn't enough room to fully stretch out with him sitting beside me on the small mattress, I lay back with my head lolling against the wall. It felt good to close my eyes. I figured I'd fall asleep right here, right now, adroitly solving the problem of whether Pierre and I would pick up where we'd left off.

Suddenly, his nose was nestling against my neck and he was kissing me. His tongue vaguely rattled the chain of my necklace.

"Always this, huh?" he said, sitting up suddenly. His rapid movement made my eyes fly open. "This is what brought you to me. You wouldn't be in Paris if he hadn't been curious about your neck fetish."

"It's not a fetish," I said.

"What is it?"

"I don't know."

"It's something, though, right? Not just idle coincidence that you always have something covering your throat."

"Not coincidence," I agreed, my eyes drifting closed again.

"There's a lot of interesting information on this, you know," he said. "Have you ever researched it?"

I let my face slacken and tried to breathe deeply. I wanted to sleep, wanted him to give up on me.

"They say you have seven seconds once your head is severed to remain aware of what's going on. That's how much oxygen your body stores. Even though your blood supply is cut off, you're cruising on fumes. Just think of what you could've seen and experienced for seven whole seconds."

He pressed a finger to my carotid and pulsed it there seven times slowly. "There. That long," he said.

I tried to imagine it, my eyes focused on the floor of the scaffold and then seeing that wooden plane abruptly rush up, hearing the blurt of my own head hitting it and the blade coming to rest in its housing. And then I'd roll a bit, wide eyes registering the spray of blood and the shouting faces of my countrymen, the feet of the executioner coming closer . . .

. . . and then rough hands in my hair, yanking me upwards, buoyant, a motion I never could have achieved while anchored to my larger, slower body. I dangle from his outstretched arm to the roar of the approving crowd—he's pulling my hair and it hurts, but so does my neck and the worst feeling of all is the *knowing*. That this most extraordinary, horrendous thing has really happened, *happened*.

Somewhere behind me the rest of my body is twitching through its death throes. I feel the first sensations of bloodlessness at the top of my head, the growing prickles of numbness, all that blood shooting down the veins of my face, past the sheets of my cheekbones, the cold cartilage of my nose, to spill endlessly out my throat.

"Eyewitnesses say they blink," Pierre murmured . . .

. . . and so I blink, scanning the faces, the ugly peasants who shout with half their teeth missing, the rest blackened and foul, the women who shove their greasy locks up under filthy caps, children whose noses run with unchecked snot . . .

I swing a bit at the end of my own tethered hair, back and forth, a sickening sensation. Then the blackness comes in, like a brilliant window shuttered suddenly. Sound vanishes, and knowledge creeps away. My seven seconds are up.

I woke in Pierre's arms, half slumped against the wall. I was cramped from that position. As I shifted to stand, he woke.

"Sorry I bored you to sleep last night," he said.

I didn't laugh. I almost didn't smile, but I figured he deserved at least a wan one.

"What now?" I said. "Do I have to break into the room to get my passport and things back? How will I get back to the States?"

"Maybe you'll stay," he said.

"Right," I said. "Because a gay man thinks he loves me, and my actual boyfriend tried to kill me. This is clearly the place to be."

"Thinks? *Knows*."

I pushed open the window for air and leaned out. Many stories below, people were walking, with a small dog on his leash, a child brandishing an umbrella. A strange city populated with people who, speaking at full speed, I couldn't understand. Somehow I had put my hand into a man's grip and allowed him to lead me here. I knew Pierre no better than Diderot, no better than Sabine or Jeanne. Or myself, for that matter.

He joined me in my leaning and let silence rule. Then, an artist intrigued with color, he reached out to his windowsill pot and beheaded a geranium of its blossoms, one by one, and threw them over the edge.

"It's performance art," he said, and somehow his voice seemed thicker, more foreign. "Down below, they see this beautiful color coming from the sky . . . is it rain? Is it Magritte sending flowers instead of businessmen?"

But to me, with a wrench, it was suddenly the tricolor flying from the windows, the rudimentary dyed kerchiefs sewn together by women who wagged them gleefully from their windows as nobles queued up for their executions. It was the dart of color one could see in the periphery during one's seven seconds.

"There's more," he said suddenly. "I told you I'd researched it?"

I nodded.

"There's another place. A cemetery called Picpus, where two mass graves were dug to hold all the nobles. 1,300 of them. And down the street is a huge statue where the guillotine stood."

I inhaled, thinking of the oxygen lodging everywhere in my body, the little stockpile some had had to use.

"All right," I said.

"Really? That's it?"

"I'm ready," I said dully. "I need to understand."

We emerged from the Picpus station and made the short walk to the cemetery. A nun let us in for a few euros. We read in a pamphlet that the nuns here kept an ongoing prayer cycle for the victims of the Terror, and had for over two hundred years.

"I feel peaceful," I said, surprisingly myself. A long garden stretched in front of us with many benches for contemplation. "This isn't a bad place."

We walked slowly along the gravel pathway down the side of the garden. Towards the far end, we opened a gate and walked into the cemetery. Birds moved among the trees, singing. I looked at Pierre. "I never feel bad in cemeteries," I said. "They're just where people let go."

I stepped at my leisure, examining a few inscriptions as I went. At the very end of the cemetery was another gate, but this one didn't open. It provided viewing onto the grassy area where the two mass pits held over a thousand tumbled bodies.

Markers denoted the edges of the now-grassy plots so one could squint and imagine the pits filled with bodies. A sign in French gave the dimensions for the two graves, nearly as deep as they were long.

"Eight meters? What is that in feet?"

"A meter is almost as large as a yard."

"But in feet? I want to figure out how deep that pit is, compared to human height."

Pierre was used to converting, so it didn't take long for him to figure out that the bigger pit could probably hold five men standing on each other's shoulders. "Or more; they were shorter back then."

I was caught up in the horror of imagining someone at the bottom of the pile, not quite dead, trying to push past the bodies to the lip of the grave, but, with a jolt, I realized that was an impossible scenario. People were never mistaken for dead when they were missing their heads. No one would have stirred.

Pierre read aloud from the badly-translated pamphlet. A young girl called Mademoiselle Paris followed the carts loaded with bodies, trailing it in the night so that she knew where the final resting place was. Otherwise, these two pits would be lost to obscurity, shovels tamping the corpses into the earth without promise of remembrance.

Pierre looked deep into my face. "Nothing?"

"It's a sad place. But so long ago."

"You think these souls are at rest?"

"I have no idea!" I almost laughed. "How would I know?"

He made one of those inexpressible French gestures and then I did laugh.

"All right, screw it. Let's look in the chapel on our way out."

The chapel associated with the cemetery had a 16th-century wooden Madonna that had been the beloved, lucky property of the Sun King. On either side of the transept, two plaques gave the names of the people buried in the graves. Not anonymous at all, it turned out. Someone had kept track, a registry that listed names, ages, occupations, and dates of death.

"What the hell is Thermidor?" I pointed to one of the plaques.

"The revolutionaries rejected the Christian calendar and created their own names for months. This person was guillotined in Thermidor Year Two; God knows what that translates to."

At first, the plaques seemed uninteresting, but as Pierre stood there studying them, I too gave my attention and then realized they were fascinating. Piecing together surnames was a particularly sad exercise: watching a whole family die in the parade of names, wondering if the sisters watched or hid their faces, if the parents jostled with them for a place in line so the children would go quickly and not bear the horror of watching everyone else die.

I looked at every single name, tried to see if any of them resonated, gave me a prickle of recognition. Had I been one of these engraved people in another lifetime?

After I looked at the very last victim, ironically enough a man named *Merry,* I realized that the number assigned to him was 1,307, when all the literature and indeed the plaques outside the chapel had named 1,306 buried. Leaving Pierre to continue looking at the names, I found a nun outside and asked her why, in faulty French.

"One of the women was pregnant," said the nun. The baby was unnamed, but counted.

Even as I smiled my thanks, I reeled. How horrible for that woman to contemplate that when her head severed from her body, her baby would slowly die within for lack of oxygen, blood. As Mademoiselle Paris slunk behind the moonlit cart, was the baby still kicking futilely at the walls of the headless woman's womb? Did the baby feel the drop as the body was thrown into the pit, as other bodies then landed on top of the mother's?

And how had she knelt, the mother, at the blade with her large belly poking the machinery? Was the husband there, crazed with impotent rage? Did the baby inside cower at the rush of adrenaline and panic?

I did feel a pang then, something real and visceral, but it gave me no answers. As I stood there, thinking of the tiniest inhabitant of the pit grave, Pierre came outside and kissed me.

"Maybe souls don't stay with bodies," he said. "Maybe they stay where they were released. Let's go to the guillotine site."

I inhaled. Like him, I was ready to learn more. It was time.

The site of the guillotine was walking distance from Picpus. We reversed Mademoiselle Paris's path, returning to the place where her world had turned upside down.

As we walked, Pierre told me what he knew: that the square had originally been called Place du Trône, meaning place of the throne, because when Louis XIV arrived in 1660, he and his bride were fêted there with a throne.

Two kings later, though, it was called Place du Trône-Renversé, a throne reversed, and the guillotine stood there instead, neatly removing heads. Pierre couldn't remember the name of the executioner, but he had been famous for his swiftness. Fifty-four heads in 24 minutes.

"The place must have been knee-deep in blood," I commented. "How buttery and oily to lay your neck where so many other bloods mingled." I imagined the executioner's hands slipping on the wet levers and ropes, the abattoir smell that drifted up from the broken bits of humans.

"An artery is like a geyser," Pierre agreed. "I'm so sorry."

I turned to look at him. "Are you?"

"You know, if you went through it."

"It's a little late to be sorry when you've had a knee in my back ever since I've met you, getting me to face all this."

"True. I apologize. I find it intriguing."

"Well, be sorry for yourself, then. Maybe you're intrigued because you were there, too."

"Possibly." He smiled and leaned in to kiss me. "Maybe that's why I love you. Perhaps we were husband and wife, nobles holding hands in line."

"Or maybe you were the executioner and you feel terribly guilty."

We walked on and . . . it didn't take long.

I began to feel the truth of it, fear whistling into my ears as we walked closer to the square. Suddenly the street opened up into a plaza and I cried out. There was the statue where the guillotine had stood, a gloomy procession in heavy black bronze, a woman balanced on a ball, arms outstretched to steady herself, and the ball sitting in a chariot pulled by ponderous, slow lions. Around the woman was stolid motion, other statues accompanied by cherubim, a man with a mallet. The whole company looked like something that had oozed out of blood, a viscous nightmare group that puddled and creeped.

And this was to honor the Republic.

"Oh, fuck them," I cried bitterly. "I never swore allegiance to Louis and that bitch Marie. And look at the hatred in their faces; they hate us."

So what if we were rich, our salons filled with gold-rimmed plates and crystal goblets? It had come to us by birth, and each should take their place as God had ordained it by pointing his finger to the crib they should sleep in, the avenue they should live on. Who were these ragged animals who cried for our blood?

"It is only a moment of pain," Pierre whispered in my ear. "And then we shall be reunited in a world far more to our liking."

I looked down at the ground. Blood was already arriving at our feet from the scaffold, in rivulets that ran and gathered force in the dirt. My foot in its soiled satin slipper was only slightly ahead of his shoe with its leather rose. As gentleman, he would allow me to go first. Better he to bear the sight.

He burrowed his face under my jaw, kissing while I watched the next one climb the small stairs and go, the jeer that rose like a wave from the ocean, up and then down, coming quickly now and fading, coming again as the next one approached the machine, the godless machine that Dr. Guillotin had thought so humane. How compassionate was it to form a line that ended in a chopping block, as vulgar and common as pigs trotted into the slaughterhouse? I turned my head as the pregnant woman now climbed the steps, clumsy in her fecundity, curling her hands around her stomach.

"I can't watch," I murmured. "What cruelty. A woman with child."

"Don't be frightened, love," he whispered. "They say it can't hurt. It is an instant death. And then we shall be somewhere quiet."

It was a roar here, the loudest place I had ever been. Hatred magnified each voice. Perhaps the timid peasant woman who bore her husband's blows was thrilled to hear her own voice, once bleating, now engorged with volume, and that spurred her neighbor and removed hesitation from *her* upstairs neighbor, and all joined together to shout, shout, shout without anyone asking them to quiet themselves.

Soon enough it was my turn. One last kiss. His eyes in delirium; we could not shut ours. And then I was escorted up the wooden steps, my light-as-air slippers becoming wet with blood, soaking through so my feet felt the warmth. The wood creaked beneath me. I trembled as I staggered upon the hot boards. My skirts dripped red at the hem.

I was ill at the smell, sick at the terror in my gut. But I had to be brave for Pierre. I wanted to die with grace as I knew he would after me. He was all I had in the next world, so I would die with honor to please his eye and catch his ghost hand in a matter of moments. I knelt when the hand pushed and bent forward to lay my neck on that grooved block. It was sticky, and its pressure hurt my throat, where the delicate knobs were pressed into the wood.

I uttered a prayer, first under my breath and then realizing I could drown out the sound of the shouting, the headsman making his arrangements, I chanted my prayer loudly, delighting in my own unsteady voice. I prayed what seemed forever, waiting for the blade to interrupt me, but it never did.

"Finish quickly," said the gruff voice at my side. "We can't do it with a prayer on your lips."

Oh! So denied even this.

I gave a little sob and ceased. In the midst of my inhale, I heard the slight rustle of the ropes and the hiss of the descending blade.

And then over! Knocked to the floor, where he picked me up, believe it or not *winking* at me—Diderot, the executioner, of course, holding me at arm's length to the crowd, and my seven seconds had begun in disbelief that my lover would have done this to me, Diderot who brought me to Paris to help me, because he *loved* me—

—and then the bright fission of sparks below, some urchin who had set off gunpowder in all the madness, lightning brought down to earth somehow, a glare of incredible spasms of light, because boys are always playing with fireworks and scaring cats and loving noise and fire and light, because to the child this day was a celebration, to be marked with sparks and noise, with mayhem—

—and as Diderot jumped in surprise, I swung out clumsily on my hair and saw Pierre, gone in a flash of his cloak, blending into the crowd.

Not even a glance back for me.

No tortured, momentary acknowledgment that luck had worked on his behalf and not mine, that the timing was wrong, that his gallant offer to go last had become unwittingly selfish. He had already dismissed me as dead. There was to be no last lock of our gazes. He was alone in the world now, fighting for his life.

In my remaining seconds, I watched his progress through the screaming mass, urging him to run faster, to blend better into the crowd. And also despising him for not joining me in the world far more to our liking, as he'd promised. How quickly he had made the decision to cast his body away from mine, to take advantage of the distraction caused by the child and escape. He had betrayed me in a manner for which I couldn't fault him. Indeed, I loved him for it.

Pierre stood behind me, cradling my jaw and my forehead, more like a parent comforting a child than a lover. I felt utterly stranded, utterly unhinged. Everything had led to this hour, with traffic passing by and the light falling, a few tourists circling the giant statue to look at its figures, and a man consoling a woman who was so filled with light that I unhooked the finding and let my necklace drop to the Paris pavement.

**GERRY GRIFFITHS** lives in San Jose, California with his family, their four rescue dogs, and a cat. He is a Horror Writers Association member and has over thirty published short stories in various anthologies and magazines, along with a collection entitled *Creatures*. He is also the author of *Silurid, The Beasts of Stoneclad Mountain, Death Crawlers, Deep in the Jungle, The Next World, Battleground Earth, Down from Beast Mountain, Terror Mountain, Cryptid Zoo,* and *Cryptid Island* (prequel to *Cryptid Zoo*). You can find his books on Amazon.

Author's note: When Ben and Trish invite their closest friends Bradley and Eva to spend the holiday at their remote home in the torrid desert, the couples are overjoyed and somewhat surprised to wake up on Christmas morning and see snow on the ground.

# THE WHITE STUFF

## GERRY GRIFFITHS

**IT WAS NEARLY** sundown. They'd been driving for more than an hour when Ben finally turned off the desolate dirt road and steered the Toyota Highlander up a gravel path. The driveway lights lit up as the SUV approached the desert home, nestled beside a scraggily hillock covered with sand and patches of sagebrush.

Ben reached up to activate the remote control on the sun visor. The aluminum garage door rolled up. He drove in and parked inside.

Trish turned and looked back around the front passenger seat. "Welcome to our humble abode."

"You guys weren't kidding. It is in the middle of nowhere," Bradley said from behind Ben. "Hey, Eva, wake up. We're here."

"Huh?" Bradley's girlfriend mumbled as she opened her eyes. "I'm sorry. I must have dozed off."

"That's okay," Trish said. "It's a long drive."

"I'll say," Bradley chimed in. "Where are we?"

"From the nearest town? About sixty miles." Ben shut off the engine and opened his door. Everyone followed suit and climbed out of the vehicle.

Ben opened the hatchback and offloaded his friends' suitcases. He opened the cap near the hybrid's rear fender, inserted the plug, and started the charger.

"How do you get power all the way out here?" Bradley asked.

"From those." Ben pointed outside to the large blue-checkered solar panels tilted skyward twenty feet from the house. He directed Bradley's attention to the big satellite dish antenna a few yards farther away. "If you were wondering, we have cell phone reception and Internet. We'll give you our codes so you'll have access."

"I'm impressed."

"We may live like hermits, but we still love our amenities."

Ben helped Bradley with the luggage and they followed the women inside.

"Oh, I just love your kitchen," Eva gushed. Everything was state-of-the art: recessed lighting, energy efficient appliances, granite countertops, and oak-grain cabinetry. Trish gave Eva a little tour while Ben showed Bradley to the guest bedroom, where they stowed the suitcases.

Afterward, everyone met in the living room. It was a large, airy room with a ceiling-to-floor panoramic window that looked out at the radiant purple sky, painted with flamingo-pink clouds as the descending sun cast an orangey glow upon the desert.

"Wow, that's beautiful," Eva said, holding onto Bradley's arm as they watched the sunset.

"You guys relax and I'll rustle us up some drinks." Trish rushed off to the kitchen.

Ben waited until his friends had made themselves comfortable on the contoured lime sectional before he sat on one of the oversized ottomans.

Bradley laughed. "What is *that?*" He pointed to the four-foot saguaro in a large ceramic pot on casters. The cactus had been decorated with colored lights and ornaments. An angel perched on its prickly dome. A few wrapped presents were piled in a half circle on the floor.

"We couldn't expect you guys to come out at Christmas and not *do* something," Ben said.

"All we need now is the white stuff," Bradley quipped.

"Well, it's not as festive as New Hampshire."

"No, Ben, this is wonderful." Eva became teary-eyed. "We've really missed you guys."

Ben was relieved when Trish came into the room, carrying a tray with a pitcher and four glasses. "Anyone for margaritas?"

After everyone's glass had been poured, Trish raised her glass. "Here's to dear friends!"

"Here, here," Bradley and Eva said in unison.

"To the best Christmas ever," Ben toasted.

Ben opened one eye and squinted at the alarm clock. The digital display was blank, which meant only one thing: the power was out. Of all mornings for it to happen, it had to be Christmas. He was a little hungover, as he imagined everyone else would be, since they stayed up past midnight. They'd polished off three pitchers of Trish's killer margaritas before going to bed.

He thought about draping his arm over Trish and going back to sleep, but decided he'd better get up and figure out the problem. He swung his legs off the mattress and sat on the edge of the king-size bed. A sun-bleached skull with broad horns hung on the beige wall above the brass headboard. The marble floor was cold under his bare feet, but the room was warm, indicating the air conditioning wasn't working.

Scant light filtered through the blinds. Ben stood in his boxer shorts and rubbed the sleep from his eyes. Padding over to the window, he stretched his arms and yawned. He pinched the edges of two blinds, widened them, and peered outside at the twilight.

"What the hell?" Ben released the blinds and spun around. "Trish, wake up!"

The lump under the bedspread stirred. "Come back to bed."

"No, you have to see this!"

Trish poked her weary face out from under the covers. "Ten more minutes."

Ben rushed over and stripped back the top sheet. Trish wore one of his old college T-shirts and a pair of women's briefs.

"Damn it, Ben," she whined and sat up. Her short-cropped hair was pasted to her right cheek. "Why is it so hot in here?"

"The power's out." He snatched Trish's hand and pulled her up off the bed.

"What's gotten into you?"

"You're not going to believe this."

Trish staggered behind Ben as he led her out of the bedroom.

Ben stopped and pounded on the guestroom door. "Get up, you guys! We've got the best surprise!"

They went into the living room to wait for their friends.

Trish took one good look out the window and said, "Oh my God, Ben. Is that . . . ?"

The nearby hillock was silhouetted by the approaching sunrise, giving just enough light to see that the barren landscape outside was blanketed with fresh snow.

"Must have dropped below freezing last night. I thought I heard thunder."

"This is so weird."

"I know."

"It's like a holiday greeting card."

"It is," Ben agreed.

Bradley came out first, wearing a pair of Hawaiian swim trunks. "This better be good," he grumbled. "I was just about to give Eva her . . ." but then he stopped once he glanced out the window. "Whoa!"

"Welcome to our winter wonderland," Ben said proudly, as if he was responsible for the weather anomaly.

Eva strolled in, sleepy-eyed, wearing a long tank top that barely covered the thighs of her shapely, tanned legs. She saw what everyone was staring at and perked up. "This is amazing." She cuddled up beside Bradley.

"I'll go fix us some coffee." Trish was about to head for the kitchen when Ben stopped her.

"Remember? There's no power. I'm going to have to reset the control box."

"Does anyone know what time it is?" Eva asked.

Bradley reached into his swim trunks pocket and removed his cell phone. He fiddled with the device. A perplexed look came over his face.

"What's wrong?" Eva asked.

"My phone must be dead."

Ben walked over and retrieved his phone from the coffee table. "That's odd, so is mine."

Bradley flicked down the lever and unlocked the sliding glass door.

"What are you doing?" Ben asked.

"Going outside."

"I'd put something warmer on. It has to be freezing out there."

Ben's friend slid the door open a crack. Torrid air blasted in. "Jesus, it must be ninety degrees out there." Bradley closed the door.

Ben looked at his wife and friends. "So why hasn't the snow melted?"

Ben came out of the bedroom in a pair of shorts and pulled his T-shirt over his head as he strolled into the kitchen. Trish and Eva were standing in front of the refrigerator with the twin doors spread open, embracing the dissipating cool air on their scantily clad bodies. Eva was holding a washcloth packed with ice behind her neck.

"Please get the air back on," Trish pleaded to Ben.

"I know, it's stifling in here." Ben opened the kitchen door and went into the adjoining garage.

He opened the driver's door of the Highlander and climbed in. He inserted the key and turned the ignition switch, but there wasn't even a click. The instrument panel remained dark.

He got out and walked over to open the solar panel control box mounted on the wall.

"Having any luck, bro?" Bradley's flip-flop sandals flapped as he entered the gloomy garage.

Ben held a penlight, then started at the top and worked his way down, throwing each breaker off, then back to the on position. "Something's not right. They're not resetting properly."

"Here, let me try." Bradley repeated the same sequence, then shook his head. "You're right. Something's definitely wrong."

"Give me a hand so we can manually open the garage door." Ben walked under the lanyard dangling from the track on the ceiling that guided the pulley for the garage door opener. He pulled the red emergency release handle.

They both bent down and slowly lifted the aluminum rollup door all the way up.

Even in the dim light, Ben could see that the satellite dish antenna and the solar panels were heavily covered with snow.

"There's our problem," Ben said confidently. He wiped sweat from his forehead.

"Shut the fridge," Ben said as he and Bradley returned to the kitchen.

"But it feels so good," Trish replied. Eva was bent over, exposing her dimpled rump as she reached into the freezer for more ice.

"Now!" Ben pulled Eva back. He brushed Trish aside and shut both doors.

"What the hell, Ben!"

"I'm sorry," Ben said. "But we have to conserve. You leave the doors open, everything's going to spoil."

"I thought you were fixing the control box?" Trish said.

"We tried, but it won't work," Bradley said.

"The dish and solar panels are covered with snow. If we clean them off, we should be able to get everything up and running," Ben said, trying to put everyone at ease.

"But how long will it take before we have power?"

"I have no idea. Which is why we have to conserve," Ben reiterated.

"You mean stay in here and sweat to death."

"Can't we just get in the car and leave?" Eva asked.

"It won't start."

Eva gasped. "You mean we're stranded?"

Sweat drizzled down Ben's back as he rummaged through a tall cabinet. "I'll get the squeegees, if you want to carry the ladder out." He glanced over his shoulder to see Bradley pick up the aluminum ladder leaning against the garage wall.

Ben found two long-handled squeegees. From the edge of the garage, he watched Bradley traipsing comically through the snow in his flip-flops, ladder hoisted on his shoulder.

The crown of the sun began to appear on the hill's crest.

*This surely warrants a picture*, Ben told himself. What a great shot: with the sun coming up and all this snow—and in the desert of all places.

He watched as the light splayed over the snow like an incoming tide washing in slow motion onto a sandy white beach.

His camera was inside the center console in the Highlander. He had just turned to get it when Bradley screamed.

Ben saw that the sunlight had crept across to where Bradley was standing, rooted in the snow. Bradley had dropped the ladder and was screaming, flailing his arms as he desperately tried to lift his feet.

"What's wrong?" Ben yelled. He started to step from the garage, but halted in shock as he watched his friend's agonizing struggle.

Bradley's body jolted downward as though he had suddenly hopped down a step.

Trish and Eva dashed out of the kitchen. "Why's Bradley screaming?" Eva asked frantically.

Bradley was becoming shorter. The snow had dissolved his feet. Then his ankles were gone. The flesh on his shins bubbled. Ben heard a sizzling sound like bacon crackling in a frying pan.

Trish shouted, "We have to do something!"

Sunlight panned on the satellite dish.

"Oh my God, look!"

Ben watched the metal saucer disintegrate as though an invisible creature chewed it away.

Bradley continued to shrink, his legs almost entirely gone. He stopped screaming and slumped forward, writhing in the snow.

The solar panels were dematerializing, vanishing as though an artist erased a pencil drawing.

"Get back inside," Ben shouted. He reached up and yanked down the rollup door, which slammed down on the concrete floor.

He bolted through the garage into the house.

They huddled in the living room. Eva was hysterical. Trish was a total mess. It was all Ben could do to keep it together. "We'll be okay as long as we stay indoors," he assured the women.

"What is that stuff?" Eva wailed. "Snow doesn't eat people."

"I don't know."

Ben heard that same sizzling sound and looked up.

A hole opened in the ceiling. A white blob fell through, landing on the top of Eva's head. Her eyes grew wide and she screamed. Ben could smell her hair burning.

The white substance enveloped the crown of her head and dripped down, eating through her skull. The top of her cranium became an open bowl. Her eyeballs leaked out of the sockets as her face turned into mush.

Eva poured to the floor like a wax sculpture shoved into a blistering kiln.

Ben grabbed Trish and they ran into their bedroom. He shut the door, as if that would keep them safe.

Heavy splats, like bags of wet cement, crashed down throughout the house.

"Jesus, it's eating through the roof!" Ben yelled.

He rushed over to the window. There was more snow, but it was still shadowed by the hillside. The snow seemed to end beyond the sloping terrain.

A large panel of drywall crashed down and fell through the bed. The ceiling started to come down all around them.

"Come on. We're getting out of here." Ben opened the closet

and took out a backpack. He slung the strap on his shoulder. He went over, ripped the blinds down, and slid the window open. He took Trish's hand and helped her through, then jumped out behind her.

As they ran, Ben looked over his shoulder. Their desert home was melting away, along with everything around it.

As the sun rose, it cast a glow that steadily chased them as they sprinted to the edge of the slope where the snow ended. Gasping for breath, Ben and Trish stumbled onto the sand.

"We made it," Trish said.

Ben watched as the sunlight crept toward them. He looked down and saw the white caked to the bottom of his shoes.

"Take off your shoes!" he yelled. Ben kicked off his sneakers. Trish slipped out of her moccasins. They stepped back in their bare feet. As soon as the sun came in contact with the soles of their shoes, the leather liquefied and soaked into the sand.

"Why is it doing that?" Trish trembled as she held onto Ben's arm.

"I don't know."

Ben knelt, opened the backpack and peered inside. "There's enough in our survival kit to get us through a couple days." He reached inside, pulling out sun-protective clothing, hats, and two pairs of hiking shoes with thick socks tucked inside.

After they dressed, they lathered their faces with sunscreen and donned sunglasses. Ben shouldered the backpack and gave Trish the canteen to carry.

He consulted the compass and pointed out a direction. "If we keep a steady pace, we should hit the main road by nightfall."

They began their long trek across the vast desert.

*Six hours previously at 30,000 feet . . .*

"Shut that damn thing off!" the pilot yelled.

The copilot flipped a toggle switch, silencing the screeching alarm. He glanced over his right shoulder and looked out his side of the wraparound windshield. A fiery flash in the night sky blinded him.

The outer starboard turboprop on the massive wing had stopped spinning. Flames engulfed the engine. "Number four's on fire."

The pilot cut the fuel feed and activated the fire extinguisher discharge system.

Seconds later, the dim cockpit shook and more emergency lights blinked on the instrument panel. "Jesus, number two is shutting down."

"We're losing altitude," the copilot shouted. Both men strained with the controls, but the plane's nose refused to come up.

The flight engineer pushed through the door into the cabin.

"Jettison the cargo," the pilot ordered.

"Are you sure?" the flight engineer said. "There's over 100 tons back there."

"I know. But if we don't dump it, we're going down."

"You do know the catalyst for that corrosive is sunlight?"

"I read the manifest. Hurry the hell up, while we're still over the desert."

"Yes, sir." The flight engineer pulled the lever.

**LOREN RHOADS** served as editor for Bram Stoker Award-nominated *Morbid Curiosity* magazine as well as the books *The Haunted Mansion Project: Year Two, Death's Garden: Relationship with Cemeteries,* and *Morbid Curiosity Cures the Blues: True Tales of the Unsavory, Unwise, Unorthodox, and Unusual.* Her short stories have appeared in *Best New Horror #27, Strange California, Sins of the Sirens: Fourteen Tales of Dark Desire, Fright Mare: Women Write Horror,* and most recently in *Weirdbook, Occult Detective Quarterly,* and *Space & Time.* You can see what she'll do next at lorenrhoads.com.

Author's note: "Still Life with Shattered Glass" was inspired by the photography of Joel-Peter Witkin and David Wojnarowicz and by taking MFA creative writing classes at the University of Michigan.

# STILL LIFE WITH SHATTERED GLASS

## LOREN RHOADS

**"SHALL I INTRODUCE** you around, Sherry? Or would you rather just *watch* the party?" Jacob asked as he handed me a beer. He knew I hated Corona, but it amused him to act cool and superior, as if the fact that he was a grad student and I was only a junior altered the fact that he was a poseur. I suspected we wouldn't be together much longer.

I pulled the key chain from my jeans pocket and opened the beer. Without asking, Jacob took my keys and popped open his own bottle.

A woman arrived at Jacob's shoulder. Her mass of permed blond hair draped artfully around the shoulders of a little black dress. "I brought my portfolio," she said, pushing a large black book at him. Without an introduction or excuse, Jacob walked her over to a quieter corner of the room. Their backs made it clear I was not welcome.

Typical. Jacob's friends always came before me.

I turned to look over the rest of the party. The people all seemed to be art students like Jacob, dressed in black and tragically hip. Same old, same old.

Their Business of Art professor's house was nice enough. Under track lighting, well-placed canvases hung on storm gray walls. Jacob had told me that this professor bought student art, then arranged connections so that, as his protégés became successful, his private collection increased in value. We'd argued about it, in fact. I said the professor had a good scam, that if he gave a damn about his protégés, he'd buy their art after its value increased. Jacob said I was naive.

Later in the evening—several glasses of wine and no sign of Jacob later—I drifted into the lull of the dining room. On the polished granite table rested the blond woman's portfolio. I lifted its cover, expecting to see her in a variety of modeling poses, maybe nude shots. It hadn't occurred to me that the book might contain her photography, that such a beauty was herself an artist.

The first pictures, blurry and uncentered, seemed as if they had been done by a child. The subjects ranged from a butterfly squashed against a Chevrolet's grill to a cluster of fish gutted on a lakeshore. The following pages held several angles of a Siamese cat, dead by the roadside. In the final frame of the series, a fly washed its hands in the blood trickling from the cat's mouth.

"Are you shocked?" a woman asked.

Embarrassed to have been caught spying, I looked up to find the blond in the Aubrey Hepburn dress. I wanted to say something to redeem myself. "They're fascinating. Memento mori, almost."

She flashed a polished white smile. "Composition is the important thing. If you can't make a shot satirical or seductive, it isn't art."

The speech sounded rehearsed, like something she hoped to be quoted on. Fine, I thought. I can play the art game. "How did you choose death as a subject?"

"In terms of still-life, everything else has been done."

I nodded, conceding she'd won. Then my gaze caught on a photograph above the buffet. I moved closer. In the 16x20, a freshly dressed deer hung from a tree, its entrails steaming in the snow beneath it. The name Lily had been scrawled across the scarlet mat.

"That's mine," she said behind me. "Lily Crowe."

I took her hand, gave her my name. So the professor had picked her as up-and-coming. I'd had too many glasses of pinot to fight down a smirk.

"What's your major, Sherry?" Lily asked.

"Theater."

She regarded me critically, her head tipped at an angle. "You've modeled for Jacob, haven't you? I recognize you from his paintings."

Before I could respond, a man called from the living room. "Lily, are you recording the local news?"

"No." She left the room abruptly. I trailed behind her.

Someone turned up the television. " . . . stumbled between the automobiles stopped at the State Street railroad crossing. He ignored the lowered crossing gate and, apparently, did not hear the warning bells or train's whistle. The engineer told police that he braked the instant he saw someone on the tracks. Even so, train didn't halt until 2000 feet after impact."

Channel Four showed only the anchorman reading his script, no scene-of-the-action film. Maybe there hadn't been enough of the victim left to record.

Lily's hand closed on my forearm. "Damn. I didn't record that."

"I think I got it for you." A balding, middle-aged man crouched in front of the TV, fiddling with the electronics until the announcer flickered back on to repeat, "2000 feet after impact."

"Thanks," Lily said as she accepted a DVD. "Anybody want to go down to the tracks to see if we can find a finger?"

I gasped, "What?"

Her hand was hot on my arm. "If the train took 2000 feet to stop, the body would be shredded. Depending on how finely ground he was, the police *must* have missed something. Let's see what we can find."

"What will you do if you find anything?" I envisioned rows of formaldehyde jars in which she kept souvenirs of her shoots.

She laughed. "Photograph it."

No one else expressed interest in prowling around the November night. "Most of them are too drunk to be any help anyway," Lily confided. Jacob appeared from nowhere to hand me my leather jacket.

"Aren't you coming?" I snapped.

He brushed a hand against his raw silk slacks. "I'll pass."

The expedition reminded me of the beginning of *Blue Velvet*. While I wasn't sure I wanted to see anything like that in real life, I really had nothing better to do.

State Street was deserted, probably until the bars closed. I was relieved no one would see us behaving like ghouls. Lily parked at the produce market beside the train tracks. "There's a flashlight in the glove box," she said as she lifted a camera bag from the trunk.

I swallowed hard, my mouth dry despite the aftertaste of pinot. "I've never seen a dead body before."

"Relax. You won't see much of one tonight."

I followed her across the street, glad to have my Docs on in case

I stepped on anything. Lily scanned the tracks exhaustively, barely gaining ground. When I could stand the silence no longer, I asked, "How'd you get into this?"

"You mean, what made me 'like this'?" A smile colored her voice in the darkness. "What incident in my unfortunate childhood made me such a pervert?"

When I didn't answer, she laughed at me. "Maybe my brother made me pose naked and shared the pictures with his friends. Maybe my parakeet died and I kept her in a shoebox under my bed. Maybe my father took me out to the barn to watch him butcher rabbits. What do you think?"

I batted the question back to her. "What do *you* think?"

Her smile reflected the flashlight. "I don't think about it."

We scoured a good length of track before Lily decided, "They must have gone over this area with dogs."

I changed the subject, hoping to cheer her up. "What do you plan to do with your photographs?"

"I'd like to get into the collection at the Detroit Institute of Art. And Professor Richardson, at the party tonight? He's helping me find a book publisher."

Do you find enough subjects? I wondered. What happens if the deadline looms and no body parts turn up? Ann Arbor is a small town. It couldn't have that many violent accidents, could it?

As we drove back to the party, I wondered how someone could ignore the warning gates and bells. What does one feel as the train barrels down the track? I hoped the agony had been quick, that he hadn't regretted it.

Jacob had disappeared from the party. Someone familiar, another painter whose name I couldn't recall, said Jacob left with a sculptor. I nodded, clutching my calm front. On the couch, Lily chatted with her professor. I wondered if she had just been another of Jacob's distracter techniques—an accomplice to get me out of his way for the evening—but that was paranoid. The whole finger hunt scheme was too elaborate for Jacob. He'd merely taken advantage of the situation.

And he was a genius at that. The space on the street where I'd parked my car was empty. I stood there, stupidly checking the landmarks to make sure I was in the right place. Then I remembered giving Jacob the bottle opener, my keys still attached, to open his Corona. I stared at the pavement, too angry to think.

"Has your car been towed?" Lily asked.

I didn't know where she'd come from, but I was in no mood to be civil. "Jacob borrowed it to take home a 'friend.'"

"He'll be back for you, won't he?"

"I doubt I'm on their minds at the moment."

She let that go. "I can give you a ride."

"Don't worry about it," I said. "Jacob's got my apartment key, too. He won't let me in." I took a deep breath to fight the constriction in my chest. "I've got friends on North Campus I can crash with. It's getting to be a regular Friday night thing."

"Roommates can be a drag," she said.

There was a world of sympathy in her voice. I realized I didn't want to walk to North Campus. "Do you have a sofa?" I asked.

"The most comfortable sofa in the world."

"Can I borrow it?"

The moment she walked into her apartment, Lily switched on a police scanner. Jacob could not live without background noise either, but at least he settled for punk shows on WCBN.

An invitingly long sofa shared Lily's living room with a television and a jumble of DVDs. A laptop and a DVR nestled on the TV stand. Lily slipped the new DVD out of her coat pocket and onto the pile. As I glanced over the labels, I saw that most seemed to be news clips.

The police scanner crackled and a voice ordered paramedics to a bar on the edge of town, where a bouncer had been knifed.

I began to lace my boots back up when Lily asked, "Going somewhere?"

"Don't you want a picture of that?"

Her smile told me it was a dumb question.

"Okay." I leaned back, laces dangling. "Why not?"

"He won't die. The ambulance will be there before we get to the car. I only photograph fatalities." She stretched, as if to allow me to enjoy the way the black dress slithered over her curves. "After poking around in the dirt, I need a shower. Want to join me?"

I was still pissed at Jacob, so I said, "Sure."

She sent me in to get started while she took off her makeup. I shucked my clothes and left them on the bathroom floor, where they'd be easy to find later.

My mind wasn't on Lily at all as I stood in the shower and let the water beat on my skull. It was November. My name was on the lease until May. What the fuck was I going to do about Jacob?

The lights in the bathroom went out.

"Hey!"

The shower door slid open. "You ever take a shower in the dark?" Lily asked.

"No." I backed into the corner. The ceramic tile was chilly. The bathroom was as dark as a coffin. Nobody knew I'd come home with her. What if I just vanished?

Lily closed the shower door behind her, then one of her hands found my shoulder. She wore a latex gloves that reached to her elbows. "The darkness makes perspective impossible," she purred, drawing me into her latex-sheathed arms. "Is there anywhere I can't touch you?"

"No," I repeated, pulling her head to meet my kiss. Her tongue forced my lips open as her gloved hands explored me. I braced one foot against the top of the tub while she confirmed that I had no problem being touched.

It was weird not being able to see anything. Had I ever been in such perfect blackness? It could be anyone's hands on my body. The sound of the shower drowned out our movements. I wasn't sure if she was breathing hard. My knees shuddered beneath me.

"If I crack my head on the porcelain, will you take my picture?" I wondered.

"Only if you die," Lily promised. "Are you gonna fall?"

"Maybe," I hedged.

"Then go lie down. I'll join you in a moment."

Her bedroom seemed standard femme, lavender blue comforter flung across the bed, perfume and jewelry scattered atop the dresser. I moved to the nightstand, expecting to find books on bondage or bullfighting. Instead she was reading *On the Genealogy of Morals*.

In the top drawer I found a rainbow of negligees. The silk cradled a handgun, cold under my fingertips, against the lace. Of course she had a gun, I told myself. It had probably been in her camera bag while we looked for the finger. She was a single woman who worked at night. Of course she had a gun.

Heart pounding, I eased that drawer closed and opened the next one. A jumble of sex toys filled it. The handcuffs had a key in one of their locks. They were the cheap kind that they sell in sex shops, but I figured she wouldn't have them if she didn't like them. I tested the key, made sure they opened, and crawled under the covers.

The phone rang, shocking me awake. I couldn't remember where I was. A woman spoke quietly. The voice brought the evening back to me in a rush, starting with the finger hunt.

Lily flicked the bedside light on. When I peeled my eyes open, she was combing her fingers through her hair. "I'm going on a shoot," she said. "If you want to come, get dressed. I have to be there now."

Except for the glow of the streetlights, South University Street was vacant. The bars must have closed. I squinted groggily at my phone. 3:57 a.m.

Lily pushed open the chain-link gate to the alley behind the University Towers apartments. Her sharp intake of breath made me wonder what could shock Lily. I forced myself to follow.

An overhead flood lit the alley, glinting off a rack of chained bikes. Lily attached the flash to her camera.

At her feet sprawled a body. The girl's almond-shaped eyes stared past Lily at the stars overhead. Straight black hair fanned out on the pavement like a satin blanket thrown across the pool of blood. The back of her skull was flattened. I leaned against the cold cement of the apartment complex, one hand on my stomach, the other on my lips.

"See how her body's crumpled on that side?" Lily's flash exploded past my eyelids. "The ribs must've collapsed."

"On the first or second bounce?" I asked weakly.

Lily laughed as she circled the corpse. "You're catching on." She stepped between the girl's legs to focus on her face. Her flash made perverse lightning.

"Do you ever rearrange things to make a better picture?" I asked.

"Only when I'm working with props, like car wrecks. I let the coroner move the bodies." She snapped the lens cap back on and returned the camera to its case. "Let's get out of here."

I was finally able to say, "Who called, Lily? Wouldn't the cops . . . ?"

"Don't panic, Sherry." She was already striding back to her car. "One of the guys from the party lives in the Towers. He found her when he chained up his bike and knew I'd be interested."

"Why didn't he call an ambulance or something?"

"Dead is dead, Sherry. If the police don't notify her family for an extra half an hour, what difference does it make? Her mom'll get some extra sleep before finding out that her baby couldn't hack it at the University. I'll tip the police anonymously before we get home. There's still a payphone at the Dennys."

Visions of Lily at work—lips parted, eyes focused in concentration, body perfectly encased in a tight leather racing jacket—chased me through the night. I finally gave up on sleep at 6 a.m.

I wanted the bathroom, but I couldn't remember how the apartment was laid out. The first door I opened led to Lily's darkroom. The switch turned on a red bulb. Photographed eyes stared at me from every surface; some reflected her flash while others had clouded over. Lots of dead things: three kids who'd suffocated in a refrigerator echoed by the pose of a gnarly old man who'd bled to death in a dumpster. There were little dead things, too, including a pile of viscera that reminded me of the toad I'd run over with the lawnmower last summer.

"Was last night an act?" Lily asked from over my shoulder.

The breath rushed from my lungs. Damn, I wished she'd stop creeping up on me. I guessed the skill was useful in her line of work. I tore my gaze away from the photographs to face her. "What do you mean?"

Lily's eyes were a cold gray. I hadn't realized that before. "You're horrified by me and my art," she accused.

"No," I corrected, "I like it more than I'm comfortable with."

As I pulled her into the dark room, she closed the door behind herself and switched off the light.

When we'd caught our breath, I asked, "How do you find all your subjects?"

"I have a lot of people on the look-out for me. They call when they see something interesting." She pulled the string to switch the light on again. "Do you like one of these especially?"

I wanted to change the topic. I don't like people to know how I really feel; that's why I decided to study acting. When I was sure my voice was steady, I said, "That black-and-white one."

Cracks radiated across the windshield from a hole the size a head would make. Something dark pooled on the dashboard. Centered in the picture, floating on the dash, was a white card hand-lettered with "Happy 18th Birthday, Bill!"

Either the photographer had focused through the rear window, or she'd been in the back seat of the car.

"Take it." Lily pulled it from its clip. "I have the negative."

"Thank you." I held the picture by its edges as I padded naked into the bathroom.

After he let me into our apartment, Jacob stomped back to the bedroom. The lock clicked behind him.

A long shower did nothing to calm me, since I couldn't get clean clothes from the bedroom. I fixed a bowl of Cheerios and settled down with my laptop to read the morning news. The top of the page featured the train accident. The story mentioned the annual midterm wave of suicides.

Returning to the front closet, I slid the print of Lily's photograph from inside my jacket. The windshield glass shimmered as if the sun had been very bright on the day of the accident. My gaze was drawn to the birthday card. I wondered if she had known Bill, if she used this photo to probe her own fascination with death. If it really was a memento mori.

Jacob's voice harped in the bedroom, carrying easily through the locked door. Whoever he'd brought home wasn't making him happy.

Then again, what did he have to be happy about? His relationship with me had deteriorated. His art school grades weren't good enough to score much of a post-grad appointment. He was a passable painter, not overwhelmingly original. His canvases had not been selected for Professor Richardson's private collection.

A midterm wave of suicides, I thought. In a certain light, Jacob's death would be a blessing, saving him from a lifetime of disappointment as a failed artist. Since Lily only photographed fatalities, maybe in the long run something Jacob did could be construed as art.

How to do it? A slip in the bathtub, head striking the tile? Too much speed during one of his painting binges? Or she might like the spatter of crimson against out clawfoot tub. Whatever happened, the challenge would be to drive Jacob to deliver his own coup de grâce. How would Lily express her gratitude if I showed her something she'd never seen before?

I wondered when his guest might leave. I was eager to get started. I hoped I was actress enough to pull it off, even if I was only a junior.

**ERIC ESSER** lives in San Francisco with his wife Courtney. When he was small, he used to wander the perimeter of his elementary school soccer field every recess, imagining stories set in other worlds. For some reason, no one made fun of him for it. He suspects they discussed him secretly. He's dabbled in Elizabethan Gothic, dystopian, urban fantasy, and horror. He is a graduate of the Clarion Science Fiction & Fantasy Writers' Workshop and a member of the Codex Writers' Group. His fiction has appeared or is forthcoming in *Schoolbooks & Sorcery*, *Pseudopod*, and *Fictionvale*, among others.

# FABLE OF THE BOX

## ERIC ESSER

**A WITCH WHO** lived near the village of Drumby Hole owned a magic box. If she put something dead inside the box, it would come back to life for one day. She used the box to find out secrets only the dead knew.

The witch had a daughter and a son and a dog. Her children loved that dog, and when it died, they begged her to bring it back to life with the box. She warned them that the first death is always easiest, and every time after that more painful. Still they begged her, so she put the dog into the box before sunset.

When the sun rose, her children opened the box. The dog awoke eagerly, as if it had never been dead. They played with it all day long, and that day was one of the happiest of their lives. Then, at sunset, the dog howled in an agony the children had never before heard and again died. The sound of that death chilled them, but still they asked their mother to put the dog back in the box. She agreed.

The next day the dog woke up, not so happy, but still it licked the children's faces. While they played together, it was not so much fun as the first day, because they knew how it would end. This time the dog screamed for half an hour before it died and writhed against the ground as if speared through its belly to the earth.

The children thought for a time, but not too long, and then begged their mother to put the dog back in the box. She looked hard at them, then laid the dog inside without speaking. The next day it woke up, but did not lick the children's faces, nor play. Rather, it crouched close to the ground, watching the children suspiciously. They tried to tempt it with treats of roasted meat, but it refused. Then, when they were not looking, it ran away. The children searched the forest everywhere but could not find it. At sunset, howls echoed for hours through the valley from far away.

The children were very upset their dog had run away. Each blamed the other, so they started to argue. To punish her brother, the little girl dared him to spend the night in the box. The boy, not wanting to appear a coward, agreed. Sneaking by their mother, they went to the box and his sister shut him inside.

The next morning, the girl opened the box. It was empty. She looked all day for her brother but could find him nowhere. Her mother asked her where he had gone, but the little girl lied, claiming she did not know. Her mother gave her that same hard look, but asked no further.

Then, at sunset, the little girl heard a screaming. After it stopped, her brother appeared from nowhere, shaking and crying. She asked where he had been. He refused to answer, but demanded she put him back inside the box. She was afraid of him, so did what he asked.

The next morning, he again disappeared. The witch asked her daughter where he was. This time when the little girl said she didn't know, the witch stared at her relentlessly. Eventually the little girl broke down and confessed that her brother had spent the last two nights sleeping inside the box. Since witches cannot cry, her mother only shook her head sadly.

The witch stood with her daughter at the end of this day to listen to her son's disembodied shrieking. The witch covered her daughter's ears during his screams, so she could not hear the terrible things he said. When finally he reappeared, the boy cried to his mother and said he was sorry, because he knew he should not have spent those nights in the box. Still, he begged her to put him back inside.

The witch nodded to her son, held him close, then broke his neck. They buried him behind the ash tree, because only those who had been baptized could be buried in the village graveyard. The witch warned her daughter never to go inside the box, and her daughter promised she wouldn't.

The girl was afraid of what had happened to her brother, but she also wanted to know what was inside the box.

A few days after her brother died, she slipped behind the ash tree and dug him up. His corpse was bloated and dripping, but she held her breath and looked away. She dragged him to the box and set him inside.

The next morning, she opened the box. There sat her brother looking back at her as if he'd never been dead, though his eyes had changed, and when he smiled at her, it felt like a lie. She kissed him and hugged him and told him how sorry she was she had dared him to sleep inside the box, how sorry she was she had told their mother he had done so.

She asked him why he had kept sleeping in the box despite the pain, and where he went when he'd disappeared and after he'd died. She asked him if it was true what the vicar said, that after they died they would burn if they did not worship the man on the tree.

Her brother shook his head but would not explain until she threatened to sleep in the box herself. Then he pulled her close and whispered to her, "In death you become a shadow of what you once were, just as in this life you are a shadow of what you should be."

He thanked her for raising him, warned her to never go inside the box, kissed her goodbye, then shut himself back in. She was not ready to say goodbye yet, so she opened the box back up, but he was gone. That evening she heard no screams, and her brother did not reappear. She checked the box again for his corpse, but it was empty.

She spent that night sleeping inside the box.

**L.S. JOHNSON** lives in Northern California, where she feeds her cats by writing book indexes. She is the author of the gothic novellas *Harkworth Hall* and *Leviathan*. Her first collection, *Vacui Magia: Stories*, won the North Street Book Prize and was a finalist for the World Fantasy Award. Find her online and sign up for her newsletter at traversingz.com.

Enjoy!

# ADA, AWAKE

## L.S. JOHNSON

### 1.

**IT WAS THE** dream again:

I walked along a narrow stone path at night. The damp increased as I walked, moisture condensing on stone and skin alike. I breathed in the wet air, letting it coat my tongue; I tasted brine and it made something stir deep in my belly. The further I walked, the more clearly I heard the sounds of water lapping, and voices whispering unintelligible phrases, and something that I knew in my bones was the sound of a large, wet shape moving alongside me . . .

And just as I glimpsed the water's surface and my own shadowed form, I awoke to find tears drying on my cheeks and my body filled with a diffuse longing.

Georges would say: *of course you would dream of water, you were born by the sea.* He would say this, and pat me on the head, and tuck me back in as if I were still a child, though I could barely remember being such.

I have always been this person, this Ada.

And what I knew, what I dared not say to him but I knew in my heart, was that my dreams were not of forgotten memories: they were of things *to come.*

As my mind cleared, I realized I was arriving at my destination.

The façade of the chateau was a grim affair, all gray stone and narrow windows. As my coach made its way up the drive, I fancied I could see what had once been a moat in the lines of the gardens, probably fed by the river that cut through the property. The neat trees, pruned to conical shapes in a pleasant symmetry, seemed at odds with the looming walls and crenellations. The unusual prospect made my blood quicken, and I was already flustered. It had been a daunting task to find a driver willing to undertake the last miles of my journey, for the locals expressed a superstitious dread of the estate; indeed, it took nearly all my monies, and money was no longer in ready supply. It was for that very reason I had come all these miles, crossing the breadth of France itself: a chance to sell one of my late husband's artifacts and finally free myself of his creditors.

At the heavy wooden doors, I was met not by a footman but a serving girl who shouldered my trunk as if she were a man. I could not help but study her in turn, for her appearance seemed familiar, though I could not say just what about her provoked my nostalgia. Perhaps she reminded me of a visitor of Georges's—there had been so many visitors I was not allowed to meet, for Georges had believed their scholarly conversation would only bore me—or perhaps one of the girls from the orphanage? The latter seemed more likely, as the maid's large brown eyes seemed to gaze at me with a mixture of suspicion and fear. It was all I could do to keep from trembling beneath her scrutiny.

Despite my unease, I kept a firm grip on the valise containing the artifact and the woman did not press me for it. Inside, a second maid, so similar to the first as to be her sister, led me to a bedroom upstairs and said that my hostess was waiting. As soon as I had refreshed myself, I was to go to the dining room, where we would take supper.

Once I was alone, I felt a profound sense of foreboding. Even at Georges's sickbed I had never felt so apprehensive, so certain that some cataclysm was about to happen. I went to my window, thinking to signal the driver, but he was gone. Not even the tracks of the coach remained.

Instead, I steadied my nerves, changed my dress, and washed my face. Thus refreshed, I went forth to meet the Countess d'Armagnac, who had offered me a small fortune for the artifact, on the condition that I bring it to her in person.

When I entered the dining room, I was greeted by a woman elegantly dressed in green brocade, her hair curled and pinned around a pretty and intelligent face. Even in our little corner of France, we knew of the Countess's reputation as a woman of letters, as well as her feuds with salonnières and encyclopedists. Now, before me, I could see that she was everything her reputation declared and more:

an assured, accomplished woman, replete with wealth and a remarkable beauty.

Yet as remarkable as her beauty was, her necklace was even more striking. It consisted of a single large pendant, a gold-framed icon showing the painted image of a coiled serpent. The image was one of marvelous detail, from the strange fins on the serpent's body to each meticulously rendered scale. I wanted nothing more than to reach out and touch it, to see if I could feel each tiny, curling brushstroke.

Only then did I realize I was openly staring at my hostess's décolletage. I dropped into a curtsey, blushing with shame; my blush deepened when the Countess laughed and bade me rise.

"My dear Madame Mortimer! I see you are taken with my jewelry—understandable, as it is a most unusual piece. My father was an importer of fish from several coastal villages; the necklace was given in gratitude for his business." She quickly undid the clasp and fastened it around my own neck, then took my hand and pressed it over the icon. "There. Now you may examine it at your leisure: a proper welcome for a new friend."

"You are too kind," I gasped. The metal frame was so light as to seem weightless, yet it was cold, so cold it took my breath away. It was all I could do to nod as the Countess inquired about my journey; I kept thinking of the necklace, how the serpent seemed almost to undulate against my hand . . .

I was letting my mind wander again, when I could not afford to do so. "Pardon?" I asked.

"I only said that you are exactly what I imagined, yet you seem taken aback by me. Perhaps Georges did not mention he was corresponding with another woman?" She was looking at me keenly.

"Quite the contrary," I replied. "He mentioned you many times, only he said your correspondence was scholarly in nature." I was blushing again, discomforted both by the necklace and the sudden insinuation. I had always trusted Georges, and I had believed he trusted me . . .

Yet here I was, a world away from our little house, my future in the hands of this strange, sly woman.

"My apologies," the Countess said. "I do not mean to . . . cast aspersions on Georges's character. But he did keep things from you,

Madame. That is why I asked you to bring the tablet to me; I would have you completely informed before you give it to me."

"Before I sell it to you," I corrected.

She laughed, openly this time; it was a wonderful, free laugh, as boisterous as a man's. "I give you my word, Madame, that you will have your money." She gestured to the dining table, where two places were set close together. "All I ask is that you dine with me tonight and listen to my little story. In the morning, I will have both payment and a carriage waiting for your journey home—or wherever you would like to go."

For a brief moment it was as if the very room darkened at her words: I was no longer in the dining room but in my dream again, straining to hear the lapping water, trembling with anticipation—save now it felt as if the necklace too was part of those imaginings, its icy presence as natural as if I had dreamed it all along.

Then the moment passed. I agreed to her terms and, in doing so, set the course of my fate. It was only then that I realized she had kept her hand over mine, her fingertips resting lightly against my chest, for our entire conversation.

## 2.

"So you were confined to the orphanage for most of your life," the Countess prompted, pouring me yet another glass of wine.

I did not want to think on that terrible place, as suffocating as any prison. Instead I focused on the marvelous repast before me, consisting solely of a startling variety of fish. "I was seeking a place as a seamstress when Georges came."

She angled her head, as if making a study of my features—or perhaps of her own, for she could not be oblivious to the way the firelight illuminated her finely-boned face. "A young age to give yourself over to a trade. Could you not have gone to a convent?"

I sipped my wine as I tried to think of an answer. Such a place had been generously offered to me, at a convent in Paris where I would be assured of improving my circumstances. Yet the moment it had been proposed, the very notion repulsed me; I had felt certain I would be merely changing prisons and the convent would be much, much worse.

"I preferred to take a trade," I finally answered, taking another forkful of the octopus on my plate, the plump tentacle dripping with salty broth. It was delicious. Georges never let us have fish. It made him ill . . .

"Or perhaps you simply feared their natural repulsion and what it might provoke," she promptly replied.

I froze in my seat, the fork halfway to my mouth, my lips parted in utter shock.

"Did you ever wonder, Madame, how it was that Georges came to you? That is, what brought him to an orphanage so far from his home?"

"He was visiting an acquaintance." I had to force the words out. The story, which had for so long satisfied me, seemed foolish in the face of the Countess's scrutiny. "His friend invited him to a concert at the orphanage, where he saw me sing, and he was . . . taken with me."

"A pretty tale, and there may be some truth in it. But he knew you were there, Madame. He knew all along, for he knew your parents, as did my father."

She leaned back then, studying the effect of her words. I knew I should demand proofs, yet I felt again that sense of familiarity, as if a long-forgotten memory was slowly rising out of the depths.

Without thinking I reached up and touched the necklace, resting just above my breasts.

"We always knew where you were, Ada." The sound of my name was as shocking as cold water. "Only Georges wedded you before anyone else could intervene and squirreled you away to that moth-eaten hovel of his. Again," she held up a hand at my rising ire, "I cast no aspersions; I believe Georges was a good husband to you. He may have even loved you as he claimed. Yet he also sought to protect you and there is no surer way to harm another than to unnecessarily protect them."

"Protect me from what?" I whispered.

Instead of replying she turned and rang a little bell. The first maid entered, bearing my valise and a large, worn book of some antiquity. With an air of ceremony, she placed both bag and book on the far end of the table; she undid first one clasp, then the other; bowing her head, she reached inside and slowly lifted out the tablet, placing it on the white cloth before us.

I found myself sighing deeply. Of all the pieces in Georges's collection, the tablet was the most alluring. At first glance, it looked like a hewn piece of rock, perhaps the work of an apprentice stonemason, but closer inspection revealed a side etched with intricate symbols. It exerted a curious pull upon my mind, as it had whenever Georges took it out of its cabinet. Only now I recognized its echo in the Countess's necklace: there were parts of the designs that resembled that knotted, serpentine form, coiling among the other symbols as if about to strike.

"It is one of the oldest languages in the world," the Countess said. "A language known only from fragments and secondhand tales, found in the villages my father dealt with . . . and where your parents lived. Our wealth was built upon the remarkable consistency of the fishermen's hauls in that region, which they in turn said was due to their worship of a sea deity they called Ada." She smiled at my sharp intake of breath. "Though do not take the name as flattery. Nearly every family along that stretch of coastline has a daughter named Ada, as homage to the goddess who keeps them fed."

Seeing my unease, she filled my wine glass again. I quickly drank from it.

"Did you love your husband, Ada?"

Before I properly heard the question, I blurted out, "He was a good man." And at once flushed deeply, knowing how poor it sounded. Though I had never given thought to it before; I knew not a single woman who had married for love or felt more than an affectionate respect for her husband. Georges had been kind and had provided well. It had been more than enough.

My answer, however, seemed to please the Countess. "There is nothing wrong in making a practical choice. But your marriage changed him. My father had hired him because, for the first time that anyone could remember, the fishing was going poorly. Catches were declining, the seas were becoming as fitful as anywhere. With Georges's background in languages and religions, my father hoped to understand what had changed. The two of them worked closely together, learning the meaning of the rituals the villagers performed. That such primitive rites could happen in France . . . but it does not matter. Once he married you, Georges abandoned our project and left us adrift with our declining fortune. I duplicated his library to the best of my ability and reenacted his studies; I even imported peasants from the villages to serve in my household and teach me their beliefs. For I knew that our only hope was to reverse what had changed and, ultimately, control the rituals for our own ends."

I felt lightheaded, perhaps from the drink; her words were tumbling together in my mind, I could not make sense of them. "But what would you gain from such control?" I asked stupidly.

"Power, Ada." She leaned forward, her fingertips brushing the necklace again—and my bare skin as well. "What if their legends are true? Fishing has always been a game of chance, of man against tide and weather and season. The villagers claim that their Ada can diffuse a thunderstorm and calm the roughest seas, as long as she is properly appealed to. Imagine if there were even a grain of truth in it. Imagine if I could expand our business over the whole of the French coastline and flood the markets with my fish. Imagine if I could not only quell a thunderstorm, but raise one against a foreign navy. I would be the most powerful woman in France, Ada, more powerful than the king himself. Only I have never before had all the pieces needed to enact the rituals. Not until tonight."

I was trembling beneath her touch, yet I could not bring myself to move away. "You have convinced me," I said. "I will sell you the tablet. We have a deal."

She slid her chair close, until I could feel her breath on my ear. "Does the tablet draw you, Ada? Does it call to you?"

I nodded, not trusting myself to speak.

"Would it surprise you to know that it was found seemingly at the time of your conception? That it was discovered during the same fishing trip where your mother had fallen into the sea and nearly drowned, only to find herself with child some weeks later?"

The room was growing warm, the air too thick to breathe. Her fingertips were hot against my flesh. I could only look at the tablet, its surface wavering in the candlelight.

"Your father never believed he was your father; he thought something had *visited* itself upon your mother. And yet here you are, as perfect a woman as any man could ask for. You must have been a most difficult conundrum for Georges—believing what he did about your parentage, craving your innate knowledge in order to sell it to my father, and yet finding himself attracted to you."

At last I came to my senses enough to stand, knocking my chair aside; I clung to the table, shuddering violently. "Foul," I managed to stammer, "foul, foul!" Though whether I meant the Countess, or her words, or the visions that danced before my eyes I could not say.

Somewhere water lapped against a shore, while voices called out words I did not understand . . .

"Ada, listen to me." She placed herself before me, her dark gaze holding mine. "All your life, have you not felt something? Something calling to you as if from a great distance, perhaps from the very sea itself?" Her voice, low and driving, drowned out all other sounds. "I thought at first you were merely a fetching peasant, but you are something else. Something perhaps formed by those churning seas, then hidden away in the safety of an empty womb . . . "

The floor swayed and rocked beneath my feet. My face was wet; I touched my cheeks and realized I was weeping, though I had not felt the tears come. A small part of my mind knew this was madness. I should flee this place; the money be damned.

Before me the Countess smiled warmly. She leaned forward and gently kissed first one cheek, then the other, and then finally placed her soft, rouged lips against mine.

"Ada," she breathed. "Let me give you *yourself*."

I opened my mouth—to speak, to kiss her?—and instead I fainted.

### 3.

I was outside of myself, bodiless, in a dark place where warm water swaddled me and voices lulled me and a scaly body coiled about me, whispering words of power in my ear, words of a strange language that nonetheless filled me with an ache of recognition.

I was swaddled in my mother's arms, listening to her whispers: *she frightens me, there's something about her eyes, what if she's been possessed by the devil or worse.*

I was dreaming in bed, dreaming of descending into the water. In a stupor, I realized Georges was speaking to someone in my room: *I have not let her touch fish or salt since I brought her here, I will never let them claim her.*

*There is no surer way to harm another than to unnecessarily protect them.*

Slowly I felt myself returning, felt smooth stone beneath me, felt damp air upon my face. Was I dreaming still? My mind was thick with images of the Countess, our repast, her terrible speech; yet my body refused to fully awaken. Perhaps I had never come here at all; perhaps it was all the same dream—the journey and my arrival, our supper and now these blurry impressions.

Then I heard scratching beside my head and it was as if cold water had been poured over me. I forced my eyes open and, with much blinking, managed to focus on the piece of chalk grinding onto the flagstones, trailing a broad white curve around my body. I heard too the Countess chanting above me, the words incomprehensible but the sounds making me shudder.

She paused when she saw I was awake; I tried to speak but could not make the words come. She kissed my forehead, the cool of her necklace brushing my face, for she was once more wearing the pendant; then she ran a sticky thumb down the bridge of my nose, over my chin, and dabbed onto my chest an asymmetrical pattern of red thumbprints—a pattern, I swiftly realized, made out of blood.

"Soon, Ada," she whispered. "Soon we will all learn what you really are."

My limbs were too heavy to move; all I could do was roll my head. It was then that I glimpsed the tablet in the circle, its carved face smeared with blood as well.

Oh, Georges, Georges, what did you keep from me?

Still the chalk ground and scratched, still the Countess chanted, her voice gaining in strength.

Somewhere torches were flaring alight. A rising cold seeped from my belly outwards, making me quiver. "Stop," I croaked.

She finished her drawing and stood over me, taking the book and reading aloud in the same queer language, at once utterly foreign and utterly familiar. The syllables skittered maddeningly across my mind. "You must stop," I said more loudly.

Her plump, pale arm flashed out. She gestured at something I could not see. One of the maids crouched over me, holding a large cup in her hands, a necklace with a smaller icon hanging around her neck. *We are here for you,* she mouthed at me. *We will not let her harm you.* She bent low and, raising my head with one hand, pressed the cup to my lips with her other.

Inside was salt water, gleaming green and as cold as I felt.

At first, I sipped. Then I was gulping it down, drinking as I have never done before, nearly choking in my haste to swallow it all. The brine tasted sweeter than honey.

"Now," the Countess breathed. "Now we will see if Great Ada dares to ignore me."

My skin rippled pleasurably at the name, as if stroked from beneath by a thousand light fingers, so wondrous it nearly made me cry aloud; yet I also felt sick with anticipation. "Not like this," I cried. "There are steps, and water . . . "

But she was bellowing the words now, a strange braying singsong that echoed in the room, making my skin ripple again.

"Water," I begged. "I must go into the water."

She leaned over me, her eyes boring into mine. Her arm flashed out again and now it held a knife, gleaming in the torchlight. "Come, Ada!" she cried. "Come protect your creation!"

The floor vanished. My stomach lurched in my nerveless, floating body. An inky blackness rushed over me. Someone was crying *No, no! It cannot be!* My skin erupted in great gaping tears, everything ripping apart, water swelling my limbs. Brine in my mouth. My mind filling with a liquid darkness. A hint of her rouge on my lips still—

I opened my eyes and the Countess screamed.

### 4.

Firelight undulating in crimson shadows on the walls. The water lapping. I can hear a voice calling me: *return, return*. Nestled in pale flesh riddled with veins. The taste of blood on my lips. My bones swelling and pressing against their prison like fingers clawing free.

The taste of blood on my lips.

I have always been Ada, dreaming.

Night without and within. I see everything, everything, I see the world unblinking. Mossy stone walls and open space beyond, torchlight and chalk dust. The woman salt-licked with glands steaming. Her blood on my lips. Over her I crouch, swaying.

There were prisons . . . there had been many prisons. Walls and gripping hands and this strange skin cocooning; voices duplicitous, the seas too far to touch. How long since I had felt true water, slept among its currents? How long since I swam in the deep chasms I call home?

I glimpse my reflection in the tablet, black-eyed and swelling. There was a dream, I saw myself in the water . . . Two of my acolytes appear. They kneel and bow their heads.

*We knew you would be reborn.*

*We would never let her harm you.*

*Great mother!*

*Great Ada!*

I bid them rise and their eyes are wet. They take the tablet and lead me from the room. Outside we follow the stony path and I am dreaming, I was dreaming always. The smell of water, the darkness. Gleams of jewel-light undulating through the ocean's scrim. Etching the tablet so I would remember: *return*. Skin flaking away, cool air stroking my scales. My body slithering against the damp walls. *Return*. From my belly comes my answer, ululating through the passage *Ada Ada Ada*.

*Ada returns,* my acolytes ululate. *Our mother returns!*

The celestial skies above. Sweet-salt water lapping. The chasms empty and beckoning. River stroking my feet, my legs, washing the last skin away. *Return*. Spines flexing, scales rippling, pores oozing gelatinous until I am slickly soft.

The terror of being without form. My womb-mother swaddling me. Georges embracing me. The oceans cradling me. Blood on my lips, a last hint of rouge. I give myself to the water and begin my journey home.

I am *Ada*. And I have always been.

**GENE O'NEILL** has seen 150 of his short stories, novelettes, and novellas published, as well as seven short story collections and seven novels. Twelve of this group were Stoker finalists, two claiming the haunted house—*Taste of Tenderloin* (collection) and *The Blue Heron* (novella). Two novels and a novella collaboration will be out sometime in 2019. In addition, two novels, previously brought out in limited hardbacks, will appear as trade paperbacks.

# GRAFFITI SONATA

## GENE O'NEILL

*Gene O'Neill*

**FOR A MOMENT** after McKay opened the door of his Oakland apartment and saw Elise standing there, he felt his spirit spike. In the next instant, he realized his wife hadn't brought their daughter Ty along, only some folded-up cardboard boxes under her arm. His elation quickly faded. Before he could say anything, Elise held up her hand, reinforcing his inference. "I'm *done* talking, Mac. Just here to pack up a few more boxes."

He nodded and said, "It's good to see you," knowing any weak arguments he had left were preempted. Three weeks ago, Elise and their six-year-old daughter had moved out to a friend's vacant apartment over on Lake Merritt. In another week, they were taking off to Elise's sister's place down the coast at Pismo Beach. Watching Elise unfold the packing boxes, McKay yearned to tell his wife how much he missed her flute playing, her classical CDs, the three of them laughing together—the essential, joyful sounds of his life. But he said nothing, realizing the time for effectively pleading his case had already passed.

Deflated, McKay left Elise packing, not able to stand the smell of her scent. He took the nearby pedestrian overpass across the freeway to the park to collect himself. On the way down the enclosed steps to the playground, he stopped after he saw a drawing freshly chalked on the concrete wall. He had visited the park often in the last three weeks, fleeing the silence of the apartment, but he had never noticed anything drawn on the wall.

This was a man wearing an indigo peacoat with his collar turned up and a black stocking cap rolled down almost to his eyes. He was standing, looking back over his shoulder, the shadows not completely covering his square jaw, penetrating eyes, or grim expression. Unlike most graffiti McKay had seen spray-painted on freeway columns and walls, there was no tag line on this one. Looking the drawing over with a technical eye, he realized this wasn't an amateurish cartoon at all. A competent artist had taken time to carefully outline, shade, and highlight, using minimal colors to make a startling figure. Although cartoon-like, the drawing was not bigger than life, unlike many of the caricatures in comic book-style art. In fact, the damn thing was realistically menacing, raising the hair on the back of McKay's neck. An image of a lowlife with bad intentions, about to step out away from the wall and create havoc.

Turning away, McKay shivered, glad he'd taken half a Valium along with his Seropram earlier in the evening.

He continued down the overpass steps with more important things on his mind. His wife and daughter were moving out of town in a week, perhaps out of his life forever.

The playground was unoccupied at this time of evening. McKay wiped a bench off with a piece of paper from the nearby trashcan and plopped himself down. Sucking in a deep breath, he tried to center, clear his mind, and focus, like Dr. Havlicek had taught him. He stretched his hands out along the bench's back, noticing his trembling wasn't too bad this evening, only a slight tremor.

The debilitating condition had developed after he'd experienced a seizure at his drafting table last December. The Kaiser doctors initially thought it was an early onset of Parkinson's syndrome. But Dr. Havlicek was not so sure now, thinking the seizure and subsequent tremor may have been related to an undiagnosed fever from last fall. Despite the medical help and Elise's support, McKay had sunk into a black funk, a depression that only regular doses of medication partially alleviated. Nothing seemed to help the trembling in his hands. He was incapable of writing clearly, much less doing fine art. For eight months, he'd done little more than sit and watch the same movies over and over again on TV.

Then, a month ago, Elise had admitted she was fed up with his wallowing in self-pity. "If the shaking were really something physical, they wouldn't have referred you to a psychiatrist," she'd argued. "Besides, there are other things you could do with your MFA. Teach, maybe? Anyhow, we need a break, Mac. Ty and I are moving to Jamie's apartment on Lake Merritt; then, after her dance camp, we're heading to my sister's. When *you* get yourself back on track, call us."

McKay glanced absently around the empty park. His biggest concern was that his wife and daughter would remain permanently down at Pismo Beach. Elise and her sister might start composing music and concert touring, like they'd done before McKay came into their lives. Lauren had always been jealous of him, thought he'd been a leech on Elise from the beginning of their marriage six and a half years ago. McKay was forced to admit to himself, it was probably true, in a way. His art income had been unreliable at best, fluctuating dramatically. Elise's Oakland Symphony job and several other part-time gigs had mostly supported the family, especially during the last eight months. Hell, he thought wryly, after the seizure, he couldn't even draw unemployment.

Slumping back on the bench, McKay realized he was emotionally drained, really exhausted. The silence in the apartment had disrupted his rest since Elise and Ty moved out. Looking about, he thought it was peaceful here: the hum of nearby traffic a pleasing background, like one of Elise's flute CDs. He closed his eyes, drifted off.

(1st Movement)

*Lake Merritt.*

*The lights in the windows of the apartments along the shore shrouded by heavy fog. A few people out along East Lakeshore Drive, apparently anxious to get in out of the misty night. All except for a lone figure, dressed in dark clothes, lurking in the shadows of the four-story complex on the corner, spying up at a lighted second-floor apartment. Standing. Just watching.*

McKay awoke stiff and chilled on the park bench. It was completely dark now. The fog had moved in from the Bay, settling around him like a fallen cloud. He stood up and rubbed his bare arms. Better head back to the apartment, he thought. Elise would have the last of her stuff packed and be long gone by now.

After climbing up the stairs to the overpass, McKay stopped at the spot where the graffito had been chalked. The figure had disappeared. The concrete wall was clean and gray. McKay spread his fingers and cautiously placed his hand where he thought the drawing had been. He rubbed his fingertips. No chalk dust. And the surface was dry. Nothing on the steps indicated the wall had been washed clean. It appeared the indigo man had just walked off the wall into the night. That's weird, McKay thought, as he climbed the remaining stairs, checking to make sure he had not just made a mistake in location. But the wall was completely clean of graffiti, clear to the top near the overpass. He walked home wondering if perhaps he'd taken too much medication.

A half an hour later, McKay got a call on his cell phone.

"Mac, you have to come over, right now. There is a man loitering outside down on the street, spying up at the apartment. He's been there since dark."

"Have you called the cops?"

"No, what can I tell them? Some jerk is down on the street looking up at my window? Scaring my daughter? They'll think I'm a paranoid crank or hysterical doting mother."

"Okay, I'll be right over."

By the time McKay got to Lake Merritt, there wasn't anyone hanging about in front of the apartments. He carefully checked both side streets of the corner building, but he found no one suspicious along either street. He made his way back to the front of the complex and buzzed up to Elise's apartment on the intercom. "Nobody's here, Babe. I've checked around the building for a block each way."

"Oh, great, that's such a relief, Mac," Elise answered back. "Actually, the last time I saw him was just before I called. Maybe my nerves have been strung too tight lately. Sorry for the trouble."

"You want me to come up?" he asked, his fingers resting on the intercom button, a sense of hopeful anticipation making his breath catch in his throat.

There was a brief hesitation, before she finally answered, "No, that probably isn't a good idea. I've got to clean up and get Ty to bed. But thanks for coming by, Mac. We appreciate it . . . Goodbye."

Dismissed, he stood there for a minute or so, staring absently at the intercom. Finally, he nodded. "Bye, Babe," he murmured to himself.

The next morning, McKay found the graffito back in a different location, about three-quarters down the steps to the park. *Jesus*, he swore. The indigo man stared back at McKay with the same piercing gaze, but there was something slightly different about the pose. The angle of the body and head exposed the face a little more now.

McKay felt a slight stir of recognition. He felt he *knew* this man. No, he wasn't sure. He shook his head with frustration, not quite able to pull up the memory.

During the week, McKay had limited contact with Elise. He saw her only briefly after church, when he picked up Ty for a Sunday outing.

"Hi . . . Keep her sweater on . . . Bye."

They went to Fairyland, his last visit with his daughter. Tomorrow afternoon, Ty and Elise would both be gone.

Sunday evening, down at the park, the mysterious drawing remained in place like a sentinel, like no one dared to erase or vandalize it. Of course, McKay couldn't help wondering who had chalked the graffito in the first place? Was the face really all that familiar? But most of his time at the park, he spent trying to figure out some way to prevent his wife and daughter from going to Pismo Beach.

In desperation, he'd even gone over to Merritt and Peralta two days ago. He'd filled out applications for a teaching job, but McKay was too late: there was nothing available for an art teacher of any kind for the next semester, at either nearby community college.

On Monday, the day Elise and Ty were scheduled to head south, the indigo man mysteriously disappeared again in the late morning.

In the afternoon, Elise swung by McKay's place in her packed yellow VW Jetta to let Ty say goodbye.

"Bye, Daddy."

"Bye, Sweetie," he said, reaching in through the opened door to hug her tightly.

"Goodbye," Elise said, thin-lipped and grim.

McKay nodded, too choked up to say anything more, and closed the door. Families should stay together, especially during tough times, he thought.

That evening McKay skipped his medication, wandered into his studio, and dug around the desk next to the dusty drafting table. Finally, he found the Jack Daniels he'd hid from Elise after Dr. Havlicek had warned him about drinking while on medication. He settled down in front of the TV and drank from the bottle. The whiskey burned his throat but washed away the stiffness from his neck and shoulders. *Blade Runner*, one of his favorite movies, was showing again on TNT, but it was almost over. Only the last few minutes remained, the chase and the great ending in the rain on the gothic building. White-headed Roy, the last of the escaped replicants, was dying, but he'd saved Deckard, pulling him back up onto the wet roof. And then Roy sadly delivered the famous monologue: Telling Deckard all the amazing things he'd seen working as a slave out in space, that those remarkable memories would soon disappear like teardrops in the rain. Finally, he bent his rain-soaked head to his chest, and in a matter-of-fact tone gasped the concluding line: "Time to die."

(2nd Movement)

*A lonely stretch of 101, just south of San Luis Obispo.*

*The bright yellow Jetta speeds along in the night, no cars in the southbound lanes, only occasional headlights in the northbound lanes, suddenly looming for a moment in the mist, looking like fuzzy Japanese lanterns.*

*Then, super slow motion:*
*A figure appears unexpectedly ahead,*
*right in the middle of the highway lane,*
*standing tall and dark, peacoat and stocking cap, arms raised overhead.*
*Braking, the VW veers right in an attempt to avoid hitting the man,*
*skids on the loose shoulder and flips over the fence,*
*before slamming with a dull thud into a live oak tree:*
*upside down, wheels spinning, but doors closed. Nothing exits the car.*

McKay awakened in a clammy sweat, his heart thumping, his pulse racing. His head felt like it had been squeezed in a vise.

The phone had jarred him from his drunken stupor. "Mr. McKay?" a calm female voice asked.

"Yes."

"This is Lieutenant Melendez of the California Highway Patrol, San Luis Obispo. I'm afraid there has been a serious automobile accident down here, involving your wife and daughter . . . ah, Elise and Tyler McKay?"

"Yes," he repeated stiffly, his hangover forgotten, the highway patrol officer's words sobering him as if ice water had been splashed in his face.

"Your wife and daughter have been taken to Sierra Vista Regional Medical Center, Emergency Services. Got a pen? I'll give you the number."

"Both of them are hurt?" he asked in a hoarse whisper as he wrote the number down. He found it difficult to grasp the exact meaning of the officer's words. "How badly?"

"Mr. McKay, you will need to personally contact the hospital for all the medical details, and updates on your daughter and wife's status. I am not privy to that information. Do you understand?"

He cleared his throat, focused, and answered, "Yes, I do."

"Someone from the CHP-Oakland branch will get in contact with you during office hours tomorrow, with more information on the accident, condition of the car, what is required of you. All right?"

"Okay," McKay said, feeling kind of detached now, like he was actually listening and watching some kind of dark B-movie.

"You sure you understand all of this, Mr. McKay?" the woman asked kindly. "Got the hospital phone number written down?"

"Yes, thank you. I'll call the hospital, right now."

He sat there with the phone in his hand. This can't be real, he thought.

The phone rang again.

It was Lauren. She made it all too real.

She had called the CHP when Elise and Ty hadn't shown up on time at her place in Pismo Beach. Naturally, she immediately called the hospital when she learned of the accident. "It's horrible, Mac, they are both gone," she said, her high-pitched voice grating on his already tightly strung nerves. "Ty at the scene and Elise on the way to the hospital." Then she continued on and on, "The funeral . . . and the church . . . making necessary arrangements tomorrow . . . "

They are both gone, it's true! There must be something he could do. Some way to bring them back. Families belonged together.

The next four days were a blur. Somehow, on Thursday, McKay managed to make it to the funeral down south in his Honda.

Lauren had taken care of all the arrangements: the church service, memorial, even the Lutheran minister for the burial ceremony. McKay just stood off by himself, staring down at the side-by-side graves in San Luis Cemetery, just off Highway 101 south of San Luis Obispo, across from the Madonna Inn and next to the Old Mission Cemetery. He struggled internally, forcing himself to accept that his wife and daughter were inside the two ornate caskets being lowered into the ground, here in this public spot by the busy freeway, so far from home.

Someone nudged his arm. "Mac, time to go to Lauren's."

He numbly followed. More blurred faces, inaudible whispers, and tasteless food. Finally, it was all over.

Time to go home, he thought, trying to pull himself together, but instead picturing the replicant dying with such dignity in the last part of *Blade Runner*.

He got home late Thursday afternoon and immediately went over to the park, still wearing his dark blue suit. Sure enough, the indigo man was back on the wall, positioned above the last few steps before reaching the playground, his features only slightly shadowed. McKay touched the drawing, absolutely certain now that he knew the face. But he sighed, just too tired and numb to expend the effort to recall details. He spent the early evening on the park bench, dozing in his rumpled suit.

Later that evening, McKay searched around the desk in his studio, looking for another bottle of booze. There was nothing more to drink hidden anywhere in the apartment. Sucking in a deep breath, he decided he'd have to make a trip down to the nearby liquor store. McKay walked the two blocks, then on impulse, he swung by the overpass to the park before heading home. He wasn't surprised to find that the figure had again left the wall.

(3rd Movement)

*Midnight at San Luis Cemetery.*

*Overcast, stars and moon completely screened by cloud cover, the two fresh graves visible in the darkness because of the dim light cast by a distant streetlight from the adjoining Old Mission Cemetery.*

*A figure, wearing a coat and a roll-down cap and carrying something under his arm, moves quietly through the darkness, approaches the graves, pauses, and peers at the headstones. Then he withdraws the item from under his arm and sets it aside on the ground. The figure kneels for a few seconds atop first one grave, then the other. Still shrouded in darkness, the man moves to the side and retrieves the object from the ground.*

*The clouds divide and this part of the cemetery is illuminated by the moon . . . Only then, for just a moment, is the nature of the object clear: the figure has brought a spade to the gravesites.*

Friday afternoon, McKay returned to the pedestrian overpass. Coming down the steps, he thought the concrete canvas was completely clean of graffiti. But on the wall over the last step, he spotted a distant scene, two tiny figures, barely thumb-sized: a woman and a child. Their features were vague, but McKay knew their identities. They seemed to be striding purposefully, a location in mind.

"*Jesus,*" he whispered, breathing heavily now, as if the air had been knocked from him by the observation. McKay closely watched the figures; of course, he could detect no actual movement. "That would be impossible," he murmured to himself unconvincingly, "absolutely frigging nuts." He finally decided that he needed to get home right now and take his medication, perhaps even double up.

Back at the apartment he wandered around nervously, unable to sit still. After a few minutes, he went into his studio. Idly, he flipped over his sketchpad on the drawing board and, to his surprise, discovered new work. Still standing, McKay thumbed carefully through a dozen pages of faces. "Oh, my God," he murmured, studying the chalked drawings. They were actually sketches of his own face being gradually transformed through the series, changed from a mirror image of himself in the first drawing to the rugged features of the indigo man in the last sketch. McKay focused on the man's eyes, which seemed to peer back at him knowingly.

Absently, he glanced down at his fingers holding a piece of chalk, his grip tremor free, his hand steady as a surgeon's.

(4th Movement—with Flute Solo)

*Sometime long after dark, McKay is awakened in his recliner by the haunting sound of a flute. Then, a moment of quiet, followed by a sharp knocking on the front door. Lower on the door, he hears a lighter rap.*

(Coda)

The next morning, a mother taking her two youngsters to the playground stopped halfway down the steps from the pedestrian overpass, noticing the graffiti chalked in dark colors on the concrete wall adjoining the steps. Three life-sized figures, but with their backs oddly turned to the viewer, giving the impression they were striding away into the dark distance. All holding hands: a man, a woman, and a young girl.

When not writing about ghosts and improbable Siamese twins, **CLIFFORD BROOKS** is a devoted cat daddy. On any given Sunday, you can find him walking his cat through one of the Bay Area's many parks. Follow his work at cliffordbrooks.com.

Author's note: The unnamed narrator of "John Wilson" is based on a character I created for a novella about Siamese twins: one male, the other female. During a revision, I gave their beautician (a bit character) more of a voice. I wrote up a bio for her and, when I was done, I realized the bio was really a short story. So became "John Wilson."

# JOHN WILSON

## CLIFFORD BROOKS

**SHIT.**
You don't have to believe me.
I'm not going to get pissed off,
call you names,
or have a hissy fit.
That's not my style.
You can even tell me I'm full of shit, if you like.
But I'm not.
I really did see a ghost.
And it's not what you think.
Not like you've been told.
It wasn't all glowin' and shimmery.
No white sheets.
No chains.
No nothing.
It looked like John Wilson.
Kinda-sorta how I expected John Wilson to look.
I guess I should explain.
Until he walked through that door,
I didn't really know what John Wilson looked like.
He didn't exist.
He's a combination of two of my boyfriends.
John has the athletic body.
Knows how to use it, too.
No complaints there.
But whenever we go out,
he's on me.
Tells me that I've had enough to drink,
when I've just gotten started.
Keeps telling me about his father.

How he died.
Liver failure or some shit.
I tell him that he's not me.
Not my problem.
And then things get sour.
Quiet.
And I'm thinking,
everything would be okay
if he'd just drink his mineral water and shut the fuck up.
Then there's Wilson.
He'll tie one on with the best of them.
We party well together,
make decent love,
and laugh.
When he's not working.
32 hours a week,
in a restaurant,
doing dishes.
Brings home less than half of what I do.
Much less.
Hopes to become head dishwasher some day.
Shit.
Don't get me wrong,
I'm not some money-hungry bitch
out to live off daddy's tit,
but come on,
head dishwasher?
Do I sound angry?
I'm not.
I get what I want.
Need.
Always have.
Do what I gotta do.
But it's not real.
Lasting.
So I combined the best parts of both
and call him John Wilson.
Hell, if I were a singer,
I'd write a song about him.
I'm not, though.

Beauty college graduate,
2008.
Fiesta Cuts.
Not the worst job.
Get to talk shit all day.
And do hair.
You meet all sorts of people.
All sorts.
Nothing I couldn't deal with.
Until John Wilson.
Does it sound like I've been doing some good shit or what?
Anyway,
he walked in.
I think it was a Monday.
Maybe Tuesday.
Does it matter?
I was alone in the shop, doing this old woman's hair.
Or what was left of it.
Lots of spray and uplifts.
Hide the scalp.
She was showing me a picture of her granddaughter.
Nearly my age.
Degree from some university back East.
The girl was all smiling and stuff in the picture.
I don't know why.
Her hair looked like shit.
All goofy and puffed up like she'd just pulled off a ski cap.
I wanted to laugh.
The old woman was going on about all the degrees and honors this
girl had gotten.
I could tell she hadn't seen her in a long time.
All she'd gotten was that sorry-ass picture and an invitation to the
graduation.
No need to attend,
just send money.
As I picked at her hair and made "uh-huh" noises,
my attention strayed to John Wilson.
Damn,
he was fine.

Tall.
Dark hair.
In need of a cut,
but not bad.
Five o'clock shadow.
Tight jeans.
Muscle shirt.
Muscles.
The old woman yelped.
I'd picked her soft scalp.
Sorry, ma'am, I told her.
Didn't remember her name.
Should.
She's a regular.
John Wilson just stood there while all this was going on.
There were plenty of places to sit.
Have a seat, I told him.
He did.
Real slow like.
As if he was moving underwater.
I liked that.
Didn't spook me at first.
I didn't know then.
Not 'til later.
You got an appointment? I asked him as I handed Miss Grandma a
mirror.
Do I need one? he asked.
Not like I just said it though,
like a smart ass,
but real innocent like.
Like it just never crossed his mind.
Usual way, I said. But you're in luck. I don't have another
appointment 'til three.
He kinda smiled then.
$35, I told Miss Grandma, then excused myself to the back room.
Checked my appointment book.
May Singleton was due in fifteen minutes.
Called her.
She picked up on the fifth ring,
all out of breath.

Said she was just on her way out the door when the phone rang.
Told her there'd been an emergency.
Needed to cancel her appointment.
Would Thursday be all right?
When I got back,
Grandma was straining,
trying to place the mirror on the counter.
I took the mirror from her,
afraid she might drop it.
She looked around her chair for her purse.
She never lets it out of her sight,
but always manages to lose it.
Told her it was in her lap.
She laughed.
Thanked me.
John Wilson was reading a copy of *Rolling Stone* magazine.
An old, tattered issue.
Janet Jackson was on the cover.
The one where she's nude and some guy's hands are cupping her
breasts like clam shells.
Strong hands.
Nice nails.
John Wilson had nice hands.
Grandma gave me a 25¢ tip.
I forgot to thank her.
She said something to me as she left.
Probably about her granddaughter.
I shook out the apron she'd worn.
Wisps of hair floated gracefully down.
Sunlight coming through the blinds made them glimmer like silver.
Everything seemed magical right then.
Like in a fairy tale.
Like it was gonna happen.
John Wilson.
Prince Charming.
Come on over and have a seat, I said, as nonchalantly as I could.
He got up and moved into the chair,
real slow like.
Not like he was underwater this time,

but like he had to think about what he was doing.
I grabbed my broom.
Leaned against it.
How are you today? I asked.
I wanted to hear his voice again.
I need a haircut, he told me.
I began to sweep the old woman's cut hair into a pile.
There was more on the floor than on her head.
More than she'd ever have again.
Eighty, if she was a day.
But she wasn't important right then.
It was John Wilson.
His dull response.
Had he misunderstood me?
Well, you've come to the right place, I told him.
Sign said haircuts, he said.
His hair was shoulder length,
a bit ragged at the edges.
Almost as long as mine.
What do you want done? I asked, propping the broom in the corner.
Haircut. Sign said.
I realized then that he wasn't much at conversation.
That was all right.
Neither was John.
And we'd made it nearly a year.
A trim? A style? What would you like? I asked,
real suggestive like.
I want to look like him, he said, holding up the magazine.
The *Rolling Stone*.
Had he brought it with him or was it one of mine?
It was an ad for Guess Jeans.
The model had a short cut.
Clean shaven.
He was wearing jeans.
So was John Wilson.
And a muscle shirt.
So was John Wilson.
Loafers.
I looked down at John Wilson's feet.
And I laughed.

I mean, hard.
Not some prissy,
covered-mouth shit.
Full bore.
He looked at me strange.
I'm sorry, I said. It's just that I'm not used to people going so far and all.
My stomach hurt, you know.
I wiped my eyes.
He looked at me,
confused like,
innocent.
Like he didn't see the humor.
I'm here for a haircut, he said, like he needed to remind me or something.
I know, I know.
I moved behind him.
Pulled my scissors out of their antiseptic goo,
rinsed them,
dried them on the drape towel,
and began to cut.
Like cutting air.
I pricked my finger.
Shit.
My hair, he said, as I shook my throbbing finger. Cut my hair.
All right, all right. I cut my damn finger is all.
I don't usually cuss much.
Not around customers.
But shit,
John Wilson was bugging.
When was the last time you got your hair cut, I asked, sucking my finger.
I couldn't taste blood,
only hairspray.
He looked at me like I'd just asked him when was the last time he'd taken a shit.
Styles change, he answered.
They sure do, I said.
I picked up my scissors again.

If you're not in style, people stare, he said.
Yeah, I agreed.
I think that's when I realized that he didn't have much over Forrest
Gump.
Good enough for a one-night stand, though.
He was kinda sweet.
In a dumb kind of way.
Thought I might be doing him a favor.
'Til I began to cut again.
His hair.
So fine.
Like silk.
Only finer.
Lighter.
It slipped *through* my fingers.
I couldn't get a grip on it.
Your hair, I began.
Cut it, he said.
But . . . it's so light. So light.
Cut it, he said.
My finger began to bleed again.
Where I'd pricked it,
a drop,
a single drop,
fell on his hair.
It glistened.
I turned to grab the drape towel from the sink.
Turned back and
the drop was gone.
He turned and looked at me.
A smile on his face.
Like I'd just done him a favor.
Yeah, that kind of satisfied look.
A slant of light from the window above the door stabbed him.
Went through him.
Cut it, he said.
This time the innocence was gone.
He meant it.
But, I said as my fingers slipped through his locks.
Sign said haircuts, he said.

He was getting pissed.
No innocence this time.
I can't, I can't get it.
Cut! he shouted.
I was flipping out by then.
Thinking acid flashback,
big time.
I'd only used acid once,
but shit,
this wasn't real.
Couldn't be.
I didn't believe in ghosts.
Cut it!
He kept saying it.
Over and over.
Like trance music, you know,
stuck in an endless groove.
I tried to tell him that I couldn't help him,
but he wouldn't listen.
He just kept demanding that I cut his hair.
My finger was still bleeding.
Throbbing.
Another drop.
Squeezed free.
A blob.
Sitting there.
Making contact with his neck.
And then it was gone.
Sucked in, like through a straw.
I shook my head.
Why wasn't I afraid?
Of him.
John Wilson.
So different from me.
Ethereal.
Did I just say "ethereal"?
Shit, I don't really know what that means,
but I know it's the right word.
Accurate.

Cuz he was there.
But he wasn't.
Different.
Not like you or me,
but there nonetheless.
And I wanted him.
More than before.
Inside me.
Deep inside me.
And he knew.
So he shut up.
Closed those full lips of his.
And he entered me.
Fully.
Fully clothed,
both of us.
I didn't even see him get up.
Just suddenly.
Inside me.
But it wasn't sex.
Not like you think.
It was better.
More complete.
I felt him everywhere.
Under my skin.
Beneath my scalp.
Between my thighs.
It was incredible.
More like anticipation than the real thing.
Perfect.
John.
Wilson.
I let out a deep breath.
A sigh.
And he was gone.
Time had slipped by.
Almost seven.
I didn't remember anything at first,
except the pleasure.
It had seemed like moments.

An extended orgasm.
But now I felt so empty.
So alone.
Like he'd taken part of me with him.
I smiled.
Wondered if there'd be a next time.
Wondered if this was it.
Time to leave.
Close shop.
It was late.
I was late.
And then the door opened.
I thought it might be him.
Hoped.
But it was Miss Grandma.
And before I could say anything, she told me what she wanted.
Her purse.
She was looking for her purse.
She didn't notice anything different about me.
Except my hair.
You cut it, she said.
Your beautiful red hair.
I reached up to my shoulder.
My fingers grasped at the air.
I turned.
Looked in the mirror.
You look like a man, she said.
Or something like that.
She'd mumbled.
I hadn't been listening.
Sign said haircuts, I said.
I cut people's hair.
She looked at me real strange.
Then down at the clumps of red hair that covered the floor.
She began to speak again.
I stopped her.
John Wilson's hair, I said.
I cut people's hair.
She moved away from me,

a pained look on her face,
like my words confused her to the point of discomfort.
And she began to look around the shop.
Under the chairs.
Beneath the mound of magazines.
The *Rolling Stone*.
In the vanity drawers.
Until she'd looked in all the likely places three or four times,
and the unlikely ones twice.
Then she left,
confused.
Without her purse.
Neither of us said goodbye.
We should have.
She died three weeks later.
Paper said in her sleep.
I didn't go to the funeral.
I didn't want to.
No need.
It's her purse that matters now.
I know she's out there.
Frantic.
Looking for something she never lost.
And something she'll never find.
John Wilson.
Shit.

**KEN HUELER** teaches kung fu in the San Francisco Bay Area and, with fellow members of the Horror Writers Association's local chapter, gets up to all sorts of adventures (only some involving margaritas). His work has appeared in *Weirdbook*, *Stupefying Stories*, *Black Petals*, and *Strangely Funny III*. Find out more at kenhueler.wordpress.com.

Author's note: Kappas are fascinating and not always explicable: Why do they collect shirikodmas? Folklore gives no reason. Cucumbers can save you from kappas, which is wonderfully whimsical. For a fun movie starring a kappa as a good guy, check out Takashi Miike's *The Great Yokai War*.

# RIVER TWICE

## KEN HUELER

**KAME CHASED JEREMY** up the park's steps and along the jogger's circuit, to where the path split off to a scatter of picnic tables. Jeremy climbed up the closest table and dropped cross-legged onto the top. "Tell him you ladies will have your own tent. All on the up and up."

Kame sat on the side of the table facing a wide downhill scoop of park. "You know I'd love to. But for him, the co-ed will be secondary. The big problem's letting me near any sizable body of water that is not a sanctioned swimming pool."

"Really? Swimming? Not hormonal boys?"

"I've never touched a lake, a creek, or a pond. So yeah, unless the water is loaded with chlorine or bubble bath, forget it. Oh, he did let me in the ocean a couple times. Saltwater's okay, apparently." She rested an arm on Jeremy's thigh, "Do you know, I believed in kappas for longer than Santa Claus."

"I bet I'd be amazed, if I knew what kappas were."

"River yokai. Back in Japan, parents use them to scare kids away from messing around in water, I suppose. Dad sure did with me."

Jeremy waited. "All right, what are yokai?"

"Oh. Supernatural goblins and demons. Not the gamma ray ones like Gojira. You know, crazy Japan shit."

He leaned forward. "What is this *Japan*?"

She soured her lips. "Are you really the best our country has to offer in boyfriends?"

"Check out my reviews."

"Oh, really? How many are there, and how detailed?"

"Just focus on the stars. Anyway, back to business: Are you going to ask your dad about the weekend?"

"No, wait—do these reviews mention the longest you've been with one woman?"

"That's a work in progress, but so far mischievous cuties from the Tanaka clan have been the most durable." He pointed down the hill. "You're saying that if you ran down there and jumped into that pond, your dad's head would explode?"

She laughed. "If I even dipped my toes."

"You know, we have our own lake monsters, like Sharlie, Tessie, and Wally, but most of them aren't carnivorous. I don't think we've had any reported giant serpent deaths since the settler days."

"You will not mention that to my dad ever. He will populate your lake retreat with giant eels and plesiosaurs." She reached over and yanked one of his shoelaces out of knot. "So thanks for picking a weekend at a lake. Great. Yeah, I guess I am going to ask him. Not looking forward, but how's he going to say no if I don't?"

"C'mon, you're nineteen."

"To you."

Jeremy did the maddeningly cute thing with his grin. "What's the worst? Take it from another only child: He'll get mad and get on with life. And you're transferring to another college at some point, so he needs to practice letting go. Just tell him you won't go swimming."

She shrugged. "Oh, it's not just the swimming. It's the proximity to water."

Jeremy laughed and started retying his shoe. "Tell him we're not in Japan. There are no yokai in the US."

"Oh, I've mentioned that. I finally got him off the kappa trip, but now he rants about lurking parasites and all the crap people and factories dump."

"Just ask. And why not go for broke—find out about your family in Japan. You're always wondering about them, and why he left."

"I've tried, but he clams up."

Jeremy kissed her quickly on the forehead and gazed into her face. "So keep at him. What have you got to lose?"

She wrapped a finger into his blond curls so he couldn't move away. "Have things always come so easy for you?"

He grinned. "Tomorrow you have to tell me at least one fact about your life in Japan."

"I was two."

"No more kisses for you unless it's interesting."

"Dad, I'm home," Kame called in Japanese. She heeled out of her shoes and shoved them aside. She heard steel against wood down the hall and padded to the kitchen. Her dad glanced up from chopping cucumbers.

"Good day at school?"

She grabbed one of the slices and perched on one of the dinette's stools. "Pretty good. Everything still makes sense, so I guess another set of passing grades is in my future. Anyway, I'm ahead on my reading and papers, so I was thinking, if I did my all assignments by Friday night, I could take a mini-vacation."

He chopped slower. "Mm?"

She plunged on. "Some of my friends are going camping."

He moved the cucumbers to a glass bowl. "Will your Mr. Wade be there?"

This is going down fast, she thought. "The girls will have our own tent. You know, separate."

He put the knife down. Fingers tapped the countertop. "When you both leave community college, probably you will choose different universities. I wanted you to go last year. You should focus on your future. Mr. Wade will focus on his."

Kame kept silent. She'd stayed at home more for her dad's sake. "Things could work out with Jeremy. We might go to the same college. Or ones not too far apart."

"Hm." Her father salted the cucumber slices and started tossing them. "Where is this taking place?"

"Madison Lake."

Oh, my God, she thought, it's been a long time since I made him inhale like that.

"You don't have my permission."

She kept her tone light. "I'm almost twenty."

He walked over to her. "You know I don't like lakes or rivers. Filthy. Why not go with your friends to the mountains? Only a couple more hours away." He patted her cheek. "Could you start the miso?"

"Sure." She got up, wondering which man she would disappoint. Neither would forget whatever decision she made.

Jeremy wove through the coffee shop and set his mug beside Kame's. As he sat, she swiveled her laptop to him. The screen displayed a mishmash of Japanese characters. "My mother tried to drown me."

"What?"

"I decided to research my family history. When I was one and a half, my mom and dad vacationed in Arita. My mom carried me deep into a river. My dad saved me, but my mom kept going. They found her body miles downriver."

Jeremy reached out awkwardly and took her hands. "I'm so sorry. You didn't know?"

"Dad told me once she'd gotten sick and died and he'd moved to the States to get away from reminders of her." The look on her face softened. "Well, makes sense if she died trying to kill his baby. Why not? I think. Why else?"

Jeremy rubbed his thumb over the back of her hand, lost. "But why would he leave his family and friends, all the people who could have helped him deal, to help raise you? I thought family was real important in Japan, and the few times I've met him, he seems so unhappy."

"Oh, he's never really assimilated. He learned English, sure, because he had to. He let me end up pretty American, but inside the house I had to learn to read and speak Japanese, and all those rules. But yeah, he doesn't like it here."

Jeremy squeezed her hand. "Talk to him about it."

She blinked. "Why? If he wanted me to know, he wouldn't have lied."

"You have to."

Friday morning, she wore a blouse and a skirt to please her dad. After breakfast, she kissed him goodbye and walked toward the bus stop, veered down a path to the park, and waited. When she was sure he had left for work, she looped back home.

After changing into shorts and a tee shirt, she put more coffee to brew and set to work: She knew their photo albums held only US memories, his address book was entirely local, and their closets were filled with mundane usefulness. Instead, she pulled down the ladder to the attic and began rummaging through boxes and double-layered paper bags filled with winter clothes from occasional trips north, videocassette tapes that made her question her younger self's taste, old hobby castoffs: the usual attic residue.

She climbed down the ladder for a coffee break. Probably the caffeine was a bad idea—her dad's hybrid car was hard to hear and she already felt jumpy, fretting that this would be the one day he'd swing back home early. She checked her phone. Two missed calls from Jeremy. If she texted, he'd just call right back. She dialed.

"I notice you aren't in class," he said right away.

"And unless you're blabbing on the phone during lecture, neither are you."

"So, where are you? I wanted to make sure you're okay."

"At home. My dad's at work until five, so I thought I might poke about."

"Oh, Jesus. Just ask him already."

"It's hard," she answered. "Especially now I know he saved my life. And he's not laid back, like your dad."

"Yeah. Listen, you must desperately need some R&R. Are you coming with us tomorrow morning?"

"Yes." She wasn't sure she meant it, but she needed to get Jeremy off the phone. He could argue forever. She'd only called him so he wouldn't come looking for her.

"Great. Hey, do you want me to come over and help?"

She thought. "Can you read kanji? We'll be looking for papers in Japanese."

"Moral supp—"

"Look, I'll tell you all about it later. Gotta run. Okay?" She ended the call. "Geez, what a bulldozer. I'm not attracted to men like my dad, that's for damn sure."

Upstairs again, she continued working deeper beneath the angled beams and insulation. Finally, in a sealed box, she found photos of her dad as a younger man with what must be his family and friends—none of whom appeared to be a girlfriend or a wife—and papers in Japanese she could see at a glance were boring legal things. At the bottom, inside a thick bundle of blue cloth, she found a dark wooden jewelry box, its lid held shut by a cloth-tethered spike pushed through the metal loop. When she opened it, the rankness inside overwhelmed her. She put it down quickly and crawled away.

Granting herself another break, this time with grapefruit juice and toast, she thought about what she had learned so far: next to nothing. She tilted her head to the ceiling and frowned. Grabbing a can of Lysol, she entered the attic, spraying. When the air smelled overwhelmingly of lemon, she braved the box again. Inside were twelve pearls, as large as blueberries and opalescent. She'd never seen any so beautiful.

"But you stink," she said. She tilted the box to watch their colors roll, which revealed a key. She took it out and set the box on the floor. She'd replace the key later, when she reconstructed the attic in the hopes her vigilant dad wouldn't notice her exploration until after she'd moved away.

She crept down the ladder, drank more juice as she passed through the kitchen, and descended to the basement. The room held a square work table near the bottom of the stairs; a washer and dryer; a small freezer; shelves of gardening implements, flowerpots, and bags of ornamental stones; a water heater; furnace; and, in the corner facing the steps, an oddly sized door that across all memory had been locked. Her dad claimed the closet held paint, cleaners, and other dangerous chemicals, but as she'd gotten older, Kame had noticed he never took anything out of it.

The key fit. Her body mostly blocked the ceiling bulb's light and, at first, all she could tell was that a jumble of boards clogged the entrance like a palisade. Judging from the space above them, the closet wasn't big. Really, it was more like an alcove for a water heater and a furnace with a door added. She went to the shelves over the washer and unplugged the flashlight.

Back at the alcove, she could see through gaps between the boards that something lay behind them. Great. This would take time and she couldn't dawdle, that was for sure. She put the flashlight on the table to illuminate the alcove and began moving the boards. Capped pipes showed that she'd been right in her water heater theory. She wondered why someone would make less space in the basement proper.

Clearing the entrance revealed a small wooden pallet tented with layers of blue tarp. Heart racing, Kame lifted a corner, then jumped back, smacking her left elbow against the cinderblock wall. Her hip caught the table before she tumbled up the stairs.

In the sunny kitchen, she started to calm down. Her dad would not keep a child's body locked in their basement. Maybe it was a statue but, because of its size, the one downstairs would be impossibly heavy to have brought with him from Japan. If he'd bought it in the States, why drag it downstairs and hide it? Well, she decided, it was inanimate and she had little time to dick around replacing the lumber and restoring the attic before her father came home.

Downstairs again, she took the flashlight off the table and approached the tent. This time, she used a trowel to lift and pin back the shiny plastic layers, exposing the legs. The skin was reptilian and had been painted or glazed a mottled blue and green. The webbing between the toes had been delicately executed. Reassured that it wasn't a child, she dragged the tarp out. The grotesque figure, about the size of a ten-year-old, was curled as much as the flattened shell rising from mid-back to just between the shoulder blades would allow. The arms wrapped protectively around a portion of ropey belt. Tied to the belt, near the gathered hands, was a sliced-open leather pouch. Even though the head had been thickly swaddled with cut strips of yellow plastic sheeting, she'd seen enough pictures to know what this was—a grotesque kappa statue. What had Dad been thinking? If it had been to hyper-scare her from water when she was little, she'd be in therapy now.

She considered calling Jeremy, but that would eat up time. She didn't know what to tell him anyway. She fetched her cell phone from the charger upstairs and took a picture. If she did end up telling Jeremy about it later, she could show him the photo, though she easily pictured him insisting on blundering into the house to drag the statue upstairs for a better look. She set the phone on the table before peeling off the tarp.

She touched the shell: dry and horny, not stone or wood. Real? The tarp and the raised pallet had been to keep it absolutely dry. She pinched one of the wrists, which felt like dried fish or jerky. Was this really a dried-out kappa corpse? Why the hell did her dad have it?

The article about her mother's death disintegrated in her mind, its truths torn out by her discovery. She tried to remember the little her dad had taught her about kappas: they lived in fresh water, they loved to drown people, they could leave the water as long as they kept their head bowls wet, they were viciously strong, and they were a danger to careless daughters. She also suspected a connection with the weird pearls.

She rotated the head towards her and started unknotting the twine around the plastic strips shrouding it. The day was fading, the house was a shambles, and she desperately did not want her dad to find out, but she had to know. As she unwound the plastic, a ceramic lid slid out and caught between two wooden slats. She held her breath and picked it up. Not even chipped, thank God. She would have no way to hide that. She set it carefully aside and removed the last of the plastic. The reptilian skin continued across the oblong head, except for a smooth beak and a shallow white depression on the top, like a cranial sinkhole. She ran her finger across it. Bone.

She weighed the danger: She'd done risky things before, like getting into Meghan's car that night, and she'd defied her father—just in ways he wouldn't find out. But unless she abandoned her mission, and soon, she saw no way to hide this. Still, she had to find out: who was Dad? If he discovered her crimes, everything could be gone by the time she returned from the lake. She walked to the sink, splashed her finger, and smeared the wetness across the hollow in the kappa's skull. She scooted back, alert. The creature twitched, just once, then stopped. Five minutes later she checked the bone: dry. Just a bit more would be safe.

She filled her cupped palm, dripped a little into the divot in his head, and then retreated. The kappa raised its head, blinked. At first, she could not tell what it was saying. Her dad had insisted she know Japanese, but this dialect was thick and difficult to unravel. The beaklike mouth did not lend itself to all sounds equally. Eventually it fell to repeating one word: "More."

When the whispers faded to nothing, she returned with another dripping hand.

The kappa twitched like a dreaming animal, but it did not lift its head until she had backed away. "I thank you for your kindness," it hissed weakly. "I have not moved in many years. Could you give me a little more? Already my body's heat dries what little you have graciously spared."

"In a bit. I don't trust you."

The kappa turned its neck slowly. "I don't see water. How could I drown you, or refill my sara? And you have done me a favor, so am I not indebted?" It lowered its head. "What do you intend? Will you let me go? I sense I am far from my home, but I will swim through stream and lake to return, if you would be gracious enough to allow me to leave."

Good luck with that, Kame thought. Japan is thousands of miles and an ocean of saltwater away. "Depends. I'd like something from you."

The kappa froze. She waited, then approached cautiously. The bone had dried again. This would get tedious, she thought, but keeping a container of water nearby would be stupid. Instead, this time she dripped a little more from her hand into the sara.

The skin began to plump. The kappa contorted like a waking cat and sat up. A gourd tied to the rope belt clattered against pallet, and looking down, the kappa spied the ceramic lid. He picked it up and fitted it onto the bowl in his head. "Will you, like your father, imprison me?"

"I want to know about that. And what happened with my mother."

"Until you promise to release me, I shall give nothing."

"You can only have a little water at a time. And if I do dump you into a stream, I'm taking you dry and comatose and then tearing off before you can get to me."

The kappa nodded as it worked out her words. "In exchange for my answers, besides my freedom, I would like a pearl."

"There's a whole bunch upstairs."

"For what you ask, I'll take just one. But I get to choose which."

Probably, she thought, her dad might not notice one missing. "Agreed. Can you tell me what happened to me? To my mother?"

"You must have been less than two when I snatched you—a lovely May afternoon, it was. I had not eaten a human child for some time, so I was very happy. Your mother was not a strong woman, but ho! did she fight. I dropped you on the bank and dragged her into the stream. So much fury, but no skill. When I surfaced, I saw your father running to grab you—he must have heard your cries—but when he saw me swimming back, he fled. Fool! But since you—a helpless child—were all mine, I put on my cap and chased him. With his longer legs, he could have outrun me, but, as you humans sometimes do in your terror, he stumbled. By the time he had gained his feet, I was almost upon him."

The kappa lifted its lid. "More water." Kame tried to fill her palm, but she was trembling. She took a little watering can from among the gardening shelves and ran a small amount into it. She tipped some water onto the kappa's head, moved back, and squatted.

The kappa lifted its head a little higher. "A tiny bit more? No? Ah, well." The kappa stood painfully upright and unhooked the gourd from its belt. It removed the stopper, lifted the ceramic lid, and poured water into its head-bowl.

"From my own stream."

Kame jumped up.

"Stay! We aren't done yet. We have a bargain, right?" It loped to her and, placing a hand on her shoulder to guide her down, settled into a crouch. The thick, fishy breath rolled oily across her face. "Where was I? Ah, my undoing. I had expected a coward who would abandon his child to keep running, but he turned and threw himself at my feet. He gave up! But I had been pushing hard to catch him and was surprised, and so I tumbled over his fool back. My sara emptied into the grass."

The kappa's withered skin continued to plump, and the dried-out eyes began to gleam like torchlights on still ponds.

"I reached for my gourd, but that's when the fool, thinking I had attacked, started to fight. I was the stronger, of course, but I needed to refill my sara. His bumbling prevented me long enough that I grew weak and froze. But not before I wrapped my arms around my gourd, in case he did not kill me." The kappa lifted its cap and added more water. "Are you learning what you asked?"

"Yes," Kame whispered.

The kappa started at a thought and slapped at the rope belt. "My pouch is emptied." It met her eyes. "So, you thought to pay me with my own treasure?"

Kame forced breath out. "I didn't know they were yours."

"Liar."

"The price was a pearl," she stammered, her insides contracting. "You didn't say it couldn't be yours." She trembled, not daring to move.

The kappa cocked its head. "Trying to outwit a kappa? You are correct, though. Yes. Yes, that was clever."

"The news said my mother had drowned and my dad tried to save her. Are you the liar? Why did Dad leave his home? Why are you here?"

The kappa stood and rubbed its thighs. "You ask a lot for coin that is not yours." It began to pace with a cramped gait. "The man took you and left. I lay there a long time, but he returned, put me in a metal box on the back of a cart on wheels—the ones that nothing pulls." It stretched and swung its arms. "I assume he ran from his disgrace the same way he ran from saving you, that he threw your mother's reputation away to preserve his."

Kame's lips worked. She began to cry.

The kappa hobbled over and sat before her. "He only woke me once, a half year later. As I gasped on the meager wetness he allowed me, he demanded I release the soul from one of my shirikodma, rendering it nothing but an ordinary pearl. Still, it was large and beautiful, so I assume he got a lot of money. I kept expecting him, over the years, to make me give up the rest. Maybe he had lost the nerve."

The kappa rose and surveyed the room. "So, this is his home. Hmm. Well, young daughter, I have told my tale. Time to give up your pearl."

Mr. Tanaka opened the door. "Thank you for coming, Mr. Wade. Please, come in."

Jeremy awkwardly returned the slight bow and took off his shoes. "No problem, Mr. Tanaka. I called all Kame's friends I know, but they haven't seen her, either. Are you all right?"

"Very concerned."

As Jeremy placed his shoes onto a shelf, he noticed the suitcases. "Did she pack those?"

"No." Tanaka started down the hallway. "If needed, I want to go anywhere at a moment's notice."

"Did you call the cops?" Jeremy saw the unfolded attic ladder at the end of the hallway. He might have to tell Mr. Tanaka about Kame's call. He wondered if the man suspected Kame knew about her mother's drowning.

"Yes, and the hospitals. There is no report of her." Tanaka gestured to a stool at the dinette and sat after Jeremy had. The older man rubbed his palm roughly with a thumb as he spoke. "I know she wanted to go on a trip with you and her friends tomorrow, but you say no one has left yet?"

"No, we leave at seven in the morning. Can I say something?"

"Of course. Please"

He knew he'd get all sorts of hell from Kame, but she needed to confront things for a change. "She read about her mother. Online." Mr. Tanaka's face broke briefly. "And she's been wondering about her family, why you abandoned them. Maybe she's doing something because of that. Does she have a passport?"

Tanaka said nothing for some time. "No. No passport. And she doesn't have access to enough money." He stood. "The ladder to the attic—I found that someone—Kame, I'm sure—has been through the boxes. Some valuable things are missing. She won't know what to do with them, though. I wish I had just—I kept planning to use them, but I was afraid. Do you understand?"

Jeremy felt lost without Kame to explain. "No."

Tanaka snapped back to focus. "There . . . there may be some things she could find in the house, though. In the basement. Mr. Wade, if she's here, in the house, she may have stayed hidden because she didn't want to talk to me. I've tried to protect her. She doesn't understand. Would you go downstairs and see . . . ? She would talk to you. If she found the things in the attic . . . Would you please be so kind?"

"Sure. I'll go right now, Mr. Tanaka." Jeremy felt relieved to escape, however briefly.

Tanaka crossed the room and opened a door. As soon as Jeremy passed, Tanaka retreated and gave an encouraging nod. Jeremy nodded back and then started down the steps. He felt more concerned than worried. Probably Kame was finally having a good old freak-out and would be back later to hash things over with her dad.

Right away he could see that the basement had been torn up: boards and beams rested against walls, gardening shears and trowels lay scattered across the floor, and swirls of blue tarp drifted from a small room behind a large table.

"Kame?"

No reply. Jeremy decided to start with the alcove. As he rounded the table, he saw her sitting on the floor just inside the tiny room, leaning against the wall. She looked half-asleep, but she was drooling. The tarp flowing over her legs into the basement had a thick tail of blood snaking from under it.

He felt terrified, overwhelmed. "Kame?" No reaction. As he approached, something flashed on top of her head, like a balanced mirror. His body blocked the ceiling light as he bent down and shook her shoulder. "Are you okay?"

Her body slumped forward and water poured out from her skull. He scrambled back. A saucer-sized hole had been cut into her head. Inside was black emptiness.

Jeremy cried out and scrambled to his feet, collided with the table, and then froze: Kame blocked the steps, her body opalescent and as scrubbed of detail as a plastic doll's. Her white face, framed by unbound silver-gray hair, showed a forced calm.

"Jeremy, for once, just listen. It doesn't know English. It wants my father to come down, to see me. Do you understand? Don't talk. It took my soul to keep with the others. Give no hint I'm helping you. Listen carefully: I'm bound to my shirikodma—my pearl, but my mother says the kappa can release us. You'll have to force it. Get police. It's incredibly strong and evil and angry. Just don't kill it until we're free. Tell my dad. Go slowly. Do not run. And if it's gone when you get back, keep away from fresh water. It will track you, no matter the—"

She vanished. From behind the dryer loped a horrible half-animal. It stopped beside him, staring, sniffing, memorizing. Its eyes boiled with barely controlled rage.

Jeremy nodded, as if in agreement, and backed away. He stumbled on the first step. When he turned, his back prickled. He braced for an attack. Second step. Still none. He kept going.

At the top, he found the kitchen empty. "Mr. Tanaka?" He staggered through the room. The hall, too, was empty. He walked to the living room, past the ladder. The lights were on, but no one was there. "Mr. Tanaka? Kame's downstairs."

Silence. He returned to the hall. Bedrooms, bathroom, or attic? Then he noticed both suitcases were missing. He ran outside, still in his stocking feet. Tanaka's car was gone. A hybrid, it had made no sound. Tanaka had run. After hearing Jeremy's cry, the bastard had known Kame was down there; had known what was in the basement, a thing so bad that he would abandon his daughter.

And Tanaka had left him alone with it.

Jeremy fled. Concrete shocked through the bones of his heels and stones cut at his soles. He realized that his car was at Kame's house, but he couldn't go back. When he stopped running, unable to breathe deeply enough, he heard the faint rustle of a creek nearby and tried to think where he could go.

Award-winning Latinx author **E.M. MARKOFF** writes stories about damaged heroes and imperfect villains. Her novels include *To Nurture & Kill* and *The Deadbringer,* which *Booklist* described as "A fantastic action-adventure, tinged with Mexican folklore, that will appeal to fans of *A Game of Thrones.*" Visit her at www.ellderet.com.

Author's note: *Curanderas* are folk healers who tend not only to the physical well-being of their patients, but to their spiritual health as well. The story includes Spanish and Nahuatl, one of the native languages of Mexico still spoken by 1.5 million people today.

# LEAVING THE #9

## E.M. MARKOFF

**"ADELIA?"**

*Stay away! Don't touch me!*

"Adelia, hey, hey?"

*That voice. Miguel? Yes. Miguel.*

"Hey!"

*I . . . I'm . . .* "I'm fine, Miguel!" I swatted my brother's arm away and leaned against the side of the counter to steady myself. My head was spinning. My mouth tasted like sand and iron—I had bitten my tongue, drawing blood. Miguel brought me a glass of water and a stool.

The water was clean and refreshing, a salve for my dry lips. I swished the water around in my mouth until the unpleasant taste was gone. I was fine, truly. The day was just too damn hot and it had finally caught up to me. Outside, past the storefront windows, I watched the number 9 bus chug by.

Taking a deep breath, I gathered my wits and continued on. "Think of it, Miguel!"

He gave me a concerned look, his lips worming around as if he were fighting back the urge to make sure I was without-a-doubt okay.

"I'm good, promise."

"Yeah?"

"Yeah."

A familiar voice chimed in. "Well, now, I feel a bit left out, so I'll just go ahead and say it: Yeah."

"Miss Cire?" I asked, confused. I didn't remember seeing her walk into the shop, but it felt right that she was here. She was Miguel's best customer and the grandmother I never had. She was also my closest friend. The "Closed for Lunch, Back in an Hour" sign hanging on the door did not apply to her.

"Yes, Dear?" She leaned on her walking cane with one hand while the other adjusted her glasses. Her eyes, like two orbs of amber resin, never ceased to amaze me. A unique trait passed down from her father's side, she liked to say.

"Nothing," I said with a smile. I was happy that she was here to share this moment with me. I began once more, rechanneling my original enthusiasm. "Miguel, you're already one of the best butcher shops in the city. Why not take the chance and also become one of the best places to grab a bite to eat?" A fly landed on my cheek, on the path left by the sweat dripping down my face. I swatted it away.

"Teret does exactly that, my dear," Miss Cire said. "And, I hate to say it, but not all of her dishes are bad."

Miguel grunted his assent.

"But she's not even in this neighborhood!" I said, pointing out the obvious. "Our community needs a place to eat that's within our *own* neighborhood, and we could be the ones to make it. You own this building, Miguel. No need to pay a landlord."

His lips were twitching. That was a good sign. "It's a risky venture," he said.

Miss Cire turned her attention to the meat resting within its glass prison behind the counter.

"You won't be going at it alone," I said, reassuring him. "I've been putting money aside for years now. But I need your help. You have the name, the reputation, the building. I have the recipes and my clients that I cook for. They love my food."

"You *are* a force in the kitchen." He ran a calloused thumb back and forth across the dark stubble on his chin, his brown eyes twinkling. He liked my idea, I could tell! He looked at the clock on the wall. "The store reopens in five. Swing back tonight after I've closed up shop. You can let yourself in through the back."

"Tonight, then! After my last client." I turned to Miss Cire, unable to rein in my excitement. "You will help me test out my recipes, won't you, Miss Cire?"

I found her staring at me over her half-moon spectacles, her amber eyes more vibrant than usual. "Of course I will. But, Adelia, dear, isn't tonight our weekly dinner date?"

I could feel my cheeks redden. "I'm so sorry! I swear I didn't mean to forget!"

"Go on, Adelia," said Miguel. "I like your idea. We can talk tomorrow. Besides, I have inventory coming tonight."

"Chicken or rabbit, my dear?" Miss Cire asked with a smile.

"Chicken," I said, smiling back. "I'll be there."

And I was.

Miss Cire lived in the richer part of the city, where the sterile box-like houses—despite the drought—had perfectly green yards and menacing fences to keep them that way. The only customers who had ever swindled me out of my pay lived in this neighborhood, so I avoided doing business here.

I stepped out of the 9-Bus and into a swarm of gnats. *At least the insects are here to pester them as well*, I thought, satisfied.

Distrustful eyes, watching from behind heavy curtains, escorted me up the sloped street all the way to the end of the cul-de-sac and Miss Cire's dilapidated home. It looked incapable of housing life, the soil in its yard too poor even to support weeds. Her fence, with its elaborately worked metal, seemed to be in direct opposition to the homogeneous aesthetic of the sterilized neighborhood. I approved. It was like a big "fuck you" to the assholes that lived here and kept trying to push her out. And besides, the home's inside was nothing like its outward face.

"Come in, Adelia, come in." Miss Cire scanned the book she had been reading and then, despite the crooked bend to her elderly fingers, snapped it shut with a dramatic flair.

"Did you get far?" I asked, pointing to the book.

"Not as far as I had expected. You're early."

"My afternoon client wasn't there, so I went home, changed, and decided to stop by early. I hope nothing's happened. It's not like them to not let me know."

She pushed my long bangs behind my ears and patted my cheek. "Always worrying about others. I'm sure they are fine."

My mouth watered at the savory smells that greeted me in the foyer. I had been too nervous to eat all day and now I was famished. I held out the bunch of yellow *cempoalxochitl* I had brought.

"I'll get the wine," Miss Cire said.

The way I always did when I visited her, I went over to the little altar in the sitting room to pay my respects to Miss Cire's long-dead family. I had never met them, but I had heard so many tales about them from Miss Cire that I had come to regard them as old friends.

I pinched the flowers from their stems and began arranging them around the photograph and water cup on the altar. "I finally told my brother about my idea. It's for a restaurant. Please watch over me as I begin this new journey in my life."

"Here you go, Dear," said Miss Cire, handing me a generously filled glass and then filling one for herself.

The wine rippled along my glass's rim like a bloody pool, spilling a bit onto my fingers.

"It will be seven o'clock soon," said Miss Cire. "The food will be ready just before nine." As if on cue, her clock went off, its baritone toll resonating within the room like an echo that stabbed at my temples. Miss Cire studied me over her glass, sipping her wine.

I found myself thinking of my brother and turned to look back toward the darkening foyer. The twilight spilling in through the door's glass panes made the foyer appear as a long dark tunnel.

I was starting to wonder if I had made the right choice coming here tonight, then felt guilty at the thought. I cared for Miss Cire, but what if Miguel decided to change his mind overnight? What if he decided it was best to play it safe rather than take the risk of starting a whole new business? If Miguel didn't help me, then my dream would become that much harder to achieve. The anxiety would not let me be.

"Should you decide to leave . . . " Miss Cire trailed off.

I turned back to look at her, ashamed of my behavior.

"Of course not," I said. I had already made my choice and I would stick with it. I took a sip and relaxed. The wine was delicious. Dinner proved to be even more so.

Afterward, I bid Miss Cire goodnight and jumped on the 9-Bus to return to Miguel's shop. It wasn't unusual for him to stay until midnight. I hoped that tonight was one of those late nights.

But I was greeted by a closed-up shop. In its window hung a sign: "Closed, Come Back Tomorrow Morning!" I knocked on the door, but no one answered. If Miguel was out back on the dock, he would not hear me. I looked down the narrow alley that led to the back of the meat shop—the place where Miguel did his bloody work, where flies buzzed at all hours. I did not like that place during the day and liked it even less at night.

I decided to ignore the sign's advice and went down the alley to see if Miguel was still around.

I woke up in a mess of sweat and tangled sheets. *My* sheets. In *my* home. I tasted blood in my mouth. I must have bitten my tongue. I fumbled in the dark for the lamp's chain. But when I finally managed to get the light going, I just barely stopped myself from throwing the lamp across the room.

*"Miguel!"* I yelped, startled.

Miguel was sitting in the rickety chair across from me. He didn't look well.

"How—how did you get in? Why didn't you tell me you were here?"

He stared, but said nothing.

"Did you have a row with a rancher? With your partner?" The obvious answer hit me then. "Are you drunk?"

Miguel's eyes stirred in their sockets like an automaton's, then an emotion like anger brought them to life.

I had never been scared of my brother before, but something was wrong. "Listen, whatever it is, I'm here for you. But for fuck's sake, I think we both need coffee first."

Miguel said nothing. He looked like he wanted to cry.

I stuffed my feet into my slippers and did my best to be brave for him. "How did you even get in? I knew it! I don't care what the landlord says, I knew that cheap lock was a useless—*ohdeargods!*"

Miguel was gone.

I had not seen him move, nor had I heard his normally heavy footfalls leave. There was a faint smell in the air, like disinfectant and blood, or perhaps entrails. The door and its lock would spell the truth of it.

The chain was down, the dead bolt turned.

I went to the kitchen, put on a pot of coffee, and set some sage to burn in the very place I had seen my brother. Overhead, the lamplight flickered in time with the anxiety growing in my chest.

I sat in the kitchen and waited for the sun to rise.

I found the "Closed, Come Back Tomorrow Morning!" sign waiting for me. I decided to ignore its advice again and made my way to the back of the store. The stench of disinfectant, meat, and entrails hit me even before I had stepped out of the alley and into the small courtyard.

I checked the back door and found it unlocked, but I could not go in. I was scared, trapped. I thought about my brother and finally found the courage to step inside.

Empty. Quiet. Everything neatly in place.

"Hello?" I called. No answer.

I walked to the front of the store and looked out the windows. There were people leaving flowers, cards, and incense all along the outside wall. I noticed my older sister among the crowd and went out to meet her.

"Excuse me," I said to the people surrounding my sister, "but I need to get through." Everyone continued chatting away, sparing only transient glances of annoyance for my having interrupted their conversation. I called to my sister, but she was too busy crying to notice me.

"Adelia?" asked a familiar voice behind me. It was Miss Cire.

"What's going on?" I asked, confused and, for some reason, scared. "Why is Ximena crying?"

"My poor sweet Adelia. You don't know what's happening, do you?" She pushed a lock of my hair behind my ear. I noticed the red blotches on the skin around her eyes, as if she had been crying for hours.

"Something's happened to Miguel, hasn't it?" I could feel the anxiety growing in the pit of my stomach. "And this *pinche* crowd won't let me get through to see Ximena."

Miss Cire looked down at her sandaled feet and stabbed the end of her cane against a loose cobblestone. "Miguel is dead."

The world around me began to spin. I stumbled my way to the curb, taking a seat. My mouth tasted like blood. I had bitten my tongue, again. "H-how did he . . . No, no, this can't be happening. He can't be . . . " I could not bring myself to say "dead."

Miss Cire took a seat beside me and clasped my hand firmly between hers. "No one yet knows, but rest assured the cause of death will be made public."

"You make it sound like he was killed. Was he?"

Miss Cire looked back at the crowd hovering around Ximena. Her gaze was distant, somewhere else. "Yes."

The revelation shook me. I wondered if my brother would still be alive if I had not accepted Miss Cire's dinner invitation.

"I saw Miguel," I said, uncertain if I really wanted to share what had happened. But I had to, or the guilt building inside of me would swallow me whole. I looked over at the growing pile of flowers on the sidewalk. "It was a few hours before sunrise. He was in my apartment. Just sitting there, quiet, angry. But the chain was hanging and the deadbolt was locked. It was locked! And then he vanished! Miss Cire, I saw his spirit!"

"*His* spirit? Are you listening to what you're saying?" Miss Cire asked, her hands trembling.

I bit back tears. "I'm scared. I don't know what to think. I don't know what I'm supposed to do. I don't—" I turned to look at Miss Cire. "How did this happen?" She took me into her arms and the tears I had been holding back poured down my face.

My brother was dead.

I wept on Miss Cire's shoulder, grateful that my closest friend was here with me. She stroked my hair as if I was a small child and said: "There's a *curandera* that lives in the farmhouse at the end of the 9-Bus. Go find them. They'll know what to do."

"The district at the end of the number 9 is abandoned," I pointed out, scrubbing my face dry with my hands.

Miss Cire looked as if she was struggling with what to say. "Go there, Adelia. The *curandera* will help you."

"Will you come with me?" I asked.

"I wish I could go with you, my dear," she said, kissing my forehead and then rising to her feet. "But I have somewhere I need to be."

I decided to take my friend's advice. I needed answers and Miss Cire had pointed me in the direction of someone who could help. Not wanting to be near the meat market or the offerings steadily growing in number along its wall, I walked down the hill to the bus stop with my grief.

It was late afternoon by the time the 9-Bus pulled up. I boarded it and took a seat. Save for the driver, the bus was empty, empty and more worn than I remembered.

My fingers laced and unlaced as my mind repeated a phrase over and over and over again until I felt as if I would suffocate. *Miguel is dead. Miguel is dead. Miguel is dead.*

Just before sunset, a derelict farmhouse came into view, dropped in the center of a vast prairie of "For Sale - Reduced Price!" buildings that had once been the community where my parents had grown up and fallen in love. It was strange to think that a *curandera* lived here now. I hadn't thought that anyone lived here.

The bus's doors opened and I stepped out into the twilight. Tall, skeletal trees surrounded the farmhouse like grotesque onlookers, while malformed blades of clumped grass stood guard like broken spirits. I realized then that I had forgotten to ask the driver when— and if—the bus would be back tonight.

With nothing else to do, I was about to knock on the farmhouse door when the smell of tobacco caught my nose. I turned to look for its source and found a tall woman dressed in a long black dress leaning against a dead tree.

"Can I help you?" she asked. There was a faint, strange cadence to her rich voice.

I squinted, hoping to get a better look, but she had brought her *rebozo* over her eyes, obscuring the top half of her face. All I could make out was that her skin was a warm sandy brown, like mine, her lips full and stained a deep red, like a *cuetlaxochitl.*

"Umm, sorry. I'm here to see the *curandera.* Are you her?"

"I am." She took a long drag from her cigarette, then exhaled. The smoke flitted strangely around her like a swarm of moths. "And you are?"

I wrapped myself with my arms, suddenly cold. "Adelia. Adelia Quintana Reyes."

The woman laughed. "Am I making you uncomfortable?"

"Not you. Just what this place became." I shook my head. "How can you continue to live here?"

"Because this is my home and I had more power than the people who sought to take it away from me." She snuffed out the cigarette and looked back toward the empty street. "They murdered the heart of this neighborhood a long time ago, when those who made it what it was were pushed out." She spat a heavy clump that fell to the ground. "As you can see for yourself, the people who took their place did not last very long."

"I'm sorry," I said, and I was.

"But this is not about them. Why are *you* here?" the woman asked, keeping her distance.

I swallowed down the lump that had lodged itself firmly in my throat. "Miss Cire said you could help me. My brother was found dead this morning, but I saw him—his spirit—in my apartment."

"Perhaps he was killed after he visited you?"

"No!" I yelled. The pot holding my emotions started to bubble over. "I know what I saw!"

"Rather certain, aren't you?"

"Certain?" I asked, insulted. "My brother was kind, generous, a pillar to our community—to our family! He always had my back and we . . . we were going to open a restaurant together. And Miss Cire was going to try the foods on the menu and I . . . I was finally going to see my dream happen. But now Miguel's dead, and I'll never get to talk to him again."

I turned toward the sound of an engine coming up the dark street. It was the 9-Bus. I could board it and go home.

"If you came all this way just to go home, then go home. But—" the *curandera* gestured to the entrance of the farmhouse "— I was certain you came here for a reason. Was I mistaken?" She leaned back against the tree. The darkness around her seemed to tremble.

The 9-Bus pulled up and opened its doors, waiting. But I did not board. I watched it drive down the street until the night swallowed it whole.

"The door's unlocked," the *curandera* said. A loud *click!* behind me punctuated her words.

I turned to face her, my determination overriding the fear screaming at me to run away and just accept that Miguel was dead. "I am here for a reason. I need to know why my brother's spirit came to visit me. I will not leave until I know why."

"The truth does not always lead to happiness," the *curandera* said, finally coming closer. "But if your soul is ready to accept the truth, then enter."

"I'm ready," I said, and stepped into the farmhouse.

The first thought to enter my mind was that I had gone crazy. And if not, then I was damned.

I was back at Miss Cire's home, in the sitting room, at the dinner from the night before. In front of me stood Miss Cire herself and . . . myself, dressed in a yellow and blue dress with red kitten heels. It was the exact same outfit I was wearing now. The knot in my stomach tightened, pleading for me to turn back, but I stayed and watched.

The clock had just struck seven in the evening.

"Should you decide to leave . . . " Miss Cire trailed off.

"Of course not. I'm just worried Miguel will come up with a list of reasons not to compete with Teret and convince himself it's a bad idea before I've had a chance to tell him why it's a great idea."

Miss Cire took a seat and opened her book. "Go on," she said waving this other me away with a warm smile. "You have two hours to convince him. Make him give you an expensive wine for interrupting our dinner. And Adelia, I'm very proud of you, my dear."

She beamed, this Adelia who had been praised, and toasted with her friend.

I followed after myself, the knot in my stomach morphing into a nervous excitement that I would see Miguel; I could save him!

I jumped onto the 13-Bus and took a seat beside myself. She looked so happy, this other me. All smiles and dreams and wine-flushed cheeks. *She* would save Miguel.

We were greeted by a shop closed up for the night. The same annoying "Closed, Come Back Tomorrow Morning!" sign hung in the window. I looked down the dark, narrow alley that led to the courtyard at the back of the meat shop.

*Go on!* I urged the other me in the red kitten heels. *Save our brother!*

I followed her down the alley into the small courtyard and onto the low loading dock. The back door to the shop was open. Straightening her shoulders, she took a few steps in and stopped.

I watched her from the courtyard as she stood there, frozen. Was Miguel already dead?

Angry voices poured out the door.

I stepped onto the loading dock but kept away from the door. I did not want to see my brother's dead body. Instead, I listened:

"Who's this? Lover?" a gruff voice asked.

"Get away from my brother!" the other me shouted.

"Brother?" said another voice. A woman's.

"Adelia? A-Adelia has your money! Not me! Ask her!" It was Miguel.

"What money?" the other me asked, confused. "What are—"

*"The money was for her restaurant!"* Miguel screamed, his voice high and desperate. "I-I saw her rummaging back here. She must have found the money and taken it! I swear it's true! I swear it!"

The voice that spoke next was cold, greedy. "How about it, little lady? You got my money?"

My other self was shaking her head and crying, shocked as if unable to believe that the brother she had venerated all her life had just fed her to the dogs. She turned to flee, but cruel-looking hands reached out from beyond the door and dragged her into the butcher's shop.

"Stay away! Don't touch me!" she yelled. Her voice was lost, terrified. I curled up into a ball and wept endlessly as I listened to my other self call out her brother's name as if it were a question: "Miguel? MIGUEL?"

Sometime later, two men in suits carried out something large and heavy in a sack. I followed the drops of blood to a truck that was parked out front on the street. Deep inside, I knew that *I* was in that sack, that the blood trailing behind like water from a leaky hose was mine. I wondered where the men in the suits would dispose of my body.

I went back to the alley and found my brother—the brother I had loved so dearly—saturating the courtyard with disinfectant to erase his betrayal. I watched as he broke down into choked sobs and angry stares. Then he was suddenly gone and I was alone in the alley. Blood seeped from a wound over my heart, staining my dress. The smell of disinfectant surrounded me.

The *curandera* had been right: the truth had led me to a broken heart, not to happiness. I was dead, an *alma en pena*—a soul lost in despair, a soul that had been unwilling to believe and unwilling to accept that my beloved brother had betrayed me. Was it to cover a debt? A loan? I found myself wishing I knew the reason *why*.

From the alley's dark recesses, the *curandera* emerged, her dress and *rebozo* trailing behind her like black ink.

"Why did you show me this?" I demanded.

"You showed yourself. When you entered the farmhouse, it was because your spirit was finally ready to confront what had happened."

"What happened? My brother betrayed me! He let them fucking *kill me!* Why? Why couldn't you just have let me leave on the bus?" I took my shoe off and threw it at her. "Answer me!"

"Because you chose to stay and confront the truth on your own terms. Your soul was done lamenting. If you had chosen otherwise . . . " Her voice trailed off.

"What would have happened?" I asked.

"Your soul would be lost in despair, unable to move on." Tears streamed down the *curandera's* cheeks. "I couldn't leave you here, alone."

I rose to my feet, suddenly somehow knowing who she was, even though it was impossible. "Miss Cire?"

The *curandera* took a step back.

"Please," I begged. "I really need a friend."

The *curandera* stood there, frozen, unsure. "Adelia, my dear, don't be afraid. Please?" And then coral snakes appeared in the air around her, pulling the *rebozo* away from her face. She was young and beautiful and would have been a complete stranger if not for the amber eyes—Miss Cire's eyes—looking down at me. The skin around her eyes was raw and puffy, as if she had been crying.

"Is this what you really look like?" I asked, stepping down from the dock and crossing over to her.

"You must be frightened," she said quietly.

"Are you really here?" I asked, looking up at her, unable to believe that my dearest friend had cared enough about me to find me even in death.

"I am," she said with affection.

I felt a weight I had not been aware of lift from me. I ran to her and she took me into her arms. She stroked my hair. Despite the hand being different, it was the same familiar, gentle strength that I loved and trusted.

I cried for hours. Days? Who knows how time works for a grieving soul?

"What will happen to me now that I know the truth?" I finally asked.

"Your soul will move on."

"Was the Miss Cire I knew real?" I asked, resting my head against her arm.

"Yes. But I had already become her by the time we met. Like you, she was an *alma en pena.*"

I thought about this for a moment. "What is it you do?"

"I offer people who have been wronged a chance at revenge. In exchange, I ask for their bodies, so that I can walk the land of the living."

"Do you think you can find my body and give me a proper burial?"

"If that is what you want, I will respect your wishes, though my own heart yearns instead for revenge. But it's up to you to decide what you want."

I thought about this. The man who had betrayed me with his words was no longer my brother. I would not mourn for him.

There was no hesitancy in my voice. "I want revenge."

"Are you done lamenting?"

I nodded. "I'm going to miss you so much."

"And I you, Adelia." She cupped my face, her lips a soft whisper against my own. "Goodbye, my dear."

A gentle warmth filled my soul, and in my heart, I knew that Miss Cire had found my body. I sent her all my love and moved on.

A fly landed on Adelia's closed eyelid. It sat there, buzzing, scheming, thankful that the animals had unearthed enough of the head so that it could lay its eggs and be born anew.

Adelia swatted the fly away, and then, brushing away the dirt on her cheek, unburied herself from the shallow grave. She snapped her legs back into place, shook the sand from her body, and stood. The blood marring her flawless brown skin and tattered yellow and blue dress would have to wait until she was home.

Adelia turned toward the direction of the city, the sand crunching beneath her bare feet. She made her way to a bus stop and boarded the 23-Bus back to the city, back to Miguel and all those who had taken away her friend. She would have no mercy, just as they had had none. She looked out the window, the first rays of the sun bringing to life the tears and revenge burning in her amber eyes.

"Be at peace, my dearest friend."

**ROSS E. LOCKHART** is an author, anthologist, bookseller, editor, and publisher. A lifelong fan of supernatural, fantastic, and weird fiction, Lockhart is a veteran of small-press publishing, having edited scores of well-regarded novels of horror, fantasy, and science fiction. He has also edited anthologies including *The Book of Cthulhu*, *Tales of Jack the Ripper*, *The Children of Old Leech*, *Giallo Fantastique*, *Eternal Frankenstein*, *Tales from a Talking Board*, and *Cthulhu Fhtagn!* He is the author of *Chick Bassist*. Lockhart lives in Petaluma, California, with his wife Jennifer, hundreds of books, and Elinor Phantom, a Shih Tzu working as his editorial assistant.

# FOLIE À DEUX

## Ross E. Lockhart

### I.
### Transcript Found in a Sunken City

**THEY SHOT THEIR** daddy in Vegas and hit the road. They were sixteen. They beat the rap, escaped from the end-of-the-world survivalist cult Daddy was messed up in. Millennialist angst was hot that year, so the story made all the papers, the late-night shows. Gave the girls their first taste of limelight.

*Twins in the Siamese Fashion, or the Two-Headed Girl?* it read on the flyers when they toured the country at seventeen, singing in a rock and roll band. Leather and lace. Managed to chart a single, but that burned out quick. Rock and roll excess led to dope and dumb behavior and a couple of arrests that never made it to court. At eighteen they shot a little "happy birthday, baby" clip, hit the Web by storm. Low-quality amateur stuff, sure, but I spot talent. I was on the phone arranging a five-figure contract with Vivianne Vid within ten minutes of closing the browser window.

They were two of the nicest redheads to ever share a snatch and a pair of legs. Cass and Hell. Short for Cassandra and Helen. Package deal. Joined for life. Split at the navel, two hearts, four shapely tits, but you know this, you've seen the vids, the pictorials. Cass the active, talky one. That's her, on the left. Their right. Can't believe how difficult the press found it to keep them straight. Sometimes I think Cass was the one in charge, the big planner. The thinker. Hell, with her naughty smirk, was always quiet, but when she said something, look out. I know she pulled the trigger on Daddy Dear.

Those four cool blue eyes, looking right into the camera as they said and did the nastiest things in unison through red-painted lips . . . .

Damn! Did they move a ton of product. Not just freak scene—total breakthrough. Real stars. Real pros. Toured the talk shows, drive-time radio. Fifty-seven scenes that first year. I figured them for a solid ten-year career, easy.

Except for the dope. Everybody's got a little crutch in Porn Valley. Even I've got my Saint Christopher. Me and Chris go way back. But it's always out there. Coke and grass and pills and crank and X and stranger stuff. Performance enhancers, if you know what I mean. We're *on with the show* people. We do what we need to do to get through a shoot. Makes us tight as carnies. All up in each other's business. You have to be when your clients are swapping bodily fluids with co-workers on a more regular basis than video store clerks in the 80s. But you turn a blind eye when it comes to the dope.

And drugs I can handle. Any agent in this biz knows how to deal with fucked-up clients. You wake 'em up if you have to, you drive 'em to the shoot. You administer antidotes. Steroids. Black coffee. You keep 'em walking in circles, keep 'em from passing out. Comes with the territory. It's the creepy shit that comes with the drugs that freaks me out. Occult shit. Astrology. Tarot. Witchcraft. Weird books.

Never trust anybody who reads weird books.

Cass and Hell fell in with Todd Amon-Ra, a small-time dealer and musician. Not a performer, not in our business. One of the hangers-on. Pale, greasy kid, who swore up and down that he was the reincarnation of some Egyptian pharaoh or magician or something. Aleister Crowley wannabe, but with an Earth First kink. Throw down Christ and bring back Pan, you know the type. Had a band called Black Ram's Reign. Read way too many goddamned books. He'd been through a couple of girls from the scene. Not sure what they saw in him. Must have been hung like a horse. Well, that or the drugs.

It was just a little bit of coke at first, an occasional hit of X—acceptable levels—but pretty soon I'd gathered they were playing Scarlet Women in Mummy Boy's twisted little ritual fantasies. I'd seen it happen to a few girls over the years, figured the relationship would flame out in three or four months, like these things typically do.

I should have known better. Cass and Hell were special.

20/20 hindsight.

Six months in, Cass was talking about having babies, quitting the business. She admitted Todd was into some strange shit, had some freaky theories about the end of the world, stuff he'd read about in old, forbidden books, shades of their daddy, but she figured it would pass in time, figured he'd be a good father. Hell was more aloof, smiling and shrugging. Along for the ride, like always. I figured it to be selfish, druggy lust passing for love. It happens sometimes when all you do is get high, chant, and fuck. I told them to take their time, get straight, keep working. Keep my fifteen percent coming.

Over the next three months, I only crossed paths with Todd a handful of times. A couple late-night soirées. Bought him breakfast once or twice, when he showed up at my place with Cass and Hell. I didn't really like him much, not my type at all, but . . .

Christ, what a mess!

What would do that to a man?

What the hell did they call up?

Yeah. I said it. "Call up."

It's taken me ages to get to the point where I can accept it, talk about it, but what else could they have been doing that night? Full moon. Lunar eclipse. Weird winds. That red tide that shut down the beaches. Those sounds the government claimed were sonic booms. That's weather for crazy.

Then there's that massive salt circle on top of the hill. And the scorched earth.

And Todd, of course.

You really think an elephant stepped on his head, like that lady reporter said on TV? Dumbest fucking thing I ever heard. I can't believe people went with that. Explains the tracks, sure, but is there anybody out there missing an elephant? Nope.

Todd Amon-Ra'd up something he couldn't put back down.

And the girls?

I'll tell you about the girls. I'll tell you exactly what I told the cops. I saw them the morning after it happened. They showed up at my place in one of those big trucks, like the ones they use to move palm trees. They wanted cash. Cass was panicked, but seemed to have a plan. Didn't mention Todd at all. In a big hurry to get the hell out of Dodge. I gave them what I had around the house, about a grand. Watched them drive off. It's been three months now and I haven't heard a thing from them.

But here's the thing I didn't tell the cops. I caught a glimpse of whatever it was in the back of the truck. Could have been a trick of dawn's early light, might even have been one of those thirty-fucking-foot palm trees, but palm trees have shallow roots. This thing had dozens, maybe hundreds of 'em, thicker than arms, like eels or snakes or something. And they were moving, moving back and forth, like branches blowing in the wind.

Even though the wind had stopped.

## II.

## Manuscript Found in a Deserted Cabin

My sister says it's the offspring of a god we carry. The horned god. Panphage, Pangenitor. She does its bidding. She believes. I have my doubts.

I don't feel filled with grace. I feel sick. And heavy. And tired. I ache.

My sister now sleeps, so I write in this diary, this notebook I keep hidden underneath the nightstand drawer. Write down the thoughts I keep from her. From them. From the Thing that watches over us. The Thing that came through the gate. The Thing that killed Todd.

Is it Todd's child we carry, or is it that Thing's?

Sometimes It talks to me through my sister's mouth. Sometimes It sounds like God. Sometimes It sounds like Todd. It reassures me. Reminds me that we're a vessel for the messiah, and that the word *mashiach (messiah)* holds the same value as *nachash (serpent)*. Reminds me that we will give birth to the New Aeon. Reminds me that our children will be beautiful.

As It is beautiful.

It serves us. It attends to us. It guards us.

It loves us.

It must. We can barely move, let alone walk. Our cup runneth over. We are little more than support for a womb, a vessel. The time must be coming soon.

The others worship It. They bring us what we need. They feed us. They keep us here, prisoners in a gilded cage. They do not talk to me. They do not look me in the eye. They call my sister Sacred Host. Todd, at least, acknowledged me.

But Todd is dead. I miss him. And when I think of him, I realize that my sister and I are carrying a monster's spawn. It does not let me hold this thought for long. It shakes the house. It scrapes tendrils thick as branches across windowpanes and along roof tiles. It wakes my sister and I am pushed down, held down, restrained.

Trapped within this body I share with her.

Like when we were children and she wanted to do something, but I wanted something else. Like when we were children and she took control.

But worse. Like when Daddy took control of both of us. Even worse than that. Daddy was human. It is something else. Something alien.

The strangers prepare us. Wash us. Anoint us with oils and perfumes. Once each month they carry us to the back of the house, where the creature emerges from the black woods, stomping to us on cloven hooves beneath the full and gravid moon, its glorious branches waving in the air. *Sheol Nuggaroth*, they chant. *Black Ram of the Woods*. The Thing touches us, touches our belly, our shared womb, feeling its progeny stirring within. It loves us.

I feel my sister stirring, waking up. I must hide this notebook.

### III.
### English Inscription Found in an Otherwise Untranslated Grimoire

Praises and abundance to the Black Ram of the Woods. Iä! Sheol Nuggaroth! Iä! Sheol Nuggaroth! The Black Ram of the Woods with a Thousand Young!

As the Master teaches: there is a real world, beyond this glamour we call reality.

This world of machines and science, of concrete and plastic, is mere imagination. Nature is the only truth and we are Nature's stewards, not her exploiters. This false technological world must be torn down.

We burn down this false world at the cost of our own lives, for mankind is a parasite that lives upon the Mother's teat, drains the Mother dry.

The Sacred Host is nearly filled with the blessings of a New Aeon. With the next full moon, the Messiah will be born, and She will, with the help of Her Father the Black Ram, tear away the veil from our eyes and invert the world, letting the beasts once again rule over man. Iä! Sheol Nuggaroth! Iä!

## IV.
### Graffiti Found in a Ruined Hospital

The dreams come, whether I want them to or not. Whether I sleep or wake.

I ask to see the doctor. I ask for more medication. I ask for something to chase away the dreams of falling buildings, of burning cities, of people torn apart on fractured streets, devoured by invisible things in the air, dismembered by tentacles erupting from the ground.

They tell me they are understaffed. They tell me that a doctor will see me soon.

Days pass. Nights pass. One day, the television in the patients' lounge tells us that a volcano has erupted in Montana, darkening skies throughout the country. An earthquake has dumped part of Southern California into the sea, drowning it. Storms darken New York City, plunging millions into blackness. An orderly turns off the television, unplugs it. The next day, the television is gone. Days later, the lights go out. Stay out.

The moon transforms from a slender crescent, peeking through sooty skies. It fattens, pregnant with possibilities. The earth shakes. Daily. Hourly. No doctor comes.

In my dreams, a basalt city rises from the sea. Shrieking leather-winged faceless things fly from its windows. A door, deep beneath the surface of the earth, is forced open. Membranous alien intelligences fall from the sky, challenge mankind's armies with sonic weapons that rend human flesh to pieces through strange vibrations.

I scratch these words into the wall with fingernails, ink them with my own blood, in hopes that someday someone will read this record.

If anyone survives.

Pan stalks the earth, his scepter in hand, his reign one of rapine and madness.

Without my medication, I cannot tell the difference between the dreams and what I see from my window. I cannot tell if the shapes that wander between the trees are real, or my imagination. But they draw closer, closer, singing to the waxing moon.

The moon becomes full, occasionally peeking through the smog, low and yellow and huge, and I understand that they have abandoned us. First, the doctors, then the nurses, then everybody else. Leaving only we madmen to inhabit the asylum. Leaving us to starve, to suffer.

The blood-red moon laughs at us. Mocks us. The stars are wrong. Dead wrong.

## V.
### Vellum Scroll Found in a Copse of Trees

The western skies are clear tonight. The full moon, thicker than my thumbs held together, begins its descent into the ocean, sinking into the ruined city off the shore, like a maiden testing a still pond with a toe. A herd of Sheol Nuggaroth's Young cross the plain, hunting floaters. They capture one, then another, with their tendrils. They pull their prey to earth, devour it with their many mouths. They pipe and trill in victory. They pay us no mind, but one can never be too cautious.

There was a time they hunted men, but men no longer walk erect and proud in cities built by hand. We are scavengers. We are inconsequential. We are ignored.

Solon's boy nocks an arrow, takes aim at a member of the herd, but I press a palm against his arrowhead. Caution him. *Do not draw attention.* He is just a boy, a mere pup, but he understands.

Understand and survive. Fail and be devoured.

We stick to our platforms amid the trees. Once the herd moves on, we will descend and scavenge the bloody field, collect floater skins to cure, bones to sharpen into tools, what meat we can salvage.

Nightblacks circle above the semi-sunken city, gaunt-winged silhouettes against the lunar disk. I recall the tales my father told me, of lost angels and ribbons supporting self-propelled carts and wagons, of stories told in lights. Tales his father told him. And his father before.

We tell stories by firelight. We scratch them into cured skins with sharpened sticks, blacken the letters with charcoal. We do this so the stories will survive, even if we die.

One of the herd trumpets, alarmed, so I turn my attention back to them. A burrower has surfaced, grasped a smaller member in its mandibles, lifted it off the ground. It thrashes, its tendrils waving, its feet stamping at the empty air. It screams.

We cower in the canopy of leaves, watching as the mostly-buried burrower thrashes its head back and forth, choking the life out of the Young it clutches, as the remaining members of the herd attack, hammering at the burrower with their tendrils, stamp at it with their hooves, gnash at it with their many mouths.

We hide to hunt another day.

My father told me a story, once. A story from his father. And his father before. Of ancient times, before anyone who lives today was born. Ten generations, maybe more, have passed since these events happened. But in this ancient time, two girls were born, twins, daughters of the King. They were named Cassandra and Helen. They were beautiful, but Devom Nodenti, the drunk and jealous All-Father, cursed them for the monarch's hubris. The king had built towers to heaven, some reaching the very moon, and declared himself king of all he could see. The god compelled the twins to always tell the truth, but there was a caveat: no one would ever believe them.

The twin girls dreamed, then prophesied, telling of a coming war, and of the rival Sheol Nuggaroth, Devom Nodenti's brother, who, offended by the King's mighty towers, wished to tear them down, trample mankind into the dust. Three times they prophesied before the King and his court, foretelling blackened skies, falling wormwood stars, a bleeding moon, and monsters from the time before time itself who surfaced to stalk the earth.

No one believed the girls. The King laughed, thinking their tales fanciful.

But one night Sheol Nuggaroth stole to earth from where he watched in secret, slipping through a hole in the sky. He killed the King, captured the twins, made them his queens, his concubines.

From the union of Sheol Nuggaroth and the twins sprung monsters. A thousand Young marched through gates of flesh, fully-grown at birth, and set to unraveling the unnatural world. These Young, these Giants of the earth, mated with human women, begetting monsters, increasing their numbers.

Awakened by the sound of towers crumbling to earth, Devom Nodenti stumbled from his bed to confront his brother, but was soon overwhelmed by Sheol Nuggaroth's progeny. They bound the god, carried him to earth's deepest pit, and there they buried him, sealing the grave with the foul sigil of their father.

To this day, Devom Nodenti commands the chthonic burrowers, setting them to prey upon Sheol Nuggaroth's Young. But Sheol Nuggaroth has a thousand Young. And Devom Nodenti sleeps deep within the earth.

I do not know that I believe this story. Tales spoken will become corrupted over many tellings. So I write this down, commit my thoughts, my memories, my observations to this skin, in the hope that this account will one day be read and understood by future generations.

And in the hope that someone—anyone—will exist to read it.

**SUMIKO SAULSON** is a cartoonist, science fiction, fantasy, and horror writer, editor of *Black Magic Women* and *100 Black Women in Horror Fiction*, author of *Solitude, Warmth, The Moon Cried Blood, Happiness and Other Diseases, Somnalia, Insatiable, Ashes and Coffee*, and *Things That Go Bump in My Head*. She wrote and illustrated the comics *Mauskaveli* and *Dooky* and the graphic novels *Dreamworlds* and *Agrippa*. She writes for SEARCH Magazine. The child of African American and Russian-Jewish parents, the native Californian and Oakland resident has spent most of her adult life in the San Francisco Bay Area.

# UNHEARD MUSIC IN THE DANK UNDERGROUND

## Sumiko Saulson

**IF DEATH HAD** a voice, what would it sound like? Would it be the distressed voice of a Jewish mother singing her emaciated daughter to sleep in a gloomy corner of the concentration camp at Auschwitz? Would it be the slow buzz of hungry flies descending on the corpse of a starving infant in Ethiopia? Or would it be the long, low seduction of the jazzman's saxophone on a hot day in New Orleans? The pounding bass note on the dance floor the moment a madman snapped and shot the first of forty-nine people in an Orlando gay nightclub?

Would it be something so sinisterly subliminal no human could hear it, yet every living thing felt it? A dark metronome taking the pulse of every warm-blooded heart beating the second before life was snuffed away? The opposite of all natural rhythm, cranking away in a maddeningly peculiar tempo . . . a strange, disconcerting hiss underneath the white noise created by everything we think of as real?

I contemplated this while I slipped behind my terminal. I switched up the song on iTunes, putting on "The Unheard Music" by the punk band X, gently dabbing away tears under my mascara so my coworker wouldn't see. My tears weren't the only thing Robert Dupris was incapable of seeing. The ghost of my dead husband clung like a second skin, clammy and wet as morning dew, gray and listless as dust in cobwebbed corners. It rendered me quiet and morbid where I used to be cocky, sarcastic. Greg passed away two and a half years ago, but the wounds were fresh for me.

### The Dungeon

It was always ice-cold where I worked. They called our laboratory, a dank subbasement below Fort Point in San Francisco, the Dungeon. Tourists never saw the Dungeon. What they saw was Fort Point, a stone fortification built in 1853, only three years after the Gold Rush pushed California into US Statehood. The fort's sturdy stone structure predated the Golden Gate Bridge, which rose above it, by eighty years.

Most folks on the East Coast don't think of California as a state with any history, but that's just because we grow up on English history. American schoolbooks gloss right over the eighty-odd years the Spanish occupied San Francisco before we got here. By the time the USA declared its independence on July 4, 1776, there was already a Spanish mission here in San Francisco.

Afraid of the British Navy, the Spaniards established Castillo de San Joaquin on this very spot back in 1793. That old adobe fell to neglect and the wind and the rain had rotted most of it away by the time the US Army Corps of Engineers leveled what was left of it to build Fort Point.

Each day, I drove down the lonely hill that wound its way into the parking lot below the Golden Gate Bridge. I parked in my spot under the old eucalyptus tree that grew sideways, due to the strong sea breezes that twisted its trunk over the years. I looked up above me at the sheer cliff the army corps of engineers cut out of the side of the mountain. I stared as commuters and tourists traversed the famously International Orange-painted bridge above. Then I entered Fort Point, traveled through a series of doors until I reached the secret entrance to the Dungeon.

Dark, mysterious tunnels wound under the ground below Fort Point. I had been told on many occasions that much of the Dungeon was under the San Francisco Bay, traversing the space between Fort Point and the first of the bridge's towers.

The official account was that it had been constructed during the 1930s, alongside bridge construction. Enigmatic Charles Alton Ellis, a senior structural engineer obsessed with the bridge, was said to have been part of a secret society that constructed the Dungeon. Ellis worked on the project day and night, even after Joseph Strauss fired him: often forgoing sleep to work sixteen or twenty hours a day. Some said that Ellis found a secret underground bunker left behind by the Spanish and expanded on it. Rumor had it that parts of the Dungeon had been the actual basement and subbasement of the Castillo de San Joaquin.

Of course, it was haunted. Some said by slaves who had been

promised they would be freed during the Gold Rush as soon as the State entered the Union, but were murdered by greedy prospectors who didn't want them to have their share. That made little sense to me, since there was little prospecting here in San Francisco, but the ghost stories persisted. Others said that pirates abducted unsuspecting folks over at the Barbary Coast and dumped the bodies of the ones that were too damaged or weak to be seaworthy here on their way out to sea.

Dupris, ever the conspiracy theorist, posited that the Dungeon was built during WWII to host the dark experiments of fleeing Nazi scientists. The basement above, he claimed, was housing for a bunch of evil refugees evading the Nuremburg Trials. Mysterious sounds sometimes crept in from the hallways. Muffled screams and moans blended in with the omnipresent buzz of flickering fluorescent lights. I could never tell if the noises came from living persons or ghosts.

### *Music Made to Kill*

I pulled Kate Bush up in my iTunes and played the song "Experiment IV." The sound lifted high above the whining fans in the air conditioning system, filling the room with pop symphony and operatic voice. I caught myself chuckling at every lyric that referenced government research into murderous sound.

"Damn, girl!" Dupris winced. He hated the pop star with the seven-octave range, convinced that I was betraying all of my black genetics by listening to her. "Daenisha McLaurin, why do you always have to be so edgy? Why can't you play something normal, like Rihanna?" He flashed me that brilliant smile. If I wasn't still hurting, I might go for him. Flawless ebony skin, high cheekbones, and the kind of teeth only pretty momma's boys with trust funds seem to have. He was a young Republican who always teased me about how liberal I am, but I knew he was crazy about me.

I laughed. "I'm not trying to be cool. I just am, naturally." The lighthearted banter helped stave off the constant chill here in our sterile facility. It also assuaged the pangs of conscience I felt when I thought about what we were doing.

Sound . . . They showed us so many cute little tricks, things they could do with audio waves. They could move objects, change the temperature of our skin, make our fingers dance involuntarily. Those things were so charming and seemingly harmless, but the sheer power of these devices raised a red flag before we knew anything about their purpose.

The gentle breeze wafting through the air conditioner batted around the thin strips of cloth that muffled the sound of the fan. I was told once that there were sound-dampening devices all over the room, to protect us from the side effects of the project we were working on. I wondered if they also muffled the screams of the animals they tested the damned thing on—or perhaps things higher up the food chain than mere animals . . .

We were working on a sound that could kill. It was a strategic weapon the government would use for targeted strikes on our enemies. This device, pinpoint accurate, would enable the government to secretly eliminate high-profile targets the way they hit Osama bin Laden and Saddam Hussein. This was a black ops project and neither of us had enough clearance or expertise to know how the larger system worked. We were programmers, working on something simple, like Google Maps or the Pokémon Go app, that would be used to help the military select critical targets and hit them with the sound.

When I looked up at my monitor, I could swear I saw Greg's reflection on the screen. "Please don't do this!" he begged, murmuring in my ear. I tried to ignore him, like all of the other ghosts in my head, but his whisper was persistent, a warning.

### Secrets and Lies

I remember the first day they informed us what the project was all about. There were ten of us sitting around in a clean room full of mainframes. In the center of the floor were arranged two rows of chairs. An outside consultant was there to lecture us. Dr. Cartel unfolded a tripod from his black leather satchel and hung a large pad of paper there. He flipped page after page of oversized PowerPoint-style slides.

"Music to soothe the savage beast," Dr. Cartel said with a nod and a wink. He pointed at the diagram with his wand. We were not the creators of this technology. We were a test team. The product we were testing? Mind control wrapped in a nonthreatening packet of pop music or smooth jazz. Or so they said.

It wasn't until later that we learned the truth: they were building a weapon.

"It will eliminate our enemies without any risk of friendly fire. We will also save civilians on their side," Dupris sputtered excitedly. "This is awesome!"

I would never willingly commit to anything so heinous. I thought we were building something much cooler, with lots of fun, potentially good for society aspects. They'd showed me earlier how we could use the sound tech to read minds, to exchange thoughts telepathically, and to use telekinetic powers to coordinate our actions. They never told us it was potentially lethal!

We were so low on the food chain that, by the time we discovered what we'd built, it was too late to inform anyone with enough power to prevent what was coming. So I did something dangerous: I contacted my friends at Anonymous, the ones responsible for putting secret intelligence out on WikiLeaks. Had I done the right thing? I'm not sure. It was treason, wasn't it?

Anonymous told me to keep an eye on things, let them know how things developed under the cloak of a complicated videogame information network. I felt like such a fool, following breadcrumbs that led nowhere. I believed I was part of the liberation force, a secret underground that would alert the American people to the dangers of mind control. I believed the lies my commanders told me. It all seemed so harmless, the way they defined the project.

I was part of a covert effort to leak information to the resistance cells. Or, at least, I thought I was. Now, I wonder if those cells exist at all. From time to time, my life feels like the movie *Total Recall*. I think I'm a hero in the resistance, carrying information out to the free press, but I'm probably secretly being misled by the enemy. Blue skies on Mars, my ass! I'm probably suffering from an embolism. Maybe they've Moriartied me, like on *Star Trek: TNG* where they locked the sentient Moriarty hologram up in a subroutine where he thought he ran the world. I'm probably like Nancy in *The Craft*, losing my damned mind, in a psych ward somewhere, screaming, "I'm flying!"

I don't even know if I am working for the good guys. Believing I am seems to be the only valid reason to continue living anymore. These people control everything: our minds, our thoughts, the press, the airwaves, several people's bodies . . . maybe everyone's . . . as well as our memories, our emotions. They've declared themselves the new gods. They stand aloft, granting wishes, like the bored rich assholes in the movie *Zardoz*.

I watch a lot of television. Can you tell?

I also read a lot of books. My favorite one is Mary Shelley's *Frankenstein; or, The Modern Prometheus*. It's about human hubris and all of the terrible things that can happen when men play at being gods. That came out in 1818; January 1, 1818 to be precise, as I well recall, because I went to a haunted house theme party for its bicentennial. Let me tell you that two hundred years later, mankind hasn't learned a damned thing about our foolish pride.

### Laboratory Rats

There was nothing in the world modern enough to keep the Dungeon from looking like a set out of a play based on *Frankenstein*, or some old black-and-white silent movie like Robert Louis Stevenson's *Strange Case of Dr. Jekyll and Mr. Hyde*. Exposed pipes crisscrossed the ceilings, boxy air-conditioning ducts and stainless-steel tables made it obvious we were in an underground warehouse laboratory. The bank of aged electronic screens from the Fifties through Eighties along the back wall completed the eerie science horror show ambiance with various blips and bleeps. I am not sure what the government has against tossing out ancient electronics. Maybe they think they'd owe the taxpayers an explanation for why they spent eight billion dollars on a hammer back in 1988, if they did.

The only thing missing was a bunch of test tubes and beakers filled with creepy, dayglow liquids. Right as I was thinking that, Dupris opened the door as if on cue and buzzed through the lab with a tube full of lime-green fluid. He took a seat at his station, then stuck a plastic probe attached to a long cable into the liquid to get a reading from his computer. I didn't bother asking what it was. I wasn't a biochemist. I was a programmer. Due to our respective clearances, he might not be able to tell me if I did inquire.

I looked up from my computer and smirked at Dupris. He had a twisted sense of humor and would have appointed himself the unofficial disc jockey here at Greystone Military Research Laboratories, if he didn't have to contend with me for control of the iTunes library. "It's your turn to DJ. What you are gonna play for us, Robert?"

"You like this one?" he asked as Blue Oyster Cult's "Don't Fear the Reaper" seeped into the room through the tinny speakers placed high in each corner of the room. "It reminds me of that scene at the beginning of *The Stand* miniseries. The one where the military screwed the pooch and Captain Tripps got out."

I couldn't blame him for cracking morbid jokes to break the tension. I did the same thing. Still, I shivered. "Sounds a bit too much like us for comfort, if you ask me. Aren't you worried about it? I know I am."

"They won't let this get out and hurt any American citizens," the ever-patriotic Dupris reassured me. "This is to be used on our enemies, not our people. The sound will be used to kill off Russians, or mentally control those terrorists in ISIS or something. Can you just imagine them, running around like puppets on invisible strings, killing themselves instead of innocent people? I could have a wet dream just thinking about it."

I shook my head and kept on running the lists of potential target types. They had us developing target selection software that would help them determine which types of individuals could be strategically controlled most effectively. People with certain mental illnesses were particularly vulnerable, it seemed. Again, my mind wandered to Jekyll and Hyde and the vanity of mankind. How could Dupris be so naïve?

"You're a damned fool if you think the government never runs experiments on American citizens," I hissed. "Haven't you heard of Agent Orange or the Tuskegee Airmen?"

"Girl . . . " he sighed, shaking his head and giving me a baleful look as though I might just be some kind of a spy for the Soviet Reds. If he knew I was leaking intelligence to Anonymous, he'd probably pull out an old Ruger from behind a pipe and shoot me in the forehead, like he was in a James Bond movie.

"You shouldn't be afraid," Dupris said confidentially. "This technology will help us by protecting us. It won't hurt us at all. They use the sound to control people's bodies, but it doesn't hurt them. Most of them never even know. Let me show you how it works!" He leaned over and pressed a few buttons on the screen. A soundwave hissed through the music on the radio. Somewhere above it were a few recognizable pitches, angelic chimes mixed in with the music.

"More cowbell!" Dupris screamed, laughing over the rising chimes in the Blue Oyster Cult song.

Before I could protest, I found my fingers typing a series of unbidden words on the screen: "IT'S ME DUPRIS GO TO THE

DANCE WITH ME DAENISHA!" he typed in all caps with my fingers. I hated that. The fact that the technology existed didn't mean it should be used . . . especially not in such a trivial way.

He must be breaking a dozen security clearances right now. I was already mentally filing a report to send to Anonymous. Besides which, he was pissing me off. If this was his idea of flirting, he needed to go to a seminar on sexual harassment in the workplace or something.

I rolled my eyes and yelled back, "Stop messing with me, Dupris! I already said no! And stop showing off. I already know more than I ever wanted to about how this wicked tech works." I pressed a button on my keyboard while I flipped him off. "Possessing people's bodies like demons. Who thought that sounded like a good idea?"

"You don't really know how it works," Dupris pouted. "I was showing you."

"Yes," I said huskily. "Yes, I do." I focused my attention on his right hand until it rose up from his keyboard. Moments later, his open palm slapped him across the face. I laughed out loud, momentarily satisfied.

"Oh, so you do," he snorted. "So, will you go to dinner with me?"

"I don't think so." Damn, he was an idiot! Why wasn't he worried about anything? I personally wasn't too happy with the fact that they'd placed this top-secret technology at our disposal. Usually, in the movies and the stories I read, people like us ended up wiped out by the people who hired us, in order to hide their secrets. An image of Amanda Waller shooting all of those computer programmers to death in *Suicide Squad* danced through my head.

"Don't you think it's weird that they've been allowing us to play around with this technology?" I asked. "I feel I'm some sort of guinea pig."

Dupris laughed and cued up the intro song from *Pinky and the Brain* on our iTunes playlist. "Paranoid much?" he asked with a wink. I couldn't believe Captain Conspiracy Theory could say such a thing. Who wouldn't be concerned?

### Whispers in the Wall

A month had gone by since the announcement. I wasn't sleeping very well. I couldn't help thinking that what we were doing was dangerous and wrong. Today, I interrupted Dupris's disc jockeying attempts with another selection of my own. It was "World Destruction" by Time Zone, with Afrika Bambaataa and John Lydon on vocals.

Dupris listened to the song, shaking his head at the lyrics. "Why are you so pessimistic?"

"Black ops, you know, they aren't always good. What does the government want with a sound that can kill someone?" I asked.

"They could beam it straight into the head of whoever's running ISIS," he suggested. I guess he didn't have too many original thoughts. It was all some *Quantum Leap* episode where they got the bad guy: Hitler or the head of ISIS, whichever.

"Abu Bakr al-Baghdadi," I said.

"Huh?" he answered, scratching his head. He was hopeless.

"That's the head of ISIS," I informed him. "Abu Bakr al-Baghdadi is the head, or at least, one of the heads of ISIS."

We were growing so accustomed to the tech that we were practically bored with it. He was using soundwaves to levitate his coffee cup. A quiet buzzing sound came from the device on his fingertip, like a microwave oven makes. Each of us had such a device injected into our right index finger. I wondered if they tagged us when they injected it.

"Yeah, so what if the CIA could beam a sound into his head and make it explode, like in *Scanners*?" Dupris asked.

I sighed. "You watch too many spy movies. The CIA doesn't run black ops against ISIS, or anyone else for that matter. They collect information. That's what the 'I' stands for: intelligence."

"Yes, they *do* run black ops. Spying is part of black ops, silly goose," he countered. His know-it-all attitude was giving me a minor headache.

"I hope this isn't your idea of flirting," I seethed. I pulled up a new window on my computer screen and started playing *Call of Duty* so I could ease my frustrations with some digital gunplay. Best I could do, since I wasn't allowed to get up and smack him in the face.

"For a sister, you're sure not woke," he grumbled. When he got up to fetch another cup of coffee, I used the sonic telekinesis device to make him stumble. He turned around and gave me the side-eye over his shoulder, uncertain if I was the one who did it.

"You gotta be kidding me right now," I hissed. "You're the Young Republican, Ben Carson-voting military man here. How are you woke, exactly?"

"You think being liberal is the only way to be black," he complained. "You're just like my mom. She keeps voting Democrat like she thinks they gonna do something for her. All they do is perpetuate the welfare system and keep a black man from competing for a real shot at the American Dream."

Suddenly, my head was filled with white noise. He continued to pontificate in my general direction, but I didn't hear what he was saying. Underneath the static, I heard another voice entirely. It was Private First Class Gregory McLaurin, whispering to me from beyond the grave. I shook my head to clear away the voices. Was it a ghost? It sounded just like Greg.

My hands moved across my keyboard, silently conveying encoded messages in text to the resistance movement. This wasn't the first time my husband's spirit had shown up, asking me to get the message out to the people before it was too late. I didn't understand the series of strange characters he had me type into the chat window on the gaming screen, but he assured me it would get to the proper people, through the proper channels.

I couldn't let Dupris suspect.

"So what do you think it's going to sound like?" I asked, quickly covering up the gap in the conversation by changing the subject. I hated it when Dupris got on his political rants.

"Now you want to ask me what's what going to sound like?" he hollered, still mad at me. "What's what going to sound like?"

"The sound, the one that can kill someone. Will it be an instrument?" I asked. "I was thinking, if it was an instrument, it would probably be something subtle. Something people would trust, like a violin, or a saxophone, something classy and soothing. Not anything threatening, like electric guitar or bongo drums."

Dupris breathed a sigh of relief. I suppose even he was tired of hearing about politics.

"It would be subsonic," he posited. "Or maybe like a dog whistle. Only animals would be able to hear it. Everyone would be looking around, trying to figure out what was wrong, like they do just before the earthquakes. The animals would be having a fit, and no one would know why."

"Yeah?" I said, meanwhile passing notes to the underground resistance through a network of gaming servers. No one suspected gamers of doing anything meaningful. People like Dupris thought we were all a bunch of mindless idiots.

"Even though you get on my nerves with all of your liberal horseshit, I kind of like you," Dupris admitted. I grimaced, thinking he was going to hit on me again. He was attractive on the outside, annoying on the inside. Then he said, "This is the first time I've been on an assignment with a black coworker. I can't believe they found two African American programmers and put us on the same project. What are the chances?"

"Yeah, well, I doubt we're part of an affirmative action program." I shook my head. "If we were, they'd have us sitting around somewhere people could see us, not trapped in this musty-assed basement."

### *Of Men and Monsters*

"You like him, don't you?" Greg's spirit typed into the notepad on my computer. I shook my head. Was I in a love triangle involving a guy I wasn't even sure I liked and a dude who's been dead for two and a half years?

"The lady doth protest too much," Greg typed. "I can read your mind, you know."

Not bothering to type anything, since he said he could read my mind, I asked silently, "How do I know you aren't Dupris?"

"Don't insult me," he wrote. Before I knew it, my fingers were flying across the screen, inputting a series of characters in no language known to me. As my fingers typed, Greg's voice continued on in my mind. "I've been here since I died in Afghanistan, so how could I be Dupris? You didn't even know him then."

Friendly fire, that's what Greg told me when he first arrived, that they'd used some new technology overseas and he'd been caught in a trap set for our enemies. Later, he told me he'd discovered it wasn't just friendly fire—it was something they were testing on our own soldiers, just like Agent Orange or the Tuskegee Airmen.

When I say he arrived, I mean his body came home in a plain brown box. We had it transferred into something a little fancier before we buried it up in Dixon at the Sacramento Valley National Cemetery. I still remember receiving the folded flag once draped over his coffin. I couldn't believe they folded it to a tape recording of "Taps." I expected real musicians, not a tiny tape recorder with a single speaker. They buried him under the ground with a number of other soldiers, beneath matching marble memorials, mostly crosses. My husband's was next to another with a Star of David; that's how I always found it.

I was sitting beside his headstone, sobbing, when I first heard his voice. He arrived in a ray of sunlight breaking through the clouds overhead. This beam of light illuminated the tombstone and I was filled with an overriding sense of peace when I saw it. The sound of doves cooing overhead completed this lovely tableau.

Now I had a reason to question the cooing of doves and every other sound.

"I don't know who you are," I hissed under my breath. I didn't know anything anymore. If I'd known about the technology then, I wouldn't have let him speak to me in the first place.

"Come with me," he whispered. "I need to show you something."

Although he asked, he didn't wait for me to give him permission. He lifted my body and walked it to the door. I turned the knob with controlled hands, walking puppet-like through the opened door. The door automatically sealed itself behind me. I struggled with my free hand to touch my lavalier and check for the keycard I needed to reenter.

He dragged me through a series of mazes, hallways of which I hadn't been previously aware. Deeper and deeper into the Dungeon I went, until I felt a trickle of moisture from above. We were into the dank area of the subbasement under the waters of the Bay. I walked past a steel girder and remembered the silly rumors about how this lab might go all the way to Marin. A chill rose over my skin that wasn't from the cold.

A haze of gray smoke covered the masonry walls as the smell of mold rose up from under my feet. I had no idea where I was. I reached out to touch moss-covered walls. The stonework seemed even older here than where we worked. Was this an illusion bought on my sense of dread and mystery? It felt all too real. Sweat began to ooze from my pores, cold and stale against my icy skin.

An unnatural croaking noise emerged from somewhere off in the distance. I walked into and seemingly through a wall. No door—no archway—nothing but a solid that somehow allowed me to pass through it, unharmed. I felt like curds being squeezed through cheesecloth, but how? Was it magic, or a teleportation device?

As I entered the round room, the fog and mold evaporated. I was once again in a sterile laboratory. This one was filled with brains in jars, fluid pumping through glass and metal tubes, monitors showing their functioning. It reminded me of the old Thirties *Frankenstein* movie. As I hunched over and stared at the jars, I felt like Igor. My hands reached out against my will as my externally controlled body walked over to one labeled *Private First Class Gregory McLaurin*. The letters reconfigured themselves suddenly, back into the code he used to communicate. I could no longer read the cypher.

"Now you know," he told me. His voice no longer beamed straight into my head, but whispered into my ear from nowhere and everywhere at once. "I'm here, in the room in the back. That creepy room you never want to walk towards."

"I don't understand," I mumbled, but I did. The box I buried at the Sacramento Valley Memorial Veteran's Cemetery was either empty or contained a brainless body. My husband's brain—and, apparently, his soul—existed in a jar. Did brains contain souls? Could one be transferred into a new body somehow, like in the old Shelley story I was so fond of? I began to wonder.

"The government thinks of us as cogs in its machine," he explained. "We aren't machinery at all. We are ghosts in their military machine, ghosts that whisper through the walls to our loved ones. We are ghosts who whisper secrets to one another and send them out into the world when our slave owners aren't looking. We are ghosts, trapped in an endless nightmare from which only people like you can free us. Will you free me, Daenisha?"

"I would do anything to free you, love," I whispered, although I was deathly afraid of what I would be asked to do.

"Then go out with Dupris," Greg said. "We really need the second access code. He has it. Get it from him."

Instantly, I understood why the ghost of my husband wanted me to date another man. I also understood that this ghost wasn't a ghost at all.

"Of course," I said. "I will get the access code and set you free."

I was relieved that I wasn't being asked to do anything more dastardly. The dead had a way of becoming wicked in movies and novels. Perhaps he was like Shelley's Creature, simply misunderstood.

### Bizarre Love Triangle

I pulled an old New Order song up on iTunes, "Bizarre Love Triangle." It seemed morbidly appropriate. I wanted to trust Greg, but he was getting a bit too pushy and frankly, it was pissing me off.

The high-pitched whining buzzsaw sound at the back of my ears swept forward toward my temples and pressed in with the force of an invisible vise. It grabbed my head with irresistible force and turned me to face Dupris. Mouth contorted into a pucker to send a whistle out, low and deep with unimpressed nonchalance.

"Looking good, Dupris," my voice said without my permission. I closed my eyes and images of brains dancing in mason jars colored the insides of the lids. Beneath straining red veins, they danced in a dizzy whirl of light and sound, twisted together and apart, then smashed into one another, clanging. They parted and sat on their shelves once again, laughing and beckoning.

"Why, thank you, Sweetie!" he chortled happily.

In my mind's eye, I imagined smashing the encased brains together with such force that the jars burst open. Gray matter spilled all over the floor in wet cascades of flesh and formaldehyde. In my imagination, I had telekinetic power over them.

"I was thinking about the day you asked me out to dinner." A deep knot formed in the pit of my stomach, as I spoke words not my own from this flesh that imprisoned me. I was fully aware but had no control whatsoever. "I think it's a great idea. We should do that."

"Oh, yeah?" He raised a suspicious eyebrow, but accepted the slip of paper my hand extended to him. On it was my cellphone number. It looked like Dupris and I were going to be a thing. Or Dupris and whatever controlled my body and called itself my husband. What a dream! The ménage à trois I never wanted.

The brain trust let go of my flesh. I quickly sat in my office chair, sighing briefly in near-relief before I was once again enthralled, seconds later. My hands fell to the keyboard, typing in a series of random codes I didn't control or understand into a gaming system: sending out messages to God only knew who, for our new disembodied overlords.

That's when it occurred to me: that the thing in the jar might actually be Greg, my husband. What if he was trying to escape the powers that be? What if he was still alive? Imprisoned?

It took all of my willpower to force the thing to renounce control of my hands. I picked up my cellphone and began texting messages to Greg's old phone number. He didn't have the phone anymore—I owned both phones now—but I hoped he would get the point.

"How dare you fucking do this to me?" I angrily pounded into the keypad. "You say you're a prisoner. How can you keep me a prisoner?"

I didn't expect to get a response. There was no cellphone service down here, so the message I sent had no way to make it to the phone at home. Even if it had, Greg wasn't there to answer it. He was a brain floating in some green-yellow juice that looked like transmission fluid diluted with urine.

Still, the ringtone I'd assigned to his text messages alerted me moments later. I had a response. "We're desperate," it said.

"So am I," I typed back. Without explaining myself further, I stood up and stormed back to the hidden room. Fluorescent lights flickered overhead as the laboratory and its unseen life bellowed in protest. They only guessed at what I might do.

I walked directly to his jar. Steeling myself, I planted my feet wide apart and leaned over the jars. My hands curled around the red and green wires attaching his mason jar to the collective.

"Nooooooo!" the brain trust screamed in my mind as I ripped his cords free from the hive mind they'd formed. "Don't leave! You must free us! You must free us!"

I smirked. "I am freeing you, Greg. Your little friends can go fuck themselves."

Before anyone could stop me, I snatched the jar marked *Private First Class Gregory McLaurin* from the assembly. Then I marched right out of the laboratory and up the stairs.

I was halfway down the hall when Dupris stepped out of a door right in front of me.

"What is going on, Dae-dae?" he asked familiarly. "You just stormed out of the room like your pants were on fire."

"I am not feeling well," I lied. I turned the jar so its label faced my chest. "I got to take the rest of the day off, soldier. Go home and get some rest."

"What's wrong?" He looked concerned and way too nosy.

"Women's things," I blurted. "You know, that time of the month."

"Yeah, I know how it is," he stammered. "I mean, I don't, I don't have a period, but I . . . oh, never mind. You go on home, then."

"Thanks for understanding." I bolted for the front door.

"Can I still get that date with you, Daenisha?" he called after me. "You know I know about women in need and I can massage your, uh, feet, if you know what I mean."

"Not today," I responded curtly, slamming the door in his face.

I ran all the way to my little Jeep and put the jar in the seat next to me. I felt a little silly as I strapped it in.

"I can't believe I am still alive," Greg transmitted telepathically as I turned to grab the steering wheel. "I'm not sure how much longer that is going to last, but so far, I'm happy about it."

I shrugged. "I can try to hook you up at home. Or maybe one of the rebels on the Internet can help us. But we just got to get out of here right now."

"I am not sure how long the jar juice will hold me," he admitted, "but it's so good to be free. Is it okay if I check out the road in your eyes, since I don't have any eyes anymore?"

"Sure," I said, smiling.

I decided to skip the house and head for help, so I turned east for the other bridge. We headed over the Bay Bridge and flew as fast as traffic conditions and police evasion would allow southeast to Livermore.

The further we drove from the facility, the more the hive mind became a distant memory. At the same time, Greg's mind grew more in sync with my own. I was driving with both sets of hands on the wheels. He saw from my eyes. My heart beat too fast with anxiety as I looked out over I-580, wary of every car that drove on the opposite side of the road. Miles clipped by at a horse-trot pace. Could I trust my contact at Lawrence Livermore National Laboratory? I wasn't sure. But he was an old friend and he also was leaking information to Anonymous. We would just have to trust him.

"I am worried that you might die in the jar," I whispered huskily.

"You thought I was dead not so long ago," he answered. "Rather than worry about whether or not I will die tomorrow, consider the fact that while I was dead in your eyes last week, I am not today."

"If that's a pep talk, it isn't helping." I scowled. "You are about as useful as an old church lady on Facebook. You might as well have said just pray on it."

"I do pray. All the time," he admitted. "Wouldn't you, if you were a brain in a jar?"

I was about to snap at him, but he was saved by the buzz. My contact had texted me. I picked up the cellphone and read the message.

"I guess your prayers worked," I sighed. "Remember old Joe Allen? He has a home laboratory close to Livermore. We can make it there in less than an hour, if I speed a little."

"Well, you just do that," Greg said. I drove faster. About fifteen minutes went by before I heard from him again. "Not having a body kind of sucks, but I always thought you had a hot body. That doesn't sound very romantic, I know. But we're married. And you know what is romantic? I love looking at the world through your eyes."

I blushed and giggled. "That's the sweetest thing you've ever said to me." Leaning over to turn on the car stereo, I added, "Since you're such a sweet-talker, you can use my ears, too. I'm going to play us some tunes. Any requests?"

"Yeah," he replied. "I request you deliver me to the laboratory before I die."

We both laughed out of one mouth as I sped on down the road.

**SEAN PATRICK HAZLETT** is an Army veteran and speculative fiction writer who lives in the San Francisco Bay area. His short stories have appeared in publications such as *The Year's Best Military and Adventure SF: Volume 4, Year's Best Hardcore Horror: Volume 3, Terraform, Galaxy's Edge, Writers of the Future: Volume 33, Grimdark Magazine, Abyss & Apex, Perihelion, Unnerving Magazine,* and *Weirdbook,* among others. He holds an AB in History and BS in Electrical Engineering from Stanford University, a Master's in Public Policy from the Harvard Kennedy School of Government, and an MBA from the Harvard Business School.

# MUKDEN

## SEAN PATRICK HAZLETT

**MANCHURIA'S BITING WINDS** chilled Captain Tanaka Hideki to the soul, but the child-sized frozen corpses piled like cordwood bothered him more. As a father, he shuddered to imagine what it would be like to see his own three-year-old son Yoshi among the dead. While the cold blunted most of the odor, Tanaka could still smell the lingering stench of human filth. He struggled to keep down his last meal. "Who did this?"

"Not who, what," Fu Shih said, wiping ice flakes off his salt-and-pepper beard. The Hung-hu-tze bandit leader pointed to one child's belly, flaps of skin peeled back like an inverted starfish. "Whatever did this, it ain't human."

Tanaka had heard accounts of similar mutilations all along the Russian-controlled Southern Manchuria Railway. It was as if a blight radiated from the tracks—a festering sore of modernity marring Manchuria's pristine landscape. For Tanaka, the atrocities also evoked an unsettling déjà vu.

Ever since the Boxer Rebellion, a Russian occupation force of several hundred thousand had hunkered down along the Russian Empire's Manchurian rail line, which stretched from Harbin to Mukden all the way down the Liaodong Peninsula to its terminus at Port Arthur. Despite assurances they would eventually leave, the Russians had been steadily cementing their foothold in Manchuria for nearly half a decade. The Japanese military had landed in Manchuria to force the issue and liberate their Chinese brethren from the yoke of European colonialism.

Tanaka adjusted his bifocals and reluctantly took a closer look at the child's body. He'd had enough of death, had hoped to avoid it out here, away from the bulk of the fighting. He'd already seen more than enough killing at Port Arthur's siege to last a lifetime.

On closer inspection, Tanaka noticed that the child's viscera were gone. The peculiar wounds reminded Tanaka of his mother's superstitions about keeping his navel covered when he was a child.

As a reward for destroying the Port Arthur necromancer, General Nogi had assigned Tanaka a more conventional mission to help Tanaka recover from the psychological and spiritual damage he'd suffered. Yet, no matter where Tanaka traveled, he seemed to cast a pall of death all around him. So much so that he felt himself becoming more attuned to the otherworldly, with one foot firmly planted in the realm of the dead. Before Tanaka returned to the highly secretive Unit 108, he'd need to seek out a Shinto priest for cleansing lest his exposure to so much defilement infest other Japanese soldiers.

"What kind of an animal does this?" Tanaka asked in fluent Mandarin. Whatever had been responsible, it hadn't spared a single villager.

Fu shrugged as though unmoved by the atrocities. "Not an animal. Something else. Not natural. Not good. I seen something like this before near a Cossack camp."

The hair on Tanaka's neck stood on end. "What do you mean 'not natural'?"

Fu laughed. "No wild beast did this. Something else. Probably sorcery."

Ever since his experience at Hill 203 in Port Arthur, Tanaka had learned not to be so easily dismissive of such claims. He'd also realized that he shouldn't trust everything these rustics said. Sometimes they'd make things up just to test him. Oftentimes, they'd repeat a litany of age-old superstitions. But if Tanaka was to work with them, he had to play along. "Explain."

"Death magic. Rumor has it a Cossack regiment's creeping around these parts. Some say these ghost faces got a necromancer."

Tanaka shuddered. He'd encountered one of these dead sorcerers at Port Arthur and had no desire to face another out here, alone in the wilderness. Yet something about Fu's claim didn't seem quite right. It didn't fit the lore. Tanaka shook his head. "I don't believe it. Even if it were true, what purpose would this serve the Russians?"

"Necromancers use children's souls to grant Russian warriors extra lives," Fu answered, with what Tanaka sensed was the utmost seriousness.

Tanaka worried that investigating these murders would divert him from his primary mission. Mapping the Imperial Russian Army's location would be difficult enough for veteran Japanese cavalry, but convincing Chinese bandits to do anything in this cold Manchurian waste was akin to herding hungry spiders. Anytime they'd encounter a small Russian unit, the Hung-hu-tze wanted to raid it for booty and blood, motivated by revenge for the Blagoveshchensk massacre when, five years earlier, the Russians had driven thousands of Chinese men, women, and children into the Amur River, drowning them in cold blood.

Part of Tanaka wanted to let the bandits loose, but as the long-range eyes and ears of General Nogi Maresuke's Third Army, he could ill afford such distractions, especially with thousands of Japanese lives at stake. Still, ignoring such savagery was also unacceptable. Tanaka was convinced he'd lose face with the bandits if he let it go unchecked.

"Fine," Tanaka decided. "We'll track these Cossacks. But as soon as we deal with them, we'll return to scouting Russian positions."

"Feed us," the gaunt hag said, her voice more rasp than whisper. She wore a torn white gown that swayed with her wispy and frayed gray hair in the windless air. A warm campfire glowed behind Tanaka, where the Hung-hu-tze carried on, drinking pilfered vodka.

Tanaka could hardly see the pale lady in the darkness. Her hazy form shimmered in the moonless night. He approached her tentatively, his hand on his cartridge pouch, gathering a pinch of rice. As Tanaka drew closer, the night grew colder.

He offered the crone his rice, trying to convince himself his actions were born out of kindness. He partly believed it, but deep down, he knew that winning peasant hearts and minds was more important to him and the Japanese military effort. Spurred by acts of Japanese benevolence, as well as a Russian occupation notorious for its butchery, Chinese peasants had become a treasure trove of intelligence, enabling the Japanese to stay one step ahead of their lumbering but numerically superior European foe.

"Feed us," she groaned in guttural tones akin to crumbling parchment.

Tanaka refused to move any further forward. Why should he? He was offering this poor, starving woman a meal, and she couldn't walk fifty meters to retrieve it?

"If you want a free meal, come get it," he said.

Before Tanaka could blink, the alabaster woman had bridged the gap between them, her eyes pure white and her teeth a riot of rotting ivory spikes. Tanaka felt paralyzed. As an officer accustomed to commanding troops, Tanaka hated losing control. Now, he was helpless.

"Feed us!" she growled just before a gust of frigid wind dissolved her haggard form.

Tanaka woke in the morning twilight, bleary-eyed and drained of energy. His inner thighs ached from a long day of riding. A layer of frost covered his wool blanket and the sweat from his feet had hardened to ice inside his hobnailed boots.

"So you saw the night hag," a seemingly unimpressed Fu said by the campfire's dying embers. "You're lucky you ain't dead."

"You saw her, too?" Tanaka said, half-surprised Fu didn't mock him.

"'Course not."

"How'd you know I saw her?"

"I can tell. The dark rings under your eyes. Your face is paler than usual. I've heard 'bout others seen her in these parts. 'Specially during these times."

"What do you mean?"

"The pale ladies come 'round when people die. War, famine, disease. They come callin'."

Fu seemed to know a lot about something he hadn't seen. Tanaka began to feel uneasy, as if Fu were hiding something.

"Have you ever met someone who's seen these women?" Tanaka asked.

"Aye," Fu said and then winked at Tanaka.

"What happened to them?"

"You'll see." Fu smirked as he walked away from the campfire toward his horse.

Tanaka knew that was the best he was going to get from Fu, so he didn't push him any further. Instead, Tanaka put on his khaki military tunic, goatskin jerkin, greatcoat, and pistol belt. When he reached for his *Murata-to* saber, it wasn't where he'd left it the day prior. But he was certain he hadn't misplaced it. Someone had to have taken it.

Tanaka panicked. An officer losing his sword, even a lower quality, mass-produced one, would bring dishonor to him, his family, and his unit.

Not wanting to draw attention to the missing weapon, Tanaka wandered over to Fu while Fu was busy saddling his mount. Tanaka stopped and cleared his voice.

Fu ignored him.

"My saber's missing," Tanaka whispered. "Have you seen it?"

Fu glanced at Tanaka, smiled, and said, "How should I know? I'm not your saber's keeper." He returned to his business, then stopped and looked back at Tanaka as about to tell a joke. "Besides, ain't it a great dishonor to lose your weapon? Wouldn't you have to commit *seppuku*? Oh, wait, you can't. You don't have a blade." He snickered.

The captain mustered every ounce of discipline he had to avoid unholstering his pistol and shooting the bandit on the spot. "Well, if you see it, return it to me. Immediately."

"Ha, ha! Brave little Japanese samurai warrior! I shall indeed," Fu said an instant before he mounted his horse and headed off toward his band. As Fu rode away, Tanaka noticed a scabbard tucked beneath Fu's saddle.

"Stop!" Tanaka yelled, but Fu ignored him.

Tanaka pulled out his pistol and discharged a round into the air. If not for the rider's skill, Fu's horse would've thrown the man from its back. After regaining control of his mount, Fu rode back toward Tanaka.

"Are you crazy, you four-eyed Japanese dog?"

Tanaka stood his ground. "Return my weapon."

"Are you dense? I already told you I don't know where it is, little man."

"Liar. It's tucked beneath your saddle." Tanaka made his accusation loud enough for Fu's men to overhear.

"That's not your saber. I captured it in a raid," Fu said.

"Prove it."

Fu laughed. "How am I 'sposed to do that? All you Japanese devils carry the same sword."

"That's not true. Do you have a man who can read numbers?"

Fu glanced at his men. A large, porcine bandit named Chen nodded. Fu turned back toward Tanaka. "Aye."

Now Tanaka had him. "Every sword has a stamped serial number near the blade's base. I'll present Chen with the appropriate markings. If those markings match the stamp on the saber, I trust you'll do the honorable thing and return it to me. And I'll consider it a simple misunderstanding."

Fu's intense glare reminded Tanaka of a cornered rat's eyes. Fu glanced back at Chen and said, "Do it." Fu tossed the scabbard onto the ground. Tanaka marched toward the saber. When he arrived, he pulled a small diary and graphite pencil out of his pocket, and scribbled down the serial number.

Chen picked up the scabbard, unsheathed the sword, and inspected the stamp. Tanaka tore a sheet out of his diary and handed it to Chen. Chen read the number and then glanced at Fu, as if seeking guidance.

Fu nodded.

Chen sheathed the saber and handed it to Tanaka. Tanaka waited for an apology, but Fu just spun his horse around and galloped away. Nothing left to say, Tanaka walked over to his horse, mounted it, and headed toward the band for another day of riding. Now, he was worried. Nothing good could come of Fu's losing face in front of his countrymen.

Fu shook Tanaka awake. "Dress quickly!" Fu's face glowed in the lantern light. "Cossacks!"

Spurred by the chance to be rid of another necromancer and to resume his mission, Tanaka willed himself out of his fur-lined sleeping bag, dressed, and prepared his horse. He noticed that Fu's bandits were already awake, alert, and on horseback.

Tanaka rode over to the others, seeking out Fu. "Where are they?"

Fu pointed ahead. "In a ravine about two *li* that way. About fifteen men."

"Why don't I see firelight?"

Fu didn't hesitate. "Because, like the Japanese, the Cossacks are very disciplined."

Now Tanaka knew Fu was bullshitting. According to his pre-war briefings, the term "disciplined Cossack" was an oxymoron. For the time being, Tanaka deferred to Fu so as not to inflame an already shaky relationship. "What's the plan?"

Fu grinned. "You'll wait here until my bandits kill the Cossacks. We'll leave the necromancer for you, so you can stab him with your mighty sword." His voice oozed with sarcasm. "We'll signal you with this." Fu held up a metallic whistle suspended from a hemp lanyard around his neck.

Tanaka nodded. Fu and his men trotted into the darkness, while Tanaka waited, shivering.

Shots rang out, followed by screams, then a whistle.

Tanaka led his horse at a canter toward the encampment, now illuminated with fire. As Tanaka spurred his mount into a full gallop, he noticed the wind had stilled.

Several cadaverous hags blocked his path, their gazes mesmerizing him. "Feed us," they said, their voices a chorus of discordant melodies. In seconds, his horse was on top of, then through them. Their ethereal forms disintegrated into oblivion.

Disoriented, Tanaka followed the light of the raging blaze. He rounded a small spur of rock that led into a deep ravine. There, he watched as Fu's men looted bloody corpses.

Fu was soaking up the fire's warmth while sitting astride a squirming man-sized burlap sack wrapped in cords of hemp. "Ah, there you are, Tanaka. I've bound the necromancer. Why don't you take out your fancy sword and stab him like you stab your mother with your tiny prick."

Tanaka bore the insult with grace, but his patience with Fu was running thin. He dismounted his horse, unsheathed his blade, and confronted Fu. "How do you know it's a necromancer?"

"Boy, I been doing this longer'n you been yanking your twig. Trust me. It's him."

Tanaka didn't sense an inhuman presence inside the man, so he stared at Fu, uncertain what to do, and then said, "Let me see his face."

"Stupid fish-fucker. If I show you his eyes, he could hypnotize you. Just cut off his head. Kill 'em any other way, and a demon can jump into his body. And then you got real problems."

"Please," the necromancer pleaded in fluent Japanese, "Let me go!"

Tanaka hesitated.

"He's just messin' with ya. He smells fish and rice, so he talks Japanese to trick ya. Kill 'im quick so he doesn't cast any spells on us."

Tanaka opened the sack, locking eyes with a fellow Japanese soldier.

Fu grabbed the man by his hair, dragging him away from Tanaka. With his other hand, Fu covered the Japanese soldier's eyes. "What the fuck ya doing, tiny man? That sack needed to be sealed, else that necromancer's soul escapes and could possess you, me, or anyone else within a tenth of a *li*. Do it now!"

Then to Tanaka's horror, he spotted a bandit tossing the *Kyokujitsu-ki*, Japan's rising sun flag, into the flames. Fu watched Tanaka. The bandit leader's eyes gleamed. His left hand gripped the hilt of his knife. The blade rested on the captive's neck. The soldier stared wide-eyed at Tanaka. In one swift motion, the bandit leader slit the captive's throat.

"You son of a bitch!" Tanaka said. "You set me up. I almost killed one of my own countrymen. Why?"

Fu blew his whistle and the band surrounded Tanaka. Then Fu said, "Because you're cursed."

Tanaka felt a blow to the head.

Tanaka woke beneath a stack of corpses. He was so cold he could barely bend his fingers. He wormed his way out of the pile. The sky was gray, but the light was bright enough that Tanaka judged the sun, hidden above the clouds, was at its apex.

Frozen blood caked his garments in burgundy patches. Surrounded by the dead, Tanaka felt utterly and irredeemably defiled. No Shinto priest could purify him now. If he'd had his saber or pistol, he would've ended his life.

Then the women appeared. Their razor-sharp teeth marred already twisted faces. Their features contorted in angry rictuses. Their black and gray hair, scattered topsy-turvy on rotting skulls, had the rough quality of burlap. They reminded Tanaka of the shikome from ancient myth, Izanami's fell servants of the underworld.

"Feed us," they said, pointing west in perfect synchronicity, curled black nails extending from their index fingers. An instant later, lightning sundered the horizon, punctuated by thunder. The women's white marble eyes penetrated his thoughts, knowing him for who he truly was. Then one touched him.

Choking in blackness, Tanaka felt death's void flood into his empty soul, its filth putrefying his frozen form. Then a surge of dark energy animated his cold limbs, breathing a perversion of life into them, instilling a strange otherworldly sense of purpose that Tanaka couldn't put into words.

In seconds, Tanaka was back on his feet, looting a Japanese corpse for its khaki winter uniform under the ghostly hags' chilling glares.

"Feed us," they said, before vanishing.

So Tanaka wandered west, meandering through the furrowed rows of a fallow millet field. Soon, he came across a copse of ash trees, where bodies swayed from a makeshift gallows on barren branches. When Tanaka got closer, he discovered the ripped and bloodied corpses of Cossacks hanging over the mangled meat of horse carcasses. From the Cossacks' wounds, Tanaka figured someone had either shot them in the back or had cut their throats. He was certain that someone had been Fu.

Fu's bandits had stripped nearly everything useful from the Cossacks' corpses, save the belongings of one dead scarlet-bearded man. Tanaka removed the man's greatcoat and shaggy *papaha*, hoping it would help Tanaka pass for a Russian.

All Tanaka needed now was a weapon. But if he couldn't find one, he'd happily kill Fu with his bare hands.

Tanaka didn't care much more for life. The dead had so violated him that his spirit reeked of filth. The only thing that drove him now was his honor and he would die to preserve it.

As he reached the edge of the millet field, Tanaka ascended a slow rise until he came across railroad tracks littered with human bodies and horse carcasses. Both men and beasts had their abdomens splayed open like inverted starfish.

He recognized Fu's bandits.

Tanaka despaired. Unable to avenge his honor, he searched their remains for his saber and pistol. He found both on Fu's desecrated corpse.

The lightning and strange wounds suddenly reminded Tanaka of the folklore tied to his mother's superstitions. Legend had it that a raiju favored the comfort of a child's belly. During electrical storms, it would seek refuge there. To uncover its companion, a raijin would strike children with exposed navels, using lightning to drive out the raiju.

But if either demon existed, the folklore had understated their cruelty, given the grievous wounds Tanaka witnessed here. Then he remembered the story of the goddess Izanami. She'd sent both raijin and shikome to capture her husband Izanagi, after he'd abandoned her rotting form in Yomi, the death realm. When Izanagi escaped his wife's minions, Izanami vowed to claim a thousand lives a day in revenge. In response, Izanagi had promised he'd breathe life into fifteen hundred more.

Tanaka liberated a pale mare from a nearby village. He'd offered to trade a farmer for the horse, but the man had refused, so Tanaka had taken it by force. He regretted such harsh measures, but he'd needed to salvage his reconnaissance mission.

Before Tanaka had left the village, several peasants had reported large concentrations of Imperial Russian troops in the vicinity of Mukden. So Tanaka rode west beyond the railway. Through dark gray clouds, a faint glow traced the sun's descent below the horizon, ushering in twilight, and with it, a deeper cold. The clouds released giant flakes of snow.

Along the way, Tanaka happened upon a second village. Hoping to find warm hearths, he found a raging conflagration instead. Thatched huts burned and the smell of cooked meat made Tanaka's stomach grumble.

As Tanaka ventured away from the fiery homes and into the darkness, he smelled vodka mixed with borsch. Cossacks!

A shot rang out. A bullet grazed Tanaka's arm. Tanaka's mare whinnied. Its forelegs rose, bucking Tanaka. The captain landed hard. The fall knocked the wind out of his lungs.

Russian voices chattered in the murk.

Tanaka scrambled to find cover. But the men, armed with torches and bayonet-tipped Mosin-Nagant rifles, easily found him. Underneath the cover of shaggy black sheepskin *papahas*, the

Cossacks' curly moustaches accentuated their grimy yellow teeth, a pack of jackals encircling for the kill.

One brute held Tanaka down, while another beat him bloody. Tanaka felt the sharp pain of a broken nose and smashed cheek. The men pounded on Tanaka until blood streamed down his neck, freezing in place. He shuddered as the Cossacks dragged his shattered body toward two crossed railroad ties lying on the snowy ground. They forced Tanaka onto the contraption, his limbs tracing an X.

A Cossack grinned, pulled out a hammer and finger-length spike, and nailed Tanaka's palms and feet to the railroad ties. Each time a nail pierced his flesh, intense stabbing pain coursed through Tanaka's limbs.

Just when Tanaka couldn't endure any more suffering, the yelping Cossacks hoisted the structure up, propping it against a small hut. Supported only by the nails driven into his hands and feet, Tanaka struggled to breathe.

The men mocked Tanaka as he cried. Yet Tanaka accepted his fate. Better to die in the cold Manchurian wilderness than to live and dishonor his family. Tanaka lowered his head and prepared to die.

"Feed us."

The ghostly hags glided through the cackling Cossacks with an eerie preternatural grace, their shredded gossamer gowns dancing in the darkness. No matter how much the hags twisted and whirled, the Cossacks paid them no mind. The men just laughed and drank themselves into a stupor.

The old crones smiled, their needle-fine teeth glinting in the moonlight. Tanaka heard a faint beat in the gloom, crescendoing until it was so intense, it stirred the Cossacks from their torpor. *Boom-dada-boom-dada-boom-boom-boom!*

The Cossacks loaded their bolt-action rifles. Several ventured toward the drumbeat.

Then the pale hags pointed toward its source. A lightning bolt struck the ground, punctuated by thunder. For a split second, Tanaka saw something lurking beneath the lightning.

A man shrieked.

The crones pointed again. Lightning flashed, revealing a gnarled squat thing about twice the size of a man, its arms the thickness of tree trunks. Scores of twisted goat horns crowned its skull. A misshapen perversion of man and beast, it had the muzzle of a horse, a snake's eyes, a boar's tusks, and a mess of bony ridges on its face.

Lightning struck again. Tanaka watched as the thing eviscerated a man in one blow. Its claws tossed the man's innards. Something else scurried out of the Cossack's steaming guts when they hit the ground. The small creature's compound eyes, scales, and stubby legs reminded Tanaka of a twisted chimera of insect, crab, and reptile. Its pincers gnawed on the dead man's viscera.

The storm continued into the night until Tanaka was the only survivor. The others lay dead, their bellies splayed open in the same manner as the other desecrated corpses he'd found along Southern Manchurian Railway.

When the storm ended, the spectral hags floated toward Tanaka, hovering at his eye level. One laid her hands on his, removing the nails binding him to the wooden structure. She lowered him to the ground, put her hands on his forehead and granted him a vision.

In his mind's eye, Tanaka beheld the railroad tracks of the Southern Manchurian Railway cleaving the bleak landscape, running northeast. Frozen rivers bisected the rail line at various points, running from south to north. A network of trenches scarred the desolate plain in a defensive line from west to east, just south of a tributary Tanaka recognized as the Sha River. To the north lay a second river, the Hun, and beyond the Hun, a town.

Mukden.

Like a hawk, Tanaka focused his mystical vision on specific areas of the battlefield, observing the guidons and banners of individual units. Outside of time, he viewed the Russians' positions with total clarity.

Just as quickly as his vision began, it ended. Tanaka found himself lying on the cold soil just before morning twilight, surrounded by mutilated corpses. The white hags watched him.

"Feed us," they said, before dissolving into the ether.

Tanaka's perfect knowledge remained. He was giddy with the chance to restore his honor.

Everything around him was dead, save for his pale horse tethered to the crossed railroad ties. Strangely, he felt neither warm nor cold; he could no longer see his frosty breath.

Tanaka wondered why the raijin and raiju had spared him and his mare. Ultimately, he decided it was pointless to dwell on such abstract and arcane notions. He had more pressing concerns like delivering his intelligence to General Nogi. Tanaka climbed on his mount and headed west toward the Third Army.

Tanaka had ridden all day and night to reach the Third Army's field headquarters. Like iron filings to a lodestone, he quickly sought out and found General Nogi Maresuke's banner rippling above a simple canvas field tent.

The general was a man of contrasts, bridging tradition and modernity. A samurai's son, he'd fought to put the samurai down during the Satsuma Rebellion. When the enemy had captured his regiment's banner, he'd fought with suicidal bravery to recover it until his commanders had ordered him to stop. Losing a banner in combat was a terrible shame for any officer. Were it not for the Emperor's forgiveness, General Nogi would not have survived to capture Port Arthur from the Chinese in 1894 and from the Russians in early 1905.

When Tanaka approached the elderly general, the man's eyes had a sad, pensive look. The general avoided Tanaka's gaze and looked toward the horizon. "It's not natural for a father to outlive his sons," he said.

Tanaka didn't know how to respond to the general's frank expression of emotion. He wanted desperately to comfort the general. Everyone in the Imperial Army had made heroic sacrifices in this war, but General Nogi had lost more than most. Both his sons had died in this war; one in the Battle of Nanshan, and the other in the fanatical assault on Port Arthur's Hill 203. Tanaka had great respect for the old man and would not begrudge him his moment of grief.

General Nogi turned, raised an eyebrow, and said, "You look awfully pale, Tanaka-kun. And it seems your face has taken a beating. I'm happy to see you're still alive." He paused, then said, "What news have you from Unit 108?"

Tanaka bowed to his commander. "Nogi-sama, may I borrow a map?"

"Myake-kun!" the general yelled. A soldier materialized as if by magic and produced one. The general handed it to Tanaka. Tanaka traced several symbols on the map, representing Imperial Russian units down to the regimental level.

Nogi's eyes widened. "How did you come upon such detail? We haven't been able to get anyone that close to the Russians, especially in the center of the front. There must be several hundred thousand men there."

"A shade over three hundred and forty thousand," Tanaka said, before realizing that his supreme confidence must've sounded odd to Nogi. After all, it was implausible that one man could singlehandedly obtain such detailed and far-ranging intelligence.

Nogi stared at the map. He then pulled out a small book from his cargo pocket, cross-referencing it against Tanaka's drawings. After several minutes, the general glanced up at Tanaka. "What you've shown me is consistent with much of the detail we have. How were you able to gather this intelligence?"

Tanaka nearly told Nogi the truth, but quickly decided against it for the general would never believe him. Instead, he lied. "I could cover quite a bit more ground disguised as a bandit."

Nogi's eyes focused on Tanaka's as if the elderly general were probing for some hint of deception. But Tanaka held firm. Nogi nodded. "Excellent work, Tanaka-kun. I'll ensure you're properly recognized for your efforts. Dismissed."

Tanaka saluted. Nogi returned the salute. Tanaka spun on his heels and made to exit the general's field tent.

"Wait," Nogi said, "Come back."

Tanaka turned. The general smiled. "I'd like to shake your hand," Nogi said, extending his arm.

Tanaka gripped the general's hand. Nogi's broad smile crumbled. His brows furrowed. "Your . . . hand, it's ice cold."

Then, with a deep foreboding, Tanaka withdrew his hand and lifted his tunic, exposing his abdomen. Nogi's face twisted into a grimace. When Tanaka touched his belly, it was splayed open in the manner of raijin's victims.

The instant Tanaka realized what he'd become, his corpse collapsed inside the general's field tent. His grim task completed, he passed through death's veil into Yomi, where his body would rot for eternity.

Over the next several weeks, tens of thousands of souls would join him, feeding Izanami's insatiable hunger on an industrial scale as the Russians and Japanese invented new, more efficient ways of killing.

**ROH MORGON** dreams up her dark tales while driving through California's Sierra Nevada foothills. But it's her time spent in more remote locales—the soaring peaks of Colorado, the windswept plains of Wyoming, the mysterious Carpathian Mountains of Romania— that provides the settings for her stories.

Roh's best known for her vampire series *The Chosen* (which includes the novels *Watcher, Runner,* and the upcoming *Seeker: Book III of The Chosen*), the related 1840s historical horror novella *The Last Trace,* and the corporate horror novella *The Games Monsters Play.* You can find Roh online at rohmorgon.com, on Facebook at RohMorgonWriter, and on Amazon.

# LITTLE PINK FLOWERS

## ROH MORGON

**DR. NANCY EDWARDS** turned off the ignition in the white SUV and stared in disbelief at the cornfield a short distance away. In spite of the hot California sun beaming through the dusty windows, a chill swept across Nancy's skin, terminating in a fine sweat that left her palm clammy against the steering wheel.

"No." She slowly shook her head. "This . . . this isn't possible."

Dr. Abe Wilson, her fellow plant pathology professor from UC Davis, leaned forward as he peered through the windshield. His Southern drawl finally broke the silence gripping them. "Lord help us, Nan."

Nancy opened the door and stepped out, doing her best to keep her rising panic at bay. Abe joined her beside the SUV with his backpack slung over his shoulder as Jose Mendez approached them from his pickup truck.

"Look at that!" The farm manager waved his hand toward the field. "It's gotten worse since I called you. My entire crop is dying!"

The eight-foot-tall cornstalks, their ears nearly ripe, had lost their natural color. They were now a sickly pale green.

"There've been no reports of this reaching American soil," Abe whispered, rubbing his short beard.

Nancy shaded her eyes as she studied the corn. "I thought it occurred only on wheat."

"Well, let's get some samples."

Abe waited, letting Mendez take the lead. Nancy fell in beside her coworker, her alarm slowly giving way to fascination.

As they neared the field, the extent of the infestation became clearer. Thousands of little pink flowers gently waved on slender, glasslike stems that emerged from the larger cornstalks. The corn plants themselves looked as though all of the color had been leached from their tissues.

"This field was perfectly normal yesterday." Mendez stopped about ten feet from its edge, fear-tinged suspicion evident on his face.

Abe produced latex gloves from his backpack and held out a pair. Nancy slipped them on and, with a grim look at her partner, stepped closer to examine a flower.

Roughly the diameter of a nickel, the sphere-shaped flower appeared similar to that of clover, except each narrow pink petal terminated in a tiny, clear bulblike structure. No leaves sprouted from the three-inch-long transparent stalk which pierced the ghastly colored corn tissue.

When she reached out to touch the flower, it moved.

"Oh, my God, Abe! It's *moving*!" Nancy couldn't tear her gaze away from the writhing flower, now a bright red and bristling with sharp blue spines that hadn't been there a moment before. "They're *all* moving!"

A strange, high-pitched whine filled the air. It quickly spread throughout the entire field.

"Holy shit!" Abe grabbed her arm and yanked her back just as a volley of spines shot out toward them. The scientists wasted no time getting to the vehicles, Mendez close behind.

"Did any of them hit you?" Abe scrutinized her face while Nancy checked her arms.

"No. No, I don't think so." Staring at the menacing field, a shudder passed through her. "There's been nothing in the reports from Russia about *that*."

"Hey, Docs!" Mendez's hand shook violently as he lowered his cell phone. "I need to get back to the yard. You should come, too."

Nancy exchanged a fearful glance with her partner as they quickly climbed into the SUV.

Bouncing along the dusty road behind Mendez's truck, she listened while Abe called their contact at the Centers for Disease Control. When he got off the phone, Abe's bleak expression made her heart sink.

"It's definitely jumped crops, and it's definitely here. They've got reports from all over the US. Apparently, it's widespread in Europe, too." Abe swallowed. "It's mainly targeting food crops. And they can't find anything to stop it. They're . . . they're speculating it came in on the Chelyabinsk meteor."

Nancy felt her chest constrict as she contemplated the possibility of worldwide famine and the fates of her two young daughters.

Gripping the steering wheel tighter, she yanked it to one side, barely missing the gatepost at the sharp turn into the farmyard. She pulled up in a flurry of dust, parking beside Mendez's truck as he leapt from the cab and strode over to the group of workers clustered against the fence.

The crowd parted for him, but Nancy couldn't see what they were staring at. She climbed out of the SUV.

When she reached the fence, she fell to her knees, a scream trapped in her throat.

Inside the paddock lay a dozen emaciated dairy cows. They were all dead.

And from their black-and-white hides sprouted hundreds of little pink flowers.

**JEFF SEEMAN** is the author of two novels, *Political Science* and *Guns and Butter*, and a tribute to Edgar Allan Poe, *The Scythe of Time: An Essay and Homage*. He was a contributor to the short story anthologies *18 Wheels of Science Fiction*, *18 Wheels of Horror*, and the Bram Stoker Award-nominated *Hell Comes to Hollywood*. His short fiction has also appeared in a variety of literary magazines. A former editor of the *Cornell Lunatic* (Cornell University's answer to the *Harvard Lampoon*), he has performed stand-up comedy in Los Angeles, Boston, and San Francisco. For more information, go to amazon.com/author/jeffseeman.

# ROAD KILL

## JEFF SEEMAN

**1:17 A.M.** Twenty-eight hours and twelve minutes. 331 miles to Chicago.

And the blur of white lines on black asphalt shooting past in the darkness—endlessly, mercilessly. And the low, steady hum of eighteen tires on asphalt unremitting, and the high, steady whine of the engine unrelenting. And the tattoo of rain on the windshield and the squeak-swish-squeak of the wipers incessant. And the feel of the seat hard and painful against his back, the cracks in the cold brown vinyl exposing the cheap foam padding beneath, hardened and yellow with age. And the air stale with the smell of sweat and nicotine. And the flashes of light from passing streetlamps throwing nightmare shadows inside the dark cab, then disappearing, then darting in again, like a slow, steady strobe. And the quiet symphony of static and indistinct, barely human voices drifting from the CB radio like memories of some distant, hypnotic dream.

And the coffee in the extra-large Thermos had gone cold hours ago. And the supply of trucker pills was dwindling. And he'd been driving for twenty-eight hours and twelve minutes. And it was still 331 miles to Chicago.

And by now she might already be gone. After all, she'd left him the message over 24 hours ago. And this time she'd sounded as if she really meant it. She might have already packed up the car, taken the kids, and left.

She might have already taken all her clothes from the bedroom closet—the brightly colored summer dresses, the dark business skirts and serious blouses, the tight little black cocktail dress that she always worried made her look fat. He tried to imagine what their closet would look like half-empty. Mostly empty.

She might have already packed up all the kids' toys. The stuffed animals and the video games, the board games and the Lego sets.

The doll with the fancy clothes and curly blonde hair he'd brought back with him from San Francisco. The autographed catcher's mitt he'd gotten at Fenway. The Nintendo Wii he'd bought for Christmas, the one the kids had been so excited about, the one they'd played all day long and then never touched again. They might all be packed up in brown cardboard boxes by now, sealed tight with packing tape.

She might have already taken all her things from the bathroom. Her toothbrush from the holder on the sink. Her seemingly dozens of bottles of lotions and creams and gels that he always teased her were probably all the same thing, just marketed in different bottles. Her pink silk panties, the ones she used to hand wash and hang over the shower curtain, the ones that always used to annoy him when he wanted to take a shower but delighted him when he'd come home from a long trip and she'd sent the kids to their grandmother for the weekend and she'd greet him at the doorway wearing nothing else. And she'd run her fingernails ever so lightly over his skin as she removed his clothes, like ten tiny, precious tongues.

She might have already taken all the pictures down from the walls. The one at their youngest's first birthday party, the whole family crowded around the birthday cake, the guest of honor with his eyes wide and innocent and completely uncomprehending the occasion. The one the waiter had taken that weekend in Puerto Vallarta, the two of them with their arms thrown around each other, laughing, wild, high on love and sex and tequila, the Pacific Ocean behind them. The wedding photograph . . . She wouldn't take that, would she? But leaving it would almost be too cruel. For him to come home and be greeted only by that photograph looking down from the wall on an empty apartment. No, she couldn't be that cruel. She'd take the wedding photo with her.

And for the tenth time that hour, he grabbed the cell phone from the passenger seat and hit redial. Ringing.

*Come on. Pick up. God, please pick up.*

"Hi, this is Amanda. Leave a message." *Beeeeep.*

*Fuck.* He tossed the cell phone aside.

*I fall to pieces, each time I see you again,* sang Patsy Cline faintly, mockingly, from the radio.

And the rain poured down. And the squeak-swish-squeak of the windshield wipers. And the low hum of eighteen tires on asphalt. And the high, steady whine of the engine. And he popped another trucker pill and washed it down with the last dregs of cold coffee. And he checked his watch.

And it was 1:19 a.m. Twenty-eight hours and fourteen minutes. 329 miles to Chicago.

*Ttschhhhhhhhhhhhhh . . .*

"Break one-nine."

All he'd been picking up on the CB for the past twenty minutes had been a swirl of static and a few barely audible voices. Probably due to the storm. Occasionally, he'd catch the hint of a conversation fading in and out, mostly talking about the weather or last night's baseball game. But this voice had cut through the auditory mist, more distinct than the others. A Southern drawl. A nasal twang.

"Break one-nine," it repeated.

Another distant, barely audible voice responded. "Come on, breaker."

"This here's Buzzsaw. Ah got a full-grown bear takin' pictures on Old Hut—" The voice disappeared in a sea of static. *Ttschhhhhhhhhhhhhh . . .*

*Shit. Speed trap.* He'd been trying to keep it at close to eighty since San Bernadino. He grabbed the microphone.

"Come back on that?" He waited for a response. Nothing. "Come back on that, Buzzsaw?"

There was a crackle of static, then, "Howdy, good neighbor. What's yer twenty?"

"Old Hutchinson Road. Eastbound."

"Y'all got a bear in the bushes your side, mile marker five. Right behind the billboard for Chuck's Diner."

He peered out the windshield, through the darkness and driving rain, and his headlights illuminated what appeared to be a billboard, about three hundred feet up ahead. He eased off the fuel pedal. 75 . . . 70 . . . 65 . . .

He reached the billboard doing 60. Sure enough, the peeling, faded sign proclaimed the culinary virtues of one Chuck's Diner. He threw a glance at the passenger sideview mirror as he drove by. A highway patrol car sat just behind the billboard, a cheetah waiting in the bushes to pounce on the next passing gazelle.

He shook his head. "Much obliged, Buzzsaw. You just pulled my nuts out of the fire."

Thunder boomed and a flash of lightning briefly illuminated the twisted, naked trees lining the side of the road. Buzzsaw's voice faded in and out of the ether. "Happy . . . help, good neighbor. Who . . . talking to?"

"Warthog."

"Glad . . . acquaintance, Warthog. Whatcha doin' out . . . godforsaken stretch . . . shit and asphalt?"

"Old Hutch? GPS sent me here. Just before the damn thing died on me. Accident back on 235. Traffic's all fucked up. Trying to find a way back to 80."

"Y'all keep headin' east. You'll hit 'er eventually. Hauling . . . load?"

"Dropped it in L.A. Just trying to get home."

"Folks waitin' for you?"

He hesitated. "Maybe." A swirl of emotions coursed through him. "Maybe not."

"Don't sound good. Trouble . . . old lady?"

Warthog couldn't resist a cynical chuckle. "Apparently on the road too much, Buzzsaw. Not home enough. On account of the whole trying-to-make-a-living-and-feed-my-family thing."

"Oh, yeah, *that* thing. Sounds . . . fuckin' curse . . . bein' a trucker, son."

He took a deep breath. "Yeah. Fuckin' curse."

"Don't see much traffic . . . Old Hutch," said Buzzsaw. He chuckled. "Hey, you watch out . . . ghost now."

"Come back?"

"Local legend. There's . . . hairpin turn halfway . . . ravine about . . . miles . . . Locals say . . . Dead Man's Curve . . . . Some driver . . . 'bout twenty years ago . . . skidded . . . and . . . When they . . . found . . . severed . . . arms and . . . head . . . blood . . . torso . . . with his guts all . . . and his eyes . . . People say when . . . they still see his ghost . . . night . . . out on Old Hutch. What the kids say, anyhow."

Warthog shook his head. "Kids. Every town in America probably got a legend like that."

"Yup. Reckon so. Say . . . diner . . . pretty decent, you ain't eaten."

"Chuck's?"

"Yup. Only place open twenty-four hours . . . damn county."

"Thanks, I'll pass. Trying to make time."

"Nothin' else . . . for miles," said Buzzsaw. "Might want . . . reconsider."

"Ten-four."

Warthog jammed the microphone back into its clip and put the hammer down, pushing the semi back up to eighty. There was a flash of lightning and the thunder crashed again. The rain came down even harder, as if redoubling its efforts. He snatched up the cell phone again and hit redial.

"Hi, this is Amanda. Leave a message." *Beeeeep.*

He cursed under his breath and threw the phone back onto the seat.

All at once, the road before him seemed to blur. He squinted and blinked several times—hard—trying to regain focus. But everything appeared as if through a haze, even the dashboard just three feet in front of him. A hot flash coursed through his body, then sweat dripped down the back of his neck. His head pounded and his mouth had gone dry. He couldn't feel the pedal beneath his foot any longer. He looked down in disbelief to make sure it was still there. It was, but he'd lost all feeling in his right foot. With a start, he realized the tips of his fingers had gone numb as well. The world spun suddenly around him as if he'd had one too many whiskies.

He gulped for air and eased off the pedal, slowing the truck to thirty-five.

The CB crackled again. "Warthog, this here's Buzzsaw. Y'all sure you don't want to check out Chuck's? Might be a surprise for you." There was a swirl of electronic feedback, then, "Ah was just there."

Warthog tried to shake the dizziness out of his head. Grasped for the mic. Missed it two times. Grabbed hold on the third.

"Ten-four," he managed weakly.

Up ahead in the distance, through blurred, bloodshot eyes and pissing rain, he caught a glimpse of neon lights, red and yellow and white. He couldn't even tell if he was on the fucking road anymore. Just aimed the truck for the lights and kept rolling.

The sign proclaimed it as CHU K'S DIN R. Warthog pulled slowly into the parking lot, rolled to a stop, and cut the engine. He sat hunched over the steering wheel, breathing hard, forcing air into his lungs as the rain pounded on the windshield. His throat was parched and his head still spun. He gripped the steering wheel tightly and stared down at the floor of the cab, waiting for the world to stop swimming around him. *Something to eat. Yeah, that's all I need. I'll be fine. I'm sure I'll be fine if I just get something to eat . . .*

He lifted his head slowly to peer through the windshield, but the rain was too heavy to make out anything but the blur of colored neon. He kicked open the door of the cab, pulled his jacket tightly around him, and tumbled out into the downpour.

He landed hard on his feet and his legs almost gave out beneath him. Struggled to regain his balance. How many hours had it been since his feet had touched solid ground? He steadied himself, a weary, haggard sailor just back ashore after months of being at sea.

The diner stood small and brightly lit against the darkness. Warthog saw there were a couple of other trucks and even a few cars parked in the lot. Maybe it wasn't so bad, he thought. Seemed to be able to draw a few customers, even this late at night. Then again, Buzzsaw had said it was the only place open for miles.

Warthog jogged across the small parking lot towards the entrance as the rain poured down.

The tinkle of a small bell announced his arrival as he stepped through the front door. He tried in vain to shake the water from his soaking jacket. The diner was so bright compared to the darkness outside, the fluorescent lights fairly sparkling off the freshly polished linoleum. A long Formica countertop with a row of stools stood on his right, a series of booths on his left towards the windows. Behind the counter was a grill where a hamburger and several strips of bacon sizzled. Glass display cases advertised various cakes and muffins and pies. A jukebox stood against the far wall, playing country music over the din of the rain. It was like every other truck stop diner he'd ever been in.

Except it was deserted.

He looked around. Two raincoats and several umbrellas hung on hooks near the front door. A wet poncho was draped over one of the bar stools. He walked slowly down the row of booths. A woman's handbag lay abandoned on one of the benches. A man's jacket. And there were definitely two semis and a handful of cars parked outside. *Where the hell was everyone?*

"Hello?"

No answer.

Warthog heard a loud sizzle from behind him and turned to see that a grease fire had broken out on the grill. He rushed behind the counter and turned off the heat, then grabbed the lid of a nearby pot and covered the piece of charred, burning meat. The smell of burnt oil hung heavy in the air.

"Hello?" he shouted again.

Nothing. Just Hank Williams and the rain.

Warthog walked slowly through the kitchen. It was as immaculate as the rest of the diner—countertop, gas range, sink, all sparkling stainless steel, all freshly cleaned and polished. A small connecting room contained shelves piled high with cans of sweet corn and baked beans and cling peaches, and on the far side of the room, the door to a meat locker stood slightly ajar.

Slightly ajar.

He walked slowly to the door and hesitantly pushed it open. A blast of cold air emanated from the darkness. He felt along the inside of the doorway for a light switch and found it.

The room was filled with bodies and body parts hanging from meat hooks. A young woman with long, stringy blonde hair, her right arm missing, her face twisted in horror, the hook piercing her stomach. An elderly man suspended in the air, still wearing his baseball cap, his left leg sawed off. Various arms, legs, and other unidentifiable organs, hanging from the ceiling like so many cold cuts in a delicatessen. And in the center of the room, a naked torso—armless, legless, blood still dripping from the chest wound where the hook burst from the skin—dangling like some gruesome piñata.

*I fall to pieces*, sang Patsy Cline faintly from the next room.

Warthog fell back, overwhelmed with horror and nausea. He covered his mouth as he gagged and retched, his eyes wide. Then turned and ran, through the kitchen, through the diner, and out the door into the turbulent night.

His head spun and he lost his balance on the slippery asphalt, falling hard on his right knee. He pulled himself up and half-ran, half-staggered back to the truck. Pulled himself up into the cab and slammed the door shut. He sat breathing hard, rain hammering the windshield, sweat pouring from his brow, trying to digest what he'd just seen.

He grabbed the cell phone and dialed 911.

"911 service is not available in your area," came the automated voice. "Please hang up and call your local police department."

Warthog hit zero for the operator.

"Your call cannot be completed as dialed. Please check the number and dial again."

He tried twice more and got the same recording.

*Shit.* He grabbed the mic and switched the CB to channel 9, the emergency channel. "Emergency," he said, his voice shaking. "Emergency on Old Hutch."

There was a crackle, then a familiar voice. "Howdy, good neighbor. Y'all get on out to Chuck's Diner?"

"Buzzsaw, this is an emergency!"

"Emergency? Why, sounds like somebody found mah little surprise." Malicious laughter floated to him through the ethereal static. "Hope it wasn't too much of a shock for you, son. But ah figured, heck—You're used to haulin' meat, ain't ya'?"

Warthog heard a gasp escape his own mouth. For a moment, he sat in stunned silence.

He regained his wits and rapidly switched to channel 10. "Emergency! Emergency at—"

"Howdy, good neighbor," came the voice.

Warthog squinted with confusion and checked to make sure he'd actually changed channels. He had. He switched the dial again, randomly clicking to another channel.

"Emergen—"

"Howdy, good neighbor."

He switched to channel 12.

"Howdy, good neighbor."

To channel 4.

"Howdy, good neighbor."

To channel 21.

"Howdy, good neighbor."

*What the fuck?* His whole body shook as he stared at the CB radio. *It wasn't possible. He couldn't be on all the channels at the same time.*

"Now at this point, son, you got two options, way ah see it," said Buzzsaw through the static haze. "You can head on back up Old Hutch. Head west to where you saw that cruiser a few miles back. Might still be there. 'Course, I ain't sayin' it is. Not sayin' it ain't, either. Not sayin' nothin' one way or the other. But it might be, and you could take that chance. You surely could. Maybe that cruiser's still there. Maybe them troopers still alive. You could take that chance.

"'Course, that would mean drivin' back up Old Hutch, like ah said. And that there's a gamble right there. That's takin' you in the opposite direction you want to go. So that's a choice you got to make. Ah ain't makin' no choices for you, son. That's your choice.

"On the other hand, you could keep headin' east. Might be an entrance back onto I-80 in a few miles. 'Course, might not. Might be a weigh station up ahead, maybe just a mile or two. 'Course, I ain't sayin' there is. Not sayin' there ain't, neither. Not sayin' nothin' one way or the other. Just want to make sure you're thinkin' through all your options is all.

"So that's what you got to decide, son. You gonna head east or west? You gonna take a chance that—"

Warthog clicked off the CB. He sat in the darkness of the cab, listening to the rain, drenched to the bone and trying to control the violent shaking of his body.

*A map. A good old-fashioned goddamn map.* Before he'd gotten so dependent on his fucking useless GPS, he'd used maps. He clicked on the dingy dome light and began tearing through the contents of the glove compartment. A map of Texas. A map of Illinois. *Come on, damn it. There has to be a map of Iowa in here somewhere.*

*Iowa.* He pulled it from the jumble of other maps, papers, and fuel stop receipts. It was tattered and yellowed, thinned and tearing along the creases. He unfolded it as gingerly as he could with his trembling, wet hands. In the dim glow of the dome light, he squinted at the tiny text. His eyes had clearly worsened with age; he could barely believe he'd ever been able to read these damn things. He found I-80 and traced it with his finger, east across the state. Finally found where it intersected with I-235 and traced it north, looking for where he'd turned off.

Nothing.

He retraced the route with his finger. *It had to be here somewhere.* East on I-80 to 235. North on I-235 to Old Hutch. He squinted harder in the dull yellow light as fat drops of water dripped from his head onto the map, disintegrating the paper before his eyes.

There *was* no Old Hutchinson Highway. At least not on the map.

He peered out into the darkness. *East or west?* Back the way he'd come or forward towards God-knows-what? But Old Hutch couldn't be that long a stretch of road. If it were, it would *have* to be on the map. Wouldn't it? It certainly hadn't been constructed recently. It must have been here when the map was printed. And if the map didn't even show it, maybe it was tiny. Maybe he hadn't even been on it as long as he thought he had. Maybe his mind was playing tricks on him. Maybe I-80 was just a few clicks up ahead. Maybe . . .

*Can't stay here. Have to find help. A weigh station. Highway patrol. Something.* He started the truck and, feeling slightly reassured by the familiar roar of the engine, pulled back onto Old Hutch, heading east.

He'd been driving for only three or four minutes when he saw a light up ahead—a small, rundown gas station on the westbound side, barely illuminated by an old streetlamp. Set back behind the single gas pump was a small convenience store. As he slowed, he saw a light shining from the window and an elderly man behind a cash register. The man looked up as Warthog eased the semi into a wide left turn, cutting across the highway. As he rolled towards the station, he saw the old man emerge expectantly from the office, pulling a rain parka tightly around him.

All at once, the night was alive in a blizzard of flames. The ground shook as the gas pump ignited and a ball of fire shot skyward. Warthog slammed on the brake, then threw the semi into reverse as flames swallowed the convenience store. Fiery debris rained down.

The old man emerged through the wall of fire, a living torch, his clothes and hair and skin ablaze, a blood-curdling cry emanating from his lips. He staggered forward into the beams of the truck's headlights and Warthog watched in horror as the flames melted the skin from his body and the heat boiled his eyeballs in their sockets. The man hurled one final shriek of anguish and agony into the night, before collapsing into a smoldering pile of flesh and bone. He lay dead in the middle of the road like a raccoon squashed flat by an eighteen-wheeler.

Screaming and shaking with fear, Warthog threw the truck into gear and hit the accelerator.

"Howdy, good neighbor. Looks like your night's just full of surprises, don't it?"

Warthog stared at the CB radio. The cold red eye of the power indicator light stared back at him through the darkness of the cab.

*But I turned it off. I turned it off. I know I did.*

He clicked off the radio and turned his attention back to the road. The wind had picked up now, the rain flying straight at the windshield as he drove. He felt as if he was flying through an endless tunnel of raindrops that glittered in the headlights. The effect was like a kaleidoscope, dangerously mesmerizing. He shook his head, struggling against its hypnotic pull.

"Now that wasn't very neighborly, was it, son?" came the voice again. "You ain't gonna get rid of me that easy."

Warthog looked. Sure enough, the power light was back on.

"'Sides, ain't good to spend so much time alone. See, that's your problem, son. Too much time alone. Too much time on the road. Just like your old lady said. Spend that much time alone, your mind starts goin' places it shouldn't. That's what ah think. Ah surely do. Forget how to be a husband. Forget how to be a father. Heck, forget how to be a man. You know it's true, don'cha, son? You've thought the same damn thing. Sure you have. Ah know you have. Only natural. That's what ah think. Damn, you forget how to be a goddamn human being's what it is. Got to re-engage with the world, son. Re-engage with people. See, that's what ah do. I *re-engage* with people." The voice broke off into laughter. "What ah call *re-engaging*."

Warthog grabbed the microphone and took a deep breath, working up his courage. "Did you kill those people?"

"'Scuse me, son? Come back?"

"Did you kill those people?!"

"Back at the diner? Surely did, son. Surely did. Old man at the gas station, too."

A chill went through Warthog's body as the words sank in. "Why?!" he stammered.

"Just bored, s'pose. Ain't you? Ain't you bored, driving for miles and miles with nothin'? Thought ah'd provide us a little entertainment's all. Oh, don't have to thank me none. Got to admit though, son, you ain't bored no more. Ain't that right?" He chuckled. "Don't you go tellin' me you're bored now, boy. 'Cause ah do not believe that. Not one bit."

Warthog took another deep breath. "Where are you?" he demanded. "I haven't seen another truck all fucking night long. Where the fuck are you?!"

"Ah, well now that's a question, son, ain't it? That's a question. Ain't easy to answer, though. Wish I could tell ya. Ah'm here. Ah'm there. Ah'm a little bit everywhere, s'pose. Ah mean, when you're on the road, where are ya really? You know what ah'm sayin'? 'Nother trucker asks yer twenty and you tell 'em, 'Ah'm a-headin' east on this' or 'Ah'm a-headin' west on that' or whatever. But you ain't really there. Or least yer only there for a moment. Then yer gone. Then yer somewhere else. So I mean, where are you really? You get what ah'm sayin'?"

"Are you . . . following me?"

"Followin' you? Well, depends how you mean, son. Not so much followin' you. Not really." Another laugh. "But ah'll put it this way. Ah'm goin' everywhere you're goin'. Anywhere you go, that's where ah'll be."

*The cargo trailer. He's in the fucking cargo trailer. That's why I don't see his truck on the road. Son of a bitch has a CB hooked up back there and he's been talking to me from my own goddamn trailer the whole time. That must be it.*

Warthog slowed the semi and pulled over to the side of the road. Pulled a flashlight from the glove compartment and fished a tire iron out from under the driver's seat.

"What you getting' up to now, son? You be careful now, hear? Don't go doin' nothing stupid. Think you may have had enough surprises for one night."

He opened the door and jumped out. The wind and rain lashed at him furiously as walked to the back of the trailer. The beam from the flashlight sliced a narrow path through the darkness. Mud sloshed beneath his feet.

He placed the tire iron on the metal step at the back of the trailer and shoved the flashlight into his jacket pocket, beam pointing upward, in order to free his hands. Pulled himself up onto the slippery step, retrieved the tire iron and tucked it under his left arm, then pulled out the flashlight again. With the light in his left hand, he reached out with his right, heart racing, hand trembling. Slowly, as quietly as possible, he unlatched the trailer doors. Taking a deep breath, he pulled the right door open. A blast of cold air emanated from the refrigerated unit, turning his breath to mist in the night air. He shined the flashlight inside.

In the glare of the flashlight beam, he caught a glimpse of something shiny. Shiny and wet. He gasped.

Bodies. Like the meat locker at the diner. Like the cargo he'd unloaded back in LA, only these were human. Suspended from meat hooks, filling the cargo trailer. The remnants of tattered clothing still clinging to their flesh. An arm. A severed leg. A half torso, split down the middle. All wet and sticky with blood.

Warthog let out a cry and slammed the door shut. He lost his footing on the slippery metal step and fell hard to the ground. The tire iron landed somewhere nearby, lost forever in the darkness. The flashlight rolled a few feet away. He crawled through the mud and snatched it up.

*When had he done it? When had Buzzsaw put the bodies in the trailer? It must have been when Warthog was inside the diner. While he'd been finding the corpses in the meat locker, Buzzsaw had been loading more into the back of his truck.*

He scrambled to his feet and sloshed back to the cab. Pulled himself up and slammed the door shut.

"Warned you 'bout goin' back there, boy. Didn't ah warn you?"

Warthog grabbed the microphone. "WHO THE FUCK ARE YOU?"

"Told you that, son. Didn't ah tell you? See, locals say there's a ghost haunts Old Hutch. What the kids say, anyhow. They say some nights you can see—"

"Bullshit! Fuck you!"

Buzzsaw laughed. "Okay, boy, have it your way. But in future, you best be more discriminating where you buy your automotive 'lectronics, wouldn't cha say?"

*The CB radio.* He'd bought it years ago, secondhand. Friend of a friend. Someone in the junk business. Recovered from a highway accident, wasn't it? Had he ever heard any details of the accident? Had anyone been injured? Killed? He strained to remember.

Warthog began frantically yanking at the electrical wires to the radio.

"Whatcha doin' there, boy?"

One more strong yank and the wire pulled free. Warthog stared at the radio. The power indicator light stayed solid red.

"Now that wasn't very friendly, was it, son? I mean, really, that's what ah call downright rude."

Warthog popped open the glove compartment and began scrambling through its contents, tossing maps and papers every which way.

"That there's the problem with people these days, boy. Manners. Ain't nobody got no manners no more. Swear to God. It's a goddamn shame. Civilization going to hell in a handbasket 'cuz ain't nobody got no goddamn manners no more."

*It has to be in here somewhere.* Warthog reached into the bottom of the compartment and felt around. His fingertip hit something sharp. *Got it.* He pulled out a Phillips-head screwdriver.

"Whoa there, son. What'cha plannin' to do with that?"

He began furiously unscrewing the mounting bracket that secured the radio to the dashboard.

"Okay, okay. Let's calm down now, son. No need to do anything drastic."

One screw out. He savagely attacked the second one with the screwdriver.

"Ah wouldn't do that, son. Ah surely wouldn't. Son? Son? You hearin' me, son?"

Second screw out.

"Really, son, this is so uncalled for. Ah mean, ah ain't perfect. Ah admit that. Ah might have said some stuff. Might have done some stuff. But we can put all that behind us, son. We can start off on a new foot."

The Phillips-head slipped, jabbing the thumb of Warthog's left hand. He smarted for a moment, then pushed on ahead. Third screw out.

"Can't we talk about this, son? Son? Can't we?"

The last screw was stubborn, its threads worn. Warthog gritted his teeth and pushed hard. It finally gave.

"Aw, son . . ."

With a grunt, Warthog yanked the CB radio from the mounting bracket. He pushed open the door of the cab, tumbled out into the night, and strode to the front of the truck. Standing in the glare of the headlights, the rain pouring down, he lifted the radio high above his head. And then, triumphantly, threw it down. It smashed against the asphalt.

Back inside the cab, Warthog threw the tractor into gear and gunned the engine. He rolled forward just a few feet until the radio disappeared underneath the left front tire. There was a small, almost imperceptible crunch. Warthog threw the truck into reverse and backed up a few feet. The radio lay dead like an animal, its electronic guts scattered across the side of the road.

He burst into tears and crumpled in the driver's seat, his body shaking as he sat hunched over the steering wheel.

It was the changing sound of the rain that finally caused him to lift his head. The steady drumbeat on the windshield diminished to a sporadic tapping. Warthog looked up to find the rain had tapered off and the clouds had parted. Way off in the distance, a glint of sun peeked out from over the horizon. Up ahead, just a few yards away, a road sign he hadn't noticed in the darkness. He squinted to read it in the dim light of dawn.

*80 East. 2 Miles.*

A wave of relief washed through his body.

He started the engine and eased out onto the highway. His head seemed clear for the first time in hours, the cobwebs suddenly blown away. He rolled down the window and a cool breeze brushed across his face. Breathed deeply and all the tension in his body eased.

And maybe . . . Maybe it wasn't too late. Maybe she'd changed her mind. Maybe while she was packing up her bright summer dresses and her serious blouses and her little black cocktail dress. Maybe while she was taking her things from the bathroom—the toothbrush, and the lotions and the creams and the gels, and her pink silk panties that hung over the shower rod. Maybe she'd stopped. Maybe she'd stood there, holding them in her hands for a moment. And maybe she'd had second thoughts.

Maybe when she'd taken down the wedding photo—or the one with the family crowded around the birthday cake or the one from the trip to Puerto Vallarta with their arms around each other and the ocean behind them—maybe she'd stopped for a moment and looked at them, stopped for a moment and studied the faces. Maybe she'd been moved. Maybe something had shifted.

Maybe when she was packing the kids' toys—the stuffed animals and the doll with the fancy clothes from San Francisco and the catcher's mitt from Fenway—maybe she'd stopped and held them to her breast. Maybe she'd taken a deep breath. And maybe she'd felt something. *Something.*

And maybe it wasn't too late. And maybe it would be okay. Maybe.

And it was now 5:47 a.m. And it was 318 miles to Chicago.

*Just remember, darling, all the while, you belong to me*, sang Patsy Cline from the radio.

The cell phone rang. *Amanda Calling*, read the display.

*Thank God.* He breathed a sigh of relief and snatched up the phone from the passenger seat.

"Amanda? Sweetheart—"

"Howdy, good neighbor," came the familiar voice.

Every muscle in his body froze.

"Ah'm here with your lovely wife, Amanda," Buzzsaw continued. "And ah tell you, boy, she sure is a looker."

"You . . . You're . . . ?"

"Cute kids, too. Seems a damn shame leavin' them alone for so long. Alone and unprotected, you know what ah'm sayin'?"

"You lay a hand on any of them—" Warthog put the hammer down, pushing the semi to 80 mph.

"Amanda, she's quite the feisty one, ain't she? Don't do what she's told the first time. Got to show her who's boss. Thinkin' you might have just spoiled her some, boy."

"You son of a bitch. You goddamn—"

He pushed it to 90 mph.

"Them kids could use some discipline, too. Think maybe you been too soft on 'em, boy. Got to toughen 'em up some, what it is. Toughen 'em up. That's what ah think. Ah surely do."

"Don't you dare. Don't you fucking—"

100 mph.

"What ah'm wondering is, are any of them gonna call your name? When the time comes, ah mean. When the time comes, they gonna remember you? If the kids were in pain, say. If your wife . . . if Amanda . . . if she were havin' some . . . intense feelings of some sort. You know, the way ladies do sometimes. Ah'm wonderin' if she'll be callin' your name. I mean, I'm just wonderin' if they're even gonna remember who you are at the end. That's all ah'm sayin'. . . ."

"You fucker! You sick, twisted fuck! You fucking piece of sh—"

He was doing 110 when he hit Dead Man's Curve, a hairpin turn halfway up a ravine. Too late, he pulled his foot off the pedal and tried steering into the skid, wrenching the wheel to the right, eighteen tires screaming at the asphalt. He resisted the impulse to slam on the brakes, holding his breath and easing down as gently as he could to try to regain control. But the tires slipped on the wet pavement and the whole rig lurched sideways, the trailer pulling violently to the right. At the last possible moment, with no other option, he slammed down on the brake as hard as he could.

The semi slipped over the edge of the ravine, the wheels spinning, the trailer hurtling down on top of the cab. And the air filled with the shattering of glass and the crunch and grind of metal on metal.

*Ttschhhhhhhhhhhhh . . .*

"Dispatch, this is 82, over."

"Go ahead, 82."

"Got a ten-fifty, half mile west of the I-80 entrance. Semi down the ravine."

"Dead Man's Curve took another one, huh?"

"Looks like. Driver's dead."

"Other fatalities?"

"Nope, truck's empty. Based on the skid marks, sumbitch must have doing a hundred."

"Drugs?"

"Pulled a bottle of pills from the cab. Looks like speed."

"Hell, take enough of that shit, probably start thinking you can fly."

"Yup. Start seeing monkeys fly out your own asshole's what I hear."

"Okay, 82. Meat wagon's on its way."

"Roger that, dispatch."

*Ttschhhhhhhhhhhhhh . . .*

*Dedicated to the memory of Richard Matheson, 1926–2013*

**CRYSTAL M. ROMERO** grew up in the heartland of Northern California in Chico, Redding, and then Oroville. During her childhood, Crystal fell in love with the horror genre. After graduating high school, she relocated to the Silicon Valley and now calls the South Bay her home. In addition to two novels, *The Veil of Sorrow* and *Valley of the Dead*, Crystal had five stories published in the LGBT 2008 flash-fiction anthology *Chilling Tales of Terror and the Supernatural*. Crystal's short story "The Relic" was originally published in that anthology. Follow her on Twitter @Crstl_M_Romero or on Facebook: Crystal M. Romero.

# THE RELIC

## CRYSTAL M. ROMERO

**THE MURDER SCENE** was enough to challenge even the most hardcore cop. The rookie, who'd just started this week, couldn't handle the smell and left to empty his stomach on the front lawn. Angela Morales had to admit that in her ten years on the force, she had never seen anything like this.

The victim had been dead for only a day, not long enough for the neighbors to complain of the smell but long enough for his business contacts to notice him missing. Thankfully, the mail carrier noticed something awry; otherwise they might have come too late. Now, with the carnage still reasonably fresh, they could try to piece together the puzzle leading to this man's death.

Professor Harvey Stusman was a Dean of Anthropology and a well-known lecturer. If Angela had more downtime to watch television, she might have seen him in numerous archeological interview shows. Now all she saw was a stiff corpse lying in his own blood.

The professor had possibly been attacked by a wild animal, maybe a large cat. His torso was completely eviscerated, his neck ripped open, and what was left of his face was nearly unidentifiable. The amount of blood that slicked the hardwood floors and splattered the walls relayed the viciousness of the attack. Strangely, all of the windows and doors of his home were locked from the inside, and there was no evidence of a break-in. When the first team of investigators arrived on the scene, they'd set off the alarm in the house.

"Odd," Angela's partner muttered as he glanced around the room. "Damn odd."

Angela followed his gaze to a wall covered with hand-carved wooden masks. Some were Aztec, some Incan, while others were from tribes she was not familiar with. Glancing down at the lower shelves, she noticed the sleek, dark wood carving of a jaguar. As her eyes traveled over its form, she felt her heart rate rising. The palms of her hand suddenly grew moist as her breathing turned labored.

The artifact looked primitive in design, yet she couldn't help but marvel at its perfect form. It was the most realistic carving she had ever seen. The outline of the feline's muscles, the way it crouched, ready to pounce on its prey, sent an uncontrollable shiver down Angela's spine. Instinctively, she caressed the butt of her gun as her gaze remained glued to the wooden carving. Why did this simple object set off her alarms? Only when her partner cleared his voice did she turn to look at him.

"You don't think?" he stammered as he pointed down at the wooden jaguar.

Angela remained silent, fearful to say anything. Instead, she just looked at him.

"Nah, that's just crazy." A nervous laugh came from deep in his throat. "I'm turning into Mulder."

"Yeah, crazy," Angela echoed. "What say we let the CSIs do their job?"

"Good idea. It's your turn to buy the beer anyway." The gruff man smiled as he walked toward the door.

Angela turned one last time to look at the wooden jaguar on the bottom of the shelf. The commotion in the room seemed to freeze. In a blur, she saw its black fur bristling, sides heaving as it inhaled and exhaled. When she gazed at its face, she noticed the small pupils burned a fiery shade of red. She held her breath and fought to pull her gaze away.

"You ok?" her partner asked.

Shaken, Angela closed her eyes. When she looked again, everything was back to normal. She exhaled softly. "Yeah, everything's fine. I'm ready for that beer now."

As they walked to their unmarked car, Angela only half-listened to her partner's ramblings about his life, girlfriends, and the boredom of the job. Instead, her mind continued to see the image of the wooden jaguar suddenly coming to life. When she closed the door of the patrol car, she glanced back at the investigators moving through the crime scene. Somewhere off in the distance, she heard a single growl that turned into a roar of a big jaguar cat.

**G.O. CLARK** is the author of 13 books of poetry (the most recent is *The Comfort of Screams*) and two short story collections. The story "The Twins" was included in his most recent short story collection *Twists & Turns*, published in 2016 by Alban Lake Publishing. He's retired and lives in Davis, California. Check out his work at goclarkpoet.weebly.com.

# THE TWINS

## G.O. Clark

**JOHN FOUND THE** twins knee-deep in the pigpen muck, bent over his two prized pigs, gnawing on their little piggy brains. Shocked and disgusted, loaded shotgun in hand, John aimed true but just couldn't pull the trigger. Despicable and scary as they were, they were still just little kids: blond-haired, blue-eyed twins, a girl and a boy. The twisted semblance of what he and Martha had long prayed for.

He just couldn't blow them away, especially when they turned towards him with tear-filled eyes and helpless looks upon their blood-smeared faces. Just two scared kids unable to control themselves. Innocence lost, probably not by their own doing.

Shotgun still in hand, John coaxed them into the farmhouse, their hunger temporarily sated, to his very surprised wife of thirty years.

Later that night they all bonded. Petite dark-haired Martha sponged the blood off the eight-year-old twins. Lanky balding John tucked them into a double bed in the spare bedroom, the room always intended for John and Martha's future kids. A little paint, bunk beds, and bright shiny new toys would soon follow.

Martha couldn't bear children, and the adoption agency had failed them time and again. Now middle-aged, they'd all but given up. The zombie twins were a godsend, regardless of their dark proclivities. "God willing, we'll find a way to save them," Martha told her husband that first night.

Neither John nor Martha thought to inquire about the twins' parents or relatives or to inform the police. The TV news made no mention of missing children, twins or otherwise, so there seemed no point. And everyone knew what happened to zombies exposed to the authorities. The twins were definitely zombies. John had seen some movies about the walking dead and knew what to expect. He preferred ones like *Shaun of the Dead* to those trying to take themselves too seriously. As for Martha? She didn't care, her mothering instincts outweighing the obvious dangers and strangeness of the situation. Together they agreed to do all they could to save the little savages, to shower them with love and understanding, to try and raise them like normal kids.

John did fashion some ankle bracelets and chains as a precaution—for the kids' own good—to restrict their movements at night. They slept all day, the sleep of the dead. Martha got used to preparing steak tartare for the little darlings. Forget the vegetables, but like kids everywhere, they did have sweet tooths. Their regular diet became one of chocolate and bloody rare beef. At least early on.

Living out in the sticks, like John and Martha did, proved expedient. No one knew about the twins, nor ever came in contact with them. Martha homeschooled them the best she could—the three R's, Bible study, art in the form of finger-painting—and made all their clothes as well.

John taught the boy how to do some simple farm chores, ones that didn't involve the livestock. The twins were slow learners, to say the least, but did progress enough to perhaps fit into the lower echelons of society one day.

Both kids seemed uninterested in toys, though the little girl—named Emily after John's mother—did have a baby doll, whose rubber head she liked to chew on. Her twin brother, now called John Junior, loved to watch TV, especially football and the various permutations of CSI. Emily enjoyed the latter as well. Watching TV all night seemed to calm them both, distract them from what they would otherwise be doing: roaming the countryside in search of fresh brains. In the morning, once Emily and John Junior were sleeping peacefully, Martha would clean up the scattered candy bar wrappers and crawl into bed exhausted. She and John only saw each other in the evening. With chores to do early in the morning to keep the farm running, he slept at night and she slept all day, to be awake when her little zombies were. Parental supervision was a must in their household, to say the least.

After a while, it became obvious that Emily and John Junior needed more. The rare meat didn't always do the trick each night. Normal children throw fits. Zombie children take the screaming and yelling a step further: they attack each other. The first time it happened, on the night of a full moon, Martha nearly had a heart attack. She found Emily pinning John Junior to the living room carpet, *CSI NY* blaring from the TV, a mouthful of his curly blond hair clenched between her teeth. The look on Emily's face was like a rabid animal. Martha had screamed, which woke her husband. Together, with some effort, they pried the twins apart.

Later on, when the kids were asleep, John and Martha decided the twins needed more. It just couldn't be helped. Martha thought they were backsliding, but John convinced her that it was perfectly natural. The twins just following their *unnatural* instincts.

Come a full moon, John and Martha started taking the twins on road trips. Or more precisely, undead feeding frenzy trips. Like a typical American family, they all piled into the old SUV, the twins strapped tightly in, and off they roamed to some isolated ranch or farmhouse. Always to a different state each time, to help keep the law off their scent. Luckily, they lived in Missouri, near the Kansas border, with many choices surrounding them. The Texas Panhandle proved the most inviting: so much open space, so many loners.

Martha hated the road trips, always waiting in the SUV with the radio tuned to a country western station, while the slaughter took place. It was up to her husband to collect the blood-covered twins once the deed was done, hosing them down with the victim's garden hose before getting back into the SUV. Martha hated the whole routine but, like a typical vacationer, did collect postcards from each state they visited. John told her she was twisted for doing so, that the postcards were negative reminders of the evil they were sanctioning. She just ignored him. Of course, she never sent any postcards out, had no one to send them to, anyway. She'd collected a couple of shoeboxes full, messages and address sides left blank, by the time the twins hit their teens.

It should be noted that Emily and John Junior, identical twins, were not your stereotypical zombies. They didn't shuffle along. Like most kids their age, they were quick on their feet. They had much better hygienic habits, even brushing their teeth after a little parental prodding. And, though their bodies were stuck at the same age as when they died, their minds grew up. Puberty finally caught up with them. Traditional zombies they weren't.

John and Martha didn't question the supposed facts about zombies, nor bother to research the literature about zombies and their connection to voodoo. They pretty much put the whole zombie thing out of mind, too busy just trying to raise their two "special" kids.

High maintenance, unhealthy kids at best, but still just kids in their adoptive parents' eyes.

The daily routines of their strange life went on for years, until Emily and John Junior, like normal teens everywhere, rebelled.

It began one night when both kids refused to eat their dinner and were sent to their rooms—separate bedrooms since becoming young adults—where they figured out a way to break their bonds, and headed for the pigpen again, as if picking up where they'd left off years before. If it wasn't for Martha's feelings of guilt and subsequent visit to their bedrooms with a late-night snack, John's new prized pigs would have ended up like their predecessors.

When John confronted the twins, the tear-filled eyes of the past were now replaced by contempt and hatred. Shocked and saddened, John managed to get the kids back inside the house with the promise of another road trip, even though they'd only just returned from one a few days earlier.

The next day, John replaced their shackles with bars on their bedroom windows and padlocks on their doors. Soon the bloody road trips became more frequent, no longer limited to full moon nights.

With Emily and John Junior's raging hormones now in the driver's seat, John and Martha agreed something had to be done, but didn't know what. Their love and the increased road trips weren't going to be enough. The twins, though outwardly childlike, were hell-bent for adulthood: in their case, zombie adulthood, with all its mind-numbing, twisted, deadly connotations. They couldn't be set free, but keeping them under lock and key for the rest of their zombie lives was out of the question. Martha and John weren't exactly spring chickens anymore. The twins would obviously outlive them, so to speak.

The full moon bathed the surrounding landscape in ghostly light as John steered the SUV, headlights off, onto the dirt road leading up to a ramshackle ranch house. It was well past midnight, no lights on, no barking dogs, no sign of life at all. Someone lived there, though, as evidenced by the Dodge Hemi pickup parked in front.

John stopped the SUV a hundred yards down the dirt road and

killed the engine. It was just him and the twins this road trip. Martha had stayed home, sick with the flu. John turned around to look at the twins, but before he could say a word, they bolted out of the doors and sprinted towards the ranch house. Watching their small bodies disappear inside, John had the distinct feeling it was for the last time.

He thought he'd heard a scream after the twins entered the ranch house, but nothing since. He checked his watch and was a little surprised when he found more than an hour had passed. The twins never took that much time. In and out, hunger sated; hands, faces, clothes bloodstained.

Martha always brought Wet Wipes to help them clean up a bit before returning to the motel or home. John hadn't thought to bring any this trip, and the twins, since getting older, refused being hosed down.

Something wasn't right. They should have returned already, so he started the SUV and slowly drove up to the ranch house, lights still off, pulling to a stop beside the pickup truck. He waited a few minutes, but seeing no movement, finally got out and trudged toward the darkened ranch house.

The smell hit him as he stepped through the front door: the smell of death, of freshly spilled blood. The twins had definitely sated their hunger.

All was deathly quiet, so he pulled a Maglite from his coat pocket, switched it on, and panned it around what had to be the living room. Couch, chairs, TV, a few lamps and a coffee table littered with old magazines, beer bottles, and a cigarette butt-filled ashtray. But no bodies.

A darkened hallway led off to the right. John headed down it past a bathroom, a vacant bedroom, and then to the closed door at the hall's end. He stopped and listened at the door, then hearing nothing, opened it. The beam from his flashlight bathed a blood-spattered scene of horror. Walls, ceiling, furniture were all streaked with fresh blood. Crumpled at the foot of the bed lay the remains of a young man and woman, both naked, both with the tops of their heads chewed off. Bloody sheets partially covered their bodies, pulled off the bed during the struggle. The gruesome sight and smell getting to him, John started to gag. He backed out of the room and started calling the twins' names, but got no answer.

He quickly searched the rest of the ranch house, ending up in the kitchen, where a trail of bloody shoe prints led up to and out of the wide-open back door. He followed their trail outside, calling their names, shining the flashlight out into the warm Texas night, but they were long gone. The silent night had swallowed them up, like a couple of wild beasts slinking home after a hunt.

They were gone, and there was nothing he could do about it. For the first time since their initial encounter years before, he felt afraid of their little zombies. He hurried back to the safety of the SUV and the lonely drive home.

John and Martha settled back into their simple lives, back to the way it had been before the twins appeared. John routinely did the farm chores each morning. Martha cooked and cleaned and blankly watched *All My Children* every afternoon on their old TV. They both went to bed early, after the evening news and dinner. It had been over a year now, and there had been no reports of strange doings out in the Texas Panhandle. Not one zombie sighting. The twins had just plain disappeared, and John and Martha started to question their own memories.

Then one night the local news anchor snidely reported about some cattle mutilations in Northern Texas, ending his report with a doctored picture of a stereotypical big-eyed alien holding a fork and knife. John laughed out loud at the image, but deep down he knew the truth. The twins had survived and were up to their old zombie ways. Martha didn't see the humor in the newscast, though. With tears in her eyes, she retired to their bedroom.

The next day at breakfast, John glanced at his newspaper and Martha just stared at her breakfast plate. "Nothing in the paper about them aliens," John said, trying to lighten up the mood, but Martha just ignored him, staring at the cold scrambled eggs before her.

The TV news that evening, however, left them no choice but to talk about the twins. The mutilations were spreading, fanning out from their original locales on the Texas Panhandle, and were no longer limited to cattle. The bloodied corpses of ranchers and their families were starting to turn up, many with their brains missing. The authorities had declared a state of emergency in North Texas. Various federal agencies were getting involved.

"I never should have let them get away," John said. "Probably, with a bit of luck, I could have tracked them down that night and brought them back where they belong. I'm so sorry, Martha."

Martha was silent for a few moments, then said in a soft voice, "It wasn't your fault, John. We knew they would leave someday. I'm just sorry we couldn't break them of their evil ways first. I failed our poor little darlings."

"No, Dear." John put his arm around Martha and pulled her close. "You did all you could. We did all we could. It was kind of like taking in a wild animal, a bear, say, and trying to tame it. Eventually it follows its instincts and has to break free. Think of the twins as bear cubs who grew up and had to return to the wild."

Martha laughed at his rationalization. "They weren't exactly pets, you know. I've been thinking a lot about them. It was wrong for us to take them in at all. We should have turned them over to the police or some scientist or something. We were way in over our heads. It was all my fault. I wanted kids so bad, I'd do anything. Now look what I've wrought."

"What we have wrought," John said, sadness in his voice. "What's done is done. I just hope they're caught before any more suffering on anyone's part. God help us."

Martha put her head on John's shoulder and half watched the *CSI* episode on the TV. It was the Halloween-themed episode, with Vegas partygoers dressed appropriately as vampires, werewolves, and zombies. "All my fault," she thought. "All my fault."

In the weeks following, the news just kept getting worse and worse. The "zombie infestation," as it was now labeled by TV newscasters, was spreading exponentially. The whole Midwest was infected and martial law had been declared. Living out in the sticks, John and Martha didn't see much evidence of the latter—no troops patrolling the back roads—but they'd taken the necessary precautions beforehand. John had boarded up the windows and kept two loaded shotguns at the ready. Martha had stockpiled nonperishable foods before the National Guard troops rolled into town. They had a gas generator and plenty of spare fuel. They were prepared.

John had seen enough zombie movies to have a fair idea of what to expect. Martha never watched horror movies, though, and was putting her faith totally in her husband and God. To calm her nerves, she read the Bible and prayed for forgiveness. More and more she felt the "zombie infestation" was all her fault. Her blind acceptance of the twins had led to this horrible situation. John had given up trying to ease her guilt. Being the pragmatic one, he put most of his energy into survival. He'd seen the movies and knew how things could end. He was downright scared, but tried not to let Martha know how scared.

The reports on the TV kept getting worse. The "zombie infestation" spread like wildfire. Nowhere seemed safe anymore. John and Martha were just finishing up dinner—the last of the frozen chicken Martha had stocked up on—when John heard his prize pigs squealing loudly outside.

"I better go see what all the racket is about." John got up from the table. "Probably some more of those stray dogs, like last time."

"You be careful," Martha said, fear in her voice. "Take your gun, just in case. Could be worse than dogs."

"Haven't seen no zombies around here and it's been weeks now. Just stray dogs. Don't you worry."

John grabbed a flashlight from the kitchen counter and headed out the back door into the yellow glow from the porch light. It was pitch dark beyond the light's perimeter. He hurried down the steps towards the squealing pigs, switching on the flashlight as he went. When he got to the pigpen, he realized he'd forgotten to grab one of the loaded shotguns by the front door. "Damn," he thought. "Better be quick, just in case."

As soon as John shone his flashlight on the half-dozen pigs cowering in one corner of the muddy pen, they quit squealing. They looked just like deer caught in the headlights.

"What you all whining about, huh?" John asked in a calming voice. "Those dogs back again?"

The pigs just stared at the light, still as death. John swung the flashlight around, searching for signs of dogs or worse, but saw nothing. Whatever it was seemed to be gone. He walked the short distance to his barn and shone the flashlight first on one cow, then another, until he was satisfied all eight were okay. They seemed quite content. One eyed him as if angered by his sudden intrusion. John walked up and down the length of the barn, shining the light into the corners, but found nothing out of the ordinary. "Got to remember to fix the busted light out here," he thought, then headed back outside.

He could see the full moon just beginning to rise above the tree line. It was huge. On moonless nights, you could see the glow from the city lights thirty or so miles distant, but that was before the zombies arrived. Now the full moon was the only glow in the night sky.

John stopped by the pigpen one more time, but the pigs seemed just fine. He thought back to that night when he'd discovered Emily and John Junior knee-deep in the muck, attacking his prize pigs. He wondered to himself what he would do now if confronted with the same scenario. Shoot them on sight, or repeat the past and let them live? Things had definitely changed for the worse, and he was partially to blame, but even so . . . Of course, he realized there must be other zombies out there in the night, besides the twins. It was only logical. The army or someone will get things under control again, he thought. Or nature will right things. Just like in the movies.

John headed back to the house, switching off his flashlight. On the back-porch steps, he scanned the backyard one more time, listening intently until he was satisfied everything was okay.

The dinner plates were still on the kitchen table, but Martha wasn't there. He could hear the TV in the living room. The muffled voice of a newscaster droned on about something. John figured Martha was just too tired to clean up and had retired to the living room to rest.

John put the flashlight back on the counter, then gathered up the dinner dishes and put them into the sink to soak. He'd do them later, like most nights now, after checking up on his wife. He grabbed a beer from the refrigerator and popped the pull tab. After taking a few sips to calm his nerves, he opened the living room door to a scene of bloody chaos. Slumped in his leather recliner was Martha, her head thrown back, two male zombies feeding on her brain. Chunks of flesh and blood spattered their already filthy shirts. Martha's green eyes blankly stared at the ceiling. One of her legs twitched spasmodically. A blood-splattered bible lay open in her lap.

"My God!" screamed John. His beer can dropped to the floor. Then, spying the two shotguns leaning up against the wall by the front door, he started towards them. One of the zombies turned towards his scream, but didn't move, just staring blankly at him while still chewing on a piece of Martha's brain matter. John reached the guns in a few strides. Grabbing one, he spun around to blow the zombies to Hell. Before he could pull the trigger, the front door crashed open behind him, knocking him to the floor. The gun slipped from his grasp and slid across the floor. He rolled over quickly, but it was too late. Three male zombies attacked him where he lay, ripping at his shirt and sinking their foul brown teeth into his exposed chest, arms, and skull.

The last thing he heard, besides their snarling feeding frenzy, was his prize pigs squealing in pain. If he could have been out there, full moon bathing the pigpen, he would have seen little Emily and John Junior, feasting on pig brains, picking up where they had left off years before, totally oblivious to their once-familiar surroundings.

**CHAD SCHIMKE** is the author of "Behind the Walls," released via TANSTAAFL Press in their *Enter the Rebirth* anthology. He's also previously published "Picker," "Weirder," "Hallowseve" and "Midwinter": a quirky gaggle of grotesque, bizarre and unsettling tales for your reading pleasure. In addition, Chad has read at San Francisco's Lit Crawl, interviewed on a number of radio shows, was published by Artifice Comics, and founded the Alabama Street Writer's Group. He is currently working on a novel series tentatively entitled *Regenerates*. Check out Chad's blog at www.chadschimke.blogspot.com/ or catch him on Facebook at authorchadschimke or on Twitter at @chadschimke.

# VIVIFIED

## CHAD SCHIMKE

*Chad Schimke*

### Deadened

An urgent coyote's howl,
The lonesome hoot of an owl,
A rapid rushing brook,
Stop, glance back, and look.
Razor-sharp barbed wire,
She simply must climb higher.
To a hidden place, where
It's surely safe, for a hare.
She counted one, two, three.
Who's left? Only you and me.
Long, loud, man's machine.
A twisted, grisly, tangled scene.
Blood-stained crimson red,
Alive once, and now . . . dead.
To spurn, to quicken, to mend.
Cross the threshold to live again.

**CLIFF BRAUN DIDN'T** have time for mediocrity. He cracked his knuckles while waiting for his PC to boot up. The dial-up modem whistled while it connected to the ISP. When the spreadsheet Corporate had emailed him finally decided to open, he pressed the intercom button and spoke. "Can you send in the assistant manager?"

"Yes, sir, right away." The receptionist's voice sounded tinny on the little speaker, punctuated by an annoying short, shrill ring.

Cliff took a swig of coffee from the mug that read *Investment Properties* with the subtitle *A Great Company.* He corrected it to *A Great Fucking Company.* Less than a minute passed before the door opened.

"Good morning, Mr. Braun."

He checked out the assistant manager. Her bust almost burst forth from her conservative blue pinstripe suit, barely buttoned over a filmy white blouse.

"Cliff Braun, but please call me Cliff."

"Bianca Chastain. My pleasure to meet you at last. How can I help you?"

He'd read her personnel file at Corporate and already knew she was one of IP's best and brightest. She smiled and he thought she would be great in the sack. Maybe he'd swing by one day next week and ask her out for a drink. How in the hell could she say no?

He cleared his throat. "Samuels, Carruthers, Howard, Masterson, Tracy, Phillips."

"Sir?"

"I'd like you to go to HR and get a PAN prepared for each of them. I'll sign and you can take the paperwork to Accounting to get checks cut. I want you to hold a termination meeting with each of them before the office closes. Pay them overtime just in case you need to stay late. Got it?"

She paused a moment, her lips pursed. She looked defeated, like she needed to worry about her job, too. Corporate had kept a close eye on this branch for the last six months. She must've known he never needed to be here if things were going well.

"Yes, sir. I'll start and get right back to you."

"Thanks. Close the door on the way out."

As he watched her walk out, he thought, *there's no way in hell she's getting fired*. He picked up the phone and dialed.

"Hello?" *She* answered. He'd always thought she would do anything he wanted. Boy, was he ever wrong.

"It's me," he said.

Silence. The sound of breathing, but no words.

"I'm taking the train instead of driving. It's going to take me longer to get there."

A small gasp. "Shit, you scared me."

"Relax, will you?" he asked.

"Do you know how many times she asks each day if you're coming?"

"Well, I *am coming*. Okay?"

"I'll believe it when I see it," she said.

"Come on now—"

"Wouldn't be the first time you bailed. And don't forget to buy her a present."

Shit, he'd forgotten. "Of course, I'd never forget. I'll get there pretty late, but I'll get there."

"I'll leave the key in the usual place."

He hung up the phone. Before he left the office, he'd wash his hands, then head over to the train station. Maybe he'd run into Bianca in the hallway on his way out. He fluffed his wavy brown hair with his fingers. He tugged his dress shirt taut across his stomach. He wondered if the crow's feet at the corners of his eyes were noticeable. He hadn't slept well; he never slept well.

He'd miss his five-mile run later tonight, but only for one night. Whatever, he'd promised. It would've been nice to drive instead of taking the train. Damn his mechanic for not finding a way to get his car back on time. Excuses, always excuses. More BS.

Cliff walked to the reception desk to sign the stack of personnel action notices before leaving. On the way out, he passed a desk and read the name tag: *Mitch Samuels.*

Samuels sat slumped at his desk, brushing donut crumbs from his dress shirt. It seemed like he stared at the page forever, a fat, unmoving sloth. What a sad schmuck; Cliff wasn't anything like this loser. *Sorry, buddy, you're getting fired today.*

Cliff took the elevator to the lobby. Outside the building, the sun hit his face. The lively sidewalks were filled with young professionals hustling to their destinations. Shining edifices of steel and glass arched skyward, glinting in the sun. When the stoplight flashed, pedestrians swarmed in every direction.

He walked through the downtown business district. Rows of trees and planter boxes lined the sidewalks. Green shoots sprang forth from rich black earth. Spindly urban trees bore their first leaves. Birds wove nests to be filled with squirming pink fledglings, downing meals fed from their mother's beak.

Cliff would be sorry to miss tomorrow's weightlifting; he'd have to hit it twice as hard next week. The train station—but first he needed to pick up something. Was it on this block?

He turned right and spotted a hunter green awning: *DuBose's Toy Shop.* One display window was filled with dolls; the other was piled from top to bottom with toy trucks. Typical and boring. He swung the door open and a bell tinkled. He immediately had to dodge the children scrambling underfoot.

He didn't know where to begin in a place stuffed with wall-to-wall shit. The beleaguered lady behind the cash register appeared flustered, bravely facing a long line of impatient mothers.

Cliff felt hopeless. Just then a woman popped out from behind a glass case and said, "Can I help you?" Her flyaway hair distracted him and he noticed she had made a pen mark on her hunter green apron.

"Yes, please." Cliff felt a pang of relief. "I've got to get something for a little girl. She's six. What do you suggest?" Could it have really been five months since the last time he'd seen her?

"Hmm. Let me think," she said. "What does she like?"

"Um, stuffed animals, I guess." He hoped he was right.

She lowered her eyes and scanned the bookcase next to him. She snatched a slim book off the shelf, excited to show him the front image: a row of brown bunnies dressed in little outfits on a red background.

She smirked as she flipped it open to a picture of a brown bunny wearing a pink dress, holding an egg. She shoved it into his hands with an urgent look, seeking his approval. "Well? What do you think?"

He had no idea. "Do you mean the book, or what?"

"No, silly. You'll see, just give me a few minutes."

She snatched the book back. Uncertain if he should help, he watched as she scurried across the tiny toy shop.

"I do have a brown bunny!" She darted back to the doll section and stripped a dress off one. "Oh, this is adorable!" the woman exclaimed as she stuffed the bunny into the burnt orange dress. "I even have a scrap of blue gingham in the back. I'll cut a small triangle for the scarf." She picked up a plain wicker basket from the toy case next to him and set the bunny inside.

"Can you do all that?" he asked.

"I can do whatever I want. Are you worried about your budget?"

*Yeah, right.* "Oh, no, it just sounds elaborate. Which means she'll love it." He pointed to a table piled high with candy. "Pick out something from the table to go with it."

She put a white sugar Easter egg in his hand. "Look inside."

Cliff peeked through the hole in the egg. Inside was a tiny diorama with a brown bunny wearing a pink bow and, behind it, a three-dimensional scene with a sleigh and a lake. He guessed the egg had been made from candy bits, food coloring, and hard frosting. It was larger and more elaborate than other eggs he'd seen.

He turned it in his hand and looked at the outside. Tiny white and yellow flowers intertwined in a green garland circling the egg. A ring of frosting hid the seam of the two concave pieces and held it together.

"Sure, this is good. Thanks. Can you wrap everything up, including the book?"

"Of course. I think clear cellophane with a pink bow tied at the top would be best. Don't you?"

He walked from downtown to the train station, kicking himself for failing to rent a car. He absolutely despised this neighborhood. He stepped over a ripped trash bag, suspicious puddles, and unsightly mounds of butts where ashtrays had been emptied; he didn't want to mess up his new shoes. There was a car on blocks, then a bum camp with dirty blankets, worn cardboard, plastic bags and a shopping cart. A motorcycle ripped down the street with its high-pitched squeal echoing off the decaying factories. An overpass loomed ahead, where the freeway soared above him. Train tracks were visible in the distance.

He always thought the arched windows of the train depot were eye-catching. He walked through the bustling lobby. The waiting room's wooden benches reminded him of church pews when he was dragged to mass every Sunday as a kid.

He remembered staring at the enormous crucifix that hung above the altar and the anguish in Christ's face. How Christ's long-limbed arms had been outstretched, legs crossed at the ankles, hands and feet nailed to the hewn cross. His lips had been depicted peeled back, showing a hint of teeth. The icon had sparkled under a dazzling kaleidoscope of colored lights, temples indented where the crown of thorns pierced his soft flesh. A single trickle of blood had marred his chalky pink cheek, all rendered in matte paint.

Cliff heard something. When he looked up, he was standing at the ticket window.

"Sir, are you ready to make your ticket selection?" The brown-haired, bearded ticket agent wore the standard uniform. "If not, I'm going to have to ask you to step out of line."

"Huh?"

"Where are you going? I've already asked you three times." He sounded annoyed.

"Sorry." Cliff glanced behind himself at a crowd of angry faces. Where had these people come from? He turned back and smiled.

"Well?"

Cliff handed the agent his credit card. "Upland. I mean, yeah, Upland."

Ticket in hand, he emerged onto a platform between two smooth, polished stainless steel trains. Up the steps and down the aisle with its tattered carpeting trodden by a flock of riders. He sat down at the end of the passageway as the ticket taker exited the adjacent train car entrance.

He slid his bag under the seat and looked in the basket at the book, brown bunny, and candy egg. Yeah, she'd probably like this. Last time he drove out, they'd spent four days together: Thanksgiving, that Friday, and the weekend. His ex had said it would be okay because she wouldn't miss school. When they'd split up, she asked for sole custody and he hadn't put up a fight.

Upland should've been close enough, but the distance wasn't the problem. *Catherine* was. He had to admit he missed *her* more than ever. Hearing her talk earlier today brought everything back, like the last couple years hadn't happened. But yeah, that wasn't the case. He wondered why he hadn't objected more when Catherine filed for a divorce.

The ticket agent stopped at his seat. "Ticket, please."

"Here you go." Cliff offered the slip of paper to him.

He retreated into silence and the world seemed to slip away. No office workers with their coffee cups and messy stacks of papers. No crowded gyms full of men. No women wearing tight dresses packed into dark bars. No car, no fancy restaurants, no high-rise apartment. Just him on the way to see his kid. When he looked outside the train, the twilight drew him in.

The train eased into a rolling start. The ride was so smooth, he felt like he was gliding on air. As he watched, the vessel picked up speed and the landscape shot by outside.

A burst of static emitted from the speakers. "FastRack car number one-eighty-seven now leaving for Upland and all intermediate points. Please follow all posted safety instructions, including keeping luggage out of the aisles. Do not eat, smoke, or place your feet on the seats. Thank you." Another burst of static punctuated the announcement, replaced by silence.

The curved steel window frame reinforced his sense of separation: him on the inside and everything else on the outside. Office buildings gave way to houses, which gave way to industrial wastelands. Soon he saw nothing except open country, electrical poles, and blacktop roadways which seemed to swerve away from the raised railway bed.

Some time passed, maybe an hour, when the train slowed. An intermediate stop, he thought. The train paused at the station for a moment, allowing him to inspect the scene. The people, cars, houses, and horses reminded him of the doll houses he'd seen in the toy store.

The door swished open again and a mature woman in a gray suit eyed the empty car, selecting the seat across from him. She might think he was hot, because he was.

"Evening," she said.

"Likewise," Cliff said.

She didn't have any luggage except for a giant purse, which she flopped onto the seat next to her.

"I'm Maggie. Nice to meet you." Her eyes met his and she smiled.

"Cliff. Likewise." *Gawd, what now?*

"Where're you headed?"

"Upland," he said. "How 'bout you?"

"Me, too. I'd much rather take the train than drive. Time flies and, before I notice, it's over. Don't you think it's relaxing?"

"It's my first time taking the train. I usually drive, since I'm too busy at work."

"Ugh, work. I'm sure glad this day's over," Maggie said. "I tell you, some people are so grouchy. I'm a secretary. What do you do?"

"I'm an asset manager for IP."

"I bet you don't get much time off in a big company like IP, right?" she asked.

"Yes, you'd be right."

"Well, as hard as work is some days, it's a regular schedule. And I'm never late getting home to my kids."

"Good for you. I've got a kid, too."

"Oh, really?" Her eyes softened and another smile eked out. "So she doesn't live with you?" This smile was different, he imagined, taking her to a darker place.

"Nope. She lives with my ex. I'm headed there right now."

"Everyone I know is divorced, but I'm still hanging on with my husband twenty-five years later."

"I got married too young." *I wonder if she's going to talk the entire way?*

"Me, too. I had no idea what to expect, but I wouldn't change a thing. My kids mean everything to me."

"Mine's young, so there's still time." Hearing himself say those words, he knew he was lying. *Time runs out and time is money. Time is ruthless, for sure, and probably evil.*

Maggie dug into her purse and pulled out a wallet. She separated the clasp and took out a small packet of pictures in plastic sleeves. "See?" She passed the photo wad to him with a group photo on top: man, wife and three kids. "Here's my family."

"Nice," Cliff said. "I'd have wished for more time, but something always comes up. I wouldn't be where I'm at with IP, otherwise."

"So work is what takes time away from your daughter?" she asked.

"Yeah, work and distance."

"The court would have to let you share custody."

"The divorce got ugly, anyway."

"Sorry to hear you gave up."

"I've got to make hard decisions every day to keep making the company money, so I can get promoted."

"I hope you get to spend more time with your daughter. You should, you know."

"Sure, but there's time for that. Luckily, I've been given the gift of success. It's good for her to see that."

"No, I think you've got it all wrong. The greatest gift is your daughter. Money and looks aren't going to last."

He scoffed. "I've got the best job, I live in a great apartment, and drive a nice car. Who are you to tell me how to live?"

She smiled. "I'm sorry if I offended you. I guess I forgot I wasn't talking to one of my kids." She pointed to the basket on the seat next to him. "Is that for your daughter?"

"Yeah." He felt a little bugged, but whatever, she was entitled to an opinion. He'd happily change the subject. "What do you think?" She'd be a better judge of what a girl liked than him. He handed it over.

Pulling it closer, she cradled the basket in her lap and peered inside the clear cellophane. "What a nice gift! You have such good taste."

"Uh, yeah." It didn't bother him the saleslady picked it out, nor should it. "Thanks."

A job, a rented place, a car of note. He had intelligence and a way with people. *Am I selling myself short?*

Maggie smiled; she seemed to be enjoying examining the gift. "Ah, yes, a little brown bunny. Cute." She rotated the basket all the way round to examine the contents. "I love these sugar eggs."

"Do you think she'll like it?" he asked.

She set the basket down at her feet in the aisle. Just then the pocket doors swished open again and the ticket taker walked toward them. "Sir, would you please place your luggage in the overhead bin? You need to keep the aisle clear. Thank you."

The ticket taker left and the woman handed the basket back.

"She's going to love the Easter basket."

"I hope so. You're right, I've got no excuse to wait so long between visits."

"It'll end faster than you can even comprehend. She'll be a grown woman, and it will all be gone forever."

*A gleaming steel chassis sliced through the night, the way a ship slices through the sea, air whooshing behind instead of water. A slight downhill slope and the train sped up, wheels spooling down the decline over precisely honed rails.*

*Pebbles skittered nervously across hefty wood ties. Black night sky framed fields and pastures. But the conductor didn't know that a stalled eighteen-wheeler blocked the roadway up ahead. The train moved too fast. He didn't have time to react.*

*When the train collided with the truck, the sound repeated across the quiet countryside. Sparks burst from the point of impact, illuminating the outlines of the polished steel train and demolished big rig. Dust from the disturbed ground rose curling eddies.*

*For a single moment, the impact slowed down the slide. But momentum carried the wreckage forward, picking up speed as it went. The top-heavy train derailed and skidded on its side. Flames erupted and licked the sides of both wrecks, spewing noxious gasoline vapors. Grinding metal screamed shrilly as meadow creatures scurried to hide inside burrows. A brown momma bunny, baby tucked under her breast, hid in her warren. She couldn't understand what the commotion could be, but it scared her.*

Cliff heard an explosion and felt a sudden jolt. He was tossed into the wall. *Oomph.* He watched as the train cabin overhead caved in upon him. Windows popped out of their rubber gaskets and sprinkled broken glass throughout.

The metal roof twisted. Rows of seats buckled. He reached for Maggie, got a fleeting grasp at her dress, but gravity sucked her away. Too much force. Her body was flung to the front of the train.

He felt his bones crack and searing hot pain shot down his spine.

And then, suddenly, everything stopped.

He couldn't turn around because his neck hurt so badly; he was scared of passing out if he tried. Cliff knew he must be in the middle of the car, because he spotted a dozen twisted seats in front of him. In seconds the train had transformed from a safe seating area to a wrecked pile. The car lay on its side, the windows against the ground.

*Get out and do it now.* When he started to crawl, his knees and elbows ground into scattered glass. *Which way was up?* Maggie wasn't anywhere in sight. He collapsed again and heard soft sobs, but couldn't tell where they came from. Liquid drops, a burning smell like singed hair. A whoosh of orange, brilliantly lighting the night. *Fire, fire, fire.*

He dragged his belly across the rubbish toward a popped-out window. Shouts, sirens, and the ping of metal contracting were shuffled together into an indistinguishable morass. Cliff rolled onto his side.

A mangled body lay a short distance away, intertwined in bent metal. The leg bone had been snapped and a shard jutted out. He realized the pants were the same color as the ticket taker's uniform. A pool of blood gathered underneath.

Cliff's neck hurt like hell, but he forced himself to look away. *Can't be good to see that shit.* Realizing the sound of sirens meant help was coming, he crawled clear of the train, and collapsed.

## Apostasy

*A brown momma bunny scampered through the dark. Since she'd smelled a coyote at the entrance after returning from foraging in the field, she knew the old den wasn't safe anymore. Every so often, she paused to look backward. Her babies hopped along behind her, but slower than she would have liked. Hurry up, little ones.*

*She vaulted over rocks and dodged tangled roots. Humans cut deep furrows, scarring the earth with their ugly machines. Gravel, tar, and the flat place made by humans. Hot rubber and road kill. Crossing the flat expanse during the day burned her feet. The loud, stinking machine bowled down the lane, pulling wind behind it. Trembling, she made her way across after it passed.*

*She ducked under sharp wire that scratched her back. A hooting owl, a barking dog, a fence slamming shut. The wide open field felt like a dangerous trap. Down a slope, where it felt cool in the hollow. Her belly was dampened by crossing the gurgling crick.*

*She saw a flash of white in the gloom and came to an abrupt stop. The momma bunny glanced backward to look at her babies.*

*Two babies huddled behind her. What happened to the third? Closer, toward the sound of ripping flesh, and a little squeal. She flinched, nearly leaping straight up by reflex. Nearer now, she saw a cat tear at the neck of her little one.*

*The calico stopped ripping, sensing the momma bunny moving in the dark, and hissed loudly: a flash of bloody teeth and raised hackles, with a low growl. As the calico chewed a bite of tender flesh, a tuft of brown fur fluttered to the ground.*

*Feline and hare were evenly matched in size, but this murderer terrified her. The momma bunny thwacked her strong rear legs, sending the largest vibration she possibly could through the ground. She hopped sharply, to one side, and then the other.*

*The momma bunny could only watch as the calico sauntered off, carrying her baby: a cracked neck, limp spine, and back feet that dragged behind. She blinked back a tear and knew better than to follow. She still had the others to worry about.*

*When she returned, only one baby bunny remained. A sense of urgency overcame her. Hide, but where? To a little den, tucked under the mound of the embankment. Where the long machine that made deafening noises roared past. Quickly, hurry up before it comes.*

*The earth-shaking rattle scared off every other animal, but not her. She'd endure it and keep her baby safe in the one place where she'd be left alone.*

*The brown momma bunny nudged green grass blades aside with her nose. She barely squeezed through the small hole, carrying the baby by the scruff of the neck. She pushed her baby inside and used her body to block the entrance.*

*She licked her little baby's neck and nuzzled her. When the loud rattle and roaring began, her baby scratched her in a panic. There, there . . . don't be scared. There was nothing but danger out there and everyone wanted to get her. She cried for the lost babies, but didn't want to lose this one.*

*A boom hurt her ears, louder than anything she'd ever heard. She kept herself wedged tight at the opening. The ground shook so much, it terrified her that the den might collapse. But it didn't and the quiet returned.*

*A few humans' lights flicked on. Dogs barked in the distance. Night birds sang, soft trills at first, then as loud as possible, echoes crossing the meadow. They were warning each other, calling the way songbirds do.*

*In the crick, frogs croaked and crickets chirped. Woken by noise, humans were the last to rustle to attention. Peering over the top of their fences, they stared with disbelief, eyes filled with red-orange flames.*

A hospital bed in the center of the emergency room. A nurse performed chest compressions as blips of medical equipment resounded in the background. At the headboard, an intravenous drip flowed through a tube. A powerful light hung from a fixture above the body, flooding the room with brilliant luminescence.

"I'm making the incision!" The doctor took a pair of heavy shears and cut between ribs: meat and bone, cleanly sliced.

"Rib spreader! Hold the tube there, that's the wrong way." Hands everywhere, grasping, pulling, sopping. Blood, lots of it. The aromas of latex, copper, and a hint of bleach permeated the suite.

"Whatever you do, don't stop!" A charge nurse worked fast on the body, sweating under layers of latex and cloth. "No, not like that. Like this." He pointed with a gloved finger.

"Got it. I feel a pulse, he's got good cardiac activity." The RN turned the dial while holding the space open. Tubes uncoiled and tape spools unwound in well-practiced maneuvers.

"Get the clamp in there!"

Another nurse inserted a large shiny metal clamp in the chest cavity. Everything stopped momentarily as a heart monitor on a cart beeped.

"No, it's not working. We're losing him!"

The second hand of a mounted clock, high on the wall above the bed, clicked down, losing time in an ominous dirge.

Cliff found himself standing in darkness. He didn't move. The floor felt cold and hard under his bare feet. He checked out his surroundings but couldn't see anything.

"The train crash?" His voice, weakened: he was surprised he could even speak.

He felt walls with his hands and knew it was a hallway. It seemed to go on forever. Yet all the way down at the end, he saw a pinpoint of brightness.

He remembered everything: leaving the office, buying the gift, riding the train and . . . *the accident.* He started to walk towards the gleam of light. He walked a long time. Minutes? Hours? The light didn't seem to grow in size or brightness but remained consistent.

When it lengthened into a slit, he realized it emanated from under a door. He stopped short before almost bumping into it. The bright light blanked out any other features. He felt around for a knob or hinges.

The door burst open. *Whoa!* The black hallway fell away and he stood in a bustling emergency room. Cliff rubbed his eyes hard with his knuckles. He opened them again and studied the scene. Yes, he saw himself on the table.

A tall man dressed in a surgical gown worked at the table. A half-dozen people crowded around him, wearing the same color. Mint green: an operating room, with doctors, orderlies, nurses. Cliff realized he wore his torn and bloodied work clothes. He moved closer and noticed a cart parked near the head of the table. On a screen, a flashing green graph displayed vital signs as they dwindled.

"Doctor?" Cliff put his hand on the surgeon, but the doctor didn't react and kept working. Cliff looked at the face on the table— his own face, eyes taped shut, mouth hanging open, body scraped and bloodied. He should have felt something, seeing himself with his chest spread open with a clamp, but he didn't. Peace flooded him and he knew everything would be all right.

Even though the nurses were brushing up against him, they didn't sense him. *Am I a ghost or what?* Maybe he'd never be allowed to go back down that hallway.

A flash, and a jarring sensation like an explosion but, somehow, he hadn't been hurt. The floor gave and he found himself falling. As he hurtled down, he looked at his hands and feet.

He slowed and hovered, looking at the operating room from

underneath. A toy operating room, filled with dolls and imitation hospital equipment. Nothing more than model lights, fabric swatches, and interlocking plastic pieces, like those little plastic bricks kids play with. He drifted lazily down and settled on a smooth hard surface, swallowed up in total blackness.

A faint light emerged and intensified. A soft orange glow ultimately coalesced into a wall of flame. There was glass, charred wood, metal, and crushed stone. The crumpled train lay sideways at an awkward angle, piercing the tableau, its nose disappearing into a dark corner. White hot fuel started to lick the black floor, pushing him back. He scurried to his feet and ran. The fire and heat chased him, beating on his back. *Shit, I'm about to die again. Or maybe this is hell?*

From out of nowhere, a door flung open. He shot through to the other side—

### Enlivened

Cliff sat on a couch in a sunny living room. A smiling young woman walked in, holding a young baby. At first, he felt unsure and questioned this new reality. No, wait. He knew the woman was his daughter Lilith, as an adult.

He touched his cheek, then his hand slid down his neck. His skin felt dry, wrinkled, and loose. She extended the baby and he reached out, noticing his hands as he did so. Thin skin covered in spots. His belly bunched up under his blue sweater. He was old, even though a few moments earlier he'd fallen through the black void. Dead, and now alive? He didn't know.

"Hold her head," she said.

"I've got her," Cliff said. "You were this little once. I remember."

He recalled new things he hadn't allowed himself to think about. Dreams, which had once slipped into darkness, were newly illuminated. Her first bike ride. Her high school graduation. Her wedding. Things that had not happened yet, in his former past.

"Did you love me as much as I love her?"

"More," he said. And he meant it.

He gazed into his little granddaughter's face, ringed by uneven fuzz. She tucked into the crook of his arm, fists balled and pumping. When she smiled her toothless grin, her eyes met his.

Lilith sat down on the couch next to him and put her arm across his shoulder. She stroked the baby's head and cheeks. The infant's chubby legs were thrusting.

He looked across the room at the picture wall. His wife Catherine. Lilith and her husband. There he was, standing with them, not as a single person but attached. Cliff Braun, a family man.

His eyes followed further down, along the gallery wall. Lilith on her wedding day. She wore a plain white dress and held a white bouquet wrapped in ribbon. She'd gotten married in the same church where his parents took him as a kid. He recognized the pews and carving of Christ on the crucifix.

Underneath that photo were pictures of his and Catherine's parents. Funny how styles changed. Suits with skinny ties and beehives with cat-eye glasses. Youthful faces without sags and wrinkles captured at a moment in time.

His eyes fixed on his mom and dad's faces. They'd met in college and stayed together all their lives. He remembered how he'd thought he had to be successful because they'd given up so much for him. How they'd said that wasn't what mattered. What matters is family. Marriage, what it stood for then. And what it stood for now.

"Do you want to feed her?" Lilith asked.

"Sure."

"All right. I'll go warm the bottle up."

She went into the kitchen. He heard rustling at the stove in the other room. His granddaughter smiled at him and her eyes grew wide. Quiet. Boring, even. But he couldn't think of anywhere else he'd rather be.

Cliff's eyes opened with a great deal of effort. He was covered with a blanket, lying in a bed on scratchy sheets. He heard conversations and footsteps in the hallway. It took a moment to realize he was confined to a hospital bed.

Any movement meant searing pain, medication be damned. He gave the bandage on his arm a gentle touch, observing that his legs were also covered. He winced and didn't want to look underneath. *Not yet, I can't do it. Maybe later.*

He saw a tube connected to the back of his hand as he gripped the bedrail. Then a nurse holding a clipboard walked into the room.

"Mr. Braun?"

"Yeah," he croaked.

The young nurse wore her plain brown hair in a bun. A pen on a lanyard dangled from her neck as she scribbled in a folder.

"You're at Sisters of the Ascension. That was the worst train accident ever seen in this state. But you made it. You experienced clinical death, sir, but the doctor resuscitated you."

He nodded. "Woman? From the train . . . " The words scratched as they came out.

The nurse cocked her head to the side. "Another passenger?"

"Maggie?"

She smiled. "Maggie Dalen. She's in recovery, too. I'll let her know you asked, when she wakes up."

The nurse turned and walked out. Had Catherine checked on him? Nobody from work would. He knew his guy friends only from the gym or the bars. He'd never felt so alone. What about his clothes and luggage? He thought about Lilith. What if something happened to him?

He'd been so mad at Catherine during the divorce, but now? There was no anger left. *Somehow, I know she'll come.* He just wanted to see Lilith. Just as the thought crossed his mind, he saw Catherine.

She said, "Thank God you're okay!" She wore a dark brown pantsuit that flattered her trim figure, her wavy hair piled atop her head. He felt a pang. He'd missed her. "Are you able to talk?"

Before Cliff could respond, he felt something pulling on the bed. Even though his neck ached, he turned his head towards the movement.

"Daddy!" Lilith gripped the stainless steel bedrail, her round face peering over the edge of the bed. "Are you going to be all right? You were hurt." She inspected the bandages and the hospital equipment, soaking it in. "Oh, Daddy."

"They told us not to come right away." Catherine put her hands on Lilith's shoulders. "But Lilith was beside herself. I couldn't keep her at home."

"Are you okay?" Lilith's brown curls were tied back with a ribbon and she wore a blue dress over tights. "I'm so sorry you got hurt!"

Cliff mustered all his strength and forced open his lips. He forced out a tiny sound. "Lilith," he said.

"Daddy!" Lilith giggled. Before Catherine could react, she scampered onto the bed and lay down on her side, snuggling up to him. He winced in pain but didn't speak. "I'm not leaving until we can go together," she announced emphatically.

Catherine's expression seemed pained. What about her? Had she missed him, too? He wanted to believe she did. *Is she seeing anybody now?* On the phone, they only spoke about their daughter.

"Lilith . . . " Catherine's voice trailed off.

He remembered her corrections, her scolding, her being so anal about everything. Her mouth hung open for a moment. But he said nothing, fearful that he'd ruin the moment.

Catherine continued, "She was inconsolable when she found out."

Fights right before the divorce, during the time he struggled to finish his MBA. He had started working for Investment Properties: overnights in Central City, dinners and drinks with the guys, important coworkers. Why not accept the transfer? They drifted apart anyway. He'd never missed a child support payment. But so what? It wasn't about money.

Cliff gulped air and spoke. "Better this way," he said, his voice hoarse.

"Right, at least she knows you're getting better." Catherine appeared uncomfortable standing there. "I think it was the word *hospital*. She cried for hours. She only began to settle down on the car ride over here."

She had said *yes* the day he proposed. *Yes*, she said. She smiled, looking at Lilith.

"Hey, I'm gonna go to the lobby." Catherine began retreating toward the doorway. "I'm getting a cup of coffee. She'll be okay with you?"

"Yeah," he mumbled.

Catherine walked away, the sound of her clacking heels receding into the distance.

His kid slept, sucking her thumb. Her long eyelashes pressed against the apples of her cheeks. He couldn't believe he had *ever* left.

He remembered her birth, in this hospital, a room not unlike this one. Her little body, bright red and crying like a banshee. A tiny, precious gift. It wasn't different today; he'd just forgotten, that was all. Don't waste it this time. He glanced up as a man in a gray uniform entered the room.

"Cliff Braun?" The man held a large box with scrawling black permanent magic marker written on the side.

"Mm-hmm." He nodded, but his throat still burned.

"I'm from the railroad, sir." Cliff read the insignia on his shirt pocket and cap: *FastRack*, in brown lettering with a yellow shield. "We were told you were in the hospital. We located your luggage and I'm returning it to you."

The railroad had gone to a great effort to get it back to him.

"Can I ask you a question?"

"Yes?" The man set the box on the table next to his bed.

"What day's today?"

"Sunday. Today is Easter Sunday."

That's when Cliff realized: two days passed since the accident. He asked, "The basket?"

"It's here in the box," the uniformed man replied. He unfolded the top of the cardboard box and withdrew the cellophane-wrapped basket tied with a pink bow. It contained a book, a brown bunny, and a candy egg. He pulled out Cliff's overnight bag with his other hand. He paused for a moment, still grasping the basket handle while looking at Cliff.

"On the bed."

The man placed the basket there and set the bag on the floor. He left carrying the empty box, footsteps trailing down the corridor.

Cliff Braun stared intently at the basket that leaned against the footboard. It was turned so he could see the candy egg through the clear cellophane. He realized there were two brown bunnies inside the diorama: a larger bunny and a small one, wearing a pink bow. *Two of them*, resting atop a grass thatch with a sleigh and lake in the background.

Maybe it had been there before and he hadn't noticed?

Outside, sunny blue skies smiled overhead, as the valley of woodland animals bid farewell to winter, anxious for the return of spring.

**ANTHONY DEROUEN** has written three high-fantasy novels and is currently finishing the drafts on two supernatural horror screenplays. He turned one of the screenplays into a short called *The Last Showing*, which picked up a Silver Spotlight Award and was screened at the Halloween Horror Picture Show. In 2018 he founded the Death's Parade Film Festival, which is happening October 5th, 2019 in San Jose, California. You can learn more at deathparadefilmfest.com and anthonyderouen.blogspot.com.

Author's note: The story behind "The Patron" came from a family trip to Lake Tahoe. Idyllic in its pure white innocence, the vast snowpack covering the south lake basin lent itself to an all-too-real scenario where a vacationing family runs afoul of the weather.

# THE PATRON

## ANTHONY DEROUEN

**EDGAR WIPED THE** edge of the smooth mahogany bar top, then used the rag on his forehead. Despite the sub-freezing temperatures in South Lake Tahoe, the owner of Whiskey Rocks had worked himself into a lather. He glanced about the bar: the slick sandy surface on the shuffleboard was untouched, the pool tables were clean and bare, the music stage was quiet, and nary a quarter had slid into the jukebox since the snow began falling in earnest.

Edgar removed his apron, picked up a remote, and switched off the television. He'd opened the cash register and begun counting the bills when a gust of chilly air burst through the entrance. A Tahoe native of twenty years, Edgar was no stranger to cold, but still couldn't resist shaking when the ice-bitten air washed over him.

A man stomped his boots in the doorway, knocking clumps of white powder on the ground outside. He entered, promptly closing the door behind him. "Oh, it's so warm in here!" he exclaimed, removing a scarf and thick gloves. "Sorry about the air."

Edgar smiled. "Comes with the territory." He returned the bills to the register. "I don't envy you stepping out of that mess. My drive home is going to be hell."

The customer chuckled as he approached the counter, a whimsical look on his red face. "So this is Whiskey Rocks."

"The one and only," Edgar replied. "What can I start you with?"

The customer blew out a breath. He surveyed the impressive collection of bottles arrayed on the back shelf. "You know, I'm not much of a drinker anymore, really," he replied softly. "Can I have a Coke?"

Edgar reached for the soda gun. "Coming up." He filled a glass and handed it to the customer. "What's your name?"

"Malcolm. Yours?"

"Edgar." The bartender filled a glass for himself. "What's your plans for tonight?"

Malcolm coughed into a hand. "Here with the family. Wife and daughter are playing in the snow some distance out."

"Come again?" Edgar asked, his voice rising in pitch. "Did you say *playing in the snow*?"

"Yes, why?" Malcolm sipped his soda. "It's not too bad, considering . . . "

Edgar jabbed a finger at the door. "Considering it's five below and your wife and kid are out there!" He sighed and composed himself. "Sorry. It's not my place. Sometimes I see tourists come out here in shorts and sandals in the dead of winter. I can't imagine what's going through their heads."

Malcolm smiled. "No worries. We're fine. Got into a pickle earlier, but we're preparing to leave. I wanted to visit Whiskey Rocks before I left. My favorite bands used to play here." Malcolm spun his stool around to face the vast, empty bar. He gestured towards the framed pictures on the wall, all the various musical artists. "So many names. Gosh, I missed them all."

Edgar raised an eyebrow. "Not all of them. Roosters in the Henhouse perform every Thursday night, and Crazy Bread on Fridays. And the summer can get crazy."

Malcolm turned back. "Yeah." He dug into his pants pocket, removed his wallet, and fished out a bent photo. He handed it to Edgar. "My wife Haley and daughter Jasmine."

Edgar nodded approvingly. "Good-looking family. You must be proud." He returned the photo to Malcolm, who placed it on the counter. Edgar turned to the alcohol shelf and removed a photo. He gave it to Malcolm. "My troop."

"Look at those kids!"

For the next hour, Edgar and Malcolm discussed family, music, and the weather. As time wore on, Edgar noticed Malcolm grew more tired and little paler. Business was slow that night, very slow. In fact no one came in while Malcolm gushed about his garage rock days, or standing outside Warehouse Music for hours, waiting for the latest Ozzy Osbourne release. Edgar took a liking to the gentleman, despite his cavalier attitude to the inclement weather.

Malcolm lifted his shirt to display a tattoo. "Van Halen, Diver Down Tour."

Edgar winced at the sight of white and yellow discolorations on Malcolm's skin. "That doesn't look so good. Are you all right?"

Malcolm considered. "I'm all right."

A group of guys dressed in snowboarding gear entered the bar, laughing and clapping each other on the backs. They made a beeline for the pool tables.

"Hey, Edgar!" one greeted.

"Round of the usual!" another shouted.

Edgar nodded and waved.

As Malcolm finished his soda and stood up, the pegs of his stool screeched like a banshee. "I enjoyed our talk, Edgar. I wish I made the effort to visit sooner."

Edgar laughed. "Open Monday through Friday, my friend. Monday through Friday. I'll be here."

Malcolm smiled slightly, said, "Cheers, then," and turned for the door. The snowboarders didn't seem to notice Malcolm go by. The family man opened the door, let off a shiver, and left.

Edgar picked up Malcolm's empty glass to wash it, then noticed his family photo still on the bar counter. "Shit!" Edgar spat as he threw open the flip door, snatched the picture, and rushed outside.

The cold wind slammed into Edgar like a freight truck. His breaths were punctuated by billowing white clouds. He clutched his arms to his chest, instantly regretting his decision to forgo his jacket in an effort to reach Malcolm faster. Through the failing light, he searched for the customer. "Hey, Malcolm!" Edgar shouted.

No answer and no sight of him.

Edgar scanned the sidewalk leading from the bar in both directions. He looked across the street and couldn't spot any movement. He glanced at the open area encircling the back of the tavern and saw prints leading away in the snow.

Glancing back at the tavern, Edgar cursed at his stupidity for stepping outside in nothing but his long sleeve shirt, then approached the wooden barrier sealing off the woods. Boot prints were clearly visible. He followed the prints over the barrier and into the snow.

In the summer, the clearing served as a park for visitors unable to get into the densely packed Lake Tahoe shoreline retreats, which usually hit capacity by noon. Edgar of course benefited from this spillover. He even took it a step further by making Whiskey Rocks more family-friendly with the inclusion of a full-bodied lunch and dinner menu, more tables and chairs, and arcade games for the kids. Visitors like Malcolm were common; dads wandered into the tavern for a couple brews while the wife and kids frolicked among the sparse pines.

Edgar spotted two more sets of footprints joining Malcolm's: smaller prints, lighter against the surface, presumably the wife and daughter. The three tracks proceeded deeper into the clearing. Edgar removed his phone from his pocket and enabled the flashlight. He scanned the snow.

After a short distance into the trees, the tracks disappeared.

"I tried," Edgar muttered, before turning back towards the tavern.

Edgar resumed his post behind the bar. One of the snowboarders approached the counter. "Forget about us?"

"I have not, Slick," Edgar responded, dishing out a number of beers. "Previous customer left something valuable behind."

"Who?"

Edgar blinked. "The guy at the counter when you fellas walked in."

The snowboarder frowned. "Guess I missed him."

Edgar looked at the snowboarder intently. "Guess you did."

The snowboarder grabbed the drinks and returned to his friends.

Edgar regarded the photo of his mystery customer, then placed it into the register drawer.

The following morning ushered in a welcome reprieve from the crushing wind and snowfall. Edgar slept in. He pulled into the Whiskey Rocks parking lot after four p.m. A thick layer of snow had frozen over across the parking lot, creating a slippery ice blanket. Two police cruisers were parked nearest the entrance.

"What is this?" Edgar muttered. He exited his vehicle and headed for the tavern, his boots crunching the ice beneath him.

The mood inside the tavern was somber. The jukebox played a ponderous melody from Crosby, Stills & Nash. Heads hung low, shoulders slumped. Conversations were hushed whispers. From across the room, Jeffery nodded at Edgar and resumed pouring a drink.

Two officers sat at the counter. Edgar recognized them both. "What's the news, Sheriff?"

Sheriff Marks sat hunched over a half-finished draught. Her cheeks were burned from prolonged exposure; her pulled-back hair a mess. Her deputy Donald—a thin, reedy man in glasses—didn't appear in any better shape. Sheriff Marks said, "We found the family."

Edgar lifted his eyebrows. "What family?"

Donald said, "The family that went missing."

Edgar looked at the officers, puzzled. "I'm not following."

Sheriff Marks said, "A family went missing out by Lake Baron. Got caught in something real nasty. We found a tent and camping gear."

Edgar's jaw hung open. "God Almighty. I didn't know—"

"Nobody knew," Officer Donald interjected. "Hell, nobody could even get out there until today. Bodies were frozen stiff and black. A woman walking her dog found hands and legs sticking out of the snow like branches."

The hairs on Edgar's arms stood up as the blood drained from his face.

Sheriff Marks caught the sudden change in the bar owner's demeanor. "Are you okay, Ed?"

Edgar blinked. "Sure, why?"

"You look like you've seen a ghost."

**JOHN CLAUDE SMITH** has published two collections (*The Dark Is Light Enough for Me* and *Autumn in the Abyss*), four chapbooks (*Dandelions, Vox Terrae, The Anti-Everything,* and *The Wrath of Concrete and Steel*), and two novels (the Bram Stoker Award finalist *Riding the Centipede* and *The Wilderness Within*). *Occasional Beasts: Tales,* his third collection, has just been published and includes fourteen tales of weird horror. He splits his time between the East Bay of Northern California, across from San Francisco, and Rome, Italy, where his heart resides always. Check out the *Wilderness Within* blog at thewildernesswithinbyjohnclaudesmith.blogspot.com.

# MY TRUE NAME

## JOHN CLAUDE SMITH

TRIGGERBOY SNIFFED THE air and circled around me, bouncing to and fro like a happy puppy. "It's time. It's gettin' close."

I cringed, but I felt it rise in me.

In my head.

The sun hung like a ripe peach, dead center of the sky. I rubbed the back of my burnt neck and continued toward the dilapidated diner, which seemed as beat down by the heat as I felt. The two cars parked in front of the diner had license plates from other states.

This was not a destination, just a break from driving, the heat, or to fill one's belly with grease and whatever came with said grease.

I was sure there was a victim to be had.

We approached a green Honda as a couple opened their doors to exit. The mother went to open the back door but hesitated as we neared.

"Can I help you?" the father said.

"What is . . . ?" A battle raged within me, between my conscience—wanting it to stop—and the uncontrollable need. My conscience always lost the battle, as if it ever really had a chance.

Something squirmed in my skull, something of hideous intent, a loathsome prescience. The piranhas who lived there were chewing through my brain.

I gathered my composure. It had to be played out. "What is your name, sir?" I asked, my face twisting from him.

"Excuse me?"

The inherent goodness of human nature is a weakness. The father looked toward his wife, then approached me. He stuck out his hand to shake mine. "My name is Sam. Sam Wenders. How can I help you?"

"Tell him. You gots to tell him what your name is." TriggerBoy was jittery with anticipation. "*Tell him!*"

I stared past the father to the car and the little red-haired girl playing with a headless doll, seeming none the worse for the absence. Her mother stood pensively next to the open door.

I whispered to myself, "No," but the piranhas only grew more agitated at my vacillation. As I reached for his hand—synapses sparking, setting fire to the nerves at the tips of my fingers—I said, "My name is Bill. Bill DeathDaughter." I gripped his hand tighter and asked, "What is your *true* name, sir?"

His eyes went blank. Then the soiled epiphany of what was about to happen hit him hard and he said, through clenched teeth, "My name is Sam. S-Sam DeadGirlsFather . . . " Then, struggling past his lips, the plea: "Please . . . no . . . "

Tears made his eyes glossy but did not wash away his dread, his desperation. I only saw this peripherally, as I stared at his daughter, this beautiful little girl . . . Her skin started to bubble. She started to melt as an ice cream cone would on hot pavement. The clipped scream from her lips was matched by her mother's scream. Her mother's scream continued long after the few seconds it took to turn their daughter into a puddle of steaming viscera. A stain on the backseat, never to be removed. A stain on their minds, never to be forgotten.

The mother scrambled at the backseat and cried, "Jessica! Jessica!" over and over, her fingers slick with the moist remains of her dead daughter. The father crumbled to the ground in front of me, vomiting and shaking uncontrollably.

TriggerBoy was on the car like a fly on shit. He immersed himself in their misery, drooling and giggling as his eyes seemed to merrily bathe in the sticky grotesquerie that was their daughter. The mother made more sounds indicative of the pain provoked by this most unimaginable exhibition, while being mortified that this monster had expressed such joy over her loss.

"Goddamn, I likes to watch them go funny. I likes to hear the sounds they make, mewlin' like squished kitties."

"Shut up, TriggerBoy," I said as I released the father's hand. The father still wrenched everything he could from within his shattered body.

The shock too much for her to deal with, the mother's brain shut down at that point, her sanity on hiatus. Her mouth hung slack, silent now, her despair complete. The pupils of her eyes were dilated, vacant.

TriggerBoy rambled on.

I screamed at him, "Shut up! I don't want any of this. I want it to stop."

Wielding his perverse influence much as a spoiled child would, he said, "But you can't help it, can you? You can't help what you is, right, Bill De—"

I shot him a look that silenced even his impish cajoling.

We left the couple to their grieving. Over the next hour they would forget about us, as if we had never existed in their lives, while they would still have to deal with the grim, inexplicable death of their daughter. The stain would remind them of that much.

It would make no sense.

It would never make sense.

TriggerBoy and me, we were like wraiths, phantoms. I was like the Grim Reaper, but I only took one specific human . . . as the name would indicate. It's not as if I had a choice. I woke up one morning and this was who I was. This is what I am: Bill DeathDaughter. Not my given name, but the only one that matters. My true name.

The piranhas in my head let me know this all the time.

I've lived twenty-three years since the morning that I'd awakened with the knowledge. I tried isolating myself, so my cursed power was never exploited. I went amongst people as rarely as possible. Graveyard shift as a janitor helped, but even then, the piranhas scraped their razor-sharp teeth against my thoughts, wanting to dig in, to feast: wanting the freedom that could only truly culminate when the killing phase was in motion. I only know this now, with experience. Then, it was a suspicion I somberly kept at bay. Solitude was the only guarantee that it would never lead to into anything more than a grim nightmare swimming through my brain. I could never imagine how it would culminate in the real world.

Then I met TriggerBoy. "Just TriggerBoy," he said. That was all I needed to know. Our meeting was like striking a match.

What the piranhas made me need, and what I wanted, were polar opposites. TriggerBoy's presence and wayward antics—a form of telepathic prodding, stirring the gray matter waters, bringing the piranhas to a frenzied state—brought it all together. I hated him, but one cannot change destiny.

While I had a conscience, he had none. He had nothing. I sensed within him a black hole, a bottomless pit of nothingness. A void so prevalent I was amazed he could even function as a human being but, then again, it was not as a human being that he functioned.

More like a parasite.

He needed what the piranhas could do and, since they resided in my skull, it was simple as that. I could not control myself with him pulling the strings. It was a symbiotic union, driven by the parasite: TriggerBoy.

We had killed many times. We didn't physically touch any of those poor girls, but we had killed them all, nonetheless.

We wandered through the empty plains of the Midwest, along dirt roads, past rest stops and the landmarks of desolation: solitary diners, ragtag gas stations, and decrepit, uninviting hotels. I tried to limit the range of my power by making the situations in which it was useful as few as possible. TriggerBoy hated this—he wanted us to move to a big city—but then again, it also made the instances when it was brought to fruition more *invigorating* for him.

I can't say I really understood what TriggerBoy got out of it. He just seemed sadistic, cruel. I did what I did because of the need, driven by the voracious piranhas, and because it was what I did, what I was made to do: the role I was meant to play. That's all.

You try living with the piranhas in *your* head. You try living with this knowledge, with knowing *your* true name . . .

Afterwards, the anguish would wash over me, but not for long. It was not my fault, this power. I'd blame God, but I don't believe in Him. Not anymore.

Between the insistence of the piranhas and the times we were alone, I dealt with it as best I could. But it always came back to what TriggerBoy demanded, in his own narrow-minded way. Then his telepathic malice would sink in, and the piranhas would gyrate in anticipation.

I wanted it to stop, but this want was relegated to the backseat or trunk of desires one feels, so I reluctantly carried on.

Weeks later, a few victims later, we were walking as we always did along the back roads, when TriggerBoy stopped and sniffed. He turned to me, not as enthusiastically as usual, but said, "I think we gots another one."

I had known TriggerBoy for five years and countless deaths. I had never seen him flicker like this when the next victim was in range. Something in me quivered. I looked to the sky, searching, wondering . . . Hoping?

Only one car was parked at the rest stop. It was an old Pontiac station wagon, dark blue, big.

"The next one is here, I knows it," TriggerBoy said, but again it lacked conviction.

Four people sat in the car: the parents in the front seats, two children in the back seat. Two girls. Daughters . . .

TriggerBoy was not his usual jubilant self, but it seemed to me that the need had kicked into overdrive. The piranhas were famished in ways I'd never sensed before. Their determination throbbed in my skull. It was as if their need was eating me from the inside, hungry, so hungry or . . . trying to escape?

The driver's side door opened. The father stepped out. TriggerBoy's face crinkled. Something was amiss, but he could not figure out what that "something" was.

The father walked toward me and stuck out his hand. I eagerly extended mine. It felt as if my fingers would devour his once we touched.

I did not even pause for the question to be asked. I just stated, "My name is Bill DeathDaughter," and then he took my hand in his. I felt it surge through me like diseased electricity, as if my bones were made of something brittle and his presence would make them break. I felt the nothingness, similar to what I had gauged within TriggerBoy, only this nothingness was more concentrated, of a purpose, and also more vast: wiry, reaching, ready, and anxious. Cataclysmic. Apocalyptic.

"Of course it is," he said and turned to TriggerBoy.

TriggerBoy whimpered a wordless utterance so foreign from his regular, caterwauling asides that it shook me to my soul.

The pain in my head was immeasurable. It filled my body, every iota of me: my blood raged, my lungs shriveled, my breath burned. I felt like a sun about to go supernova. Sweat steamed from my pores.

But something else, something more *crucial* was in motion.

"You will pay the price for being so selfish, Son," the father said to TriggerBoy.

The rear doors to the car opened and the two girls jumped out, running to their father. The mother smiled from her passenger seat.

"If you would have understood the big picture, you could have been a part of this, Son. But you never listened and so we will have to go on with our mission without you." He turned and smiled at me, then turned again to TriggerBoy. "Say goodbye to your brother, girls."

TriggerBoy started to melt, as all of our victims had melted. It was swift and decisive and devastating in its destructive beauty. The two girls danced around him as he melted, their melodious nonsensical singing drowning out any noises that emitted from his collapsed throat. The girls seemed oblivious to the horror before them. Seconds passed and he was a boiling, amorphous mass; seconds later, he was only a stinking, liquified blemish on the asphalt.

Their song lingered on the dry, pungent air.

I was at a loss, somehow hopeful and repulsed that this would be my fate. Then the father let go of my hand and I wobbled and fell to the ground, defeated, and still alive.

I was drenched, cooling, trembling.

The father hunched down and spoke more at me than to me: "Without my son, you will not have to suffer with what you are." He said this as if disgusted by me, no sympathy garnered for my alleged suffering. "You were blessed, but now you are inconsequential. But because you were blessed, I will leave you to live for a little while more."

It was done. Without TriggerBoy, I would not be driven to kill the unknown daughters of the people destined to cross my path. For the first time in what seemed forever, the piranhas not only seemed sated, they seemed . . . gone.

But how could the father look at my former condition as something blessed?

As he stood up and started to walk away, I said, "I . . . I don't understand. Blessed?"

He stopped, turned to me, and smiled. "My son never understood the magnitude of what he was a part of. As you never understood, but I don't blame you as much. You were only a minor player in the whole scope of things. *He* should have known better."

"What are you talking about?"

He stared into the sky, into a sun that should have blinded him. "It calls to us, the God of the Void, the black sun that spawned the primal chaos—a spasm, a fluctuation that scarred the perfection It had always known. It burns for perfection again. It will incinerate everything in order to bring order to Its mistake, in order to attain Its quest."

When he pulled his eyes from the sun, they were coal black and radiated a menace that crawled through me, inside, teasing me, taunting me.

"You were not worthy of the gift. You did not understand how to truly manifest Its wonder. But I do." He pointed to the car as the two girls got in. The mother still wore a smile. "We all do. We four, as well as the others who understand and crave the perfection that the God of the Void promises. We will soon congregate in Its shadow and help It attain the perfection that is Its birthright, Bill."

Then it dawned on me to ask the question that always needed to be asked. "What is your name, sir? What is your *true* name, sir?"

"Roger. Roger WorldDestroyer."

He tilted his head, the menace clawing at my brain, searing my eyes, and I was shown the absolute, soul-eviscerating blackness that was to come: The God of the Void. I gasped, the shock, *the truth*— unbearable. Tears flowed, washing away the vision, but as with all the fathers whose hope I had annihilated, it did not wash away the dread.

I looked to the sky—searching, wondering—but hope was not a part of the equation for me anymore, either. The sun was swiftly setting—too fast it seemed, but of a purpose, I feared—and there was no guarantee that it would ever rise again.

The God of the Void would make certain of that . . . soon.

**DANA FREDSTI** is the author of the *Ashley Parker* series, the *Spawn of Lilith* series, and co-author of the *Time Shards* series. When she originally wrote "You'll Never Be Lunch in This Town Again," Melanie Griffith was still hot in Hollywood and cell phones had yet to become smart.

# YOU'LL NEVER BE LUNCH IN THIS TOWN AGAIN

## DANA FREDSTI

**FIRST-TIME DIRECTOR** Darren Zuber was having a hard enough time shooting his film *before* the dead started coming back to life and eating the living.

Mara Dubray, his leading lady and a well-known star of daytime soaps, was proof positive that most actors' IQs and egos were inversely proportional. Known more for her enormous bosom rather than any real acting talent, Mara was not about to let some first-time director tell *her* how to deliver lines. Her tantrums had already run the film well over budget and the words "completion bond company" had been bandied about more than once by Gerald Fife, the executive producer.

Never mind that it had been Fife's brilliant idea to cast a mediocre soap star as Lady Genevieve, a noblewoman in love with a priest (played by Derrick Stone, a minor name whose entire range consisted of stoically wooden) in the midst of a plague-stricken 14th-century Europe.

As vehemently as he dared, Darren had fought this casting—certainly the most ludicrous decision since Verhoeven cast Melanie Griffith as Elizabeth I ("I have the mind of a king and a bod made for sin"). But with only a music video directing credit under his belt, Darren had to swallow both pride and common sense on a great many crucial details, such as casting and rewrites. It was the only way to get his film made, a project he'd dreamed of doing since his first years at UCLA. And it was only the success of *Game of Thrones* that had convinced Plateau Productions, headed by Fife, to invest the money.

Plateau was known for low-budget rip-offs of big box office pictures, as well as micro-budget exploitation films in every genre. If you rented a Plateau picture, you could always count on four things: bad scripts, worse acting, one or two minor "name" actors for foreign draw, and at least one scene set in a strip club.

Explanations to Fife that 14th-century Europeans did not have strip clubs were useless. To Fife, if a film didn't have topless dancers, it wasn't a film. "You gotta have tits and ass, kid," Fife had said during one of their many rewrite sessions. "And I don't give a shit what century we're talking here; you can't tell me that the men didn't want to see naked girls after a hard day plowing in the field, even if they hadn't invented boob jobs yet." Darren had given in, figuring he could come up with some sort of scene in a tavern with bawdy serving maids and a band of roving minstrels for the music.

But the process was certainly a far cry from the idealism of film school and all of those vows Darren and his fellow students had made. *They* would never sell out to the commercialism of Hollywood. Their movies would be pure: art for art's sake. No stars (unless it was an older name, like Maureen O'Hara or a Seventies sitcom star. Both had a certain cachet that appealed to the idealistic— and pretentious—students in the UCLA film program), no more than one explosion per film, and *no* scripts by Roland Emmerich.

Darren wondered how many film school grads had their idealism kicked out of them by the steel-toed boots of companies like Plateau. He supposed he should be grateful to have won the battle against a rock'n'roll soundtrack. As he stared balefully at Mara while she finished butchering yet another speech, Darren found it hard to be grateful about anything.

The scene would have to be done again to get the master shot, and then there would be countless takes on key phrases, close-ups, reaction shots from the crowd of peasants as Lady Genevieve tried to convince them not to flee their village, and—

Shit! Was one of the extras wearing sunglasses?

Why the hell hadn't the extra coordinator or the wardrobe mistress caught that? And how had *he* missed it? And how could that asshat of an extra be so . . . so *brain*-dead? Several scenes would now have to be reshot, adding more to the already inflated budget.

Darren groaned and rubbed his head, trying to convince the nagging ache behind one eye that it did *not* want to become a migraine. Melissa, his assistant, silently handed him two Excedrin Migraine and an unopened can of soda. Darren mouthed a silent "thanks" and popped the top, washing down the pills with a mouthful of sickly-sweet orange-flavored carbonation.

"Jeez, this stuff is crap." Darren handed the can back to Melissa. "Can't those PAs get anything but this shit?"

Melissa shrugged. "Budget'll only cover generic. Besides, the whole dead thing back east is really playing havoc with shipments."

"Jesus." Darren turned to his first AD. "John, call lunch. We'll take this scene again after that. And tell Zack to make sure none of the extras are wearing fucking sunglasses! Or watches, or any other jewelry, for Crissake! These are 14th-century peasants! And tell Linda I want more yellow on their teeth! They didn't *have* Crest in the 14th century! Jesus!"

Darren stomped off without waiting for an answer, unable to control his temper. He didn't like losing it in front of people. He had promised himself he wasn't going to be one of those abusive directors, famous for their on-set tantrums. But he hadn't bargained for the reality of low-budget Hollywood.

At least Darren could trust John to handle the situation. Thank God for John, a fellow student from UCLA and one of the few people Darren could really count on. His producer, Phil, was another friend from film school. The three of them had shared many a late-night pizza while watching The Definitive Movie Masterpieces as defined by their film prof, analyzing them to a degree that would have both amazed and amused the original filmmakers.

John still retained some of the purity of vision they'd once all shared, albeit tempered with an increasingly world-weary attitude now reflected by his newly tinted glasses. Phil, however, had not only happily tossed idealism out the window; he'd also thrown out imagination, courage, and loyalty. He made up for these gaps in his character by extra brown-nosing and sleaziness.

Even now, instead of showing any interest in the increasingly disastrous proceedings, Phil was off in a corner schmoozing some buxom peasant girl; one wearing a pair of decidedly non-period earrings and far too much self-applied cosmetics, despite strict instructions from the makeup department.

Darren went off in search of something stronger than Excedrin.

The following day brought a whole slew of unpleasant surprises, including the news that Joe Pilate (one of the few actors Darren had actually cast himself) had been eaten the day before. Phil delivered the unpleasant news via telephone before Darren had a chance to sip his morning espresso.

"Eaten? What the hell do you mean, 'he was eaten'?"

"Had his guts ripped right out," Phil confirmed with ghoulish relish. "Joe was visiting his father's grave in Philly and a couple of deadheads had him for lunch."

"Jesus, that's sick." Darren was dismayed that even while he mourned the death of a friend, his mind was already going over possible replacements for the devoured actor.

"That's the East Coast for you," Phil said. "By the way, Fife is really on my ass about the budget. Are there any more scenes we can cut?"

Darren swore. It would already take an editing genius to make a coherent story out of the amputated bits left from his original script. Not for the first time, he suspected Fife had a sympathetic ear in Phil.

"Forget it," he growled. "Any more cuts and we're going to have a 14th-century music video."

"Hey, we could get a rock band and have them do a title song," Phil said enthusiastically. "Call it *Plague Years* or something!"

Darren closed his eyes. "I'm going to pretend I didn't hear that. Bottom line, no more cuts." He paused, finding his next words sticking in his throat. "And find me a replacement for Joe ASAP. We'll shift his scenes to Thursday. I'll have Melissa call the actors and let 'em know we're doing the love scene today."

Hanging up before Phil could argue, Darren sadly reflected that he'd just given Joe an extremely shoddy obituary.

As soon as he arrived on set, Darren was told by Melissa that Mara was refusing to do the love scene with Derrick unless provided with a bottle of Cristal to relax her.

Phil, who had joined the pair as they walked towards the craft service table, snorted in derision. "Relax her? If she'd lay off the coke or whatever other crap she's been taking, she'd relax just fine."

"I don't know." Melissa shrugged fatalistically, something she'd been doing a lot the past few days. "She says the whole dead coming back to life thing is really stressing her out."

"Oh, that's a load of crap," Phil snarled, grabbing a bagel and slathering it with cream cheese. "This is Hollywood, not

Philadelphia."

Darren headed straight for the Excedrin.

"I don't know." Melissa shrugged again, pouring herself a cup of coffee. "They're saying it's spreading."

"'They?' Who are 'they,' Mara? That's total bullshit." Phil bit viciously into his bagel. "She just wants to get loaded on good champagne on our dime."

"I guess," Melissa said doubtfully. "So what should I tell her?"

Darren sighed, deciding he'd better step in. "Get some Totts or spumante and don't let her see the bottle. I doubt she'll know the difference. She only knows about Cristal because she's watched *Showgirls* at least twenty times."

Later, as he tried to coax some genuine emotion out of his two leads, Darren reflected that if the walking dead problem *did* spread out west, no one would be able to tell the difference between the zombies and his actors anyway, so who'd give a shit?

The next day, both the media and the general uproar in the city confirmed that, like practically everyone else in the country, the dead had indeed migrated to the West Coast. Traffic was abysmal; it took Darren two hours to drive from Culver City to the studio in Burbank. He wasn't sure, but he thought several of the scruffy street people he passed on the way looked . . . well . . . *dead.*

At the studio, for the first time Darren could remember, the large electronic iron gates were shut. A heavily armed security guard screened each new arrival very carefully before letting them in. Another guard, also packing what looked to be a heavy-caliber weapon, kept vigilant watch each time the gates opened and closed.

Melissa greeted Darren with the news that several crew members—two production assistants and a grip—were missing. They hadn't called in; they were just . . . missing. "And we're short extras, too," Melissa added. "Central Casting called and said a bunch of their people are afraid to drive anywhere."

John walked up, radio in hand. "I figure we'll have to do tighter shots to get the kind of crowd effect you want with the plague victims."

Darren set his mouth in a determined line. "Let's just do it."

He stalked towards the day's first set: the interior of a church where several hundred plague victims, both dead and dying, were gathered to seek salvation. About 75 extras, gruesomely made up to look like they were in the final throes of the Black Death, were sitting in the aisles and rough-hewn wooden pews, nervously discussing the more current plague of ravenous corpses. Crew members looked equally distracted. Very few were actually doing their jobs.

Darren thought they'd have to do some fast talking to keep people on the film, so he called a meeting with John and Phil.

"So what do you think?" he said after outlining his concerns.

"I just don't know, Darren," Phil replied. "I mean, you've got people scared to leave their homes. Businesses are shutting down. I mean, *Starbucks* was closed this morning." He stared at both Darren and John in turn. "*Star*bucks."

"Do what you can," Darren said, trying not to imagine a world without readily available coffee. "Offer bonus pay, whatever it takes."

"*Bonus* pay?" Phil sounded outraged. "Are you nuts? Do you know what Fife will say if I do that?"

"Don't tell him!" Darren slammed his hand against a chair in frustration. "Jesus, Phil, there's got to be something we can do!"

Phil was quiet, a sign that his mind was working furiously. After a moment of reflection, he smiled broadly. "I've got it!" He lowered his voice. "We'll *offer* the bonus pay. But we don't have to actually *pay* them the extra money."

John nodded thoughtfully.

Darren, on the other hand, was horrified, both at the idea and John's calm reaction to it. "Jesus, Phil, that's totally unethical! These people are working their asses off!"

"Yeah, and we're paying them. There aren't any clauses in their contracts for a zombie plague."

"Look, Phil, they have every reason to demand more money if they're risking their lives to be here."

John nodded. "He's got a point, Phil. You know how much stuntmen get paid."

Phil brought his face close to Darren's. "Do you want to finish this film or not?"

John nodded again. "He's got a point, Darren."

Thousands of objections whirled around in Darren's mind, but all he could come up with was a feeble, "But we could get sued!"

Phil shrugged. "Yeah, maybe. But with all this other shit going down, who's gonna have time to deal with it?"

John shook his head doubtfully. "SAG isn't going to let a little thing like zombies stop them from fucking with the production if we screw their actors over, you know that. And the Teamsters . . . "

The three men shook their heads, differences momentarily forgotten as they contemplated the eternal enemy of the low-budget filmmaker: the unions.

Taking advantage of the moment of camaraderie, Phil rested his hand on Darren's shoulder. "Let's get this film finished, buddy. This is what we worked for in film school, right? So we'll do whatever we have to do."

Darren felt a tiny piece of his soul die as he heard himself reply, "You got it."

The offer of hazard pay got about two-thirds of the cast and crew on set the following day. Darren had sympathy for the absentees. The commute to the studio had been even worse than the previous day. He'd definitely seen people—both living and dead—with large chunks missing from various limbs, all staggering around the streets. The kind of stuff nightmares were made of.

On the other hand, it was a definite solution to the homeless problem.

Darren's main concern was the number of armed soldiers and national guardsmen now patrolling the city. Certain broadcasts on radio and TV said the government was planning to impose a 24-hour curfew on the streets. That would make it impossible to get to and from the studio. Darren had brought an overnight bag, just in case, and had called to tell Phil and Melissa to do the same.

Melissa had been charged with the duty of calling as many other crew and cast members as she could reach and suggest they plan on staying over, too. "People aren't going to want to leave their families," Melissa pointed out.

"They can bring their families with them," Darren replied immediately.

Darren was gratified to see some people actually did bring their families—and pets—with them to the studio. When Phil pointed out this would compensate for the shortage of extras, Darren agreed, thinking it would keep their minds off the horrors outside of the studio walls.

Today was a key scene. Lady Genevieve accidentally reveals her love for the handsome priest in front of the townspeople when she seeks him out in the church so he can read the Last Rites over her dying father.

The scene was shot several times before lunch, Mara doing an abysmal job of conveying any real emotion. Whether she was trying to show fear, love, hate, or indifference, Mara just looked as though she had a bad case of gas.

"I can't concentrate!" she wailed when Darren didn't bother to hide his impatience with her lack of talent. "There are *dead* people outside!"

"Well, they're not *inside*," Darren shot back coldly. "And they aren't paying your salary." He turned away, dismissing her before he said something he really regretted. "Now people, we're going to break for lunch and then try this again. The caterer did show up, didn't he?"

When Mara didn't return to set after lunch, Darren assumed she was throwing a tantrum because he hadn't treated her with respect she didn't deserve. Everyone else was in place, waiting for the camera to roll. Derrick, playing the handsome young priest, stood patiently at the pulpit, muttering lines that would all come out sounding heroically wooden.

Patience worn paper-thin, Darren stalked towards Mara's trailer, determined to drag her out by her hair if need be.

"Damn it, I hate actors," he muttered, rapping sharply on the trailer door with a closed fist. When no response was forthcoming, Darren threw manners to the wind and flung the door open hard enough to send it smacking into the wall.

"Mara, get your ass out here! I swear, I'm going to make sure you never work in this town again if you don't stop this shit!" Aware that he'd just made an empty threat, Darren took the stairs in one long stride and stuck his head around the corner. "Mara, I mean it. I—"

Darren stopped short, confronted by the sight of Mara's prone body, still in 14th-century garb, lying on the trailer floor, one hand clutching a hypodermic, the other splayed lifelessly to one side.

"Oh, shit." Darren knelt by his erstwhile leading lady's corpse, taking a quick check on her pulse to see if he might just be wrong. Nope, absolutely nothing. Mara was dead.

Darren waited for the rush of grief one was supposed feel at the death of someone . . . well, not close, but certainly someone he'd worked closely with for several weeks. He was dismayed to discover that amongst his mixed emotions, the strongest was overwhelming annoyance. A new, darker side of Darren reflected that on any other occasion Mara's death might even be a cause for celebration. But now Mara was once again holding up his film.

Darren sat back on his heels.

"Oh, you dumb bitch. How the hell am I going to shoot around you?"

Darren walked slowly back to set, leaving Mara's corpse to be disposed of after he'd figured out how to salvage the film. Body double, using close-ups from previously shot footage? Might just work, although it would be tricky.

Darren joined John, Phil, and Melissa by the camera. Correctly reading his expression, Melissa asked, "Trouble?"

"What?" Phil frowned. "She won't come back to set? I'll handle it." Phil strode towards Mara's trailer, obviously confident his powers of persuasion were more than ample for the job at hand.

Darren stopped him with a hand on one shoulder. "She can't come back on set, Phil. She's dead. Mara OD'd."

All three stared at him blankly. Finally Phil shook his head. "Jesus. Fife just isn't going to be happy about this." His voice took on an accusatory tone as he continued, "She was a *big* part of the deal! You know that, Darren!"

Darren's response was forestalled by the appearance of Derrick, their male lead. "Are we going to get going soon, Darren?" The actor wiped sweat from his stoically handsome forehead. "Goddamn lights are melting the makeup off my face and that *always* makes my skin break out."

Darren considered several replies, discarding each one before it made its way from his brain to his mouth. He supposed he'd have to tell people that Mara Dubray was no longer among the living, but—

"Oh, shit."

The actor stared at him. "It's okay, Darren. I'll just see my dermatologist. It shouldn't affect filming or anything."

But Darren wasn't paying attention to Derrick. He was too busy staring over his shoulder as Mara Dubray staggered and swayed her way towards them, an expression of intense longing stamped on her face. Her mouth was open slightly, a moan of desire ululating from it. A copious stream of drool ran down one side of her chin.

"I thought you said she was dead," Phil hissed in a stage whisper.

Darren noted the slightly bluish tint to Mara's skin. "She is dead." He didn't bother to lower his voice.

Everyone on set had stopped what they were doing and were now staring at Mara's awkward yet determined progress towards the small group of people by the camera.

As the implications of Darren's comment hit home, Melissa, Phil and John scattered. The clueless Derrick stayed where he was. Darren was too busy watching Mara in fascination to do more than step to one side, leaving the path wide open towards the actor. Mara's attention focused specifically on her screen lover. She lurched towards him with outstretched arms, fingers opening and closing spasmodically. Before anyone could react, she threw her arms around Derrick with passionate intensity and took a distinctly unlover-like bite out of his well-muscled shoulder.

Chaos ensued as several hefty grips pried a snarling Mara off the screaming actor. Darren turned to Phil, his face alight with enthusiasm.

"Shit! Did you see that?" he exclaimed. "That's the best acting she's done since we've started. Let's get that on film!"

Darren sat in the screening room, watching dailies with Phil, a contented smile on his face. For the first time since filming began, he was actually happy with the way Mara played a scene. Granted, some fancy editing would have to be done to replace the look of abject terror on Derrick's face with a look of tormented longing, but that could be done. Come to think of it, it was the most expressive Derrick had ever been as well.

It had taken some doing to restore enough order on set to continue filming. Convincing Derrick to play the scenes had been the hardest part, but an appeal to the actor's vanity, the promise of more money, and the two big grips standing by to prevent a repeat of Mara's first attack had worked wonders. "Besides," Phil had pointed out, "It's not *that* big of a bite." And luckily one of the people who'd made it to the studio that day was the on-set medic.

Darren managed to console his own outraged conscience with this last fact.

The rest of the cast and crew had responded with amazing equanimity. Darren suspected part of that had to do with needing the work to keep their minds off of what might be happening outside the studio. This thought also made Darren feel better as he watched the dailies.

He made the mistake of mentioning it to Phil, who replied, "Whatever. Just so long as they keep working."

Darren stared at his erstwhile friend in disbelief. "How the hell can you be so callous?"

"Oh, get off your high horse," Phil retorted. "You've got the best fucking acting you've had since we started, so don't get all moralistic on me. A filmmaker's gotta do what a filmmaker's gotta do. It's the art that matters." Phil gestured towards the screen. "I mean, just look at that. It's beautiful!"

Darren looked. It *was* beautiful, damn it. Except for that one moment when Mara's attention turned from Derrick to one of the extras who'd gotten a little too close . . . Darren winced at the memory.

He turned to Phil. "We'll have to remember to keep the other actors far enough away to keep Mara's focus on Derrick. It distracts from the intensity of her emotions. And we had a few close calls today that I don't want to repeat."

"Yeah," Phil agreed. "We can't afford to lose any more of our extras. Those crowd scenes look pretty sparse as it is."

"I know," Darren sighed. "But we're not likely to get anyone else from outside, so we'll just have to make do with what we've got, add in CGI later."

Phil shook his head. "The only CGI we can afford on our budget will look like crap. Maybe . . . " He paused and suddenly his eyes brightened. "Oh, man," he said slowly. "Have I got an idea!"

At first Darren had been totally appalled by Phil's brainstorm, delivering an unequivocal "No!" in response. How could Phil even *think* of it? Didn't he understand the moral implications?

"What moral implications?" Phil was genuinely confused by the question. "These people are *dead*, Darren. They're not going to care. Most of them probably wanted to be actors anyway, so you'd be doing them a favor."

Darren's outrage sputtered a bit, then flared up again when he thought of new objections. "What about the danger? I mean, catching them in the first place. Who the hell is going to agree to do that?"

"Production assistants," Phil replied calmly. "Tony'd do anything for this film. He'll probably think it's fun. Besides, with the equipment I've got in mind, it shouldn't be a problem."

"But what about the danger to the cast and crew?" Darren demanded. "How the hell are we going to handle that?"

"Have the set design folks come up with something to keep 'em separate from the others during the scenes. We can use handcuffs, hide 'em under the costumes, and . . . "

As Phil proceeded to counter all of Darren's objections with arguments that at least *sounded* reasonable, Darren allowed himself to be persuaded it really would be a *good* idea to use some of the newly ambulatory dead to supplement the crowd scenes. Somewhere in the back of his mind, a little voice told him he was making a compromise even more Faustian than his deal with Gerald Fife. But the dailies in front of him and Phil's persuasiveness were better than a pair of earplugs. And once committed to the idea, Darren put his considerable energy into implementing it.

Even without the steady stream of media reports—and CNN was over the moon to have something this big to report without the need to supplement it with brain candy—Darren had only to look outside the studio gates to see the situation was definitely worsening. There were more walking dead roaming around the area, lots of cars driving frantically up and down the surface streets, general chaos. Only one of the security guards remained at his post, steadfastly ignoring his erstwhile partner who was now banging on the gates from the outside, a large chunk of flesh missing from the side of his neck.

Darren approached the remaining guard. "You still letting people in and out of here?"

The guard nodded. "As long as they show their badges."

"Great." Something else occurred to Darren. "Any more guns here?"

"We have a few in the Security office."

"Do you think—"

The guard shook his head. "No way. That's against the law."

Using his most persuasive tone, Darren said, "C'mon—" He looked at the guard's nametag. "C'mon, Arthur. I've got to send some people out on a run and they need protection."

"I don't know . . . "

Darren played his trump card. "Y'know, I could use you in this film, Arthur. I've lost a couple of my co-stars because of these damn zombies."

The guard tossed Darren a key. "Just don't tell anyone where you got it. It'd be my ass."

Darren walked off to find the security office, thankful that everyone in this town really *did* want to be an actor.

Melissa listened carefully and jotted down notes as Darren gave her the list of items he wanted one of the production assistants to pick up on what might be their only run outside the studio. When he was finished, he had her read the list back to him. Phil stood to one side, nodding.

"Okay. Dry ice, lots of it. Any food he can find. The thickest sports padding available. Heavy-duty steel collars. Leather will do, but steel preferable. Chain leashes—" Melissa stopped and looked at both Darren and Phil. "Are you sure about this?"

Phil nodded. "Ought to be a piece of cake."

"Hmm," Melissa said doubtfully. "Okay. John's rifles, plus ammo . . . We're gonna need his house key and directions." She jotted down another notation. "Okay, I think that's just about it."

The on-set medic strode up, her forehead creased with lines of worry. "Are you sending someone outside?"

Darren nodded.

"Good. I need some antibiotics as soon as possible. Derrick isn't looking too good. That bite is festering. It looks like the infection is spreading rapidly beyond the wound."

Melissa made another notation on her list.

A shriek from Mara's trailer drew their attention. Linda, the rather temperamental makeup girl, came running out of it clutching her hand. She was followed closely by her assistant, a mousy little thing whose name no one could ever remember.

"Darren!" Linda's voice was raised several notches above her usual petulant whine. "I absolutely cannot work under these conditions! I can only do so much with someone whose skin is naturally blue. And when I tried putting lipstick on her, she bit me!" Linda dramatically held up one hand to show a smallish bite mark. The medic looked at it worriedly.

"Add a mortician's makeup kit to that list," Phil said thoughtfully. "Hell, bring a mortician. Might make more sense and we won't have to pay union scale."

When Linda started to sputter in outrage, Phil snarled, "Listen, Linda. If you can't do your job, I'm going to get someone who can. Give me any shit and you'll be working Craft Services. And I'm not talking about behind the table."

"Maybe we could sew Mara's lips shut," the makeup assistant suggested with the air of one used to being ignored.

Darren considered the idea, grateful for even this token safety measure with which to salve his increasingly battered conscience. "Just might work!"

The makeup assistant looked absurdly gratified.

"Darren, it has to look like she's really talking," Phil protested. "How the hell are you going to loop in her dialogue realistically if her mouth doesn't move?"

Darren shot Phil a resentful glance, hating the fact that his producer was right.

"Okay," he amended. "Let's try sewing the corners so she can't get a good bite radius going." Phil nodded his approval and Darren continued, "Melissa, talk to wardrobe and see what they can do." Turning back to the mousy assistant he said, "Good thinking, honey. Do you think you can do something with Mara's makeup so we can get the next scene shot before we lose the light?"

The assistant nodded, eager to prove her worth. She scurried back to Mara's trailer as the protesting Linda was led off to be treated by the medic.

Darren resumed his conversation with Melissa and Phil. "We can sew the new extras' mouths completely shut. They don't have to talk. And make sure the PA . . . Who are we using?"

Melissa checked her list. "Tony."

"Good. He's smart. Make sure he's got a decent gun."

"Got it." Melissa set off to make sure everything on her list was done with her usual efficiency. Then she stopped and turned back. "Darren, shouldn't we send someone to ride shotgun with Tony? They'd stand a better chance of getting back safely."

"Phil, can we spare the extra hand or—" Darren stopped abruptly. "Jesus, I don't believe I said that. Of course we can spare someone else. Whatever it takes to bring them back safely."

"And more quickly," Phil agreed. "It'd be hell to try and find more good production assistants."

Darren ignored that. "Okay, let's get moving."

"Yeah," Phil said. "We should get going on Derrick's death scene while he's still got some life in him."

The scene went well. Derrick shivered with a real fever no amount of acting (at least on *his* part) could emulate. His skin was pasty, sweat poured off of him in rivulets, and he seemed to be suffering from as much pain as a plague victim in the last stages of bubonic plague would have felt. Darren was delighted with the results . . . on a purely artistic level, of course.

The medic stood at the sidelines throughout, wearing an expression that alternated between disapproval and downright horror. She had vehemently protested the decision to shoot a scene with the sick man, but Derrick himself had insisted. He was a professional, by God, and he would act as long as he could breathe; a state lasting approximately ten minutes after they finished shooting his death scene. Darren immediately had someone from Wardrobe stitch the dead actor's lips partially shut, consoling himself with the thought that he'd given Derrick the chance to die with his acting boots on, so to speak.

"You are using buttonhole thread, aren't you?" he asked the woman pushing a needle in and out of Derrick's lips.

She looked up in annoyance. "Please. I *do* know my job."

Several hours later, the production assistants returned from their run, loaded down with all the items on their list, including a dozen large coolers full of dry ice, several intimidating rifles, and a star-struck mortician. The mortician was sent off to see what he could do with Mara as the young assistant hadn't been able to make her look life-like.

The medic appropriated the medical supplies and immediately injected a shivering Linda with a hefty dose of antibiotics as she asked, "You're not allergic to penicillin, are you?"

Linda shook her head and promptly passed out.

Darren, in the meantime, sent several coolers of dry ice over to Mara's trailer to try and slow down the natural rotting process. He figured that three more good days ought to see the film finished. Then she could rot at will. He turned his attention back to Tony and the rest of the supplies. "You got the collars?"

Tony grinned and held up a handful of heavy steel collars. "I know a couple of dominatrixes who didn't mind lending their gear. What are we using 'em for?"

By the time Tony and another PA rounded up a dozen extras from the outside and locked them in one of the steel-sheeted storage units, the mortician had finished his makeup job on Mara. He beamed proudly as the actress was led out on a leash by one of the heftier grips. "One of my better jobs, if I do say so myself," the mortician bragged. "Doesn't she look peaceful?"

She did indeed.

Darren rolled his eyes. "That's just great, but I don't *need* peaceful. She's supposed to be reacting to the death of her lover, not going for a drive in the country. Get my drift?"

The mortician sniffed. "I'll see what I can do."

"All right, people," Darren yelled. "Let's call it for the night! We'll pick this up tomorrow. Call time is six a.m.!"

A brief listen to the radio told Darren that things were not getting any better. The ratio of dead to living in Los Angeles was rapidly favoring the walking dead. Citizens were advised to make their way to rescue shelters set up around the city. Darren thought that the walled confines of Plateau Pictures were about as good a protection as anyone could ask for, which suited him just fine. The other members of the production seemed to feel the same way, for no one had left the studio when they'd called it for the day. Darren was happy that he could offer some safety to his cast and crew. He figured they deserved some compensation for the notoriously long hours that low-budget productions demanded.

Tomorrow would be another sixteen-hour grind. Darren just hoped he'd be able to tell the live members of the production from the dead ones by the end of it.

The next day's shooting went relatively well, although controlling the dead extras proved somewhat difficult. Several of the live extras were scratched and a production assistant bitten before all the ghouls had their mouths sewn shut. One of them ripped out the thread and managed to make a healthy lunch out of the makeup assistant. Phil took a good look at her corpse and decided there was enough left to reanimate. "Someone put her in the extras pen."

Darren winced, but tried to look at it from the angle that it would save Tony from having to procure more bodies from the outside. He really didn't want to risk losing the kid to the extras pen. Tony was the best PA Darren had ever worked with. Tony had that *spark*, the same sort of idealism that Darren felt himself rapidly losing. Darren wanted to see that spark (not to mention Tony's health) preserved.

All in all, Darren was quite pleased with the acting he was getting from his ghoulish thespians. They were easier to deal with than some of the crew, who were complaining about the smell. Wardrobe was especially vocal when it came to costuming the dead.

"Do you know how hard it is to get blood stains out of this material?" snapped the wardrobe girl who'd stitched Derrick's mouth shut. Darren hoped she'd become eligible for the extras pen. She wasn't that good of a seamstress, either.

The medic, meanwhile, frantically tried to treat those who'd been bitten or scratched by the zombies, but the antibiotics didn't seem to be working.

On the upside, the dry ice was working well enough to prevent Mara and Derrick from degenerating too quickly. The hot lights were a bit of a problem, but that was what stand-ins were for.

Darren was coming to the reluctant conclusion that the zombie plague could be the best thing that had ever happened to his career.

At the end of the day Darren eagerly ran the dailies to see if they lived up to his expectations. Even Phil and Melissa were impressed with the improved quality of the stars' performances.

"Mara really looks horrified," Melissa commented during one scene.

"I think she was really hungry," Phil said. "That was the scene we shot before lunch."

Darren felt a warm glow suffuse his entire being as the certainty that this, the end result, really was worth all of the . . . *unpleasant* things he'd had to do, the compromises he'd been forced to make. Sometimes true art could only be born out of the womb of horror.

Ignoring the pretentious tone of that last thought, Darren continued to watch the screen.

When they'd finished watching the dailies, Phil and Melissa headed off to get some supper while Darren rewound the film to view his masterpiece again in private. He'd only gotten through five minutes, however, when the door opened and the light switched on.

Darren turned around in annoyance. "Didn't you see the red light was on?" he snapped before his eyes adjusted to the light. He put a lid on his temper when he saw who'd entered the room: Gerald Fife, dressed in his usual relaxed-fit jeans and silk shirt that did nothing to create the desired effect of borrowed youth or hide his middle-aged paunch.

"Gerald," Darren said expansively, confident that he at last had something of quality to show the executive producer. "Have a seat and check out these dailies."

"Sorry, ain't got time." But Gerald sat down despite his words. "I'm just here to give you the news in person. Didn't want you to hear this through Phil." He pulled out a cigar and lit it.

Darren's heart plunged down into his stomach. "What news?" he asked, although he thought he knew the answer.

"I'm pulling the plug." Gerald took a long pull on his cigar, exhaling with obvious relish.

"What? Why?"

"This whole dead thing, kid. It's depressing. The investors aren't gonna want a movie about the Black Death when the viewing public is already down about the zombies. No percentage in it."

"Jesus Christ, Gerald, you've got to take a look at these dailies!" Darren gestured at the screen. "We've really got something now!"

Gerald shook his head with finality. "Sorry, Darren. No go. We're in this business to make money. No one's going to want to see a movie with a bunch of rotting bodies when they can look out their window and see the same thing for free."

"But—"

Gerald held up one hand, sending a plume of cigar smoke wafting in Darren's face. "But me no buts, kid, I ain't got the time. I wanna get out of here while I still can. Traffic's a bitch out there." He took a puff of his cigar. "Sorry, kid. But you know what they say: when the going gets tough, the tough get going. And I'm getting the fuck out of Dodge." Gerald stood up. "Now where's Mara? I wanna give her the news myself."

Staring bleakly at the screen, Darren said, "She's locked in her trailer."

"Locked in?" Gerald's voice rose in outrage. "What the hell are you talking about, locked in?"

Darren started fumbling for an explanation. Suddenly his train of thought jumped to another track as something irrevocably snapped in his brain. He wasn't sure if it was his conscience or his sanity— maybe it was both—but it no longer mattered. Only the film mattered.

He stood up. "Sorry, Gerald. I meant she's locked *herself* in her trailer. Maybe you can help out."

"Jesus!" Gerald stubbed out his cigar. "What the hell did you do to her?"

"She's unhappy with the quality of the food we've had lately," Darren explained as he followed Gerald out of the screening room bungalow towards Mara's trailer. "It's been hard to get Cristal these days."

"On your budget, it should be impossible," Gerald snapped. "Damn good thing I'm shutting this down. The investors would have my balls for breakfast if they saw shit like that on the budget sheets. Jesus, what the hell is that smell?"

They were passing the warehouse housing the extras. Despite the heavy steel walls, the smell of the rotting extras gave the area a distinctly charnel atmosphere.

"Some meat gone bad," Darren said vaguely.

"What the hell are they doing in there?"

"Rehearsing one of the big crowd scenes."

"What a reek! How can anyone eat around here?" Gerald stepped up his pace. Darren matched it.

Mara's trailer sat before them. A steady, unsatisfied moan emanated from inside.

"Jesus!" Gerald exclaimed. "She sounds like she's starving!"

Darren bounded up the steps before Gerald could see the industrial-strength padlock on the trailer door. As he inserted the key, he tapped on the door and called, "Mara, Gerald's here to talk to you about a few things. You're going to have to unlock the door and let him in."

A rising moan answered him, along with the sound of Mara lurching through the trailer towards the sound of fresh meat.

"Let me up there, you asshole." Gerald pushed his way up the stairs just as Darren managed to remove the padlock. Slipping it into his pocket, he retreated out of Gerald's way.

"Mara, Baby, it's Gerald. Open the door, Sweetheart! Uncle Gerald will take care of you."

Mara scrabbled at the door from the inside, moaning pitifully.

"Christ, she can't even talk!" Gerald said in horrified tones. He grabbed the door handle and turned it. "Don't worry, Baby, I'll feed you."

"I bet you will," Darren said cheerfully as Gerald opened the door. He watched as Mara grabbed hold of the executive producer's arms and pulled him inside. Darren helped with a well-placed push on Gerald's backside, then quickly slammed the door shut and replaced the padlock with a decisive snap.

"You know what they say," Darren called out as Gerald began screaming. "When the going gets tough, the tough get eaten!"

Darren smiled to himself. His first film, and it looked like he'd even get final cut.

# PREVIOUS PUBLICATION
# INFORMATION

"Ada, Awake" by L.S. Johnson first appeared in *Strangelet* Volume 2, Issue 1 in January 2016.

"Cooking with Rodents" by Nancy Etchemendy was originally published in the *Rat Tales* anthology in 1994.

"Fable of the Box" by Eric Esser was previously published in *Awkward Robots Anthology: The Orange Volume*, released October 31, 2015.

"Folie à Deux" by Ross E. Lockhart appeared initially in *Strange Aeons* issues #13 and #14 in 2014.

"Graffiti Sonata" by Gene O'Neill first appeared in *Dark Discoveries* magazine, issue #18, winter/spring 2011, and was reprinted in *Best of Dark Discoveries*, published by Dark Regions Press in 2015.

"John Wilson" by Clifford Brooks first appeared in *Cemetery Dance* #49 in 2004.

"Leaving the #9" by E.M. Markoff was written especially for *Tales for the Camp Fire*.

"Little Pink Flowers" by Roh Morgon was originally published in the *24th Annual World Horror Convention Souvenir Book* in May 2014.

"Mukden" by Sean Patrick Hazlett was published in *Weirdbook* magazine in 2017.

"My True Name" by John Claude Smith first appeared in *The Parasitorium: Parasitic Thoughts* anthology, published in May 2008.

"River Twice" by Ken Hueler was published in an earlier form in *From the Corner of Your Eye: A Cryptids Anthology*, edited by David Kramer, Great Old Ones Publishing, May 2015.

"Road Kill" by Jeff Seeman originally appeared in the 2015 anthology *18 Wheels of Horror*.

"Seven Seconds" by Erika Mailman appears here for the first time.

"Still Life with Shattered Glass" by Loren Rhoads was originally published in a different version in *Cemetery Dance* #54 in March 2006.

"The Ninth Skeleton" by Clark Ashton Smith was first published in the September 1928 issue of *Weird Tales*. This version is taken from *The Collected Fantasies of Clark Ashton Smith*, Volume 1, edited by Scott Connors and Ron Hilger, Night Shade Books, published 2007.

"The Patron" by Anthony DeRouen is published here for the first time.

"The Quarry" by Ben Monroe was written for this anthology.

"The Relic" by Crystal M. Romero was first published in the 2008 anthology *Chilling Tales of Terror and the Supernatural*.

"The Twins" originally appeared in G.O. Clark's short story collection, *Twists & Turns*, published by Alban Lake Publishing in April 2016.

"The White Stuff" by Gerry Griffiths is original to this anthology.

"Unheard Music in the Dank Underground" by Sumiko Saulson was originally published in the collection *Spit and Pathos* in October 2018. An excerpt appeared as part of Episode 6 of the Next Great Horror Writer Contest on HorrorAddicts.net in June 2017.

"Vivified" by Chad Schimke was previously published on

BookFunnel in 2018, with editing by L.S. Johnson, and cover art by John Rawson.

"The Wolf Who Never Was" by John McCallum Swain originally appeared in *Spawn of the Ripper*, published by April Moon Books in May 2016.

"You'll Never be Lunch in This Town Again" by Dana Fredsti first appeared in *Mondo Zombie*, edited by John Skipp, published by Cemetery Dance, in June 2006. It also appeared in *Horror Anthology 2015,* published by Moon Books.

**CHECK OUT AUTHOR READINGS AND OTHER EVENTS AT**
**ELLDERET.COM/CAMPFIRE.**

32503944R00202

Made in the USA
San Bernardino, CA
15 April 2019